Tanya Rumford

CUT AND RUN

CUT AND RUN

For cousins everywhere.

1

IMOGENE

(SEPTEMBER 22, 2018)

THE LAST DAY OF SUMMER hits Imogene harder than any other. This has been true her entire life. But this year is different—bittersweet, perhaps—because this summer will be her last.

As a young girl, Imogene found the years stretching on and on—limitless. Summer itself rode in on a long and lazy yawn and flicked out soft as a porch light, a silent farewell to a season well spent. But the older she grew, the quicker the summers passed. Soon, entire years slid by with a blink of her lashes.

Without meaning to, her hands had wrinkled, her hair faded to gray, and all the beautiful sounds around her had changed.

This house used to swell with the loveliest sounds: secret tippy toes pattering along the hall, hushed whispers and sneaky giggles, forks scraping against dinner plates as little bellies filled to excess. Tiny fingers would tug on the fabric of her dress, shouting *Watch this, Gram!* as she scrubbed a supper plate. And she stopped to watch them—always, no matter what—because nothing was ever more precious than those four perfect children.

This house has been quiet for years. Imogene can't fault the kids for that. They've grown. They've done precisely what they're supposed to do—what *every* kid does at one point or another—they get on with their lives. This doesn't trouble Imogene. She rests easy these days, proud of the adults they've become, and grateful for the summers when they'd been hers.

But, *oh*, what she wouldn't give for just one more.

New sounds fill her house now. Silence, mostly. News programs in the evenings. And Jude. She can hear him now in the kitchen, pill bottles rattling as he portions her evening doses into a flimsy paper cup.

He's a good boy, Jude. Mid-twenties, a bit of meat on his bones, a handsome face, and the straightest, whitest teeth Imogene has ever seen. Jude was a compromise; the agreement she reached with Frannie and William when they'd suggested placing her in a nursing home. Imogene blatantly refused, and they'd settled on a live-in nurse instead.

Jude pads into the living room and hands the cup of multi-colored, various-shaped pills to Imogene with a kind smile. He places a glass of water on the wooden end table beside her and bends to empty the drainage bag that hangs from the back of her wheelchair. Oh yes—a permanent catheter—another fun addition to this unfamiliar world. Jude has been with Imogene for a few weeks and will stay with her for the rest of her life, which won't be much longer, she suspects. Days? Months? It doesn't matter. She's made peace with it.

Imogene's mind is going; it has been leaving her for years but worsens with each new day. There are days she doesn't recognize a single person, or where she is, or the time, or where she left her reading glasses. She'll forget who she's talking to in the middle of conversation. She lashes out, saying ugly things she'd never think to say if not for this illness. Of course, she could always put an optimistic spin on things and say: *well, at least Wilfred didn't live long enough to see me in this condition.*

What it boils down to is that life moves too fast. It does. One day you're just starting out, making a place for yourself in the world, and next thing you know you're an old woman with more health concerns than hairs on your head.

It's not all terrible, though. There's an ease that comes with aging. A peace when you realize the hardest days are behind you. It's as though you've climbed this impossible mountain, and now you're at the top. Your legs ache, your knees are scratched, there's dirt on your face, but you've made it, and now you can breathe and enjoy the view. Imogene was lucky enough to enjoy the view with her sweet Wilfred for many years. And it was bliss. So, no, she is not opposed to aging. The thing she resents most is to reach the top and find the sun already setting. To realize that soon she'll have to go.

From where she sits, she can just glimpse the edge of the lake out the sliding glass doors beside her. The evening light washes over the inky surface of the water, glorious strokes of gold and yellow paint the canvas of her long and happy life. A smile touches her lips then; the sort of smile that comes when you've finished your chores and have the rest of the day to fill any way you choose.

Before Jude arrived, back when she had more good days than bad, Imogene concocted a brilliant plan. She'd found a way to have one last summer with her grandkids—her *Lovebugs*—even if she wouldn't technically be around for it. She's done everything she can, and the wheels of the plan spin now without her control.

Imogene has finished her chores. She needs only to wait.

"What would you like to do this evening, Ms. Baker?" Jude asks, a thoughtful glint in his eyes.

Imogene tears her attention from the glass doors and smiles. "It's the last day of summer, Jude," she says. "I think I'd like to sit outside and enjoy it."

2

EMELINE

(MAY 23, 2019)

EMELINE PULLS A BOWL FROM the dishwasher and gives it a sniff, forgetting if she ran the machine last night after dinner.

"I'm hungry! *Hurry!*" Conner shouts from the dining table, though his eyes stay glued to the tablet in front of him. Some ridiculous cartoon screeches from the tiny speakers.

Emeline grabs a second bowl from the top rack of the dishwasher and gives the bowls a quick rinse under the faucet, just in case.

Her cellphone rings on the kitchen island, and Emeline glances at the screen. Her mother. *Again.* She has a knack for calling at the worst imaginable times.

"I'm getting you cereal," she shouts over the ringing. "Turn that thing down, please. And don't talk to Mommy in that tone of voice." Conner's fourth birthday came with a few surprises, the least pleasant being the splatters of pee that forever stain the toilet lid and floor, and this fun new attitude.

Aimee squeals from the living room as she chases Sweetie up and down the hall. *Sweetie—what a horrible name for a dog who has destroyed her entire house,* she thinks. Nails clatter and scrape against the tile floor, followed by a grating crash as someone collides with a piece of furniture—the coffee table, from the sound of it. The dog barks—she never *stops* barking—and Conner scream-sings, "*I can't hear my show. I can't hear my shoooooow,*" to elevate his voice above the commotion.

"Aimee! Knock it off and leave the dog alone! Conner, please! That doesn't help."

Emeline hunches over the sink for a moment to gather herself. Surely it's unhealthy to experience this level of anxiety so early in the morning.

If only she could blame her distress on a bad day; everyone is entitled to those. However, most of Emeline's mornings take a similar turn. If anyone bothered to pay attention, they'd see that life has been squeezing the air from Emeline's lungs for *years.* Every day is a losing-battle to free herself from this inner misery, and she often thinks: *Right now, if the earth were to split open and swallow me whole, I doubt I could muster the energy to care.*

But that's the thing with being a Mom—you *have* to care. If not for yourself, for your children. You can't afford to fall apart when someone depends on you. So, you take a deep breath, and you keep going.

Placing the two bowls on the kitchen island, Emeline fills each with Cheerios. Conner climbs onto a barstool, knees in the seat, and leans half over the counter on his elbows. "Sit on your bottom, please," she snaps, twisting the red cap off the jug of milk.

Aimee appears in the kitchen then, clutching her elbow, bottom lip quivering.

Emeline's eyes widen at the sight of her. *Please hold it together,* she thinks. *I can't handle a meltdown today.* "Are you okay?" she asks her daughter tentatively. "What happened?"

"Sweetie! Scratch me!" she shouts, erupting into a full-blown crying fit.

"Oh no, it's okay! Don't cry! It's not even that bad. Look. It's okay. No blood." Emeline tries her best to soothe her, but two-year-olds are rather difficult to reason with when they believe they're about to lose an arm. "We'll clean it up and get a Band-aid on it, and you'll be good as new!"

It's not until Aimee's blue eyes widen in terror and fresh screams fill the kitchen, that Emeline remembers her daughter's newly developed, and irrational fear of Band-aid's.

"No Mommy! No Band-aid!" she cries. "No! No! No!"

A splattering *plop* sounds behind Emeline; she's afraid to look but does, anyway. Conner has attempted to pour his own milk into his cereal bowl, and it hasn't gone well. The jug is on its side and milk rushes onto the counter and waterfalls over the edge to the floor. Cheerios are everywhere.

"Conner! *No!*" Emeline wails, running to right the overturned jug. "Don't just watch it spill everywhere! Pick it up!"

Conner winces at her tone. Emeline at once feels the guilt wash over her. *Way to go. He only wanted to help. Why don't you stop being a bitch to your children?* "I'm sorry," she mutters. "I'm sorry. Mommy didn't mean to yell."

"No Band-aid!" Aimee still clutches her elbow, scrunching up her chubby, tear-streaked face.

"No. No Band-aid. Forget the Band-aid." Emeline runs for paper towels and a washcloth, careful not to slip in the mess.

The doorbell.

Great.

"Conner, can you try to soak this up, please?" Emeline hands him a wad of paper towels and makes for the front door. A lump of tears rises in her throat she tries her best to swallow.

The door swings open to Sue-Ann, a mom from carpool club.

Sue-Ann, obnoxiously cheery at any hour, has a bright smile plastered on her face, but it fades at the sight of Emeline.

And no wonder. Emeline wears an oversized t-shirt and checkered pajama pants, thick brown hair loose and unbrushed. Most mornings, she gets dressed for work while the kids eat breakfast. Emeline's expression falls. "Oh, Sue-Ann, I'm so sorry. I forgot you were picking up today. We, uh… we aren't anywhere close to ready. I'll just—I'll just bring them to school myself."

Concern creases Sue-Ann's forehead as the shouting continues in the kitchen. Emeline's cell phone is ringing again.

Conner screams, "Sweetie! No! Bad girl!"

"Mommy!" Aimee yells.

"Is everything okay?" Sue-Ann asks, craning her neck to better see inside the house.

"All good," Emeline says, a bubbly lilt to her voice. "We just had a little spill. We're on it."

"Sweetie is eating my cereal!" Conner's voice comes out in an angry cry.

"Sue-Ann, I've really got to go. I'm so sorry again." Emeline makes to close the door, but Sue-Ann stops it with her hand.

"Has Armie left for work already? Do you need some help? I can help. It sounds like you have your hands full in there."

Emeline smiles as pleasantly as she can. Sue-Ann doesn't know that Emeline and Armie have separated—*no one* knows—though chatter has been working its way through the nosy-mom circle. "I'm okay. Thank you. But I *do* need to go." She shuts the door in Sue-Ann's stunned face.

No sooner has Emeline returned to the kitchen, dragged Sweetie into her pen, poured fresh bowls of cereal for the kids and began mopping the rest of the mess with a wet washcloth, when her cellphone rings out a third time. She glances at the screen and startles when she sees Belinda's name on the display. Belinda never calls. She barely texts. Something is wrong.

"Hello?" Emeline answers the phone, just as Conner screams at Aimee for licking his arm. "Hold on," she says into the phone. "Guys! Please!" she shouts at the kids, but her voice is lost in their endless squabble. The dog is barking again; the pen always makes her go ballistic.

With no other options, Emeline slips into the pantry and shuts the door.

"Sorry about that," she says to her cousin. "What's going on?"

Through muffled sniffles, Belinda says, "Why haven't you been answering your phone?" *Is she crying?*

"I'm sorry. It's been a rough morning. Is everything okay?"

"No. Everything *isn't* okay." The phone is quiet for a moment. Belinda takes a ragged breath and says, "Gram died this morning," then breaks into loud sobs.

The words are a gut-punch. Emeline's legs give out beneath her, and she slides to the ground. She sits and listens to Belinda's tears; her own emotions creep up from low in her stomach, tightening her muscles one by one. And it is here on the pantry floor—her shoulder blades wedged between the Raisin-Bran and a box of instant rice, the sounds of her chaotic life echoing through the door and pressing their weight against her chest—where the remains of Emeline's fragile world shift off their axis and send her free-floating into space.

3

GEOFF

(MAY 28, 2019)

GEOFF HAS BEEN AT SPHEROTEK for less than four months. *It's rare we hire kids fresh out of college,* his bosses had told him. *Make sure we don't regret it,* they'd say with a chuckle and a pat on the back, but Geoff didn't miss the warning look in their eyes. So, Geoff works hard—harder than anyone at Spherotek—to make sure he earns his place.

Geoff knows they discourage requests for time off, even for emergencies like this. This is especially true during the first year of employment when they expect a full commitment. For that reason, he'd hesitated even to ask. They'd granted his request, of course—they weren't monsters—and passed on their condolences, but Geoff couldn't help but worry what they'd say about him when he left: *Told you, Boss. The young ones just aren't serious enough.*

Work isn't the only reason he's loath to leave town. Honestly, this whole thing couldn't come at a worse time. At first, he'd considered missing the funeral altogether, but Mom chewed his ass out for even suggesting such a thing. His mother has been pushed to her wit's end over the last few years, watching Gram as her dementia worsened. She paid Gram's bills, made sure she didn't hurt herself or wander off alone, that she was taking her meds, showering, and checking in often enough.

For the past eight months, Gram had her live-in nurse, but Mom still fretted over keeping her at home. *She needs to be in a facility,* she'd say. And no one could miss the way Dad scoffed, shrank into himself, every time Mom suggested shucking Gram in *the home.*

Geoff didn't see the problem. Gram was managing fine; he'd even had several coherent phone conversations with her over the years. Mom always blows things out of proportion. She worries herself into breakouts of itching hives and tries her best to pull everyone into her pit of never-ending anxieties. A part of him thinks Gram would still be alive if Mom hadn't micro-managed her illness. She got Gram into the wheelchair when she could still get around with her cane. Got her the catheter then, so she wouldn't hurt herself in the bathroom. Put her on bed rest when she caught a cold back in February, and Gram never left that bed again. An infection finally did her in. They hadn't even known she was sick.

Mom asked him to arrive over the weekend *to help with arrangements,* but that was out of the question.

Geoff arrived this morning—a Tuesday—with the funeral tomorrow.

Now, he perches at the counter, watching Mom buzz around the kitchen. She's attempting to rearrange the fridge to accommodate the assortment of casseroles and pies and pasta salads that have arrived in a steady stream since word of Gram's death broke out.

"Are you sure you don't need any help, Mom?" he asks.

She tosses a half-eaten pack of lunchmeat into the trash with exceptional ferocity and continues her work. From the moment he arrived, she's been giving him the silent treatment.

Shrugging, his gaze returns to his cell phone. To the text sent early this morning before his flight that has yet to receive a reply. And his throat tightens with what that must mean.

4

EMELINE

(MAY 28, 2019)

EMELINE CROSSES FROM TENNESSEE INTO Georgia, four and a half hours into their nine-hour road trip south. With overcast skies and oppressive humidity, a heaviness clings to the day that parallels the weight in her chest.

How many times has she imagined herself running away? Nothing but a long stretch of highway to separate her from the life she's grown so tired of and the one she hopes is waiting for her. It's a daydream, of course; she'd never leave her children. And besides, where else could she go? Emeline breathes out a sigh, mind half on the road ahead of her, and half somewhere else entirely.

Mom suggested flying. *It's quicker*, she'd said. *If you get home early, you can help with funeral preparations.*

Her mother couldn't understand the lack of appeal to everything she'd suggested: spending a fortune on airline tickets, dragging two exhausted toddlers onto a plane who cried the first two hours of the trip as it was because Sweetie-the-Devilish-Beagle-Pup had to stay behind, and planning a funeral for Gram who would have rolled her eyes at the thought of a bunch of people she hardly knew coming to *wish her off.*

No thanks.

Emeline will get there when she gets there.

5

WYATT

(MAY 28, 2019)

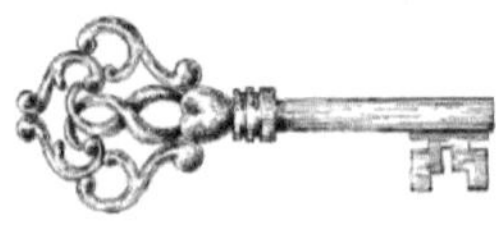

WYATT IS ALONE, AND THAT'S okay.

He prefers solitude; the quiet places where his thoughts have room to stretch and breathe.

A rerun of Everybody Loves Raymond plays at low volume on the television. A desk lamp casts a ring of light onto the coffee table where he works. Wyatt fixates on the pen in his hand, frantically trying to commit his thoughts to paper. He scratches out what he's just written, tearing the paper in his frustration, and his face falls into his palms. What can he say about Gram? How can he make people understand how special she was, how funny, how brilliant his childhood was because of her—how brilliant *she* was?

He can't.

No one saw Gram the same way *he* did, and he can't even arrange his words in a way to *make* them see. He is letting her down yet again.

Someone knocks on the aluminum door of the garage.

"Come in," Wyatt says.

Geoff.

Since arriving this morning he's spoken only two words to Wyatt: *Hey man,* and a head nod. Nine months in the same womb, over two years since his last visit, and all Wyatt gets is *Hey man.* Oh well. That's Geoff. He is *nothing* like Wyatt, and Wyatt thanks his lucky stars for that every single day.

Geoff thinks he's better than Wyatt; he thinks he's better than *most* people. But Wyatt wishes he could tell him that lucking into a job right out of college and keeping the same girlfriend from high school isn't exactly an impressive accomplishment. At twenty-two, there's plenty of time for things to go wrong; best not to get cocky.

Though their personalities couldn't be more different, being fraternal twins, they also share little to no physical similarities beyond that of normal siblings. This, Wyatt isn't *nearly* as grateful for, as Wyatt seems to have drawn the short stick in the looks department. Geoff is tall—over six feet—with an athletic build. Wyatt is a good four inches shorter and slim, verging on scrawny. The twins share their wide-set, brown eyes; but Geoff's are awake and focused—ready for business—where Wyatt's are sleepy, the surrounding skin puffy and shadowed. Geoff's complexion is fair and clear, Wyatt's tan and oily, still troubled with the occasional pimple. Both have thick, dark hair, but Geoff's is kept short around his ears and neck and professionally maintained, whereas Mom often trims Wyatt's—although he's been letting it grow over his ears for the last several months.

Geoff strolls into the room and plops next to Wyatt on the sofa. He lets out a sigh, his fingers raking through that perfect hair as he leans back, eyes on the ceiling. "Mom is driving me crazy," he says.

Wyatt grunts in response, keeping his eyes on his work.

"She's pissed that I didn't come home early to help. I was

lucky I got the time off I did."

Wyatt grunts again.

The truth is, he couldn't care less about Geoff's *work problems*. Geoff was a jock in high school—a soccer star, and unspeakably popular. Wyatt was the computer-savvy one—the nerd. Mom always told him not to worry. When he got older, all those brains of his would make him rich, and then no one would care that he wasn't cool. Yet, thanks to life's twisted sense of humor, Geoff ended up with the tech job, and Wyatt ended up in the tiny apartment he'd converted from Mom and Dad's garage.

Geoff, unphased by Wyatt's grunts, says, "I mean, she should ask Dad for help—it's *his* mother, after all—but she'd rather direct all her passive-aggressive rage at her children."

"She's *our* Gram," Wyatt finally says. "We should *want* to help."

Now it's Geoff that grunts. But at least he's shut up for a second.

"Are you speaking at the funeral?" Geoff asks.

Wyatt nods. "I am," he says, even though the paper in front of him contains more scribbles than words. "Are you?"

Geoff shakes his head. "No. I didn't have time to write anything."

Gram died five days ago. There was plenty of time. Wyatt doesn't say this, though. Instead he says, "It's early still. You can put something together."

Geoff spreads his legs and readjusts himself on the cushion. "No. I don't think so. I'll just observe."

Wyatt feels his face heat at this, though it shouldn't surprise him. Geoff didn't appreciate Gram the way Wyatt did. Wyatt has *been* here. Everyone else ran away first chance they got. But not him.

"You still working for Danny?" Geoff asks.

"Of course," Wyatt says.

"Hasn't it been long enough? Can't you get hired somewhere *legit*?"

The anger spreads from his face to his chest. "My job *is* legit," Wyatt snaps.

"Right," Geoff snorts. "You know what I mean."

Wyatt knows what he means: *Poor, sad Wyatt. Living at home. Works for his uncle because no one wants to hire an unexperienced kid with a criminal record. And look at him now—desperately scribbling out a half-assed eulogy hoping to make it up somehow to the woman he disappointed.*

6

EMELINE

(MAY 29, 2019)

EMELINE ARRIVED AT HER PARENT'S house late yesterday evening, just as everyone was shuffling into the kitchen for dinner. She dragged her bag through the front door, a sleeping Aimee tossed over her shoulder, and hurried to join them before Mom's anger worsened. The mood was tense at dinner, not just from grief, but from the unspoken resentment that often accompanies these visits.

Ah, home. How she has missed it.

Today is the funeral. Emeline stands in the church vestibule with the rest of her family as guests trickle in from the parking lot. She wears her best black dress with the silver belt around the waist. People she doesn't recognize step forward to offer condolences; she's never sure how to respond to that. *Thank you? To you as well?* It's all a silly song and dance; people saying what they *think* they should say without knowing the meaning of it.

A man approaches she's certain she knows but can't quite place.

"Emeline White," he says with a soft smile. "It's good to see you again, though I wish it were under different circumstances."

Emeline offers him a smile and a *thank you,* wanting to ask who he is, but not wishing to be rude.

The man glances at his shoes. "You don't remember me. That's okay, it's been years. Uh… I'm Skylar Hayes. We were in school together. We're uh… we're friends on Facebook."

The name clicks into place, and Emeline blushes. "Skylar," she says. "I'm so sorry. Of course, I remember you. You look so different." He's gained a few pounds around his middle and another pound or two in facial hair since she'd seen him last.

"Oh, no hard feelings," he says with a wave of his hand.

"And it's actually not White anymore. It's Baker again… or… it *will be* Baker again." It's been six years since she used her maiden name, and she hasn't spoken it out loud since the separation. She's not sure why she chooses to now.

He nods. "My apologies. And my condolences for your loss."

Emeline pulls her mouth into a tight smile; her teeth grind behind her lips.

Behind her, the giant wooden doors creep open, and an icy blast of AC send goosebumps along her calves and arms. Church officials lead the guests into the nave to take their seats. Instead of following, Emeline hands Aimee and Conner off to her mother and disappears into the bathroom, taking an extra moment to compose herself.

When she returns, she finds her family lingering near the front row. The church is quiet. Everyone uses library voices here, which Emeline has never understood; she'd rather people talk amongst themselves than be subject to the whimpers and sniffles that echo through the silence.

The room suddenly slips into an even deeper quiet that sends Emeline searching for the cause; it takes only a moment to find it. Disrupting the sea of black clothes, white tissues, and bowed heads, her cousin Belinda has floated into the room wearing a floral dress of bright teal and violet. Her long blonde hair bounces over her shoulders. She follows along the center aisle, oblivious to the barrage of disapproving glares she receives, and hugs her way through the family at the front.

When she gets to Emeline and her brothers, she serves hugs to each of them and says, "Sorry I'm late. The bus got a flat, and I had to wait for AAA."

"Is that why you aren't dressed?" Geoff asks.

Belinda's pale lashes blink a few times in quick succession. "I *am* dressed," she says.

Emeline sees when Belinda notices her mother seated in the front row across the aisle and watches her face tense the slightest bit. Aunt Dea has her arm looped around her new husband's and dabs her eyes with a crumpled Kleenex.

"Excuse me," Belinda mutters, crossing to where her mother sits.

Aunt Dea pulls herself to the edge of the pew, her third-trimester belly pushing against her too-tight dress. Belinda stoops to hug her—a one-armed hug and a swift peck on the cheek—and then returns to the other side of the aisle where she sits beside her father, Danny.

Belinda and Uncle Danny have a bond that Emeline never had with either of her parents. Uncle Danny is still young, as far as parents go—still fun. As a teenager, Belinda was allowed to make her own schedule: she stayed out late, skipped school whenever she wanted for *mental health days*, and took overnight trips with friends, *unchaperoned*. Uncle Danny took her to get the dainty bumblebee tattoo on her wrist when she was only seventeen. And as a graduation present, he bought her a used school bus at an auction. The two of them spent five months converting it into an RV so Belinda could *discover herself on the open road*.

Belinda thought her dad was the most amazing person you could ever hope to meet.

Her mother disagreed.

It was obvious which side Belinda had taken.

The energy in the room shifts as Emeline's dad says they are ready to begin. Wyatt, Mom, and Dad file into the front pew with Belinda and Danny. Emeline, Aimee, Conner, and Geoff shuffle across the aisle, joining Aunt Dea and her new husband. Emeline and Geoff share a knowing glance as they settle into their seats. *Take a look at us,* it says, *the ones who left.*

7

WYATT

(MAY 29, 2019)

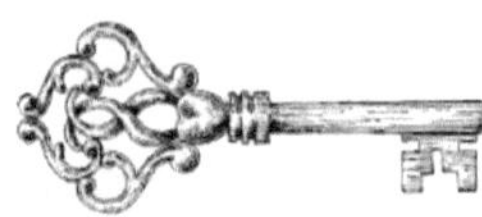

WYATT NEVER LIKED FUNERALS. NOT that anyone *does*, but Wyatt always found the idea of death and what follows rather morose. One day you're a person, an accumulation of an entire lifetime of memories and accomplishments. You make imprints upon the universe and the lives of everyone you touch. Your body warms rooms and hearts. Your arms hug and comfort. You cry tears and have deep thoughts. You take up space.

And then you die.

And your body ends up in a box in the ground or incinerated to dust. An entire *life*, and that's what the end of the road looks like for each of us: dirt and bugs, or a crackling furnace. Yes, there's Heaven and all that. But your body, your vessel, is just—

discarded—as if it never glowed with life at all.

The Pastor reads from the Bible in a solemn baritone voice. Wyatt's leg bobbles nervously as he awaits his turn to speak. The words he's written for Gram rest in a tattered notebook on his lap. He tries his best not to let his gaze linger on the casket, but it's hard to turn away. She's right there; hands crossed over her midsection, as if she's drifted off for a quick nap.

A familiar knot twists in Wyatt's stomach, so he closes his eyes and tries to think of something pleasant. Oddly enough, the memory he summons forth is from the day of his grandfather's funeral.

Wyatt was barely thirteen when Gramps died. They'd known he was sick, but his death came quicker than anyone expected. Wyatt had never been to a funeral before. Never seen a dead body. He hadn't a clue about open-caskets and closed-caskets. So, on the morning of the service, when he walked into the room and saw Gramps—his strong, able-bodied Grandfather—laying in a box, a waxen smirk on his face that looked nothing like him at all, Wyatt panicked and ran away.

He sat at a pew near the back of the room, knees tucked up to his chest, trying to make himself invisible. A moment later, Gram appeared; she was as composed as ever, as if she hadn't just lost an entire half of her heart. She sat next to him on the pew, let her smile linger on him for a moment, and in that instant, he knew she understood. Gram *always* understood.

"I know it's strange seeing him like that," she'd said.

Wyatt only nodded. He didn't want to tell Gram how scared he was. Scared because what he saw in that box didn't look like Gramps anymore. Scared because they were going to put him in the ground today. Because, silly as it was, he thought Gramps might wake up as they buried him and wouldn't be able to get out. Scared because he didn't want Gram to die, too. Or his mom or dad. Or himself. So, he nodded instead.

"I get it, kiddo," she said. "But it's okay. This is a lot for anyone to take in, and *you*... well, you've always felt things a bit *more* than most people, haven't you?" Gram gave him a soft nudge on the shoulder as she said this, and he'd allowed the tears to spill over then, because *yes,* sometimes he felt so much it frightened him. So much he thought something must be wrong with him.

Gram sighed. "That's the heck of it, Bug: when you feel that much, you're lucky, because you get to experience love a little deeper than everyone else. Of course, losses hit you a little harder, too. Right here." She pressed her index finger to his chest, right above his heart.

"But can I tell you a secret?" Gram tilted her face so only he could hear. "A heart like yours is a rare gift, and it's my most *favorite* thing about you; it was your Gramp's favorite thing, too. He loved you so very much. He loved *all* you kids, of course, but between you and me, he may have favored you a bit."

A wave of pride washed over Wyatt as he imagined Gramps preferring him to Geoff.

"And *that,*" Gram said, making a vague gesture toward the wooden casket, "some people just need to see him one last time, to say goodbye; it's how they cope with loss in their own way. But *us?* We know that isn't really Gramps, is it? No. Gramps is all around us, right in this very room. And he's going to *be* with us, everywhere we go, for the rest of forever. Here, close your eyes."

And Wyatt did.

Gram's voice eased out in a whisper. "If you sit really still and quiet, you can feel his arms around you, giving you one of those big Grandpa hugs."

Wyatt smiled. Gramps had never been much of a hugger, but on the rare occasions he pulled you in for one, the warmth of it lingered for the rest of the day. And Wyatt felt warm just then.

Gram had taken his hand after that and led him up to the casket. The fear passed. Wyatt found it easier to look at Gramps and say goodbye, same as everyone else. Now he realized Gramps wasn't there. Not laying there in that box—he *couldn't* be. Because as sure as Gram's soft fingers warmed his right hand, Gramps held fast to his left.

Today, sitting here in this pew, Wyatt has them both. Their glow surrounds him, comforts him, reminds him they are with him for the rest of forever.

Belinda nudges Wyatt, yanking him back to the present. "You're up," she whispers.

Wyatt takes a deep breath and approaches the alter. His notebook shakes in his hands. But he is ready.

<h1 style="text-align:center">8</h1>

<h2 style="text-align:center">BELINDA</h2>

(MAY 29, 2019)

AFTER THE SERVICE, BELINDA TELLS Wyatt how lovely his eulogy was, and she means it.

Out of everyone who'd spoken, only Wyatt had captured the true essence of Gram and the unique love she held for each of them.

When Wyatt was younger, he had all these nervous habits—a low-register hum he'd emit under his breath whenever he felt anxious and a terrible hair-plucking tendency that frequently left him with bald patches in his eyebrows. He'd shaken the habits with age, thank goodness, but the nerves never did quite disappear.

Today, anyone could see how rattled he'd been with those

pesky nerves—but my goodness, he was an amazing writer. The words he'd chosen for Gram had breathed much-needed life into the room, and Belinda was sure the walls between this world and the spirit realm had broken down, allowing Gram to step through as easily as if she'd been right next door.

Belinda's own tribute paled in comparison. But then, she'd expected that. Wyatt was closest to Gram; naturally, he'd deliver the perfect words to honor her.

But Belinda honored Gram in her *own* way: the floral dress.

People stared. Of course they did. In Georgia, black is the only acceptable choice for a funeral. No exceptions.

In 2010, on the morning of Gramp's funeral, Belinda sat on Gram's bed, helping her choose the dress she'd wear to the service.

Belinda's mom and dad were arguing so much back then that home felt like a war zone, and now Gramps was gone as well.

Belinda picked at a loose thread on Gram's quilted duvet, lost in grief. The morning had been full of emotions; her face already streaked with tears. At sixteen, she knew what death was. She soaked in loss like a sponge and wore it on every inch of her skin. Heartache is so much *bigger* when you're sixteen, and Belinda was living proof of that.

In jest, Gram plucked a floral housedress from the closet and said, "How about this?"

Belinda laughed. There was no stopping it.

"I'm not so sure," Belinda said with a smile. "That might draw some attention."

Gram laughed then; she had the most beautiful laugh.

"You're right. Besides, I wouldn't want to show up your grandfather. He'd want to be the prettiest one in the room."

They both laughed at that, but Gram's humor faded as she held the dress at arm's length, considering it from collar to hem. Then, with a shrug, she said, "In all honesty, Bee, I would wear this dress in a heartbeat. Gramps loved me in it. And who knows? It might add a little color to an otherwise dreary day."

As quickly as the thought had struck her, Gram returned the dress to the closet and removed a long-sleeved black dress instead. With a sigh, she tossed it on the bed.

Today, Belinda woke up and said, *screw it!* She'd pulled on a floral summer dress in Gram's favorite colors and wore it with pride. It was a special tribute to Gram only they would understand. Gram *hated* dreary days. The clouds would form, the rain would pop and splatter against the tin roof of the porch, and Gram would peer through the blinds, shaking her head in contempt. *A perfectly good waste of the south,* she'd say with a tsk.

So today, Belinda brings Gram a bit of sunshine. She may not write a eulogy as brilliant as Wyatt's, but sunshine she can manage.

9

EMELINE

(MAY 29, 2019)

A STEADY RAIN FALLS AS Emeline parks at the cemetery. *Why does it always rain at funerals?* She reaches beneath the driver's seat for her umbrella; one umbrella to share between herself and two miniature humans.

Emeline stoops as they walk, tries to keep the rain off their little heads, and Conner from jumping in the puddles and muddying his new shoes and pants. Her heels sink into the soggy grass as she totters along with short, graceless steps.

"Here. Take this," a voice says behind her. "Please."

Emeline turns to find Skylar, offering his own umbrella.

Emeline thanks him and lets Conner take hold of theirs; he trots off with Aimee, the two of them huddled close together.

Emeline moves beneath Skylar's umbrella, and they proceed to the burial site, arms brushing as they walk. Emeline is aware of a sticky film of sweat beneath the heavy fabric of her dress and hopes her deodorant is still doing its job.

The cemetery has erected a large white tent over the burial site, which keeps the attendants dry enough but traps the humidity like a bathroom after a hot shower.

While Skylar shakes the water droplets from the umbrella and fumbles with the clasp to close it, Emeline mutters another *thank you*, dashes away into the safety of the tent, and takes her place at the front with her family.

An instrumental version of *Hallelujah* plays at a low volume from a scratchy speaker. A few minutes later, the casket starts its journey across the cemetery grounds; Emeline's dad, Uncle Danny, Wyatt, Geoff, her Uncle Bart on her mom's side, and Jude, Gram's nurse, carries it from both sides. The rain falls heavier now, soaking the pallbearers through. Their hair is heavy and dripping, and they blink water from their eyes that could be rain or tears.

During the brief service, Skylar returns to Emeline's side. When she sobs, he surprises her by draping his arm around her shoulder, a move she finds odd and inappropriate, rather than the comfort he likely intended. Perhaps he's trying to be kind. But she hasn't seen him in years, and they were never especially close. She shrugs him away to fish for a Kleenex in her purse.

On Emeline's other side is Geoff, stoic and straight-backed. Emeline hasn't seen him cry *once*, which isn't altogether surprising; he is strictly against public displays of emotion. You'd suppose his grandmother's funeral might be an exception, but apparently not. During one of the Pastor's many prayers, Geoff steals a glance at his cellphone. His face tenses as he reads the screen and types out a quick response before returning the phone to his pocket.

Emeline's fists clench at her side, and she heaves a disappointed sigh in his direction. The *nerve* of him.

Between the humidity and the close quarters of the tent, everyone is relieved when the Pastor wraps his final words and nods to the staff member hovering near the side, who presses the button that lowers Gram into the ground. But as the casket begins its descent, Conner tugs on Emeline's hand and says, "Mommy, what are they doing with Great-Gram?" Emeline's voice catches in her throat. In the frenzy of the last few days, it'd slipped her mind to prepare Conner for this; to tell him what to expect. *Too late now.* She holds his little hand in hers and gives what she hopes is a reassuring squeeze, hot tears stinging her eyes.

"Where is she going?" Conner asks again, more urgently, pulling so hard on her arm she thinks he'll tug it right out of the socket. Emeline hugs him against her waist and smooths his fine, ash-brown hair with her hand, breathing gasps of air into her lungs. Motherhood is funny that way: you think you have answers for everything, but you're unprepared for more than you realize.

Unsatisfied with his mother's attempt at soothing, Conner emits an ear-splitting howl.

Thoroughly embarrassed, Emeline pulls him into her arms, but he wriggles and thrashes to get loose, to run to Gram. She catches Wyatt's eye, who pops in a set of Bluetooth earbuds as he tries—and fails—to control his own emotions; his dark hair tumbles over his eyes, but she can tell he's weeping from the quivering of his chin.

After the family takes turns throwing handfuls of dirt into the grave atop the casket, everyone drifts back to their cars. The rain has reduced to a light drizzle; the hardest drops fall from the leaves and moss as they pass beneath the trees. Despite her insistence that it was *absolutely unnecessary*, Skylar walks beside Emeline, holding the open umbrella over her head until she reaches the safety of her Buick.

As Emeline buckles Aimee into her car seat and Conner into his booster, Skyler waits on the curb behind her. When she shuts their door and turns for her own, Skylar is still there, saying, "I'm so sorry, again. For your grandma, your marriage, just… everything you're going through right now." He moves in for a hug, and Emeline, seeing no way to avoid it, hugs him back.

"Thank you," she mutters and pulls away as quick as possible without appearing rude. She opens her door a crack to signal her readiness to go. "I'll be okay," she says.

"I know you will. You're such a strong woman. Always have been."

Emeline needs to leave.

"Hey," he continues, "if you're planning to be in town for a few days, I'd love to take you out to dinner. That is… if you want to. It might be good for you to get out, laugh a little." He shrugs bashfully.

Emeline stares at his hopeful face for a fraction of a second before her expression sours. "Skylar… are you asking me out? At my grandmother's funeral? While I'm going through a divorce?"

His eyes shoot open. "What? No! I mean… sort of? I just thought maybe you'd like to go out… it doesn't have to be romantic. We could—"

Emeline cuts him off. She throws her door open, climbs inside, and thrusts the key into the ignition in one motion. "It was nice to see you again, Skylar," she says. And when she shuts the door and drives away, she can finally, *finally* breathe.

10

GEOFF

(MAY 29, 2019)

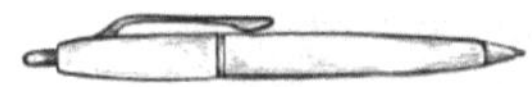

EOFF IS BACK IN HIS old room… well, what's left of it, anyway. Dad used Geoff's absence as an opportunity to renovate the space into a new home office. They had reduced his old memories to two Rubbermaid containers labeled *GEOFF* and stuffed them in the closet.

An expensive corner desk has replaced Geoff's bed, so his parents have taken the liberty of blowing up an air mattress for him.

How thoughtful.

It's these kinds of above-and-beyond accommodations that make him so grateful to be home.

He now lies on top of the stiff mattress, waiting for the call to dinner, staring at the text that, earlier at the cemetery, sent him reeling.

Three words: *I don't know.* A response to the message he'd sent before leaving Albany.

He'd left the comfortable apartment he shares with Lila Livingston, his girlfriend of five years, taken an Uber to the airport, and tapped out a quick message while he waited to board: *Will you still be there when I get back?*

Over twenty-four hours of radio silence, and the response he gets is: *I don't know.* How could she not know?

At the cemetery, he'd typed a quick response: *Call u later.* He'd earned a dirty look from Emeline for that one, but he didn't care.

Not that it mattered. He called in the car on the way back to his parent's, and again when he walked in the door, and again five minutes ago, and the ringing had given way to her voicemail every time.

Geoff has never felt such helplessness, and as someone who takes great care to know precisely where life is heading at every turn, an uncertainty such as this is more than nerve-wracking. Tomorrow afternoon they are to attend the reading of Gram's will, followed by a family dinner at Cat Tails Mom insisted was *non-negotiable mandatory.* Come Friday morning, he'll be back on a plane, and will sort everything out at home.

He must.

There is no other way.

11

WYATT

(MAY 30, 2019)

WYATT IMAGINED A WILL READING to take place in an empty conference room or stuffy lawyer's office. He imagined tense glances among family as items are read off and distributed. And he imagined bad blood lingering among them for the rest of eternity.

This isn't the case today. Well… not entirely.

There *is* a stuffy lawyer man, but he traveled to *them*.

This lawyer man is now opening his briefcase on Mom and Dad's kitchen table, arranging papers, and sipping from a mug of herbal tea that Mom prepared, as if we are the kind of family that sits around drinking hot tea in the middle of the day, or *any* time for that matter.

The family sits around the table. Leans against the counter. Perches in the doorway. Everyone is here. Wyatt has no wish to be. There's a nervousness in the room; legs twitch in secret beneath the table; fingers drum against thighs; heads crane, hoping to snatch a glimpse of something important in the lawyer's papers.

Wyatt can't stand it.

He doesn't want *stuff* or *money*.

He wants his Gram back.

She should be here. They shouldn't be divvying up her belongings like poker cards. Who gets the best hand? Who has the biggest pile of chips? This is ridiculous. It's Gram. The stress she must have endured to write the will in the first place, he can't imagine. Gram spread her love among them evenly. She'd never want them fighting over her things.

The lawyer clears his throat, and the chatter snuffs out immediately.

"Good morning, everyone," he begins. "I thank you all for assembling here today, under these regrettable circumstances. I'll try to be as brief as possible."

The room falls into a deep silence.

"Right, well," the lawyer says, clearing his throat again and lifting a sheath of paper from his open briefcase, "let's begin."

He pulls a pair of reading glasses from the pocket of his jacket, unfolds them with a flick of his wrist and pops them on his face. Strangely, he peers over the *top* of the glasses as he reads. "I, Imogene Louise Baker, of the county of Lowndes, State of Georgia, realizing the uncertainty of this frail and transitory life and the certainty of death, and being of sound mind and body, do hereby make, ordain, publish and declare the following to be my Last Will and Testament…"

The will begins with the largest items first. Gram's house and property, left to William and Frannie Baker. Mom and Dad have kept the property up since Gram fell ill, so it makes sense. Dad nods once at this. Mom's eyes drop to the table where she watches one hand work anxiously against the other. Her face is unreadable, but Wyatt senses her disappointment.

Gramp's classic Chevy that Gram hadn't driven in years, left to Uncle Danny. Also for Danny, sole ownership of Baker Construction LLC, Gramp's business—his legacy. This announcement doesn't come as a surprise to anyone, either—Danny has managed Baker Construction since Gramps passed away nine years ago—but Dad sighs and tries to disguise it as a yawn. Everyone knows Wyatt's father should have inherited the construction company. And Gramps tried to give it to him. But William Baker was not a man who enjoyed working with his hands. Nor was he a man to struggle and scrape by. So instead of following in his father's footsteps, he'd gone into finance; a bank teller first, then a loan officer, and finally the assistant manager of his own branch. When Danny expressed an interest in the business, Gramps took him under his wing, and—though he'll never admit it—Wyatt's father harbors some lingering jealousy over that.

The lawyer moves on to Aunt Dea. Gram left her the twelve-thousand-dollars she had in savings. Wyatt notices Belinda shift uncomfortably as the lawyer reads that bit aloud. Belinda isn't on the best terms with her mom since she walked out on them nine years ago, just two months after Gramps died. Wyatt is sure Belinda thinks her mother deserves nothing.

After ten minutes of reading, the lawyer circles around to the grandchildren. Crouching, he retrieves a small cardboard box tucked beside his feet, a look of guilt as he places it on the table in front of him.

He begins.

"For my grandchildren, I bequeath the following," he reads.

"For Belinda Hutson." His hand disappears into the box and withdraws a small, maroon box with hinges. He glances up, scans the room, and says, "Pardon, but which of you is Belinda?"

Belinda's hand shoots up as if marking herself present at school.

The lawyer nods and presents the small box to her.

Inside is a ruby ring. Strange, but probably worth something, Wyatt thinks. The lid of the hinged box is engraved with gold lettering, likely the name of the jeweler. Belinda examines the gift with a confusion she tries to disguise as admiration.

Next is Emeline. The lawyer hands her the old wooden hope chest where Gram stored her valuables. Empty. She doesn't even try to hide her bewilderment.

Geoff and Wyatt are last. For Geoff: a rectangular box containing a vintage fountain pen. And for Wyatt: the brown leather wallet that once belonged to Gramps.

Wyatt allows his fingertips to trail over the soft folds and deep-set creases that adorn the cover from years of hard use. Inside, he finds a photo of Gram when she was younger. She's near Emeline's age, late twenties, maybe thirty; she leans against the hood of a car, arms crossed beneath her chest, legs crossed at the ankles, an easy smile on her lips. The wind lifts a strand of her hair and blows it back across her face.

Wyatt lightens at the sight of her. Forever immortalized in her youth. He wishes she could stay here. Right here. Spend her eternity in this very photograph; young, beautiful, healthy, tireless—a lifetime of happiness and peace stretching in front of her on a loop that continues without end.

He parts the fold of the wallet. Inside he finds an old key. Nothing more.

12

EMELINE

(MAY 30, 2019)

WATER DRIPS FROM HER HAIR and soaks into the beige carpet as Emeline emerges from the bathroom. Freshly showered and alone, she finds a moment of peace.

At the vanity table in her old room, she scans her tired reflection in the mirror. *When did she lose her luster,* she wonders? Not even thirty, and yet she's dulled. The freckles of her youth still dust the bridge of her nose; a charming attribute good fortune has allowed her to keep. The outer edges of her eyes exhibit the first etchings of crow's feet; not yet a problem, but the suggestion is there. Glimpses of the girl she used to be, the woman she is, and the person she's becoming are in front of her, framed in the spotted glass of her mirror. She sighs.

The television echoes through the common wall she shares with her parents; a high, sing-song voice she recognizes as one of Conner's favorite animated characters. The kids convinced Pawpaw and Grandma to let them sleep in the *big room* tonight, and that's where they've been since returning home from dinner.

One more day in Valdosta. Morning after next, they head out.

Muffled giggles and squeals break through the chorus of a song Emeline has played in the car no less than five million times. She smiles at the sound.

This time spent with their grandparents is so valuable for Conner and Aimee. Emeline often wrestles with the guilt of moving them so far from their family. They have their grandparents on Armie's side, of course, but an entire half of their world is here, in Valdosta.

As for Emeline, this trip is less like coming home, and more like delaying the inevitable. A million decisions and problems wait for her back in Brownsville that leave her in a state of deep unrest. Once, this room inspired calm in her—her sanctuary, the stage for her wildest daydreams. Now, there is only the strong sense of being misplaced; an unexpected snooze on the bus that lands you in a strange city, miles from home. That sinking sensation in your gut when you wake and realize you aren't where you're supposed to be—that is Emeline now.

Gram's wooden hope chest rests on the glass top of her vanity. This isn't the strangest gift Emeline has ever received, but it's close. She remembers the wooden box. Remembers seeing it as a small child, sitting on Gram's dresser, situated there with the rest of her grown-up things. But Emeline had never commented on it, never mentioned liking it, or hoping to have her own someday. So why had Gram left her such an odd item?

Earlier at dinner, Wyatt was turning the old leather wallet over in his hands, his thumb fanning through the individual credit card slots, likely looking for whatever made the wallet special or worth something. Mom had shaken her head at him as she plunged into her second glass of wine before dinner had even made its way to the table. *You can dig all you want, Sweetheart,* she'd said. *There's nothing of value in there. Towards the end, she didn't have much to give away. She probably just picked things at random for you kids, so you'd have something of hers to keep, you know? Remember, it's the thought that counts.*

Mom also grumbled at dinner over finding the time to clean out Gram's house and decide what they wanted to do with the property. *The land is worth a good deal,* she'd said to Dad under her breath. He waved her off with his hand. *We can talk about it later,* he'd said.

Surely Mom isn't hoping to *sell* the house now that she's inherited it. The house is old, yes. Maybe needs a few repairs. But it *has good bones,* as Gramps used to say. The thought of another family moving in, of anyone else living there, gives Emeline an ache in her stomach she can't explain. As if someone making *new* memories in that house, will somehow erase her old ones.

A sigh escapes her lips as she contemplates the chest once more. With her index finger, she lifts the dainty golden clasp and raises the lid. Inside smells of old. Of cedar, of nostalgia, of *Gram.* As she stares at the empty space inside, something compels her to fill it. To use it. She plucks her hairbrush from the vanity and lets it drop inside.

When it hits the bottom, it makes a dull *PLUNK,* the sound not matching what she'd expected to hear.

Emeline's brows wrinkle in confusion. She removes the brush and knocks on the bottom of the chest with her knuckles—once, twice.

At once, she's on her feet, hurrying to her desk where she shoves the box beneath the table lamp. Tilting it toward the light, she presses the bottom of the box with her fingers and watches it flex beneath her touch. Emeline sucks in a sharp breath and lets the chest fall back onto the desk. She whirls, casting about for something she can use.

Emeline snatches her purse from the floor. Rifles through the layers of candy wrappers, loose change, and receipts to find the pocketknife she always carries. She'd purchased it for self-defense, though if she ever finds herself truly in need of it, she'll be dead or kidnapped long before she locates the darn thing.

At last, her fingers close around the cold metal of the knife. She fits the shiny blade into the narrow space that surrounds the bottom of the chest. At first, she worries that she's wrong, that she's going to break the last gift Gram will ever give her. But after a moment, a *POP*, and a panel breaks free.

Emeline peers into the chest, her pulse thrumming against her throat.

At the bottom of the box is a VHS tape.

With one look, Emeline is sure the course of her entire night is about to change. Because written on the top of the tape are four words: *For My Darling Lovebugs.*

13

GEOFF

(MAY 30, 2019)

GEOFF SCROLLS THROUGH A LIST of flights on his phone, hoping for a last-minute redeye, or anything that will get him home sooner than his scheduled flight tomorrow morning. He can't stop thinking about Lila, about showing up to an empty apartment and that gut-wrenching realization that it's over. If he leaves early, he can stop her. They can talk. They'll make it through this. They will.

A rapid-fire of knocking breaks his concentration.

Emeline stands in the hall with a frazzled expression, clutching an old VHS tape.

"It's from Gram," she says in a breath.

"What do you mean, 'it's *from* Gram?'" Geoff snatches the

tape from her hand. "Where did you get this?" he asks.

"The hope chest she left me had a false bottom. She hid the tape inside."

Geoff looks at her in disbelief. "Why would Gram hide something she meant for us to see? Why not leave it for the lawyer to give us at the will reading?"

Emeline shrugs. "Only one way to find out."

Reluctantly, Geoff follows her into the kitchen, where Dad is taking a break from the sleepover shenanigans upstairs. He's scooping out a heaping plateful of pasta salad from one of the enormous platters in the fridge.

"Didn't get enough to eat at dinner?" Emeline asks with a raise of her brow.

Dad shrugs. "Just something to do."

Geoff understands Dad is grieving in his own way, but he's become so detached from everything that it looks as if he doesn't care. Geoff knows that isn't true but doesn't have time to unpack everything right this second. "Do you have a VHS player?" he asks.

Dad's eyes narrow for a moment as he shovels a forkful of noodles into his mouth. "We got rid of that years ago. Who watches VHS tapes anymore?"

"People who like to keep it old school?" Geoff says.

Emeline sucks in a sharp breath of air. "People like... *Wyatt?*"

Wyatt barely has his door open, when Emeline pushes through into the room and shoves the tape in his face.

Wyatt goes paler than usual at the writing on the front. "I don't have a VHS player," he says.

Emeline's expression falls.

"But *Gram* does."

The room goes quiet for a moment, and then Emeline nods and says, "Call Bee."

14

BELINDA

(MAY 30, 2019)

THE FOUR OF THEM PILE into Emeline's Buick Lacrosse and drive the fifteen miles to Gram's house.

They'd taken this route plenty of times. Could manage it blindfolded if they had to. But tonight is different—*eerie.* Because of the mysterious tape? Because Gram is gone? Because they are together for the first time in over two years? Belinda doesn't know. But they complete the trip in near silence, each lost in private thoughts.

Emeline pumps her breaks hard, which takes everyone by surprise. She's passed the big tree, passed the dirt drive that winds back to Gram's house.

Years ago, Gram had wrapped the trunk of that tree with a

string of tiny, flickering fairy lights. Every night at seven o'clock, she would turn them on. *We could do with a streetlight,* she'd say. *But since that's unlikely to happen, I'll improvise.*

Tonight, the tree is dark. A silhouette against a black sky.

Belinda stills at the sight. She imagines all the twinkling lights that shimmer and glow inside of *her,* certain that one or two have just burnt out. The same weariness settles over the car. Emeline reverses and makes the turn in silence.

As they bounce along the drive, Belinda runs her fingertips across the VHS tape, tracing the black ink where Gram has written. The ghost of a smile touches her face as her fingers linger over the word *Lovebugs.*

She's not sure if the others recall, but Belinda clearly remembers the day they'd asked their grandmother *why* she called them *her Lovebugs.*

"Lovebugs are pests," Emeline had said.

"Oh no, Darling!" Gram had replied. "Lovebugs are magical little things. Do you know why?"

They'd all shaken their heads. Of course they didn't see the magic in lovebugs. Most people didn't. If you were unfortunate enough to live in a state plagued by these invasive little black and red bugs, you'd know that twice a year they swarm the skies, fornicating in mid-flight, and splatter the front of your car with their gooey guts. Annoying or not, it made Belinda sad to see them *POP* against the windshield.

Gram explained. "Lovebugs come in May, right before school lets out. And what happens when school lets out?"

"We come stay with you," Belinda said with a smile.

Gram beamed, thrusting a slender finger in her direction. "That's right, my girl! And I'm so happy when I see those first lovebugs drift past my window. Because that means summer is nearly here, and we get two whole months of fun together. Lovebugs aren't pests. They are the beginning of my most favorite time of year."

The sound of car doors opening and slamming shut frees Belinda from her memories, and suddenly it's nine o'clock, and they are in front of Gram's house.

Wyatt has a key. Belinda doesn't have one, and as far as she knows, neither do the others.

Wyatt lets them in, switches on the lamp by the front door, and suddenly they are home. And yet, *not.*

Walking in together is familiar, but at the same time, artificial; an imitation of the act that used to occur without effort. Belinda shrugs this idea away and tries to focus on the moment.

Belinda's last visit had been brief. Three months ago, she'd come home for the anniversary of Gramp's death; it was always a tough day for Gram to get through alone. But the Gram Belinda knew was long gone. By that point, she was hooked to a thousand noisy machines and was clueless to Belinda's presence. She'd hurried out and couldn't bring herself to return.

Now, she casts her eyes over the room and takes it in. The house is exactly as she remembers it. Gram never cared much for keeping a tidy house. *Where there's mess, there are memories being made,* she would say. There *are* signs of her absence, though. Of her age and poor health. Pill bottles stacked on the counter in the kitchen. A few cardboard boxes shoved against the side door where someone—Aunt Frannie or Uncle William—has packed away the first of Gram's things. The silver cane Gram used when her knee acted up still rests in the corner beneath the bar, though she'd been in the wheelchair for close to a year.

But it smells like Gram here, *feels* like Gram. Not the Gram from recent months—the one who had mostly forgotten them—but the Gram they grew up with. The one who danced and hummed and let them be kids and never made them sorry for it. Gram's energy remains where her body doesn't, so strong you'd believe she is only in the next room, set to bounce around the corner with a fun new game to play. Belinda taps into that energy, and she imagines the sun shining in on the wood-paneled walls, heating the house, and Gramps' raspy voice grumbling about the cost of air conditioning. She smells sunscreen and hose water drying on her skin. Can see Gram's favorite frying pan, irrevocably stained from years of hard use and *so many* fried-bologna sandwiches. There she is with her cousins, catching tadpoles down at the lake, dropping them into homemade aquariums they'd fashioned from Gram's Tupperware so they could watch them grow into frogs. Belinda thinks of bedtime stories, late-night giggles, and smothering her *itchy bites* with pink Calamine lotion. She smiles softly at these remembrances, though tears pool in the corners of her eyes.

Wyatt clears his throat. "I'll uh... I'll find the VHS player."

They move into the living room, situating themselves on the sofa, the chairs, sinking into them the way they did as children.

Belinda falls to the sofa; the brown and orange cross-stitch that everyone seemed to own in the eighties and nineties. Her hands drift across the stiff fabric, trying to drink in the remnants of her childhood through the tips of her fingers.

Geoff lingers beside the sofa, arms crossed, uncomfortable.

Emeline sits rigid in Gram's favorite green-velvet-upholstered armchair, staring at a faded stain on the carpet.

15

EMELINE

(MAY 30, 2019)

THE SUMMER OF 1999, THAT was when the stain appeared. Emeline and Belinda sat crisscross applesauce on the living room floor. Earlier that day, Gram surprised the girls with an oversized checkerboard mat, and they hadn't stopped playing. The two of them sat on Gram's new rug, the mat spread out between them.

The twins were two then—not yet talking and using only loud shrieks and mumbles to express themselves. But they were bursting with energy and bounced around all day on fat, wobbly legs.

Emeline remembers Gram was tired that day. Gramps was under the weather and kept to the bedroom. Gram brought him water, medicine, and broth whenever she had a moment to spare. The boys were relentless, and the heat rendered everyone miserable and moody. Looking back now, Emeline recognizes this as the obvious motivation for the gift; Gram had hoped they'd keep themselves occupied long enough for her to sneak a rest.

Belinda, ever needy, had asked Gram several times for juice. And each time, Gram told her to hold on—the boys had to take their baths so they could get ready for bed.

Emeline had felt especially grown that summer; it was her last year in the single digits, after all. She knew she could be helpful.

So, she crossed into the kitchen, dragged the jug of Fruit Juicy Hawaiian Punch from the fridge, plucked Belinda's My Little Pony cup from the dish rack, and made her way back to the living room.

Belinda took the cup in her tiny hands, and Emeline instructed her to hold still while she poured. What happened next should not have come as a surprise, but at nine, things appear much simpler than they are.

The jug was too full and heavy. It slipped from Emeline's hand, took out the cup, and splashed sugary red drink into Belinda's lap. *And* Gram's pretty white rug.

Belinda released a howl that rattled the walls and set Emeline's ears to ringing. She righted the juice bottle and her face flushed as she realized the horrible mess she'd made.

Trailed by Belinda's shrill cries, Emeline darted to the kitchen for paper towels. But as she hurried back to the living room, Gram was rushing down the hall with panic in her eyes.

Emeline froze, heart thudding against her eardrums. When Gram saw the juice soaking into the rug, and Emeline standing there with a new roll of paper towels clutched to her chest, and Belinda howling and pointing an accusatory finger at her cousin, Gram's jaw clenched, and for the briefest moment, Emeline thought she was going to yell. But then, just as quick, Gram's features softened. She smiled at Emeline, who was trying her best not to cry.

Gram helped Belinda—juice dripping from her bare legs—off the ruined rug and walked her to the bathroom. Gram told Belinda she could take a bath first; the boys could wait. Take off her sticky clothes, watch over the filling tub, and she'd be right in to help.

Gram then coaxed the roll of paper towels from Emeline's hands and actually *apologized.*

Gram said, "I'm so sorry, Sweet Girl. Belinda asked for juice a million times, and I should have got it for her. You tried to help your old Gram, didn't you?"

Emeline nodded because she had, *she really had,* and Gram pulled her into a long hug. At this, the embarrassment lifted from Emeline's skin.

"But what about your rug?" Emeline had asked. "Will it stain?"

Gram grinned and waved her worry away. "Oh, so what if it does?"

Emeline squished up her face. "But it's new, and I ruined it. I broke Dad's new headphones from Christmas, and he was furious. He sent me to my room."

Gram looked rather furious too. But not at Emeline. She cleared her throat and said, "I'm sure your dad was just upset about what happened. He's always been a bit single-minded. But not you. And not me, either. No, ma'am. We're all about the big picture, you and me. And do you know what I think when I see this big red spot here?"

Emeline shook her head.

"I think I have the most caring and helpful granddaughter in the world. She noticed her Gram was having a tough day, and she wanted to take a little weight off her shoulders. And every time I look at this spot, I'll remember how lucky I am."

Emeline's throat clenches at the memory as she tears her attention from the faded blotch on the rug that Gram refused to throw away. Even all these years later.

Why hadn't she come home more often? Gram had never even met Aimee (Emeline had been eight months pregnant with her daughter during her last visit). What kind of person robs their grandmother of the opportunity to know their great-grandchild?

Wyatt returns with an overstuffed cardboard box. Wires and cords drip out and over the edges.

"Got it," he says.

16

GEOFF

(MAY 30, 2019)

WYATT FIDDLES WITH A TANGLE of cords, trying to decide which will connect the machine to Gram's 32-inch fossil of a TV. He doesn't appear to be in any kind of rush.

Geoff is restless, pacing the length of the room. The minutes soar by. He shouldn't be here. Not just here at Gram's house, but *here* in Valdosta. He shouldn't have come back. Not now. Mom would have gotten over it eventually, and Gram is dead. Not as if *she* would have noticed his absence. His life back home is in literal shambles, and what is he doing? Whatever this business is with the tape, it's not worth it if it destroys his relationship with Lila. The others, what do they have to lose in being here? Nothing. But Geoff has *everything* to lose, and every second he waits, his chances to salvage it diminish.

The television screen flashes blue as Wyatt finds the correct combination of wires. "Are you guys ready?" he asks, as he feeds the tape into the old machine.

Silence falls. Even Geoff quiets his thoughts and tunes in to the television.

For a moment, nothing happens. Then the screen fills with the image of Gram sitting in this very room. She looks well. Lucid. All senses firing. *When did she film this?*

She smiles, and the warmth reaches for Geoff through the glass. Guilt swallows him as he silently berates himself for thinking he could ever miss her funeral.

"My Darling Lovebugs," Gram says in the video, "if you are watching this now—and I sincerely hope you are—that means Emeline found the tape."

Emeline's hand shoots to her mouth, and there is no missing the damp in her eyes.

"It also means, as you all well know, I am no longer here." Gram turns somber for the briefest moment before correcting herself and returning the jovial bounce to her voice she carried no matter the circumstances.

"This tape is only the beginning," she continues. "This is only one of *several* clues. Clues to *what*, you may ask. I'll tell you."

The room is quiet enough that Geoff jumps when the refrigerator clicks on in the kitchen.

After a pause, Gram explains. "There are things you don't know about your grandfather and I. Things even your *parents* don't know. Many years ago, something happened—an unexpected and *terrible* thing—and if I don't tell someone soon, everything will be forgotten. So I must. I can't bear to take these secrets with me when I go. And I can't bear to lose this story— this piece of my past—to have it ripped from me so cruelly by my diagnosis.

"Now, I could share the story, here, now, on this tape. But where would the fun be in that?" Her eyes twinkle with mischief and the promise of adventure. For a moment, Geoff's gut twitches the way it did when he was young with a fun new game to play. But his spirits sink as he remembers Gram's mental state at the time she likely filmed this video—this was *after* her diagnosis—and the sadness settles over him once more.

There will be no more grand adventure. No more games. No more fun. Coherent as she seems in the video, this is likely the ramblings of an old woman desperately holding on to what remained of her memories. A muddled mess of reality and what she wished to be true.

Gram continues, and Geoff listens. "You kids have reached the age where time and circumstances will pull you in a million different directions. Babies, marriages, moves, careers. It's already begun. I can see it. And if you don't fix it soon, the distance will grow and grow and *oh*, what a waste that would be."

Geoff senses that this reproach is directed at him alone and shuffles his feet beneath him. The silence deepens around the room. Gram's voice is everything. Everywhere.

"Those wild-eyed, imaginative kids I love so much may seem lost to you now. But I *know*, they are still in there somewhere. So, I'm asking you now: take one last adventure with me. I'll tell you the story in a way that allows you to see it through your own eyes. Perhaps you can even help me right a few wrongs along the way. If you do this for me, I promise, what's waiting for you at the end will surpass anything you could ever imagine."

For the first time since Gram began her speech, the cousins exchange glances.

"Now, Emeline already found this tape. Good girl, Emeline," she says with a wink. "But as I mentioned, this is only the first step. If I've piqued your curiosity and you'd like to take this further, perhaps the fabulous writer Edward Bulwer-Lytton could lend you a *hand* and point you in the *right* direction."

Gram over-enunciates certain words, which strikes Geoff as strange. But then, she always had a flair for the dramatic.

She smiles again and her wrinkles rise with the effort, reducing her hazel eyes to slits. "I love you very much, my Lovebugs. And if I've done my job well, you know that to be true. I do hope you'll take this journey with me."

She blows a kiss to the screen and with that, she's gone.

17

BELINDA

(MAY 30, 2019)

SECONDS PASS THAT MAY AS well be hours. No one moves or speaks. Belinda can't decide where to rest her eyes, so she stares at her reflection in the now-black television screen.

Wyatt moves to eject the tape, and the sound has legs; its echo ripples around the room and folds back onto them.

Wyatt kneels before the TV, tapping the tape against his palm.

After a long silence, he asks, "What do we do?"

Geoff answers, and he does so with a derisive snort. "What do you mean 'what do we do?' There isn't anything *to* do."

Wyatt shoots to his feet. "Are you serious? There's obviously something Gram wants us to know. Something she wants us to *see*. You aren't planning to ignore that?"

Geoff stands his ground, long legs planted beneath him as he trains his full attention on Wyatt. "That's precisely what I'm going to do. That's what *all* of us should do. Look, I miss Gram as much as the rest of you. But she wasn't exactly *well*, was she? And her instructions on what to do next weren't the *clearest*, were they? So yeah, I reckon I'll be passing on whatever little adventure she *thought* she wanted us to have."

That silence again.

Wyatt blinks and looks to Belinda, silently urging her to take his side. But what can she say? Geoff is right. He's being a total jerk about it, but he *is* right. Gram hadn't been well. Though she appeared coherent in the video; she could have filmed it before things got bad. Belinda would *love* to believe that Gram had planned one last adventure for them. Imagining that excites her more than anything has in ages. But it's a long shot. Belinda believes in taking chances and following her inner voice and embracing life's moments, and even *she* can see the odds are stacked against them on this.

Belinda considers her words before saying, "I'm not sure, Wyatt. I don't want to let Gram down. I don't. But do we honestly suspect there's more to this? She gave us a strange author's name and said he would point us in the right direction. What does that even mean?"

Wyatt clenches his jaw. He looks lost for words, or maybe just... *lost*.

"Listen," she says, in an attempt to lift the mood, "if you know what to do next or where she wants us to go, then okay! I'm with you one hundred percent! But until then... it may be smart to slow down and remind ourselves of Gram's mental state these last couple years."

Belinda's intent to smooth things over appears to have backfired. Wyatt jerks the cords from the television, face reddening beneath his curtain of dark hair. He says, "I am more than aware of Gram's mental state, thank you very much. I'm the one that's fucking *been* here!"

The VCR lands in the box with a grating crash, and Wyatt

storms from the room.

18

EMELINE

(MAY 30, 2019)

EMELINE BREATHES A SIGH OF relief when, at last, she pulls the Buick into her parent's drive and turns off the car. The silence of the trip was bad enough. Mix that with Wyatt's irritated foot tapping against her plastic floor mat, and the incessant *click-pop* of Geoff fiddling with his phone, and it was enough to drive anyone straight to madness.

The moment the car comes to a halt, Wyatt flees straight to his apartment. Geoff mutters a *see ya* to Belinda and lets himself into the house. Emeline stays behind and waves Belinda off as her bus roars to life, and she reverses out of the drive.

Inside, Emeline finds her mother alone at the kitchen counter sipping a glass of white wine, the rest of the bottle an arms-length away.

"Are the kids asleep?" Emeline asks.

Mom nods in a way that suggests getting them down wasn't easy. "Zonked out about an hour ago."

Emeline takes a glass from the cabinet and fills it with water from the dispenser on the refrigerator door. "Where's Dad? Is he asleep, too?"

Her mother shakes her head. "He went down to Danny's about an hour ago. Says Danny was taking the funeral badly." She raises the glass to her mouth and tosses back a sizeable gulp. "It's not Danny, of course. Your father has let none of this sink in properly. If he doesn't keep moving, it will all come tumbling out, and God-forbid he *feels* something."

Emeline props against the counter and swirls the water in her glass. "I've noticed he seems a bit detached."

Her mom offers a half-laugh and snorts. Emeline suspects this isn't the first glass of wine she's indulged in tonight. "Oh, sure. He's been '*detached*,'" she says, using air quotes, "ever since your Gram got sick. Every episode she had, and he couldn't bring himself to acknowledge a single one. Left everything to me, as usual. I swear, I'm just so *tired*, Em."

And she did seem tired. Emeline hadn't mentioned it, but she'd startled when she saw her mother two days ago. The extra gray in her hair; the sagging skin around her mouth that's afflicted her with a permanent frown; that muddled, directionless gaze that veers straight into anger without a whisper of warning.

"Mom, why didn't you call me if things were so bad? You should have told me if it was too much for you. I would have helped."

At this, her mom's nostrils flare, and she grips the stem of her glass with both hands. "Oh, really? Would you have?"

Emeline doesn't answer.

"How many times have I called your phone and had it go straight to voicemail?" she continues. "You couldn't even bother yourself to come out here early and help with the funeral preparations. None of you could."

Emeline blanches. Her first thought is to retort, to tell her mother how much she's dealing with at home. That it's next to impossible to raise two toddlers as a single mother when you're isolated from your family. That she doesn't always have time or energy to spare. But the move was her decision. The divorce, hers as well. It doesn't matter anyway because Mom stands. She takes her glass and her accusations and moves toward the living room doorway.

Before she slips through, though, she turns and says, "The phone works *both* ways, Emeline. You could have called and checked in on me, checked in on your grandmother, whenever you wanted. The choice not to was yours and yours alone."

The words stab Emeline like a knife. Her mother acts as though Emeline doesn't care about them. But her thoughts are always with her family, even when she isn't. She worries over them constantly and scolds herself for being a screw up daughter and a lousy sister. Yet knowing this and doing something about it, are apparently two different things. Because her mother is right—she hasn't called. She's made zero effort.

She tosses her water into the sink, snatches the bottle of wine from the counter and retreats upstairs.

In her room, sedated from a generous pour of Sauvignon Blanc, Emeline opens her laptop. To avoid thoughts of her mother, she turns her attention to the strange things Gram said in the video. It's stupid, of course. She knows there's nothing to it. But there's no harm in satiating her curiosity.

Who on Earth is Edward Bulwer-Lytton?

She plugs the name into Google and scrolls without expectation through the results. *English writer and politician.* Okay. *Born in London, 1803. Died in 1873.* Right. If Gram expected them to fly to London, she really *had* lost her mind. Emeline reads on. *Most famous quote: "Beneath the rule of men entirely great, the pen is mightier than the sword."*

Emeline sighs and rubs her face. She's so tired she could fall into her hands and sleep for a week. But instead, she pours another glass of wine.

Geoff was right. None of this makes sense. Gram was

delusional in her last years. As much as Emeline wants to believe Gram's tape leads to something more, odds are…

Wait.

The tape.

She'd found the VHS in the hope chest Gram had left her. What if?

The pen is mightier than the sword.

He'd lend us a *hand* and point us in the *right* direction. Right? Or *write?* Gram had over-enunciated both words in the video.

This is absolute insanity, but *what if?*

19

GEOFF

(MAY 30, 2019)

THE DOOR TO GEOFF'S ROOM flies open and slams into his packed carry-on bag.

"Em! *Jesus!* Knock much?" he shouts.

Emeline has a crazed look in her eyes, but her expression shifts to confusion as she takes in the sight of him; he sits on the edge of the air mattress, pulling on his shoes. "What are you doing?" she asks.

Geoff swallows and answers, "Going to the airport." He'd gotten a red eye flight into Albany International. With luck, he'll be home before noon tomorrow.

"What? *Now?*"

"Yeah, now. I've got to get back. I shouldn't have stayed as long as I did."

He expects Emeline to reprimand him for ditching early, but she only mutters, "Whatever." And then, as her eyes scan the room, adds, "Where's the pen?"

"What?"

"The *pen*, Geoff! The pen. The one from Gram. Where did you put it?"

She must realize it's packed away for his trip home—which it *is*—so she turns to his luggage, unzipping random pockets and emptying the contents onto the floor.

"Um… Excuse me? That's personal property," Geoff snaps, and shoves her aside before he needs to repack the whole damn thing. He opens the main compartment of the bag. The pen is still in the back pocket of the jeans he'd worn earlier to the will reading.

Emeline snatches it from his hands and sighs with relief.

"What's this all about?" he asks.

She makes an abrupt turn for the hall. "Come with me," she says.

Geoff sighs and follows to her room.

As he steps through her door, a stab of jealousy tears at him. Mom and Dad haven't touched Emeline's room; it's still hers, everything unmoved from the day she left.

Emeline sits at her laptop and frantically swipes her finger across the touchpad to wake the dark screen. Geoff's eyes fall to the half-empty wine bottle on the desk beside her. "Well, that explains a lot," he mumbles.

She ignores him and rambles on about Edward Bullwinkle-Lysol, or whatever his name is.

"So, I started thinking, what if the things we received at the funeral weren't random gifts? What if they were part of the game? What if they were *clues?* I found the VHS in the hope chest. What Gram said in the video leads to a *pen*." Emeline raises the pen in demonstration.

Geoff presses his thumb and forefinger to his brow bone; he suddenly has a splitting headache. "It's just a pen, Em. There's nothing written on it. No engravings. Nothing."

Emeline's head falls to her lap where she slowly twists the pen in her fingers. Her eyebrows wrinkle in concentration. Then, without a word, she unscrews the tip of the pen from the barrel and pulls it apart.

"Emeline! What the hell?" Geoff shouts. But his voice trails off because there, wrapped around the ink chamber, is a small piece of paper.

"Oh my God," she mutters.

Geoff watches in disbelief. Emeline throws him an *I-told-you-so* stare before she unrolls the paper and reads what it says:

91799 Main St.
Daytona Beach, FL 32118

Emeline clicks out of Edward Bullseye-Lugnut's Wikipedia page and plugs the address into Google.

"The Salty Siren Bar and Grill," she reads.

Geoff stares at the back of her head, at the thick, unruly waves her hair is drying into because she hasn't straightened it yet. He sighs. "Gram wants us to go to a bar in Daytona? Why do I somehow doubt that?"

Emeline's head shakes back and forth. "This makes no sense."

Geoff agrees. He's ready to get out of here. "There's nothing to make sense of," he says. "Like I said before, loony Gram didn't know what she was talking about. Let's go home and forget this nonsense."

She spins around to meet his eyes, crazed expression restored. "We can't, Geoff. This might not make sense to us now, but it's *something*. We have an address. It didn't crawl into the pen on its own. Someone put it there. If we ignore this, I won't be able to live with myself. Will you?"

Geoff wants to say no, wants to believe he can leave and put this behind him, but can he really? Could he ever stop himself from wondering if this was legit? But then there's Lila. A delay in his return will only hurt their situation. He needs to get back. Being here—unable to reach her, to fix things—is enough to make him want to crawl right out of his skin. In this moment, he resents Gram. He resents her for putting the thought of this trip in his head, for taking his ability to walk away and staining it with a big, fat *what if?* He'll carry this regret forever if he doesn't see it through.

But this is *his* life.

He can't concern himself with others. Not even Gram. Not right now.

"It's three hours and fourteen minutes from here," Emeline says as she studies Google Maps.

Geoff sighs. Takes one decided step backward, and then another. "I'm sorry. I have a flight at four AM."

Emeline glares at him in disapproval, but not surprise. It doesn't surprise anyone when Geoff makes a selfish decision. "Do whatever you want," she says, "but I'm going."

Geoff leaves the room.

20

WYATT

(MAY 31, 2019)

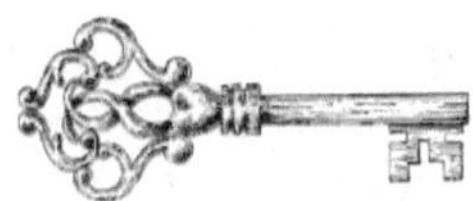

THE LAST TIME WYATT SAW six AM, he'd been awake the entire night (not by choice, but that hardly matters), and watched the thin curtain over his single window take on the blue glow of first light. His eyes had hurt. Everything hurt back then.

Today, however, he stands on the driveway, fully dressed and with a few hours of sleep under his belt. He feels okay. Maybe more than okay.

When Wyatt was younger, a certain thrill came with waking before the sun. To step outside your usual routine and start the day while the rest of the world dwelled in dreams, teased of big adventures to come.

Wyatt isn't sure how much of an adventure this will be, but it *is* different, and a tiny jolt of excitement surges through him.

"It's pretty small," he notes, after peeking inside Belinda's home-on-wheels. She'd pulled the sky-blue bus into the drive at five-thirty sharp, per Emeline's instructions.

"It's bigger than it looks," she says. "I've lived on this thing for seven years without a problem."

Belinda takes them on a quick tour, pointing out the full bed in the back and the kitchen table that folds to an extra twin bed. She turns on the faucet in her small sink and presents the running water like a model on The Price is Right. She's just filled the water tank, she says. There's even a toilet and shower.

The tour eases Wyatt's worries. It will be tight, but since Geoff left for New York this morning, the three of them should be comfortable enough if they need to sleep in the bus overnight.

It doesn't surprise Wyatt that Geoff bailed on the trip, and he isn't sorry for the loss of his company. The girls don't treat Wyatt the way Geoff does; they at least *pretend* to respect him. Geoff wears his disgust with Wyatt right on his sleeve.

Emeline clears her throat. "With any luck, we'll figure out what Gram wants to tell us before the end of the day. But, just in case, I told Mom to give us three days. Are you good, Bee? Do you need to be back at any certain time?"

"Nope. Wide open," Belinda says with a swish of her hand. "What did your folks say about all this?"

"They agree with Geoff. Thinks it's the ravings of a delusional old woman. But fortunately, Mom loves her grandkids and has no problem sending me on a wild goose chase through gator-infested Florida if it means getting more time with them."

Belinda offers a soft chuckle of agreement.

"Well, we should hit the road and try to beat the traffic on I-75," Emeline says, ever practical.

Wyatt's shirt sticks to his back with the dampness of the early morning humidity, and he is more than ready for the relief of air conditioning.

They are loading their bags onto the bus when a white GMC Yukon pulls up to the house. The back door opens and Geoff steps out, dragging his luggage behind him.

Damn it.

Damn it to Hell.

Wyatt's eyes fall to his feet as the potential of this trip takes a sudden nosedive.

"Thought you left?" Emeline asks, voice hard and unfriendly.

"I did," Geoff huffs, and stomps across the drive. His face casts judgment on each of them, as if they personally extracted him from his flight. "Or I *tried* to, anyway. I made it to the airport but couldn't bring myself to get on the damn plane. For the record, I think this is a total waste of time, and I can't wait to say *I told you so.*"

Emeline finishes his thought. "But you couldn't leave without knowing for sure."

Instead of an answer, Geoff's eyes travel to the bus. "Oh, you've got to be kidding me. We're not taking *that* thing?"

Belinda's face reddens. "This *thing* has taken me across the entire country more times than I can count. It's comfortable and can fit all of us without a problem. Would you rather sit cramped in the backseat of Emeline's Buick?" She adds, "No offense, Emeline. The Buick is great."

"None taken," Emeline says.

Geoff sighs, eyes fixed on the bus in distaste, but doesn't further press the matter.

Wyatt, already dreading the next few hours, shoulders past him and says, "You'll be sleeping on the *floor*, by the way."

As much as he'd like to turn and relish the scowl on Geoff's face, it's needless; the fury that radiates from his brother is palpable.

Wyatt smiles with satisfaction and climbs the steps into the bus.

21

BELINDA

(MAY 31, 2019)

BY NINE-THIRTY THEY ARE CRUISING along Florida A1A and getting their first glimpse of the oceanfront towers and colorful tourist shacks of Daytona Beach.

This isn't Belinda's first trip to Daytona, of course. She's driven these streets a hundred times, and plenty of other beach towns to boot; when you've been traveling your entire adult life, you tick lots of cities on the map. But towns like Daytona linger in her soul, calling her back again and again.

Belinda steers with her right hand, left arm hanging out the open window, and she relishes the way her fingers cut through the thick, briny air.

These are the towns you *must* ride through with your

windows down, she thinks. Where schedules are loose, and you feel the salt on your skin before you ever see the ocean. The warm sea-breeze dances across your fingertips and you realize you are someplace extraordinary—a place that exists in a state of perpetual summer. And really, is anything better than that?

"Main Street, next signal," Geoff clips, forehead pressed against the window as he searches out the street signs. Belinda is aware where Main Street is.

Emeline moves to the front of the bus and nearly tumbles as Belinda takes a sharp right turn onto Main; she holds on to the back of the driver's seat to steady herself. The two of them scan the storefronts for the address.

"There!" Emeline shouts, and points to a bright orange restaurant on the right.

Belinda slows to get a better look. A silver hatchback, annoyed with the delay, blasts their horn and passes aggressively to the busses left; as they zoom by, Geoff flips them the bird.

There, above the door of the building, a circular sign hangs— The Salty Siren Bar and Grill.

"Damn," Emeline mutters, reading the hours posted on the front door. "We're early. They don't open until eleven."

A general grumble breaks out on the bus, but Belinda has an idea. "That's okay!" she says with a rush of excitement. "It's Friday. We can go to the farmer's market."

Geoff makes a show of dragging his hands across his face and half-sighs-half-screams. It's no secret that Geoff would prefer to get this done quickly, but with circumstances as they are, he'll have to deal.

"Farmer's market?" Wyatt says. "I'm cool with that. Sounds fun." Belinda watches in the rearview mirror as Wyatt throws an instigative smirk in Geoff's direction.

"Where is it?" Emeline asks.

"Right across the street at the boardwalk. I sell my jewelry there sometimes."

Belinda 's worst fear is to work in a job she hates; a stuffy office with boring people and a measly paycheck that barely covers the bills. To whittle away her days, hoping her sixties bring rest and travel opportunities, seems a tremendous waste of her youth. Belinda has never prescribed to societal pressures, and though she finds herself constantly ridiculed for her *less than conventional* choices, she is happy. Her dad has paid off her bus, she's never owned a credit card, and she earns her spending-cash by making and selling custom jewelry at farmer's markets and festivals across the country.

Belinda makes simple work of backing the bus into a spot on the street and opens the mobile parking app where she pays the meter straight from her phone.

Geoff stands, arms crossed. "Fine. But as soon as the bar opens, we come *right back.*"

22

EMELINE

(MAY 31, 2019)

THOUGH EARLY, THE HEAT ON the boardwalk is stifling. Not quite eighty degrees yet, but the lack of shade or cloud cover has Emeline wishing for an umbrella. She moves along with the others and fans herself with a pamphlet on sustainable palm oil a vendor handed her farther back.

To their right are the permanent shops and restaurants of the boardwalk, while white tents and self-built stalls extend along the left. The booths advertise everything from homemade cupcakes, to vegetables, to locally sourced honey, to pet supplies, to pyramid scheme products. Half-naked bodies are everywhere, stinking of Coppertone, and trail wet, sandy footprints across the promenade.

Emeline shades her eyes with the pamphlet and looks to the ocean. Summer vacation is in full swing in this part of the state; a weekday morning, and the beach is already swarming. Families with coolers and umbrellas have staked their spots and settled in for the day. Nearby, a giant inflatable slide is planted on the backshore; a line twenty-deep waits to climb up, and buoyant shrieks sound from the riders already taking their plummet. Emeline aches for the cool rush of the water and can imagine it lapping over her toes, her thighs, soaking her hair.

The kids would love this. She hates herself for leaving them in Valdosta; they just lost their great-grandmother and now their mom up and leaves without explanation. But she can't ignore how nice it is to walk a crowded market without the worry of one or more of her children slipping from her sight or asking every five seconds for a snack or a toy or a potty, and she feels guilt over that notion as well.

Belinda bobs along next to Emeline. A peaceful smile plays at her lips as her eyes scan the market booths. She babbles non-stop to Emeline, pointing out vendors she's sold with at other markets—which to avoid, which she personally buys from—and how Ann at the artisanal popsicle booth weaseled her way into the best vendor space at the *huge* market in San Antonio because she babysits the festival director's five kids for free. Emeline hardly has time to absorb what she's said before she moves to her next thought.

Belinda is in her element here, dressed in an ivory sundress that falls to her calves and an oversized hat to keep the sun off her fair face and shoulders. She doesn't display the wide-eyed confoundment typical of tourists; she moves and speaks with the confident ease of a local. A girl who belongs nowhere, and yet *everywhere.*

Geoff stalks several paces ahead of them. Despite his best attempt to show zero interest in *anything* Daytona has to offer, his eyes now follow a rather voluptuous female who approaches in the other direction. Whether intentional, he straightens his posture, his chest inflating as she passes, and Emeline can't contain her eye roll.

Wyatt falls behind, hands stuffed in the pockets of his cargo shorts, observing without comment. Words aren't necessary to convey how out-of-place Wyatt is here; the fact that he's wearing sneakers to the beach gets that message across fine.

"Denver!" Belinda shouts, and she breaks into a half-jog-half-skip to join a young guy at one of the tents. The sign on his table reads: *Holistic & Whole.*

The guy is on the shorter side. Around Emeline's age, perhaps a year or two older. His pale hair falls in messy wisps, as if he showers and allows the wind to dry it however it pleases. As he pops from behind his table to embrace Belinda, Emeline studies him further. He's attractive, in a grungy sort of way. His eyes are a brilliant shade of blue. A dusting of sandy-colored facial hair grows patchy and unmanicured. He wears a short-sleeve, loose-fit Henley unbuttoned to his navel. A puka-shell pendant Emeline recognizes as one of Belinda's creations hangs from his neck on a long, black-cord necklace.

"Belinda! Why didn't you tell me you were coming, gorgeous girl? Are you selling today?" A faded Australian accent takes Emeline by surprise.

"No. No, not today," Belinda says, flushed and breathless. "I'm here with my cousins. We're in town for my grandmother."

Denver's eyes flick to each of us, and he smiles in greeting. Attention back on Belinda, he says, "Your sweet grandma! How is she doing?"

Belinda blanches. "She passed away last week. The funeral was Wednesday."

Denver grips Belinda's hand between both of his own and pulls her so close their faces verge on touching. "I'm so sorry for your loss, Belinda. But remember, there is no death, only a change of worlds. Your grandmother has entered through the cosmic doorway to a beautiful new life."

Belinda nods, dewy eyes fixed on Denver as though he were the Messiah; the appeal eludes Emeline, but with a voice that smooth, she can see how one like Belinda might be so easily beguiled. Geoff, however, has been tensing beside her throughout this entire exchange.

"So," Belinda says in a voice several octaves higher than usual. "How is business?" She slides her hands free and forces her eyes to Denver's booth.

Denver's face brightens at the invitation to discuss his products, which, according to him, are a complete line of all-natural, hemp-based bath and body care. His most popular product, he says, is his Vitamin-Infused Hemp-Seed Soap Bar.

Geoff gives a dismissive grunt and says, "I'm more of a body wash man myself."

"Oh yeah? What brand do you use?" Denver turns to him, interested. This unsettles Geoff, Emeline can tell.

Geoff crosses his arms. "Old Spice, usually. Whatever smells good. No offense, but my girlfriend has tried to get me on the homemade soap kick about a million times, and it just doesn't lather like body wash does."

"I hear ya, man," Denver says. "But did you know the amount of lather is actually unrelated to the level of cleanliness you achieve? Does your body wash contain Triclosan, by chance?"

Geoff snorts. "How would I know?"

Denver's eyes widen with concern. "Oh, *definitely* something you should know, my man. A lot of products add Triclosan as an antibacterial, but in actuality, this makes our bodies resistant to antibiotics, and even causes cancer in rats."

"Well, good thing I'm not a rat," Geoff says.

At this, Wyatt snorts, and the glance Geoff throws him is viperous.

Denver, missing this display of brotherly hostility, continues. "Now, *my* soaps are Triclosan free. Free of any artificial ingredients, as a matter of fact. Raw shea butter and hemp-seed oil. That's it. It's ultra-moisturizing, anti-aging, loaded with Vitamin A, and is perfect for all skin types. This is some *good* shit."

"I use his turmeric and rosemary soap. It's super exfoliating," Belinda adds with a gleeful smile.

That smile only widens as Denver rushes to her side and runs his fingertips down her arm in demonstration. "And look at this skin!" he says. "She's glowing. She's a goddess."

Belinda giggles and slips from his grasp, readjusting the thin strap of her dress that's slid from her shoulder.

Not missing a beat, Denver turns back to Geoff. "Mother nature provides everything we need for eternal health and wellbeing. It's her greatest gift to Earth's children."

The muscles beneath Geoff's jaw clench once and then twice. To no one in particular he says, "I'm getting a beer," and tramps off in the opposite direction.

"Nice to meet you, bro!" Denver shouts after him.

23

WYATT

(MAY 31, 2019)

GROGGY AND SUN-FLUSHED, THEY RETURN to Main Street and drag themselves toward the orange and white awning of The Salty Siren Bar and Grill. The front door is open now, and someone has set up a chalkboard menu on the sidewalk. Wyatt is dying for AC and a place to sit that isn't teeming with people and sweat and sand.

The sweet, yeasty smell of beer permeates the air before they even reach the door.

Inside, the restaurant itself is small and unsophisticated. Wood-paneled walls are bedecked with mismatched flotsam and nautical artwork. A long, aluminum-fronted bar runs along the left wall; an antique anchor, rusted and chipped, hangs above the sprawling shelves of liquor, and plastic stools in a kaleidoscope of colors await the day's customers. Great big windows span the front of the restaurant, each cranked open to release the smells and sounds of the bar to passersby. A dozen tables and booths sit empty.

The far wall is painted in a garish shade of purple—the backdrop to a short, homemade stage. A man with a backwards hat, tank-top and sandals sits on a stool there, tuning an acoustic guitar.

One other man sits at the far end of the bar, both elbows propped on the counter. He scrolls robotically through his phone, a half-empty beer in front of him.

Just then, the kitchen door behind the bar swings open and the waitress slips through, a towering stack of glasses balanced in each hand. Wyatt doesn't mean to stare, but he supposes he must be. She's pretty. Short and caramel skinned. Long thick hair the color of espresso. The shadow of freckles defused beneath a thin layer of makeup. As she greets them, a set of full lips pull back into an eye-catching smile.

"Hey there," she says. "You guys have a seat, and I'll be with you in just a sec."

She turns to place the glasses on the counter behind her and transforms her two towers into four neat stacks.

Wyatt isn't sure what they will find here (if anything), or why Gram has sent them to a random bar in Florida, but he can't object to the atmosphere. The waitress has another freckle, he notices. An inch beneath the hem of her denim shorts, high on her left thigh. Wyatt's flesh burns hot, and he turns his attention elsewhere.

The cousins take their seats at the bar, near the door. If the AC is on in here, they can't feel it. At least the open windows offer a slight—albeit *warm*—breeze.

The waitress drops a soggy coaster in front of each of them and takes their drink orders. Geoff orders a beer—his second of the day, and it's not yet noon. A Sprite for Wyatt, water for Belinda, and a cider for Emeline.

After a few test-strums, the man on the guitar starts in on a somewhat off-key rendition of "I Go Blind" by Hootie and the Blowfish. Wyatt's feet tap inconspicuously beneath the bar.

The waitress returns with their drinks just as a group of guys shove through the front door. They retreat to the first booth, with a surety that suggests they come here often enough to consider it *their* spot. There are three of them; college-aged, all muscles and tans and testosterone. Wyatt's feet stop tapping.

"Cami!" they shout to the waitress.

She answers with a blush and a roll of her eyes. "Be with you in a minute," she shouts to them.

"Don't keep us waiting, baby!" one of them yells.

"We missed you!" yells another.

They hoot and laugh, deep voices overpowering the man with the microphone, which Wyatt finds rude and unnecessary.

Cami places a spiral-bound menu in front of each of them with an apologetic smile. "Let me go handle these guys real quick, and I'll be back to get your order. Shout if you have any questions."

As Cami joins their booth, more frat-boy whooping and animated conversation breaks out. Wyatt keeps his back turned to the table; he refuses to watch her giggle and flirt with a bunch of Neanderthals. But more than that, he wants to hide the insecurities he wears like a billboard on his forehead. As much as he wishes to claim the attention of someone like her, it's not in his nature.

You see, to Wyatt, people fall into three basic categories: Those who are truly extraordinary; those who are extraordinary but think themselves mediocre, and (much to Wyatt's disappointment, the most *common* of the three—) those who are average and dull in every feasible way yet *believe* themselves extraordinary. Wyatt must be part of a rare, undiscovered subspecies because he doesn't fit into *any* of these categories. He certainly isn't special or extraordinary and has never been inclined to think otherwise. Even as a child, he'd walked through life as an outsider; a misshapen peg desperately trying to stuff himself into a million pre-cut holes and hating himself when he didn't fit. As an adult, he's come to accept his differences, and so he sticks to music and novels and the underrated value of his own company, to protect himself from the certain disappointment of unnecessary human connection.

With a sigh, Wyatt turns his attention to the menu, thumbing through the thick, laminated pages in silence. The man with the backwards hat transitions into Sublime's "What I Got."

Geoff lets his menu fall to the bar with a *smack!* and swivels on his stool to survey the bar. He's getting restless; Wyatt isn't the only one who's noticed. Something has been stuck in his brother's craw since he came home, and whatever it is, has turned him into more of a jerk than usual.

"Well, hate to say I was right, but…" Geoff says with a smug twitch of his shoulders.

Emeline frowns. "Shut up. We've been here five minutes. We'll figure it out."

But doubt has even wormed its way into Wyatt, and he is sure the others are questioning this trip as well.

Behind the bar, several pictures hang in a cluster: an A- score from the health department in a frame made of bottle caps; a newspaper clipping with a grainy photo of a swarming crowd, with the headline: "Owner of The Salty Siren Serves it up for Bike Week"; a framed, black-and-white snap of two young girls sitting on a dock in front of a bunch of boats.

"Interesting," Emeline says, eyes fixed on the same cluster of frames.

"What's interesting?" asks Wyatt.

She points at the photo of the two girls. "Do you see the boat in the background? Look at the name."

Wyatt narrows his eyes and, sure enough, the boat behind the girls has a name painted on the back: The Salty Siren.

"Big deal," Geoff snorts. "They probably named this place after it."

Emeline throws Geoff an annoyed glare. "I said it was interesting. I didn't say it had to mean something."

Cami returns then, notepad in hand, ready to take their order. Her eyes flash briefly to his, and Wyatt is sure he's blushing; his face heats clear to his eyebrows. Emeline comes to his rescue and asks, "Excuse me. That photograph there on the wall—what can you tell us about it?"

Geoff sighs; he clearly doesn't think there's reason to pursue the photograph further. But Cami beams. "Oh, this one here?" She signals to the black-and-white photo, and Emeline nods. "This is the owner, Greta," she says, pointing at the darker-haired of the two girls. "And the boat in the background there belonged to her brother. She named the bar after it."

"See?" Geoff mutters under his breath.

"Thank you. I was just curious," Emeline says, and returns her eyes to the menu with a hint of disappointment. "I'll need just another minute, if that's okay."

"No problem! Take your time." Cami turns to check on the man at the end of the bar.

Wyatt debates between the grilled chicken sandwich and the turkey club, but in doing so, his eyes land on something that sends gooseflesh across his arms. "Guys," he says in an urgent whisper, "look at this."

The others lean inward to see. There on the menu, in the section for sandwiches, four items from the top, is something called "The Imogene."

A fried-bologna sandwich.

Gram's favorite.

"The Imogene," Belinda reads, a note of awe in her voice.

Cami overhears this and turns back with a smile. "The Imogene! Excellent choice. That's her there, you know!" She points at the second girl in the photograph, the one beside the owner.

Glances are exchanged. Even Geoff seems intrigued. Still unsure what any of this means, or why Gram wanted them to come here, they've found a connection. And answers are sure to follow.

"Were they friends? Imogene and the owner... Um...?" Emeline sticks on the name.

"Greta," Cami says.

"Right. Greta. How did they know each other?"

At this, Cami offers an apologetic shrug. "They were friends back then, but I really don't know much about what happened. That would be a question for Greta. She doesn't get in until four today. You're welcome to come back then if you'd like."

The others ignore the loud, disgruntled puff of air that comes from Geoff.

They will come back at four.

Of course they will.

24

EMELINE

(MAY 31, 2019)

EMELINE WRIGGLES HER TOES IN the warm sand, the rolling waves of the Atlantic Ocean before her. With time to kill, they'd visited one of the tacky tourist shops on the beach and bought swimsuits and towels. Belinda had set up the white canvas tent she uses for festivals, and beneath the shade of it, the heat is not only bearable, but pleasant, and Emeline is finally relaxing. Between the friction with Armie, reentering the workforce after years of playing house, and raising two kids under the age of five, *relaxed* is not a position in which she often finds herself.

Geoff lingered for maybe ten minutes before the restlessness took hold, and he left to walk along the beach. Now he plods along the shoreline, brooding like a moody teen; Emeline can just see the sinewy stretch of his bare back bobbing away in the distance. Something is going on with him, and Emeline would bet money it involves Lila and her reason for not accompanying Geoff to the funeral. On that first night home, when Emeline noted her absence, Geoff stiffened and said *her brother's graduation is this weekend. A ton of family is in town, but she sends her best.*

Right.

It astounds Emeline that Geoff and Wyatt are twins; their differences are innumerable. Now, for instance, Wyatt sits beside the girls under the tent, his tennis shoes placed neatly beside him, white socks balled up and shoved inside. His chin rests atop his knees as he reads a paperback. Reading at the beach—you would never catch Geoff doing that.

Belinda hunches over a short length of black cord, carefully threading on three puka shell charms.

"Bee?"

"Hm?" Belinda opens the small wooden box where she keeps her paint pens and rifles through her collection.

Emeline hesitates before asking, "Do you ever feel you're missing out by traveling all the time?"

"How do you mean?"

"Like… Do you ever wonder what it would be like to settle somewhere? With a husband and kids and a mortgage and all that?" *Like me?* Emeline thinks with a heavy heart. "I know the driving around was fun when you were eighteen, but now that you're older, do you ever plan on stopping?"

Belinda is adding calligraphy to each of the shells and doesn't look up from her work when she answers. "No. I really don't. This life is perfect for me. It's not for everyone, but it's what I always wanted. I get to create things, and meet new people all the time, and wake up to views like this. I spend every day exactly the way I want, and each day is something new."

Emeline nods and retreats into her thoughts. Belinda must sense Emeline's discomfort, quickly adding, "Not that there's anything wrong with settling down and doing things the more conventional way! That's just not for me."

It's not for me, either, Emeline thinks. But she nods and says, "No, I know. I was just curious."

And she returns to her thoughts.

"Done! *Ta-dah!*" Belinda presents the bracelet to Emeline. She's painted each of the puka shells with an initial: An E for Emeline, a C for Conner, and an A for Aimee.

"Do you like it?"

Emeline smiles. "I love it, Bee." With a soft sigh she says, "Just the three of us," and lets her fingers brush over the painted letters.

"Careful!" Belinda snatches the bracelet away. "You'll smear it."

"Sorry," Emeline mutters. As Belinda cleans up, silently packing her paint pens in the box and stuffing the extra black cord into a burlap pouch, Emeline stares out at the water.

"I'm sorry about you and Armie," Belinda says after a moment.

Emeline nods. "Thanks."

"I know it's not my place to ask, but I *am* curious… What happened between you two? You always seemed so happy."

Emeline tenses. She doesn't want to talk about it, but she doesn't want to *not* talk about it, either. For too long she's been alone with her thoughts; it might help to talk. Perhaps if she shares her burden with Belinda—and Wyatt, who is listening but pretending not to—she can lighten the load in her mind. She's never put her story to words, but it's worth a shot.

Emeline shrugs and begins. "Nothing really *happened*, per se. That's the strange thing. I can't look back and pinpoint where it all went wrong. I just knew it had."

The truth is, her issues with Armie started long before they'd known they were issues. Negative thoughts and nagging resentments she at first attributed to bad moods and stress crept in one by one. She imagined herself swallowing these feelings— storing them away—so that over time they might dissipate. Instead, they simmered there inside her, permanently changed her thoughts, and dimmed the light that used to burn so brightly for her marriage. So, no—love didn't slip from her hands and plummet to the ground in one defining moment of despair. It was a slow change, an erosion, tiny pieces of them chipped away with each passing day, until nothing remained but dust.

The loss of her marriage Emeline can endure. If it were just the two of them to consider, she'd pull herself from the wreckage, accept the wasted years, and move on with her life. But it's not just *them*, is it?

"I'm not a good mom, Bee," Emeline confesses.

"What are you talking about? Conner and Aimee adore you."

Emeline snorts. "They adore me. But they deserve more than me. They deserve a mom who is *good* at being a mom. One who sets up playdates and takes them to fun places and plays make-believe, arts and crafts—all that stuff. The truth is... I love them more than anything in the entire world, but I miss my old life. I miss my job—my *good* job from before, not the stupid receptionist job—and I miss the way I used to love Armie and all our time together. Life got... *difficult* after I became a mom."

Emeline hears the words leave her mouth, and though she can't deny the truth of what she's said, she hates herself for even entertaining such thoughts, let alone speaking them out loud. It sounds like she hates her kids. God only knows what Belinda must be thinking. But she needs to go on; the rest of the story won't sound so bad (she *hopes*).

Emeline confesses that after Conner was born, she struggled to slip into her new role as *Mom*. She'd just received a promotion—the Human Resources Director at a four-star Hilton resort—when she'd fallen pregnant. After her maternity leave expired, she jumped back into her position full force. She loved her job, but it was demanding and better suited for someone with more time to spare. Still, every morning Emeline put on her expensive Ann Taylor pant suit, dropped Conner off at her parent's house, and dedicated the next ten hours to her team and the strangers who expected a flawless stay at the most recognized hotel brand in the world.

When she picked Conner up in the evenings, she realized how much she was missing, and her heart ached because she *knew* she was a despicable mother for choosing work over her own child. Then, to make up for the moments lost, she would spend her free time devoted to Conner, which left Armie on the losing end of her affections, and her heart ached over *that*, because now she was a despicable *wife* to boot. No matter what she did, there was a gnawing sense she should do something else instead.

Then, just over a year later, she was pregnant with Aimee, and was desperate for change. Armie had suggested a move to Tennessee, to live closer to his family. Emeline hesitated. With Gram being sick, she wasn't sure a move was the right choice. And what about work?

In the end, she'd been desperate enough to agree. But regretted it almost immediately.

In Valdosta, they lived on a modest piece of land at the end of a cul-de-sac. It was cozy, and everyone had a big potluck in the street on the Fourth of July. In Brownsville, they live in a gated community. Little more than an arm's length and a row of low shrubs separate you from your neighbor, and yet, Emeline doesn't even know her neighbor's names. Cars are tucked away in garages—never the driveway, or you'll find a citation in your mailbox faster than you can blink. Recycling collects on alternating Wednesdays. And all landscaping choices need prior approval from the board. Armie's parents live two streets over and visit the house *constantly,* doting over the children and offering *friendly suggestions* that are neither asked for nor implemented.

With the move, Emeline had given up her job with Hilton. She'd wanted change, hadn't she? Things would be different with Aimee. So, she stayed home with the kids, resolved to become the mom people expected her to be. But the suburban domestic life was not how she imagined, and she struggled from the start.

Emeline was never much of a social butterfly, but she *had* kept a couple of close friendships back in Valdosta. In Brownsville, however, it was a struggle to make any genuine connections. The moms at Conner's preschool were nice enough, but they'd made a full commitment to the stay-at-home mom lifestyle. They exchanged healthy, tasteless recipes, planned day trips to the children's museum or the park where they spent the whole time comparing their kid's accomplishments and milestones, enrolled their toddlers (who hadn't even mastered wiping their own butts) in soccer and tee-ball and ballet. It was too much. Emeline tried. She did. But every moment spent with these women, had her silently screaming, *I'm not the same as you! I haven't given up on myself! I have a career! I'm more than this!* But she'd watched herself stray from self-assured to lonely faster than she ever imagined possible.

To compensate for the financial hit they took when Emeline left the workforce, Armie took on extra hours. At this point, they essentially lived two separate lives, joined only in the evenings when Emeline was so burnt out she could barely muster the enthusiasm for conversation, much less anything else.

One night, she broke down to Armie and told him the homemaker life wasn't for her; she was miserable. Armie seemed to understand. Those big, green, sympathetic eyes of his had twinkled, and he told her not to worry about the dishes or the cleaning or the playdates or *any* of it. *None of that is important,* he'd said. *I just want you to be happy. You should do whatever you need to be happy. Don't worry about us.*

And Emeline believed him.

The pressure to be the perfect mother and wife had lessened. She read more. She took time for herself. Though it was miles from the high-status job she'd held in Georgia, she took a part-time job at the local Double Tree as a front desk receptionist. Whenever she didn't have the patience to put the kids to bed, she told Armie, and let him handle it instead. When she was too tired to make dinner, they got takeout or had pizza delivered. And these omissions and moments of self-care *did* make her happy. Maybe not as happy as she'd prefer, but it was a start.

Unfortunately, Emeline's new way of life had the opposite effect on Armie. He'd become resentful of her newfound freedoms; the less she did—the more she smiled from the not-doing—the more distant and colder he became.

Yes, he'd told Emeline to slack off, but he hadn't stepped up to fill the gap. The things he told her not to worry about doing simply *weren't* getting done. Their lives were in constant disarray. Armie's mother would visit and snicker at the state of the house. Of course, it was Emeline's fault. Never mind that she had a job; she was still the woman, after all, and *a proper woman keeps a proper house.*

Before long, Emeline realized Armie hadn't considered the possibility that she might not slip back into her old routines. He plainly thought this was a phase of sorts, and if he let her spread her wings for a week or two everything would correct itself. But it had taken *years* to achieve this state of unrest, and a few weeks of liberties—if you could call them that—would not flip some imaginary switch and bring her back to life.

One evening, in a frantic, drunken rant, she told Armie how far they'd grown apart, how little he seemed to know her, and how desperate she was for them to reconnect. *We don't talk anymore,* she'd said. *If we don't communicate, what do we have? I need us to be like before.*

Armie lit up at this, and for a moment, Emeline was sure he understood. At long last.

But a few months ago, Emeline had come home from an evening shift at work. The kids were asleep. She waved to Armie, who was watching a sports recap on television, and headed straight for the shower. The first half of her day had been toddlers relentlessly pawing at her face and clothes, and the second half consisting of needy customers and ringing phones. She'd driven home with thoughts of slipping into her pajamas, crawling into bed, and catching up on a few Netflix shows before losing herself to sleep.

As she rinsed the shampoo from her hair, the bathroom door creaked open, and Emeline saw Armie's blurred form through the foggy glass of the shower door. She figured he'd slipped in to grab something he needed. But a moment later, he's in the shower with her—naked—a wild look in his eyes.

"What are you d—" Emeline couldn't even finish the sentence before his mouth was on hers. Shocked, she pushed him away.

"What's the matter?" he'd asked.

This question had flabbergasted Emeline like none other. "What's the matter? I've been home for fifteen minutes, we've barely acknowledged each other, and now you think *this* is going to happen?"

Armie pulled back and looked her hard in the eyes. For a moment, that's all they did. Stared at each other. Two strangers unable to comprehend the needs of the other.

"I don't get you, Emeline," he'd told her. And it was plain that he didn't. He *really* didn't. "I've done everything you asked. You wanted a break from the chores and the school stuff, and I gave you that. You wanted to go back to work—done! You wanted me to do something special for us to reconnect—here I am. And you push me away."

Emeline's skin blazed hot, water rolling down her face in streams she was too angry to wipe away. "Something *special*? I meant a nice dinner or a trip away, just the two of us. For Christ's sake, Armie, tell me you didn't think I meant a quickie in the shower? Have you been paying attention to me at all?"

Armie's next words changed everything. The words that forced her to look inside herself and admit the thing she already knew. He said, "I have no idea what you want, Em. Just tell me what you want, and I'll do it. *Please?*"

Emeline had told him precisely what she wanted—what she *thought* she wanted—so many times. But it hadn't happened. Nothing had changed.

She felt the words before she said them. They started low, from a deep and buried place, and rose without hurry, giving her enough time to stop them if she'd wanted to, to push them down again. But she didn't.

"I want a divorce," she'd muttered.

Another God-awful silence followed. Armie looked at her, and she saw something in his eyes she'd never seen before: *surrender.* After all this, he'd finally given up on her.

Without another word, he left the shower, wrapped a towel around his waist, and exited the bathroom. Emeline shook, sinking to the tiled floor as water rained over her. And she let the tears rush from her eyes until she shook not only from grief, but from cold as well.

What is wrong with me? she thought—and not for the first time. It wasn't a stretch to say she was difficult to love, but she now found it just as hard to love *others,* and that scared her more than anything else ever had.

For the past three months, Armie has been living with his younger brother, Porter, while they sort out the schematics of the divorce.

For so long, Emeline had blamed her unhappiness solely on Armie. She thought, *If I can just get out from underneath him, I'll be a different person. Born anew.* But the freedom from marriage, thus far, hasn't eased the sadness in Emeline. Hasn't relinquished her need for escape. She is alone now. Completely alone and expected to care for two small children with endless needs. And all while pretending that Mommy is fine, and her entire brain *isn't* turning against her.

As Emeline finishes her story, she clears her throat and wipes at the space beneath the bottom of her sunglasses where tears threaten to slip out.

A quick glance at Belinda's face, and Emeline can see the mistake she's made. Belinda doesn't understand. And how could she? She lives her life in such a different way. Without a husband, without kids of her own, she can't begin to know the depths of Emeline's despair. No one can.

"Emeline, I—"

Geoff returns and plops onto the sand beside Emeline, which stops Belinda from saying whatever she meant to say. Instead, she places her hand on Emeline's knee and offers a quick squeeze of reassurance, a move that does nothing to lighten Emeline's spirit. In fact, it infuriates her. As the oldest, she should be setting an example, not accepting pity from her flighty, wanderlust cousin who has never faced a tough decision in her life. It's embarrassing.

"Right," Belinda says, and her voice breaks the tension that is sure to escalate if they continue sitting together like this, "we have about an hour before Greta shows up. If you want, we can shower on the bus and then head over."

Wyatt shuts his book, pulls on his shoes, and walks away without a word.

25

GEOFF

(MAY 31, 2019)

"**W**E JUST SHOWER RIGHT HERE** by the toilet?" Geoff trains an apprehensive eye on the small space between the toilet and the wall. The bathroom is approximately three feet long and two feet wide. "Where's the drain?" he asks.

Belinda smiles and pushes Geoff aside. "It's a shower-bathroom hybrid," she explains. "The floors are teak. The water drains right through the slats and into a tank beneath the bus. Crack the window a little before you shower, though—it cuts the moisture. The shower head detaches here," she says, reaching up to demonstrate. "So you don't have to crouch."

Geoff snorts at this. He's six feet tall and hasn't been able to stand at full height anywhere on this forsaken rig; crouching is unavoidable.

"Any more questions?" Belinda asks. Geoff is still standing there, looking at the bathroom in confusion.

"Just out of curiosity," he shifts his weight and lowers his voice, "if someone needed to use the bathroom, like... *more than pee*... would that be okay to do in here?"

Belinda gives out a toylike giggle. "Yes, silly. The bus is fully functional. But this is a compost toilet, so if you go number two, you'll need to crank the handle a few times to help along the oxygenation process."

Geoff stares in disbelief. "Wait... compost—like, you reuse your poop?"

Belinda laughs again but explains the process in a patient and matter-of-fact tone. "Compost toilets separate liquids and solids. Almost everything evaporates, but it sorts any leftover solids into a separate chamber and—*yes*—you can use it as fertilizer. But I never use it myself."

Thank God, Geoff thinks. "Neat," he says.

"Yeah, whenever I empty the chamber, I save it and give it to my friend Jade. She runs a plant nursery."

Geoff looks at Belinda with amusement, waiting for her to laugh, but she is quite serious. "Jade buys your shit?" he asks. He's never heard an idea so wild in his entire life.

"She doesn't *buy* it. I give it to her," she says.

Geoff thinks of her pal Denver from the farmer's market. "Jesus. Where do you meet these people?"

This is a rhetorical question, of course, but Belinda answers. "I met Jade at a yoni steaming demonstration a few years ago."

Geoff blinks. "I'm almost afraid to ask what that is."

Straight-faced, Belinda says, "Vaginal steaming."

He nods. "Yeah... Okay. Well, on that note, I'm off to make some compost."

Geoff hoists his bag onto the small stretch of counter beside the sink and rifles through to find a fresh towel, his shampoo, and his triclosan-filled body wash that smells a hell of a lot better than that hippy freak's dirt-soap. Belinda continues chatting away.

"It's not gross, Geoff," she says. "It dates back to the Mayans. Emeline knows about it. Don't you, Em?"

Emeline, now an unwilling participant in this conversation, shakes her head, eyes wide. "I absolutely do *not*."

A slight gasp escapes Belinda. "Oh my gosh! How can you not know about vaginal steaming? Okay, so, in short, you sit over a steaming hot bowl of water that they have infused with all these super-beneficial herbs. It completely revitalizes your reproductive tract! I swear, I haven't had a single menstrual cramp since I started doing it."

She pulls her phone from her bag and taps away at the screen. "I wonder if there are any nearby treatment facilities," she mutters, more to her phone than to Emeline. "We can go together! It will be fun!"

Emeline places her hand on Belinda's arm and shakes her head with more politeness than Geoff could have managed. "No thanks, Bee," she says. "Look around… It's ninety-two degrees and one-hundred percent humidity. Florida is basically just one *giant* vaginal steam."

"Oh my God," Geoff mutters, and gathers his things in a rush. He stuffs himself in the shower, desperate to remove himself from this conversation.

Belinda shouts after him. "If vaginas make you this uncomfortable, Geoff, I feel sorry for poor Lila."

She guffaws at her little joke, thinking herself hilarious. Wyatt laughs, too, working hard to project his loud jeers across the bus. Geoff's jaw tenses as a stinging heat spreads over him. These people don't know the first thing about anything. They are beneath him; they always have been and always will be. At his side, he clenches his fists so hard his nails spear his palms.

He continues to fold himself into the pseudo-bathroom as best he can, ignoring Belinda's request to crack the window. Let her deal with mold. See if *he* cares. And though he knows it won't stop their irritating voices from reaching his ears, he slams the door.

26

WYATT

(MAY 31, 2019)

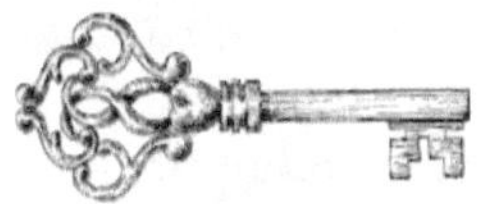

SHOWERED AND CHANGED, THEY RETURN to The Salty Siren. Cami is serving some swamp-colored cocktail to a table of three who converse loudly at one of the two outside tables.

Wyatt's heart does a little flutter; she really *is* beautiful. He catches himself smoothing his hair—a reflex. It's ridiculous, of course. He is as far from her type as one can be.

Yet, when Cami glances up and sees their group approaching, a wide smile transforms her face. "Oh good," she says, "you guys came back!" Did Wyatt imagine it, or did she look right at *him* when she said this?

"Greta just got in. She's back in the office," Cami says. "Come on in. I'll go grab her." And she tucks her drink tray beneath her arm and bustles off through the front door.

Inside is far busier than before. Cami has help now; a curvy blonde with a doll-like face and a booming laugh now tends the crowded bar. Customers fill four of the tables as well. And someone has set up a table for beer pong on the stage, the live music having been swapped for a radio channel; the upbeat indie rock that Wyatt enjoys most plays from overhead speakers.

A few moments later, Cami returns through the swinging door. She squeezes past the blonde bartender and crosses to the far end of the bar, where they stand to wait by an open window. She leans over the bar and shouts in a voice loud enough to overpower the music, "Greta will be right out!" Then, after a beat, "Noah and the Whale!" Sensing Wyatt's confusion, she points to his shirt.

He blanks, forgets what shirt he's wearing, where he is, or how to breathe.

"I love them!" she says with a smile.

Coming to his senses, he clears his throat and says, "Yeah? Me too. Well, I mean, obviously, right? I'm wearing the shirt." He clears his throat again, and then resolves to *stop* clearing his throat, lest she thinks he's full of mucus. "A few years ago, I saw them in Atlanta, right before they broke up. They were awesome."

"Oh, really? I never got to see them live! When they announced they weren't together anymore, I was so upset. I swear, the good bands never last. It's so disappointing."

"Agreed," Wyatt says. "Such a bummer."

Cami's eyes catch a sudden spark. "Hold on!" she says and skips to the cash register where her phone is plugged in; she picks it up and quickly scrolls through with her thumb. The bar music ceases, and a few grumbles break out behind her. "Oh, hush," she says over her shoulder to no one in particular. A second later, the peppy whistles that introduce Noah and the Whale's "5 Years' Time" play over the speakers.

She turns a proud smile to Wyatt that heats his face and neck, and he bobs his head up and down to the beat while he tries to ignore the sweat pooling in his armpits.

"This is *your* playlist?" Wyatt asks.

"Yeah," Cami says. "Greta canceled our Pandora subscription a few months ago, so I started playing music from my phone."

"Nice," Wyatt says, thinking this may very well be his dream girl.

"This is one of my favorites," she says.

"Same here," he agrees. "It's a good tune." He knows Geoff is staring at him, can feel his beady eyes drill into the side of his head.

Regardless, the room disappears, and in that moment, Cami is all Wyatt sees. He imagines where the two of *them* could be in five years' time if things work out in his favor—which they never do. But then the swinging door flies open again and breaks his fantasy.

The woman who enters the room is old—too old to be running a restaurant, Wyatt thinks. She gives the room a brief scan before the blonde bartender runs to her side with a question. The woman nods, turns to the Point-of-Sale system above the register, and punches in a few quick codes. "Thanks, Greta," the bartender says, printing a ticket and tearing it from the printer.

Greta's eyes reach them then, the four of them huddled in the corner of the bar against the wall. A sudden paleness dulls her face, and she freezes. With a quick glance at her feet and a deep breath, she moves toward them.

Greta looks to be in her seventies, with dyed hair that falls to her shoulders in loose, dark curls. A thin strip of black eyeliner streaks the top lid of small, wide-set eyes. Tall and slim, she has clearly taken care of herself over the years. But her face, tight and shrewd, shows a woman not to be trifled with; this is the face she trains on them now.

Soon, her features soften. She takes another deep breath, and in a throaty, no-nonsense voice says, "I would ask who you are and how I can help you, but I believe I already know."

The four of them stare on with blank expressions.

"Your grandmother," she begins, "she's dead, isn't she?"

27

EMELINE

(MAY 31, 2019)

"**I**F THERE WAS ANY DOUBT in my mind, it went out the window as soon as I saw this one here." Greta jabs a thumb toward Emeline and stares at her in awe. "You're the spittin' image of your Gram."

People had remarked on their similarities before, but Emeline never saw the resemblance much herself.

The five of them have moved to a corner booth against the back wall, set beside the stage. The *VIP table*, Greta calls it. In the middle of the table is the framed photo from behind the bar. Emeline looks it over now with renewed interest. The photo shows Gram, much younger than Emeline is at present; a teenager, she'd guess. They *do* share the same general build and body type; which is to say, average. Although Gram's legs are longer and leaner; they stretch in front of her, a slight bend at the knees, bare toes pointed, slender arms hugging her shins. Gram's hair is shoulder length and wavy—same as Emeline's—but Gram's is held back from her face with a wide headband; impossible to say if they share the same chestnut color due to the black-and-white print. Slim, straight nose—another match. The distinction is in the eyes, Emeline thinks. Gram's eyes sparkle at the camera; even in the black-and-white photograph, there's no mistaking the fizzing radiance of her stare. Whatever Gram is looking at in the photo, it fascinates her—gives her life. She was stunning, and much more remarkable looking than Emeline ever was or could ever hope to be.

Curious, she asks, "Who's taking the photo?"

A smile touches Greta's lips, wrinkling the fine skin around them. "That would be Ted Barret. Well, his name was Theodore, but we all called him Ted. He owned the fishing charter in the background there." She taps the photograph with a thin, wrinkled finger.

"Oh, the waitress said that was your brother's boat. Is Ted your brother, then?"

Greta shakes her head. "My brother," she says, pointing at the photograph again. A small male figure stands on the deck of The Salty Siren (the *original* Salty Siren, not the bar which shares its namesake). Bent over, he fiddles with something unseen on the ground. With his face pointed away from the camera, only his back and right ear are visible. "That's him there," she says. "His name was Raymond. Him and Ted owned the charter together. A few times a day, they'd take folks out for these two-hour fishing tours. This photo was taken in 1963, their first summer in business. No. Ted was… Well, I'm not sure what you would have called him at the time of this photo, but Ted and your Gram were deep in love that summer."

Emeline's heart flips at this revelation, but Wyatt looks most shocked and speaks up first.

"Sorry," he says. "I don't mean to be rude, but Gram told us the only man she'd ever loved was our grandpa. She told us she met him young, and there had been no one else for her."

"Wilfred," Greta nods along in agreement. "Imogene talked about him a lot in her letters. She talked about you kids, too. Oh, she loved your granddad something fierce. Made me just *sick* to learn about his passing. I so wanted to be there for your Gram when it happened, but…" She shakes a thought from her mind. "I ain't gonna lie to you kids, though. It was only a summer, so most wouldn't think you could love someone in that amount of time—not *really* love them, anyhow. But your Gram sure loved Ted like nothin' else. Now, that's not to take away from the love she had for your granddad!" she says in a rush. "I'm sure meeting him pulled her attention from the past, gave her a future to hold on to, grew in her a love as strong and deep-rooted as love can be. But that summer, Ted was as real to her as anything."

Emeline is done wasting time. This has been a long day already. "How did you know Gram?" she asks.

"She was my best friend in the entire world," Greta says matter-of-factly. "Like a sister to me."

This answer doesn't sit well with Emeline for *several* reasons. Above all, if Gram and Greta were so close, why had they never met her, or even heard her name? Where has she been all these years?

Greta takes the silence as an invitation to continue, but she does so in a somber tone of voice. "Last letter I got from your Gram was eight months ago. They used to come every couple weeks, or a month at most. After such a long stretch of time without hearing from her, I feared the worst."

Geoff takes up the conversation from here. "This is going to sound insane," he says. "But after our Gram died, she left us a video tape. In this tape, she asked us to take a trip through her past. The tape led us to an address—to *here*. We came out of respect for our grandmother, but to be honest, we haven't a clue why she wanted us to come here and talk to you. She's had dementia since 2015. So, as you can imagine, we aren't sure how much of this is legitimate, and we'd like to sort it out as soon as possible."

Greta blinks a few times in response to Geoff's business-like approach to their visit. But then she nods. "The dementia. Yeah, she told me all about that after her diagnosis. That one hit me hard. Most of the letters that followed, though, were just typical Imogene, far as I could tell. I had wondered if maybe they hadn't misdiagnosed her or if she was just pullin' my leg. The last one, though…" She pauses for a moment to gather herself. "She said her grandkids might be stoppin' by one day soon—which was weird enough in itself; I'd asked to come visit, to meet you kids, must be a million times over the years, and she always said no. There was always an excuse. Now she told me if you *did* show up, I should take you somewhere and tell you the story of the last summer we spent together. I knew—I didn't *know*, of course, there was no way to really *know*—but I had this sneaking suspicion that was the last time I'd hear from your Gram. She hadn't talked about that summer in years. Bringing it up *now*, after all this time, felt too final. I saw you kids standing here today and gathered I was right."

"You weren't at the funeral," Emeline accuses. "You suspected she may have passed, and you didn't look into it? A simple Google search would have brought up the obituary." Greta is old, but as a businesswoman, Emeline guesses she is familiar with Google and the internet.

Greta's eyes glass over at this, and she clears her throat to disguise the emotion. "You're right," she says. "I guess—I guess I didn't really want to know. If I didn't know, then she wasn't really gone, was she? I could just go on and keep waitin' for that next letter."

Silence falls around the table, and Emeline knows her cousins have felt those words as deeply as she has. What they wouldn't give for one more letter, one more phone call, one more visit, one more hug.

"So… this summer you're supposed to tell us about…" Geoff says, steering us back to the task at hand.

Greta stands and shouts over to the bar. "Camila, can you hold down the fort for a bit? I gotta slip out for an hour or two."

"Sure thing!" Cami yells, displaying a thumbs-up. She then returns to a line of shot glasses she fills with an unappealing brown liquor.

Greta gathers the photo and makes to leave the booth. "Come on," she says. "We can take the catering van."

"Where are we going?" Belinda asks, speaking for the first time since they'd sat.

"To the marina," Greta answers. "I'll tell you everything when we get there."

28

BELINDA

(MAY 31, 2019)

THE NARROW BOAT DOCK ON which they stand juts out from another dock only marginally wider. Hundreds of boats surround them, though this particular slip stands empty.

Giant booms and masts tower all around and cut through the blue sky. *Halifax Marina*, Greta had said.

Father back, at the start of the slip, Geoff stands alone to admire a neighboring yacht.

Greta is a statue at the end of the dock, hands resting on one of the wooden dock pilings. She stares out—not at the boats across the narrow channel, nor the sky, nor the water itself. Something *else*, Belinda thinks. Something only she can see.

This is the boat slip that used to belong to her brother, Ray.

The slip that once moored The Salty Siren.

Belinda sits in the same place Gram had sat in the photograph from 1963; she'd sought it out and lined herself up with precision, assuming the same position, even; legs extended with a slight bend, arms wrapped around below her knees. Her eyes lift to Geoff, and she imagines Ted standing somewhere near there to take the photo those many years ago. She tilts her head to the sky and welcomes the sensations. The salt air on her skin, the sun warming her face, the birds cawing from every direction, the soft lapping of the water against the boat's hulls, the ghosts from the past.

Belinda can feel Gram here with her—with *them*. Her energy remains in this place, strong as a current. She was *here*. She heard these same sounds, walked these same weathered boards, and sat beneath this same sweeping, blue sky. Once, she was here, and part of her still is.

Somehow, through Belinda's extensive travels, she's only ever driven *past* marinas, never taking the time to tour one. Never has she sat and listened to its heartbeat—something she delights in when visiting somewhere new; places—like *people*— have heartbeats, and if you sit long enough to listen, it reveals itself to you, and you know that place in a way most could never dream possible. The majority don't bother with that sort of thing; places are just *places* to them. But to Belinda, her relationship with the world is just as important as her relationship to actual living, breathing things.

Marinas, it turns out, are a blissful contradiction: a sense of urgency and preparation and journeys to be had, pocked by the quiet calm of a long summer's day; a Hurricane over ice, local radio on a scratchy boombox, and a *come and sit for a minute* attitude. She loves it. She lives for it. This is Belinda's kind of place. And her Gram thought so too, once upon a time. They were more alike than she'd ever realized, and that knowledge brings such peace that Belinda could curl up on the warm decking and fall asleep wrapped in the bliss of it.

After many years, Belinda has at last come to terms with her separation from the others—both physical and otherwise.

Emeline, Geoff, and Wyatt share the sibling bond. Belinda is an outsider, sharing a bond with no one. Dea (her mother and Gram's only daughter) split from her dad right before Belinda's seventeenth birthday. Not long after, she met Logan and ran off to Atlanta to remarry and start her life anew. Even back then, her mother called on rare occasions. Less so, now. Belinda and her dad have been alone since then. Gram always treated Danny as though he were one of her own children, but the fact remains—he isn't *blood*. And, after her mom left, Belinda sensed the divide between her and her family deepen. The notion that she and Gram share a pull to places like this—a call to adventure and travel—gives Belinda a sense of belonging she's never experienced; a connection to the family that is *hers*, but doesn't always feel that way.

Belinda trails her fingers across the engravings beside her. In the old wood that frames the dock, there are three messages carved. The first: *Greta was here*. The second: A heart; *I + T 4ever* in the middle. The third: *Ray smells*.

"I did that one," Greta says, appearing over Belinda's shoulder. "Not the most clever, but *scuzz bucket* would have taken too long to carve out." She snorts out a laugh.

"What happened?" Belinda asks. She can't guess what went on that summer, but the look on Greta's face suggests it wasn't pleasant. "To your brother? To the Salty Siren?"

Greta sighs but appears to have worked up the nerve to begin her story.

"There was an accident that summer," she says. "Ray was killed."

29

IMOGENE

(JUNE 1962)

ELBOWS PERCHED ON THE GLASS countertop, Imogene stares at the display of Swedish Fish, M&M's, and Hot Tamales below; these various sweets and snacks are the focal point while her mind wanders elsewhere, as it so often does on these slow summer days.

Who wants to sit in a dusty old theater in the middle of June anyhow? No one, that's who! Folks are busy soaking in their swimming pools, or running through sprinklers, or catching rays at the beach (exactly where Imogene would be if she had the choice). But as it is, The Sheldon Theater is where she will spend most of her seventeenth summer, same as the summer before.

Studious, introspective, and soft-spoken, Imogene is a loner in every sense of the word. She has friends, of course, but no true *best* friend; this is how it has been her entire life. There are girls she chats with at school, and through volunteering, and at church who she likes well enough, and they like her just fine in return—but not enough to transition into *all the time* friends. She tells herself it doesn't bother her, that she isn't lonely, that she isn't a girl who needs close bonds beyond that of God and her family and eventually, her husband. Imogene is a girl who works summers, saves for college, and dreams of becoming a nurse and helping people. She is a girl who always does what Mom and Dad say without question, because they know what's best for her. *This* is what she tells herself.

But deep down—*oh*—deep down there is an Imogene the world has never seen, and she wishes more than anything to be *that* girl instead. She spends most of her days with her head high in the clouds, dreaming of big adventures and wild love and long drives to new places, and all the things she's learned not to whittle her life away brooding over. But at heart, Imogene is free-spirited and fun and every woman from her favorite television programs.

A short thirty-five-minute drive is all that separates her hometown of Deland from Daytona Beach, where thousands of kids her age congregate in the hot summer sun, and she can only imagine the fun she would have there… if she were *that* kind of girl.

The bell rings out above the door and startles Imogene something terrible. She rises to attention to greet the customers. A lady enters the tiny lobby with her daughter; the daughter looks to be around thirteen and, like Imogene, as though she'd prefer to be anywhere else but here. They skip Imogene's concession stand and make their way straight into one of two theaters offered at The Sheldon.

As the duo disappears through the door of theater one, Imogene slumps back into her position on the counter and returns her chin to the cushion of her palm. The twelve-thirty showing of *Jack the Giant Slayer* is about to start; it won't sell out, not even close, not on a Thursday afternoon. A few moments later, three preteen boys come in and order three Coca-Colas and a large popcorn to share, which they have Imogene drench in butter for them. A lull follows, and Imogene thinks this will be the last of the guests for a while.

Lolita lets out in theater two. Imogene readies the broom and dustpan and heads to sweep up after the meager crowd. As she steps around the counter, the bell chimes a third time, and two girls near Imogene's age stroll into the lobby.

The first is small and petite, short blonde hair falling just below her pierced ear lobes. She wears these tight yellow pants and mid-drift-bearing top splattered with colorful polka dots. The second girl is tall with long, jet-black hair she wears tied back from her face. Thick, shaggy bangs obscure her forehead and tickle the tops of her eyelashes. Fair skin, but she is taking on that sun-kissed summer glow all the girls strive for. Both are lovely, and Imogene is at once self-conscious in her ugly theater smock and sensible shoes.

Imogene hopes they will bypass the concession stand so she doesn't have to embarrass herself, but no such luck; they approach the snack counter, giggling and knocking into each other with playful shoves.

Imogene leans the broom against the far wall and returns to the counter. In a voice smaller than her own, she says, "Can I help you girls?" feeling a hundred percent daft for addressing them this way.

The girls exchange a look—two lionesses spotting a helpless baby antelope—and turn back to Imogene with a smile. "I'll take a box of Milk Duds," the dark-haired girl says, adding a swift, "please."

Imogene retrieves the Milk Duds and places them on the counter, turning her attention to the petite blonde who says, "Oh, just a small popcorn for me! I'm watching my figure."

Imogene says, "Of course," with a smile and a nod. Though, she isn't sure what the blonde could be worried about; she is thin as any girl Imogene has ever seen.

Imogene fills a box with popcorn, *dry*, at her request. "Twenty-five cents, please," she mumbles, placing the popcorn on the counter. The blonde plucks a piece off the top, pops it in her mouth, and glances at her companion as she chews.

The dark-haired girl doesn't miss a beat. She pulls a quarter from her pocket and places it in Imogene's open palm, but she doesn't release the coin straightaway. "You have gorgeous skin," she says to Imogene. "Like Snow White."

The blonde girl nods along in agreement beside her.

"You ever go out in the sun?" the dark-haired girl asks.

Imogene blushes as the girl drops the quarter and pulls away. "Uh… I do." She drops the coin in the cash register, clears her throat and tries again. "Of course, I do. I'm… I'm here a lot, so, I don't get out much in the summer. But during the school year, I do—when I can, that is. I'm usually much tanner. It's just… I guess it's faded." She is rambling. *Stop it, Imogene.*

The girl nods, keeping her eyes on Imogene with keen interest.

Imogene breaks the uncomfortable eye contact and throws her attention to the clock on the wall. "Um… the movie started four minutes ago," she tells them. "You're late."

The dark-haired girl only laughs and gives a mischievous glance to the blonde, who giggles behind a mouthful of popcorn. "That's okay," she says. Lowering her voice, she leans in and adds, "We didn't come here to watch the movie." She winks at Imogene and lets her fingers graze the back of the blonde girl's hand. The movement is quick, but Imogene catches it and blushes something fierce, now losing her voice altogether. She nods, scurries around the corner to grab her broom, and disappears into theater two. She can hear the girls giggling as they make their way into the theater across the hall.

As the minutes tick by, Imogene cannot divert her thoughts from the two girls. She has returned to her place at the counter and dreads the moment the movie releases and the girls pass back through the lobby to leave.

Imogene knows people like that exist. Of course she does. Her eighth-grade teacher, Miss Simpson, used to live at the end of their street. Once, her mother had come home late from visiting her aunt and driven past Miss Simpson's house, and there Miss Simpson had been, sitting in her car… kissing another woman! Later that night, Imogene heard her mom and dad shouting over what her mother had seen. Imogene listened from the hallway; half-asleep, she made sense of just enough to get the general idea. Words like *ashamed of herself,* and *repentance,* and *depraved behavior* were thrown around with enough vitriol, it was obvious where her parents stood on the matter. Then her dad used a word Imogene had never heard, but it didn't sound nice, and her mom had said, *They call themselves homosexuals.* And her dad said, *It doesn't matter what they're called. It ain't right. First thing tomorrow, we're switching Imogene from that class and getting her on with a good Christian teacher.* But, to Imogene's relief, her mother had said no, not halfway through the year; she'd fall too far behind if they pulled her now.

The next day, Imogene had gone to class, expecting Miss Simpson to look different somehow. In what way—she wasn't sure. But learning what she had about her, *something* was bound to have changed. But nothing was different at all. Miss Simpson was the same lady she'd always been. The lady who stayed late to explain Imogene's mathematics assignment when she couldn't get the hang of it in class. The lady who organized the holiday recital every December and planted that tree in Abbot Park to honor the fallen soldiers. She was a wonderful teacher, and Imogene liked her fine.

Imogene didn't think of it again until Valentine's Day that year, when Miss Simpson had a bouquet delivered to her classroom. One boy in Imogene's class asked if they were from her husband. Miss Simpson had blushed, but only smiled and said, *No. I'm not married. These are just from someone special.* Imogene thought of the lady in the car and wondered if that was who she meant. It saddened Imogene that Miss Simpson couldn't just *say* who the flowers were from. That she had to keep it a big secret.

People like her parents believe anyone like Miss Simpson has evil in their soul; they won't go to Heaven because of the terrible sin they commit by living how they do. Imogene knows she's supposed to share this belief. But she doesn't. Not even a little. That day in Miss Simpson's class, Imogene vowed to never treat people like Miss Simpson any differently. But she had never met anyone else like Miss Simpson… until today.

And she *had* treated those girls differently.

She'd turned an ugly red and gaped at them as though they'd kicked President Kennedy right in the shins. And then she'd ran away quick as can be.

Shame overtakes her. When the movie is over, will they give her a nasty look? Will they leave without looking her way at all? Could she blame them if they did?

The door to theater one swings open, and the three boys run out, whooping through the lobby, followed by the mom and daughter, the latter now in much better spirits. Several minutes pass before the two girls emerge, walking shoulder to shoulder, deep in conversation.

Imogene tries not to stare, pretending to wipe the counter she'd cleaned for the third time only five minutes ago. Risking a quick glance up, she sees the two girls heading her direction. With a lump in her throat, she straightens herself, gripping tight to the rag and the bottle of cleaner.

"Hey Snow White," the dark-haired girl says.

"Hey," Imogene says, trying not to appear as tense as she feels.

"I was thinking, you should come hang out with us this weekend. Get that tan back."

Imogene presses the rag to the counter, rubs a few slow circles over the glass, not even conscious of what she's doing, and then picks it up again, clutching the soggy thing to her chest. "I… uh… hang out where?" she asks.

The dark-haired girl adjusts the sunglasses that perch on top of her head. She says, "My family vacations in Daytona Beach. We're there all summer."

Daytona! How many days has Imogene passed dreaming of the beach and the fun to be had there? She wants to say yes, but something holds her back. "I… I don't know," she says.

"Come on," the girl coaxes, green eyes sparkling from the glare of Imogene's gleaming concession counter. "It'll be fun. You like the beach, right? Listen, if you're worried about it, I promise I won't bite."

The blonde girl laughs, and Imogene knows she's gone red again.

This is her chance. Her *one* chance to have the summer she's always wanted. To have friends outside of school or church. To have an *adventure*.

"Sure," she says at last. "I'm off on Sunday."

"Sunday it is! Do you drive?"

Imogene doesn't.

The dark-haired girl thinks for a moment and says, "Well, where do you live? We'll pick you up."

A flash of panic freezes Imogene as she imagines someone like this girl—like *Miss Simpson*—showing up at her house with her parents there. "Can you pick me up here?" she suggests nervously. "Out front? I'll come and wait here."

The girls agree. Sunday at eleven.

Imogene won't be spending her *entire* summer at The Sheldon, then.

Before the dark-haired girl leaves, she turns and asks, "Just so I don't have to keep callin' you Snow White all summer, do you have a name?"

"Imogene," she says.

The dark-haired girl nods, soaking it in. "Well, nice to meet ya, Imogene. I'm Greta."

30

IMOGENE

(JUNE 1962)

SUNDAY AFTER CHURCH, IMOGENE TOLD her parents she was
going to the beach. But when they asked, *With who?* Imogene
hadn't wanted to say, *With these girls I just met at the movies*
because she knew her mother wouldn't like her gallivanting with
strangers. So instead, she said, *With Susan Bostwick from school.*
Susan is a nice girl from Imogene's class who has attended every
birthday party of Imogene's since grade five. Susan is kind of a
drag, though, quieter and more cautious even than Imogene. But
her parents would approve, she thought. And they had.

So now, three hours later, Imogene, Greta, and Greta's
"friend"—whose name she'd learned was Nancy—sprawl on
their towels on a busy stretch of beach at the south end of

Daytona. Greta's family spends their summer in a condominium right on the water; a three-story building painted in various shades of blue. Not the nicest condo on the strip, but far from the grungiest.

Greta's mom relaxes in a white, plastic chair close to the building, sipping a glass of white wine with two ladies from neighboring units; a big, floppy hat shields her face from the sun and her bare toes dig into the sand. Imogene can hear their muffled gossip from where they lie farther along the beach.

Schmoozing with Greta's mom are two other women. The first has a fifteen-year-old daughter who stretches out beside Imogene and the other girls but hasn't said much. Her name is Christine Delgado, a pretty brunette with caramel skin and gaping brown eyes. Christine's little brother, Chip, and two small children who belong to the third woman build sandcastles nearby.

"Time to roll over, girls," Nancy says, rolling onto her back and flipping her sunglasses down over her eyes. The other girls follow suit.

Just then, a boy—or should she say, *man*—appears beside them. As he passes, he kicks a heap of sand onto Greta's stomach.

"You sleaze!" she shouts and dusts the sand from her sweat-slick skin.

He trails a loud cackle up the beach as he makes his way to Greta's mom, stoops to kiss her on the cheek and snags a handful of chips from the bag the women are sharing.

Christine watches him with a wild look in her eyes.

"Stop gawking at him, Christine," Greta says. "Don't need to give him a bigger head than he's already got."

"Who is that?" Imogene asks.

"My idiot brother," Greta says.

Christine watches him walk back toward their group. "He's such a hunk," she says in a low, dreamy voice.

His steps slow for a moment as his eyes flick over their cluster of towels, baby oil, and bare skin; his attention lands first on Christine, and then Imogene, whose chest tightens and burns beneath his stare. He throws a wink in their direction and continues toward the water, where he rejoins a group of guys who toss a football back and forth.

Christine sighs, and Imogene tries with great effort to stifle her blush.

"Oh man, get a grip!" Greta complains.

Imogene learns that Greta's brother's name is Ray. He's twenty-three and moved to Daytona three years ago. He shares an apartment with his friend Ted, and they are in the process of starting their own fishing charter business. A couple months ago, they rented a boat slip at Halifax Marina and hope to have enough saved for their boat and licensing later in the year.

"Christine here has been drooling over Ray since we were girls. It ain't gonna happen, Christine," Greta says, challenging the younger girl. Christine only sticks out her tongue at Greta, and they dissolve into laughter.

"What do *you* think about him, Imogene?" Nancy asks as she pulls her glasses down the bridge of her nose and peers over the top at Imogene. She plays up the question with a suggestive waggle of her eyebrows. Greta elbows her in annoyance.

Imogene isn't sure if she would call Ray a *hunk,* but she can't deny his good looks. He's tall and slim, with a strong, defined body; shaggy brown hair, chiseled jaw, brilliant blue eyes, full lips, and a chin dimple.

Okay, maybe hunk *is* the correct word.

Imogene blushes again but tries to hide it beneath a half-hearted answer. "He seems nice," she mumbles.

"*He seems nice,*" Nancy parrots Imogene with a giggle. "You ever had a boyfriend?" she asks.

Imogene knows the truth will paint her as a total square, but up to this point, she has lived a fairly boring life, and lying will only lead to more questions, so she says, "No. Not yet… It's fine. There aren't a lot of choices at my school," she adds, trying to play it cool and aloof.

"Interesting," Nancy says with a nod. But she is already turning away, forgetting the conversation.

"What about you?" Imogene asks Nancy, desperate to win

her back.

Nancy and Greta share a wicked glance and burst into laughter.

"Oh… right…" Imogene realizes her error and is mortified. "Sorry, I forgot…"

But Greta raises an index finger to her lips and gestures to Christine, who rests with a towel folded over her eyes, oblivious to the world. *She doesn't know.*

Imogene knows, and Christine doesn't.

Imogene is part of a secret. She has friends. She has sunshine. She has cute boys to stare at… *older* boys. This summer won't be so bad after all, she thinks.

31

IMOGENE

(JULY 1962)

LATER, AFTER WORK, IMOGENE IS spending the night at Greta's. To her mother's knowledge, however, Imogene will be at Susan Bostwick's house. In fact, if you ask Imogene's mother, Susan and Imogene have been spending every weekend together for the past month.

Whatever Susan Bostwick is up to this summer, Imogene imagines it isn't *half* the fun she is having herself.

Greta's family is an absolute gas. Mrs. Green is young and spirited; you'd never guess she's a mom at all, the way she acts. Most days you'll find her smoking one of those long cigarettes and drinking something alcoholic; never in an overindulgent or classless way, but in the way people do on vacation when they're having a good time. Imogene is sometimes jealous of Greta, because her mom is so cool; Imogene's own mother is wound so tight her jaw must hurt from all the clenching.

Mrs. Green's two friends—Mildred, who is maybe thirty, and Christine's mom, Clara—are just as free-spirited and fun. For years, they've vacationed together. Without a schedule of any kind, their days consist of relaxing by the water, soaking in the sun, and sipping chilled wine. The evenings are for dressing up and going out to do grown-up things. It's a rare night that the Green's and their friends are home being dull.

Imogene loves to arrive at the condo before the parents leave. She gets a thrill out of watching Mrs. Green ready herself for the evening. Light as a feather, she sails around the room, humming a Patsy Cline song, eyes glistening from the haze of earlier drink and the endless potential of the night ahead. Fashion-forward as she is, she never misses the opportunity to ask for Imogene and Greta's opinions on her outfit choice. She brushes out her bob of short brown hair, throws a kiss over her shoulder, and off she runs. The condo feels different for several minutes after her departure—less alive somehow. Imogene wants a presence like the one Mrs. Green has—one that can change the room whenever you come or go.

Every day is a party at the condo. Imogene finds herself so swept up in the lifestyle, she struggles to slip back into her humdrum routine at home.

With her overnight bag concealed beneath the counter, Imogene watches the hands of the clock in a state of anxious anticipation. Her shift at The Sheldon is nearly finished.

Ten minutes before six, the bell chimes, and Greta strolls into the lobby, dark curls slung loosely over one shoulder.

"Ready to cut out?" she asks.

Imogene grabs her bag and joins Greta at the door, a smile on her face and a Patsy Cline record spinning in her head.

Imogene balances a plate of cheese pizza in her lap. The open pizza box stretches between them on the bed, and two half-empty bottles of Coca-Cola are on the nightstand. A Twilight Zone rerun is on the small television set on Greta's dresser but is mostly ignored by the giggling and gossiping girls.

Imogene glances at the clock. Eight o'clock already. "Aren't Nancy and Christine coming?" she asks.

Greta pulls a long string of mozzarella from her slice of pizza and sucks it through her lips with a slurping sound. "No," she says, licking the sauce from her thumb and then wiping it on a napkin. "Christine is off with a few girls her own age, and Nancy... isn't coming. Just the two of us tonight."

Imogene blanches. She assumed the other girls would be here. After all, they've spent the entire summer together so far; it makes sense they'd be here tonight as well.

Greta must notice Imogene's hesitation because she asks, "Does it bother you?"

"What?" Imogene asks, cheeks gone warm.

Greta shifts her weight, moves her plate from her left knee to her right, and says, "Being here... just with me?"

The troubling voice in Imogene's head returns—the one that says she might be treating Greta differently because of who she is. She wouldn't think twice about staying at a girl's house alone, if it were anyone but Greta.

"No." Imogene answers, swift and confident. "It doesn't bother me at all. Why would it bother me?"

Greta's eyes fall and for a moment, Imogene worries this tough, cool girl is going to cry.

"It would bother most people," she mutters, meeting Imogene's eyes once more.

Imogene isn't sure what to say. She is right, of course; most people *wouldn't* approve of her. *Has this happened before?* she wonders. And then, she suddenly realizes she knows *nothing* of Greta's life in Virginia—where her family spends the other nine months of the year.

"Do many people know?" Imogene asks.

"No." Her answer is quick.

"Your mom?"

A little snort escapes her. "No. She doesn't know. Well… she *may*. But I never told her."

"Your mom seems totally cool. Like she wouldn't mind a bit."

Uncertainty tugs at Greta's mouth, but after a moment of reflection, she agrees with a nod. "Yeah. She's cool as far as moms go. I don't reckon she'd be too upset. But I don't suppose she'd want me flaunting it around town or bringing it up at dinner, either. She's not lookin' to explain me to her friends."

A sadness washes over Greta; Imogene has never seen this look on her. Among the ever-growing list of admirable qualities Greta possesses, Imogene's favorite, perhaps, is Greta's unwavering confidence. It's never occurred to her that so much of this fearlessness could be chalked up to smoke and mirrors. But seeing this side of Greta now, Imogene realizes *no one* can be that confident *all the time*.

"You really think?" Imogene asks.

Amusement flashes in Greta's eyes. "Why do you suppose Nancy and I were way out in Deland that day, at the theater? Plenty of theaters around Daytona, right? But no one would recognize us out there. No chance anyone would see us and have it get back to my parents."

This hadn't occurred to Imogene—the *why* of it. She swallows and says, "Well, I'm real glad you came. Otherwise, I never would have met you."

Greta smiles now. "Thanks, Imogene," she says. "Same here."

"What about your brother?" Imogene asks.

"Yeah, Ray knows. I told him a few years ago before he moved out here. We give each other a hard time, but Ray's got my back, and I got his."

Imogene nods. "He seems like a pretty neat guy."

"He is," Greta says without hesitation. "He's probably the smartest and nicest guy I know. When we go back home and Ray's not with us… it's hard. I miss him."

As an only child, it's difficult for Imogene to understand the sibling bond. But she's always thought how nice it would be to have an older brother. Someone to look out for her.

"Tell him I said any of this, and I'll kill you," Greta adds.

Imogene laughs. She won't say a word. But she likes that Greta is comfortable sharing things with her brother. And she enjoys being her second confidant.

A silence falls between them as Greta plucks another slice of pizza from the box and takes a bite. After a moment of chewing she says, "You may be my best friend, Imogene."

This takes Imogene by surprise, and a warm blush breaks across her skin.

Imogene may not know much about Greta or the life she lives back home; they are new to each other and rarely discuss anything that exists beyond their little summer bubble. But in the short time Imogene has been her friend, she's seen an unyielding fire in Greta's eyes; a determination to be seen as an equal, but still stand out in the crowd. She is clever and fierce and deep… but what's more, she is frightened. Imogene has seen as much tonight.

The summer is quickly approaching an end. Greta's family will leave in just a few short weeks. Will she return? Will they see each other again after this? Imogene isn't sure. But one thing she can say with certainty: no matter what happens, Greta will live a life much tougher than the one she deserves.

How many out-of-town theaters will she visit in her lifetime? How many not-so-friendly words will be used behind her back—or *worse*—right to her face? How many bouquets must she lie about on Valentine's Day? How many people will meet her and refuse to see the brilliant girl underneath?

Imogene grabs her own slice of pizza from the box and smiles. "You're mine, too," she says. And she takes a bite.

32

IMOGENE

(AUGUST 1962)

ON THE FIRST DAY OF August, Imogene finds herself once more at The Sheldon, her desire to be there waning quicker than the days themselves. In this last stretch of summer break, the days are hot and pass in a muzzy haze. Senior year is creeping up, and the inevitability of returning to her old life makes her ill. She's the same person she's always been, of course, and yet—*different*. A change has taken place within her. This summer has removed from her the girl she used to be and opened her eyes to an alternative path—an alternative *life*. Imogene has been a fish; unaware she'd outgrown her aquarium. But now someone has opened the door and allowed her a glimpse of the ocean. And how can she ever think of anything else now that she's seen it?

Around noon, the bell above the door rings out and Greta strides into the lobby. At once, Imogene's mood lifts, and she skips around the corner to join her friend.

Without preamble, Greta says, "We're leaving."

The smile slips from Imogene's face. "What? Why? I thought you were staying through the weekend."

Greta sighs and rolls her eyes. "Not anymore. Something came up with my dad's job. They need him back this week. We're packing now. I just wanted to come say goodbye."

Goodbye. Imogene doesn't like the sound of that. She wants more time. "But… um…" she shakes her head, searching for words and knowing none will do.

Greta laughs. Her hearty chuckles fill the lobby. "I'll miss you, too, Imogene," she says. "Here."

Greta reaches into her pocket and withdraws a folded piece of notebook paper. She thrusts it in Imogene's direction. "This is my address," she says. "Write to me."

Imogene takes the paper reluctantly. "I will," she says. "Wait… you'll be back next summer, right?"

Greta winks. "Of course. But… keep in touch, okay?"

For a moment, the two girls stand and face each other. Not a word passes between them. Then, the bell chimes, a family of seven spills into the lobby and makes a beeline for the concession stand, the woman shouting at the smallest child to keep his dirty fingers off the glass. Imogene blinks, the last of her summer slipping away before her eyes. The door closing. The ocean-view lost.

Without warning, Greta wraps her arms around Imogene and pulls her into a tight hug. Just as Imogene feels herself sink into the hug and is about to reciprocate it, Greta pulls away.

"Later, Snow White," she says. And with that, she skips out the door, and Imogene is left to her work, stricken by the sinking fear that she'll never see her best friend again.

33

TED

(MAY 1963)

TED WIPES HIS FOREHEAD WITH the back of his hand. The tops of his shoulders sting beneath the unforgiving heat of a midday sun, and he's drenched in sweat from head to toe.

With a final swish of his brush, he sits back on his heels to admire his work. "Well, check it out," he muses.

Ray's head springs up in the cabin doorway. "You done already?"

"Just finished. Come see."

Ray, who had been fiddling with a length of rope, tosses it to the ground and hops over the stern to the dock. Ted reaches into the small cooler beside him and pops the top on a bottle of beer, passing it to Ray as he joins him.

The Salty Siren: Private Fishing Tours: Call 555-4010 is painted on the back of the charter in gold-stenciled letters, outlined in black to make it pop.

Ray shakes his head in amazement. "That's cool, man. Really. That's stellar. I still can't believe she's ours."

Ted pops the top on a second beer and raises it in response to Ray. They clank bottles and sit in awe of their new vessel.

A year ago, they'd rented their slip at Halifax, but they'd only just purchased their boat two months past. She's a beauty: a shiny white Rybovich sportfishing boat, 53 feet long, rod holders throughout, a giant freezer for any size catch. She boasts two staterooms, a salon, and a galley. She has everything they need—as she should, because she sure as hell wasn't cheap.

Ted and Ray both work as attendants at the Daytona Beach Golf Club. Ted has been employed there since age sixteen and had no problem securing a job for Ray when he moved to town four years ago. Since then, they've shared an apartment on Bellevue at a dinky complex called The Grove, but a month ago they dropped their lease to move into the charter permanently. This is, of course, a downgrade, as The Salty Siren is mighty cramped for two full-grown men. But the move saves them 275 dollars a month, and they'll make profit soon enough, God-willing.

As much as he wishes their meager paychecks from the golf club had clinched the beautiful vessel before them, this simply wasn't the case; at the rate they were saving, it would've been several years before they earned enough money for her. And to continue paying rent on a boatless boat-slip seemed counterproductive, so they'd known it was now or never.

Thank God they met Marty when they did.

One night, Ted and Ray were on their patio, sharing a soda and leftover spaghetti. Conversation had steered where it always did in those days—to money (or rather, their *lack* of money). A neighbor—an older fellow named Sinclair, with a penchant for fast-food takeout and eavesdropping—overheard their conversation and rushed to tell them how they might earn themselves some extra cash. Two days later, he'd taken them both to meet Marty.

Marty Camargo founded a group of men who referred to themselves as "The Company." Never more than twelve strong, they travel in groups of two or three to perform small, insignificant thefts; something anonymous, such as picking the wallets of tourists on the beach or swiping from unlocked cars in the parking lot.

Ted has to admit that *insignificant* isn't the word he would use to describe what they do, as someone is, without a doubt, affected by their actions. And though Ted never fancied himself a criminal, a certain camaraderie exists at The Company that fills him with pride and a strong sense of duty to the others.

Marty keeps things organized and fair. Everyone goes for a job at some point—some more than others, depending on their skill set. But everyone gets a cut of the pay on "distribution" days, regardless of whether they performed the specific job. Marty takes fifty percent of the earnings, and they split the remaining profit evenly amongst the other Company members.

Marty keeps his group small—both to prevent the fellas from getting loose-lipped on their comings and goings, and to ensure everyone gets their fair share. For the most part, getting on with The Company is a low-risk, high-reward gig; the very thing that makes it so damn appealing to two young kids with ambitions larger than their bank accounts.

Ten months ago, they met Marty for the first time, when Sinclair took them to his office. Marty's "office," as it was, was a pocket of space above a sleazy-looking meat market on Seagrave. They'd climbed the rotted stairs up the back of the building to a thick steel door, and Sinclair knocked in a sequence of brief taps. A moment later, the door opened, and Sinclair led them into a gloomy, open space that smelled of mildew and cold cuts. A worn leather sofa lined the left wall and beside that, a crooked floor lamp that, despite its best efforts, struggled to light the room. The man who'd opened the door nodded to Sinclair, and then returned to his seat on the cushion beneath the lamp, where he picked up the newspaper he'd left on the armrest and returned his eyes to the pages.

Sinclair led them further into the room, to another door on the far wall. He repeated the same sequence of fast knocks, and this time a man's voice beckoned from the other side.

"Open! Get in here!"

This room presented more like an office than the first, but only by the narrowest of margins. A couple of folding tables filled most of the dim space, a stained, well-tread carpet beneath their feet. The office faced an intersection, and four large windows curved around the room, which allowed a view of three adjoining streets at once; the blinds, however, were shut, streetlights glowing through the slats—the ones which hadn't snapped off and fallen away, that is.

Sat at one folding table was a man with dark, receding hair and large, tired eyes. Another guy, younger than the first by a decade or two, sat across from him, left foot propped on the tabletop.

The older man watched in surprise as the three of them strolled into the room. "Sinclair. You're not on the schedule tonight, my boy. What can I do ya for?" His attention then turned to Ted and Ray. "And who do I have the pleasure of meeting?"

The man stood to shake their hands. "Name's Marty. Pleased to meet ya," he said, and it was then Ted noticed how tall he was; somewhere in the ballpark of six-foot five, a stark contrast to Ted's own five-foot ten inches.

Ted shook his hand, trying to stand as straight as he could and grip with the proper firmness. Beside him, Ray looked uneasy, shifted his weight, and took an involuntary step toward the door.

In all fairness to Ray, the room gave off definite mobster vibes, but the man in front of them was anything but. An enormous smile broke out on Marty's face as he turned to the other man who shared the room. This guy was early thirties at most. He had dark, shaggy hair, a slight frame, a pallid complexion, and a short, scruffy beard. Unlike Marty, this man lacked in friendliness and trained a wary eye on the two newcomers. Not that Ted was an authority on the subject, but in his humble opinion—the dude was strung-out.

"Mickey, anything else you need? Or are you good for tonight?" Marty asked.

The guy called Mickey stood, trained his dark eyes on them once more, and then shook his head. "No, sir. Got everything under control."

Marty let out a chuckle. "Stop with that *sir* business, kid. Makes me feel old."

Mickey's lip twitched, which may have been his idea of a smile. "Should be back by midnight," he said.

As Mickey turned to go, Marty gave him a jovial slap on the back. "Can't wait to celebrate," he said, and after Mickey's departure, he shut the door.

Marty motioned for Ted and Ray to sit, which Ted did without pause, eager to hear what the man had to offer. It took Ray a moment's hesitation—and a warning glare from Ted—to consent to the seat.

Sinclair excused himself and allowed the three men to talk in private.

It was then Ted shared details of their fishing charter dreams and their need for funds. "Sinclair mentioned there may be an opportunity here," Ted had said.

A broad smile transformed Marty's face. "Well boys, your timing is impeccable," he'd said with a gleam in his eye.

As luck would have it, two of their guys—a Henry and a Roger—had left a short time before, and two spots had opened in their absence. Once Marty gave them the lowdown on The Company, Ted sensed Ray stiffen beside him. Annoyance coursed through his veins. Ray was going to ruin this for them. Taking chances—that's the first rule of success in business and, incidentally, Ray's biggest weakness. The odds a more perfect opportunity for fast cash would present itself was improbable, yet Ted knew Ray, and he knew he'd find fault in these methods of *acquiring* said cash. Ted had to admit, the idea of breaking the law was unappealing. But it wouldn't be forever. Only until they raised the money for the boat. Ted followed his gut; he spoke for them both that night and said they may be interested.

Marty's eyes flicked between Ted and Ray, no doubt sensing their discordance of opinions. Reservation creased his face. "But fellas, listen, you got to be serious about it if you join up," he warned. "This is my family we're talkin' about here. We have some fun. We make a little money, yeah? But it's more than that to these guys. This is a brotherhood. We look out for each other, got it?"

Ted gave an astute nod.

Brothers. Not only had Ted never had a brother, he'd also lacked a family for most of his young life. His parents died in a car crash when he was nine, and no one leapt up to take him in. There was a grandpa out of state whom he'd never met, and an aging aunt who wasn't looking to adopt the responsibility that came with raising a nine-year-old boy. So, with no other options, he'd entered foster care.

It was there he found himself in the care of Cathy Marsh, a heavy-boned woman in her mid-forties with four foster children, which turned to five after acquiring Ted, and seven a few months later when she took in a couple more. Each time Ted formed a bond with a kid, they left, and he had to start over again. So, as time wore on, he stopped trying and settled into his own company instead. He watched as the years passed and the number of kids in the house fluctuated; the disappearance of those fortunate enough to find their forever homes and the unfamiliar faces who took their place; a revolving door of abandoned kids.

Ted knew he was comparatively lucky to other kids in the system. A few had showed up at Cathy's with bruises and cuts and broken bones; the product of drunken, abusive parents or from the abuse and mistreatment they'd received at a previous foster home. Other kids had been plucked from the streets, or surrendered as babies, never knowing a world outside of this one. And here he was… just a regular ol' orphan. Old enough to remember his parents, but alone too long to miss them much. *Lucky*, see?

Ted stayed with Cathy until he aged out of the program at eighteen.

For three years, he struggled on his own. He made ends meet, but had made little of anything else. Life was just like that for some people, he guessed; made to get through—to survive. That's when Ray answered an ad Ted had put in the paper seeking a roommate. Ray and his big ideas.

The rest, as they say, is history.

Raymond Green is, in fact, the closest thing to a real brother Ted has ever had, and he has no complaints—except for Ray's tendency to drag his feet with every business decision, but that is hardly worth bickering over as Ted is more the decision-maker, anyway.

It was Ted's decision that led them to shake hands with Marty that night.

"Welcome to The Company, boys," he'd said, a toothy grin spread across his face. "Changing our lives one small, victimless crime at a time, am I right?" Marty laughed and slapped Ted on the shoulder.

Ten months at The Company, and Ted still isn't convinced about the brotherhood thing. Most of the guys have established bonds built on years of trust. Ted and Ray are still new; two more people to split the pot with.

Ted learned that Mickey from that first night in the office was none other than Mickey Lancaster of Lancaster Jewelers, only his parents run the store, not him. Ted's suspicions that Mickey was strung-out that night were, in all likelihood, correct; Mickey is a right lush and a pathological gossip. Every hidey-hole in town, every dirty little secret, Mickey knows or is sure to find out. Some say he is a rotten snake—which is accurate enough—but this has earned him his place as Marty's right-hand man.

Louis Steinfeld is another senior member of The Company. The first guy to join up with Marty, he's gone on twice as many jobs as anyone else. An eccentric, ill-tempered man; you shouldn't pick fights with Marty you don't want Louis to finish.

Sinclair Parks, their neighbor, has been with them for just two years, but is working his way up the chain with dutiful ease.

As for the rest, the guys vary in age and personality. They

each have their skills. Ted is earning a reputation as a bit of a locksmith. On his first job—breaking into the token-exchange at the boardwalk—he was quick to discover his skill in picking locks. A few months later, he and Ray were assigned to swipe from the lockers at the Daytona Golf Club. As employees, gaining access was simple. Ray was an impeccable lookout and Ted was swift with the combination locks. They cleared 872 dollars that day. 436 went to Marty—which brought a smile to the big man's face—and the other guys took home 36 dollars each, bringing Ted and Ray's total for the week up to 54 bucks respectively, which was nothing to sneeze at. A lot of weeks had passed in this way, and their savings were adding up to a fair number.

That night, after the golf club job, Marty called them into his office.

"You guys are doing a real swell job," he'd praised. "I sincerely mean that. It's been a pleasure to have you aboard."

Oh no, Ted thought. *Is he giving them the boot?*

Marty narrowed his eyes, hands clasped on the table in front of him. "You guys still saving for that boat of yours?"

Ted and Ray nodded.

"How short are you, would you say?"

Ted and Ray exchanged a quick glance and then turned back to Marty. It was Ted who answered. "Uh… after tonight… I'd guess we're about twelve-hundred shy."

Marty nodded, mulling something over in his mind. "What if I spot you the rest?"

Ted was sure he'd misheard.

"What do we have to do?" Ray asked.

Marty released an enormous laugh, slapping the flimsy table with his palm. "Do? Nothing, my boy! It's been a great couple weeks for business, thanks in no small part to you," he'd said. "Consider it a thank you for all your hard work so far."

So, just like that, Marty had given them the remaining twelve-hundred dollars needed for The Salty Siren.

And now here she is right in front of them, no longer a dream, but a reality brought to life—one small, victimless crime at a time.

Ray wipes his mouth with the back of his hand, spinning the neck of the beer bottle in his fingers. His expression turns grim. "We're gonna have to pay him back, you know."

Ted lifts an eyebrow at Ray. "Marty? No way. He said it was a gift."

"You ever get a twelve-hundred-dollar gift with no strings attached?"

"No," Ted admitted. "But there's always a first time."

Ray snorts. He makes to take a sip of his beer but remembers that it's empty and sits the bottle beside him on the deck, then wraps his long arms around his knees.

"It's about time someone sees our worth, Ray. We've been kissin' up to the golf course preppies for years, and it never got us nowhere. Look at us now!" Ted raises his bottle and motions to the boat.

Ray looks hard at The Siren, and a smile touches his lips—not a fully formed smile, but enough to count.

"Although," Ted tread lightly here, not wanting to spoil the mood, but knowing it must be said. "This means we're gonna have to hold off on quittin' for a while."

After their first job, Ray had panicked—said he wanted out. Ted had convinced him to stay on by promising they'd quit as soon as they raised enough money for the boat. Unfortunately, because of the circumstances in which the boat was acquired, Ted must break that promise—at least for a while. No way they could walk away pell-mell after Marty had done what he had for them.

Ray drops his head and sighs. He turns to Ted and says, "No money is ever free, man. There's *always* a cost."

34

IMOGENE

(JUNE 1963)

A WEEK AGO, IMOGENE RETURNED to The Sheldon. Not much has changed, except that Mr. Pickman is having Theater One renovated this summer, resulting in even fewer customers than usual since they're down to showing only one film at a time.

Senior year had been a real drag, but Imogene did well. Her abundance of anxious energy had channeled into her schoolwork, and she'd graduated top of her class. She wrote to Greta off and on, using her return address as The Sheldon. Mr. Pickman didn't mind setting the letters aside for her, and it was always a special treat to swing by the theater after school and find she had a new one.

Based on her letters, Greta's senior year had been considerably more adventurous than Imogene's. She ran cross-country track and went out for student council president (though in the end, she'd lost to *that kook Francis Powers*). Mrs. Green was selling Avon now and bought Greta her very own car, which Greta promptly christened as *Rhonda*.

Imogene had *also* bought a car this year but paid for it herself with money earned from the theater the previous summer.

The last letter Imogene received came more than three weeks ago. In it, Greta stated that her family would return to the condo on the seventh of June—which was yesterday. But still no Greta.

Today, Imogene tries her hardest to concentrate on work, but her eyes keep drifting to the door, and the empty street beyond. *Why hadn't she come yesterday? What if something came up, and they canceled their trip?* Can Imogene survive the humdrum summer she's doomed to suffer without her best friend?

The day takes its time, in no hurry to pass, and when Imogene leaves the theater that evening, a dejected lump weighs in her stomach.

As she mopes down the sidewalk to her car, a nearby engine revs loud enough to wake the dead and rockets Imogene's heart straight into her throat. Across the street, Greta steps from the front seat of a sleek red Chevrolet Impala, laughing in hysterical bursts.

"Oh my God! You should have seen your face!" she shouts, still laughing.

Imogene is so happy to see her friend, the scare is already a distant memory. In four quick leaps, she crosses the street and says, "I'm so happy you're here," and pulls Greta into a long hug.

"Okay, don't get soft on me now," Greta says, unhooking Imogene's arms from around her neck. "I came here to ask you a very serious question."

"What's that?" Imogene sees that Greta *is* serious, and a tingle of nerves vibrate through her.

"Really? You don't know?"

Imogene shrugs. The worry roots deeper.

Greta sighs and shakes her head. "Come on!" Then, "*What do you think of Rhonda?*" She throws her hands to the side and motions to her new car.

Imogene laughs then, relief swelling inside her, and Greta joins in, draping a slim arm around Imogene's shoulder.

After an extensive tour of Rhonda's *rockin' bod,* both inside and out, Greta says, "Okay, so tomorrow, me, you, and Christine are going out on my brother's boat."

Imogene startles for the second time tonight. "We are?" she asks.

When she'd dreamed of this summer, Imogene imagined more of the condo, more of the beach. Sleepovers, shopping, ice cream, pizza, late nights—all the same forms of entertainment as last year. What she *hadn't* imagined was a boat with boys.

Greta nods in excitement. "Yeah! Him and Ted finally got their fishing boat! He offered to take me and my 'pretty' friends out for free." She rolls her eyes at this and continues. "Try to get seen, drum up some business."

"I don't know how to fish," Imogene says with a frown.

A rush of laugher flies from Greta. "We won't be fishing, silly chick. Just cruising and havin' a good time. No worries."

"Oh, okay, yeah… That sounds fun." Imogene agrees to go, but the creepy crawl of doubt runs through her like a cold chill.

She's never been on a boat before. What if she gets seasick and embarrasses herself in front of everyone? Her parents won't like her being out there alone, and under no circumstances with a couple of grown men, one of whom she's never even met. And in another unfortunate turn of events, Susan Bostwick and her family moved to Michigan last year, so if Imogene is to go tomorrow, she will have to concoct another excuse.

The sky is still dark when Imogene wakes and embarks for the Green's condo.

She explained her departure to her parents by claiming that Stetson University was to offer summer courses, and sign-up was first-come-first-served. Her mother and father had beamed with pride when she told them—her mother in particular had always insisted on Imogene's education because she herself had never finished high school. *You have so many opportunities today, Imogene,* she'd say. *You kids don't realize how good you got it. If I had the opportunity to go to a college, who knows what I'd be? More than what I am, that's for sure.*

Whenever Imogene argued that her mother could *still* get an education, that it wasn't too late to make something more of herself if that's what she wanted, she'd shake her head and say, *No. God had other plans for me. It's your time now, Imogene.*

Driving the darkened streets that lead from Deland, her chest still burns with the guilt of her lie. She wishes lies weren't needed. If her parents were cool, like Greta's parents, everything would be so much easier. But they want a very specific life for Imogene, one she is no longer sure she wants for herself. The time will come when they must find out, but not today.

As her car stalls in the condo's parking lot, the sun is rising, the cool blue of dawn giving over to the soft yellow glow of a new day.

The girls pile into Rhonda—Greta being all too eager to take her friends for a spin—and head to the marina to meet the boys. *The boys.* This thought sends a tremor of nerves through Imogene. She tries to focus on the radio. On the buildings whirring past her. On *anything* else.

Absent this summer is Nancy. Things hadn't lasted with her and Greta over the school year, but Greta doesn't seem too broken up over it, so Imogene isn't worried. In the backseat, Christine puckers into the small mirror of her compact and applies a peachy lipstick.

"Easy on the bumps, huh!" she shouts, wiping a smear from her cheek for the third time in as many minutes.

Greta snorts out a laugh. Imogene suspects she's hitting holes on purpose at this point.

This past year has been exceedingly charitable to Christine;

her chest has grown at least two sizes since Imogene last saw her. She wears a daringly low-cut orange top, tied to expose her midriff, and white jean shorts that enhance her naturally tan legs.

"I wonder if Ray will still recognize me," Christine muses. It looks as though her crush on Greta's older brother is one thing that *hasn't* changed.

Greta rolls her eyes. "You look exactly the same, Christine. A couple new bumps in your blouse ain't confusing no one."

Christine makes a dismissive noise in her throat and turns her attention out the window as Greta turns right into Halifax Harbor Marina.

Imogene's stomach does a lurch as they park, unload, and follow the dock to Ray's boat. She is nervous, sure. And then there's the guilt for lying to her parents. But beneath that is excitement, and each step brings a fearlessness into her stride. She can be anyone she wants today. Anyone at all.

"Hey!" comes a deep voice. "Over here!"

Greta waves off in the distance and Imogene sees Ray dart out from behind a small shack advertising *Live Shrimp*! He half-walks-half-runs to meet them.

Beside her, Christine releases a giggle, and Imogene can see the warm red flush of her cheeks. Ray is just as handsome as Imogene remembers, perhaps even more so now. He's dressed in blue shorts and a white shirt, left mostly unbuttoned—thrown on in a hurry, she bets; he seems like a guy who simply throws himself together in the morning and finds a way to look lovely without wasted effort. His hair had been wet, either from swimming or sweat, but it's drying now and flops loose against his forehead. Imogene swallows, a trifle less fearless than she was a moment ago.

"Hey, Dork." Greta greets him with a hug.

"Hey, Ditz," he responds, hugging her back.

His blue gaze lands on us. "Ladies." He winks and gives a brief bow.

Christine's giggle is much more pronounced this time.

"Hi," I mutter.

"Follow me," he says, with a jerk of his head. "Ted is getting everything set up now. Should be about ready to head out."

Their little group follows Ray up the slip, Christine's low-heeled sandals clip-clopping across the wooden dock. To their right, two young girls with their parents wait to board their own charter, and Imogene doesn't miss the glimmer of envy in their eyes as they pass. With that, she finds her fearlessness again. Today, *she* is the cool girl. *She* is where the party is.

Ray turns, and they follow him onto the narrow strip of dock in front of the boat. *The Salty Siren,* they call it. The girls stay put as Ray disappears onto the vessel to check in with his friend.

A few minutes pass when *another* girl turns onto the dock where they wait. Imogene sees the widening of her eyes and the moment's hesitation in her step when she catches sight of the three of them standing there. She takes a breath, adjusts her t-shirt, and continues forward. Imogene has never seen this girl before, and from the surprise on the other's faces, neither have they.

The girl is black, somewhere around Imogene's age—or maybe closer to Christine's? She is skinny, flat-chested, and not very tall, either, which lends to her more girlish appearance. Her beauty is undeniable, though; large, brown eyes, an angled jaw, and full, symmetrical lips. But dressed in a purple t-shirt, hair done up in a ponytail, she comes across quite casual next to their own group.

The girl offers a tentative smile, and two dimples appear on her cheeks.

Imogene smiles back.

"Hi," the girl says. A soft southern accent drags out the word.

The other girls stand silent. It's only a moment, but to Imogene, the silence seems to stretch on forever. "Hi," Imogene blurts out, worried they already appear rude.

"I'm Athena," the girl says, and rocks onto the outer edge of her Keds and back again. "I'm a... friend of Raymond's."

The use of Ray's full name must strike Greta as strange, because her eyes narrow to distrustful slits.

"I'm Imogene," she says in a rush. "And this is Christine, and that's Ray's sister, Greta."

Now a spark of terror flashes in Athena's eyes. "Oh… his sister. Raymond didn't tell me you were coming. It's… so nice to meet you."

After another drawn-out stare, Greta gives a half-smile and says, "Yeah, you too," deciding, it seems, that the girl is alright.

"Athena!" Ray bounds over the side of the boat, both legs flinging across in unison, and cuts straight for the bashful newcomer. Athena smiles, and Ray pulls her into a long hug, the kind of hug that makes spectators feel like intruders.

Christine turns to Greta in a panic. Plainly, she wants Greta to explain what is happening, to tell her who this girl is, that it's not what it looks like. But Greta only shrugs.

Before Christine can dissolve into a full-on pout, however, the cabin door of The Salty Siren swings open, and another man fills the doorway. At the sight of him, Imogene swears the dock has fallen away. She is falling, air swept from her lungs. He is the absolute *most*.

This man—Ted, she assumes—has close-cropped brown hair. A pair of old jeans hang low from his hips, and as for the rest of his outfit… there isn't one. Imogene rarely sees men in such a state of undress and can't stop her eyes from noticing his impressive summer tan and strong shoulders. He wipes his hands on a towel and tosses it back into the cabin, then crosses to the hatch at the back of the boat. In a few effortless movements, the hatch is open, and he moves a short ramp in place to ease their transition from dock to vessel.

Imogene watches him work—or rather, she watches the muscles twist beneath the golden skin of his back. There's a shudder low in her stomach she's never felt before.

Ray, now oblivious to the rest of them, helps Athena cross the ramp, and disappears with her into the cabin. Ted—in the same heedless way one might twiddle their thumbs—chews on a toothpick, using his tongue to kick it absently around his mouth. He takes position at the hatch to help the rest of his passengers across the ramp, but Imogene is fascinated by his lips, and nearly misses her turn.

When Ted extends a hand to pull her up; their eyes lock, and

Imogene notes how boyishly handsome he is—like Warren Beatty, she thinks, with another lurch of her stomach. Though Ted's face has several large freckles speckled across his cheeks and jawline. He looks expectant and hopeful—*sweet*.

But then Imogene focuses on his eyes. The sweetness is there, sure, but there's something else. A hint of mischief.

Ted smiles at Imogene as the toothpick juts between a display of perfect teeth, and when he pulls her onto The Siren—*though how could she have known, really?*—she is certain that nothing will ever be quite the same.

35

TED

(JUNE 1963)

UP HERE, HIGH ABOVE THE world, breeze on his face, the city displayed before him, the subtle, weightless sensation of being on open water—it is magic. Pure magic. They cruise along the Halifax at a nice speed, just fast enough for potential customers to read the phone number on the back and have time to jot it down or commit the digits to memory.

Below, the stereo belts out "Walk Like A Man" by The Four Seasons. Ted is on the upper deck, in the cockpit, navigating them south on the river. Here, he is well and at peace. They'd dreamt this for so long, he and Ray, and now that it's happening, the reality surpasses all expectations.

He hears Ray on the main deck, teaching Athena how to cast

a rod. The boat is still moving, so they can't actually throw a line, but if the frustrated tone of Ray's voice is any indicator, Athena is struggling with his demonstration. In Ted's mind, he sees the scene below, and a smile finds his lips. The other three are quiet, though. It's Ted's duty to assure everyone is having fun—and *looks* it. After all, that's why they'd invited the girls out in the first place.

He powers down the engine, stands from his comfortable captain's chair, and peers over the railing. Ray's sister is stretched out on a towel, sunbathing. Ted cocks an eyebrow. *Not a bad view*, he admits. The stacked brunette is nowhere to be seen; she'd been rather moody since they boarded. This irks Ted a bit. She's easy on the eyes, sure, but little good *that* does if she's holed up somewhere moping. But then his eyes rest on the pretty girl with the cinnamon hair and the long legs. She's got on this checkered blue top that reminds him of Dorothy from The Wizard of Oz, and a pair of navy shorts. She sits on a bench against the starboard side, elbow propped on the ledge, chin resting on her fist. Lost in her own world, a peaceful smile plays at her lips. Without realizing it, Ted mimics this smile as he watches her. *Now that's more like it*, he thinks. This is what people want to see.

Before he knows what he's doing, he shouts, "Hey!"

The girl lifts her head, squinting against the sun, and goes owl-eyed when she realizes it's *her* to whom Ted is speaking. "Me?" she calls back, and touches a hand to her chest.

Ted laughs. "Yeah, you! You wanna come up here and have a look around? Much better view."

The girl turns her attention to Ray's sister, who makes an indistinct motion with her hands. He can't tell what is being said, but the girl rings her hands together and rises to her feet, moving toward the tall metal ladder that extends to the cockpit on the upper level of the boat.

Ted helps her up into the small space, noticing the unsteady tremble in her footing as she takes in the sprawling riverscape.

"Whoa," she says. "It's a little high." A sheepish grin flashes across her face.

"Scared of heights?" Ted asks, amused.

A blush washes over her. "No… not usually. A little, perhaps. It's just… this is my first time on a boat this size."

"Oh, a landlubber, are ye?" he jokes in a raspy pirate voice.

She smiles, and a rush of warmth springs out in Ted's chest. "Here, sit down," he says, and offers her a seat on the bench beside the captain's chair. "It feels less wobbly when you sit."

The girl obliges with a grateful smile.

"Imogene, is it?" he asks. Ted hopes he's remembered it correctly, being such a unique name and all.

She nods.

"I'm Ted." He wipes a palm on his jeans and extends the hand to Imogene. She gives his hand a look as though unsure what to do with it, then wraps her delicate fingers around his and offers a timid shake.

"Nice to meet you," she says.

"Same to you."

Ted grins and returns his eyes to the water ahead. This seems like a fine spot to relax for a while, so he drops the anchor to keep them from drifting. Once he's finished securing the boat, he steals a glance at Imogene and catches her staring back. The blush that follows gives her away, though she tries to hide it by quickly looking off and tucking a strand of hair behind her ear. Ted regrets embarrassing her, but my goodness, is she ever a beauty when she blushes.

"So, what were you thinking about down there?" he asks, hoping to ease her nerves.

"What do you mean?" she asks.

"Down there when I called to you. I could see on your face you were thinking of somethin'… or could it be some*one*?" Ted raises an eyebrow in her direction and gives it a suggestive wiggle.

That blush again. He doesn't even feel bad about it this time; he enjoys it.

"No," she stammers. "No—no, I wasn't thinking of anybody. I don't have anyone to think of anyhow. Or rather… I *do*. But—not like that." She clears her throat.

Ah, not going steady with anyone, then. Ted files that information away for future use.

"No, I was just fretting over the fall, I guess. How I wish there was a way to stop it from coming," she says.

Now that was an unexpected answer. "Why's that?" he asks.

Imogene shrugs. "I just love... *this.*" She motions all around us, and her face comes to life. "The sun. The water. The heat on my skin. People complain about the heat, but not me. I love it. I suppose perhaps I was *made* for summer. Everyone has a season, I think. Summer is mine. But it can't stay like this forever. Come fall, I'll be in a stuffy ol' classroom at Stetson, Greta will be gone—back to Virginia, and... I don't know." She catches herself then and shakes something from her mind. Ted hopes she'll continue, but instead she says, "I'm sorry. I don't mean to bore you."

With a look of amusement, Ted wonders how she could ever think herself a bore. "Not boring. Not at all," he says. "I might be a summer, too, or could be a spring. Cold weather is the worst."

Imogene smiles at this validation, and glances at her hands, folded neatly in her lap.

Ted asks, "What are you going to Stetson for?"

"Nursing," she says, clearing her throat. "I... want to be a nurse."

"That's something else! Really cool." And he means it. In his entire life, he's never known someone who went to college.

Another pink touches her cheeks, but she's warming to him now. "Are you and Ray the same age?" she asks.

"I'm twenty-five." Ted watches her reaction from the corner of his eye.

Imogene nods, pulls her lower lip between her teeth, and straightens her posture. Her eyes dart to the water. *Hm,* not the answer she hoped for then.

"You're eighteen? Like Greta?"

"Yes."

"Cool."

Silence fills the space between them again. But before it

becomes awkward, a loud squeal tears through the air from below. Ray's loud chuckle isn't far behind.

"You bozo!" Greta shouts, which brings about another wave of laughter. He can only imagine what Ray had done.

"Are Athena and Ray..." Imogene blanches and doesn't finish the question, though Ted is sure he knows what she means to ask. A month ago, when Athena first started coming around The Siren, he'd asked Ray the very same thing.

"Swapping spit?" he offers.

Another blush, eyes wide. "That's not what I... no—I..."

Ted laughs and Imogene joins in, looking embarrassed, but not uncomfortable.

In a lower voice, she says, "That's not the way I was going to phrase it. But, yes, that's the basic idea of my question."

Ted lets the laughter die away and, with a sigh, he says, "They are... off and on. Yeah."

Imogene nods but says nothing further.

"What do you make of that?" Ted asks.

Ted has his own opinions on the matter, of course. At the top of the list is concern—concern for Ray, and for Athena as well.

Athena Roberts is seventeen and the daughter of their former upstairs neighbors at The Grove.

Mr. and Mrs. Roberts were the quiet type, always keeping to themselves. A few folks got on their back over the years, but Ted always let them be. Athena, though, was smart and kind and gorgeous, and caught Ray's eye immediately. Mr. and Mrs. Roberts never approved of this match, however. Was that because Ray was older? Because he was white? Because he was uneducated? Who could say for sure? But they forbade Athena from seeing him. This didn't sit well with Ray—or Athena, either, for that matter.

After moving onto the boat last month, Ray and Athena had picked back up in secret.

Just last week, after Athena snuck off The Siren and headed back home, Ted cornered Ray in the galley to try and talk sense into him.

"What are you doing, man?" Ted had asked.

"What am I doing, *what*?" Ray asked, and shoved a handful of chips in his mouth, crumbs sprinkling over his bare chest.

Ted huffed. "You know what I mean. You and Athena. What are you *doing*?"

"The walls are pretty thin on this rig. Figured you could hear exactly what we were doing," Ray joked, and slapped Ted on the shoulder.

Ted hadn't found this very amusing. "What kind of future do you suppose you're gonna have with her, Ray?"

Ray's face turned stoic. In a controlled voice he said, "You're my brother, Ted. But I don't think I like what you're implying."

Ted shook his head. "C'mon, stop. You know me, man. You know I don't see her like that. But you get how things are. You've seen what's been going on up in Birmingham; the sit-ins, the marches, the violence. Any of that ringing a bell to you? It's getting ugly out there. You think people won't notice the two of you walking around smoochin' each other in the streets? Guess again. I imagine they'll have all kinds of things to say about that. This is dangerous, Ray—for *both* of you… but most of all, you. I understand you care for her, but you've got to save your own neck and stop this while you still can."

Ray ran his hands hard through his hair, and for the first time, Ted worried he might seriously try and clobber him. But instead, he spat, "To hell with them! Why does it matter to anybody else what we do? It's not their life."

Ted nodded in agreement and said, "No. You're right. It ain't. But you can bet they'll make it their business."

Ted trusted his words to stick with Ray, but here is Athena on the boat with them, so he guesses he hadn't made quite the impact he'd hoped. Ray seems happy, though, and Ted can't knock that. As long as he's careful.

Imogene turns her head toward the laughter below and smiles. "She seems really nice," she says.

Ted returns her smile. "She is. Yeah." Then he looks at Imogene and says, "So are you."

36

IMOGENE

(JUNE 1963)

THE SALTY SIREN RETURNS TO the dock at eleven AM.

Christine, who'd spent the trip in the salon pouting over Ray, is eager to go. Imogene, however, would be content to spend the rest of her days on The Siren.

After her conversation with Ted, the nervous flutters in her stomach elevated to a dizzying level. She tried to sunbathe with Greta but couldn't shake the knowledge that Ted was up in the cockpit alone. He'd come down only twice to pass out snacks and to use the restroom; the rest of the trip he'd spent on the upper deck, sitting in his chair, lost in his own world. Everything Imogene attempted to do over the next two hours earned only half her attention; the other half trained on the ladder, in hopes she'd catch Ted coming down to join them. He hadn't, though, and now the trip is over.

Ted returns to his place at the hatch and helps each of them step off the boat. Everyone has gone, and Imogene can delay no longer. She makes to pass, but Ted takes hold of her wrist to stop her. Surprised, Imogene pauses and turns her full attention to him for what she hopes isn't the last time.

"Uh—Imogene… I'd just like to say it was real nice to meet you." There is a nervousness in his voice Imogene can't understand.

"You too, Ted," she says with a smile and the coolest voice she can muster. "Thank you for taking us out. That was a blast." She gave an inconspicuous nod in Christine's direction and added, "For *some* more than others."

They both chuckle. Imogene had spilled the beans about Christine's crush on Ray and how disappointed she was to learn about Athena. *Ah, that explains the sour disposition,* he'd said. *I thought she might be a touch seasick.*

Imogene clears her throat. "Well…thanks again," she says and turns to go, but Ted's voice pulls her back.

"Hey, wait. Uh… If you aren't doing anything tomorrow, I'd love to take you out for coffee or shakes or something. If you'd be interested, that is."

Imogene's entire body tightens, the heat everywhere. "I work tomorrow at one," she says, trying to keep her voice even and light. *You are the cool girl, remember?* she thinks. "But I can go out before then."

Ted's face brightens at her acceptance. "Okay, yeah, great. That sounds good."

The following morning, Imogene wakes in a state of nerves and mild disbelief. Never has she been on anything even remotely *close* to a date. Is that what this is? She takes her time dressing and curls her hair, just in case.

Almost mechanically, she leaves her tiny house on East

Wisconsin and drives the thirty minutes to Lola's Coffee on Main. As she pulls into a parking space, her sweat glands open and perspiration wets the back of her neck. On the walk from her car to the sidewalk, an even deeper dread overcomes her. *What if he doesn't show? What if he's late? What if I'm at the wrong coffee shop? What if we can't find each other?*

Her worries are short-lived, however, because Ted is waiting at the door to Lola's. He looks real smart, she thinks, dressed in gray slacks and a striped button-down shirt.

The morning is perfect. They drink coffee and talk, then follow Main to the beach and back again. Ted asks her to dinner that evening, and she says yes.

Later, at work, her brain is only half-focused on the job; the other half is busy playing Ted's smile on a loop, dissecting his words, listening to his voice drift about in her inner ear. Imogene doesn't even notice when Greta enters the lobby two hours into her shift and is startled when she approaches the counter and shouts her name. *Hello! Earth to Imogene!*

It seems Greta has not only recovered from her relationship with Nancy, but moved on entirely; she's here with another girl. Greta introduces her companion as Marybeth, who is as petite and blonde as the last one, though much taller. Imogene notices they don't touch the way Greta and Nancy did, and Marybeth pays for her own popcorn and soda. So perhaps she's just a friend.

Marybeth goes to the powder room, and Imogene fills Greta in on her morning with Ted. "He's taking me to dinner tonight," she says. "An Irish place called Maguire's."

"Two dates in one day? Holy cow, Imogene! Ol' Ted must really be sweet on you."

Marybeth returns just as Imogene's face goes flush. "Oh, he is not. He's just being kind," Imogene says.

Greta laughs. "Oh man, you are thicker than a five-dollar malt! He'll kiss you by the end of dinner tonight, mark my words. And when he does, you owe me a free popcorn." She plucks a popcorn kernel from the top of her box and chucks it across the counter at Imogene. Imogene swats it away with a laugh, but her brain is already whirring.

Greta and Marybeth disappear into the theater and leave Imogene alone with her thoughts. A kiss. *Kissing.* Ted's lips on hers. Her face burns at the possibility. To someone like Greta, this might not be a big deal. But to Imogene, who had only had her first date a few short hours ago… well… it was the biggest deal in the world.

———

Maguire's is a cozy little restaurant wedged between a drugstore and a place that sells leather and fabric. Dozens of motorcycles line the sidewalk out front. Ted frowns as he parks but says nothing.

Inside, the restaurant is packed; most of the tables are taken and giant men in black vests and Levi's stand three deep at the bar. Imogene makes herself as small as possible as the waitress leads them to their table just to the right of the crowded bar. The noise is deafening, the room reeks of cigarette smoke, and a gentleman's backside is a mere foot from her left elbow, but Imogene scarcely notices anything beyond the beating of her own heart. Ted looks as though he wants to speak but thinks better of it; he would need to shout to be heard over the din of the place.

When the waitress returns to take their order, Ted asks about the crowd, and the waitress tells him that tonight is Bike Night, a monthly event that offers buy-one-get-one drinks until ten PM. Ted gives a polite nod to the woman, but Imogene sees his mood deflate.

A man passing too close to their table takes a stumble, and a wave of beer sloshes over the side of his glass and onto Imogene's purse. The waitress rushes to her side with a spot of club soda and helps Imogene scrub the spatter from her bag. The fuss is unnecessary, though; it's honestly not a bother. Imogene had that purse for years—a gift from an old aunt. Even if it stains, she won't much care. But Ted apologizes all the while. As if he were in any way to blame for the mishap. Between apologies, he stares daggers into the man with the beer, who remains oblivious to the entire scene.

By the time Imogene's shepherd's pie arrives, an Irish band has taken the small stage in the back of the room, and their instruments and rousing voices are tearing through the air. Ted and Imogene share a discouraged glance.

Ted looks as though he wants to crawl out of his skin. "You wanna go outside?" he shouts.

Imogene gives a vigorous nod in response. "Yes!"

Ted pays for their half-eaten meals, and they make their way out front. The sun has begun its slow descent, and golden light bathes the street.

Down the way a bit, an Italian Ice vendor sells from a cart on the corner. Ted withdraws a bill from his wallet and buys them each a cup. They continue their walk as they eat.

"Sorry about all that," Ted says, and Imogene can hear the note of shame in his voice. "I didn't realize. It's usually a real quiet place. I'm sure sorry."

"It's okay," Imogene says with a shrug. That's only part of the truth, though. The whole truth is that Imogene doesn't care *where* they are or how many drinks spill on her; she's just happy to be with him.

"I'm sorry about your dinner, too. I'm sure this isn't what you had in mind," he nods to the sweet treat in her hand.

"It's delicious, actually," she says, and takes another bite to prove it.

Ted winces. "Yeah, but you're all decked out."

This much is true. Imogene has in fact donned her best summer dress for the occasion—the yellow one with the paisley flowers she loves most.

"It's okay," she assures him. "Honest."

Ted is plainly unconvinced, and she can see how much this bothers him. He'd tried so hard to give her a nice evening, and while it hasn't gone *quite* according to plan, she is having a great time and wishes more than anything he could see that.

"Thank you," Imogene says.

"For what?"

She smiles and lets her eyes find Ted's as she says, "For taking me out tonight."

It surprises Imogene to see him flush and stumble over his words for a moment. "Oh, no need to thank me for that," he says. "Your company is a pleasure."

"Greta says it's odd to go on two dates in one day." The moment this slips from her lips, she wishes to take it back. Maybe he hasn't meant these to be dates at all.

"Sorry, I…" she stammers.

But Ted smiles. "No. I guess it *is* pretty odd. I've never been on two in the same day before… until now."

Imogene heats head to toe. "Me neither." She turns her face before Ted can see her dopey grin.

The sun sinks lower, the streetlamps kick on above, and yet they keep going, not ready to surrender the evening, or each other. Imogene has spent most of her life feeling lost in the crowd, but tonight she is plucked from it—*chosen*. She has never felt this way—this complete ease with another person; as if she's known him her entire life. She could walk with him forever and never yearn for anywhere else.

But it appears the night has an alternate plan. The wind picks up and the musty scent of ozone hits Imogene's nostrils.

"Uh-oh," Ted says with an apprehensive glance at the sky.

Without another warning, the clouds open, and a hard, warm rain surrounds them. Imogene squeals as the first drops pelt her skin.

Ted grabs her arm. "Come on!" he shouts.

They are both running now, glancing up just long enough to see where they are going. By the time they reach the car and throw themselves inside, they are soaked to the bone and shaking with laughter. For a moment, they just look at each other. Water droplets glisten in the scruff of Ted's shorn hair. And then he leans across the seat and pulls Imogene into a kiss. She has less than a second to think before it happens, but she kisses him back, and as she does, she tells herself, *You should remember this, Imogene. Remember it.*

The kiss lasts for only a moment, but she wills time to slow and taps into each of her senses. She can taste the salt in the rain drops on his upper lip and the faint trace of citrus on his breath from the Italian Ice. The humid warmth of the car wraps her like a hug. The dampened fabric of her dress clings to goose fleshed legs. Ted's palm rests softly on her cheek, his fingers curved around the base of her skull as he pulls her against him; the vinyl seat crunches when he leans in to deepen the kiss. Irish music thumps from the open door of Maguire's, but the hollow beat is dulled by the rhythmic patter of rain against the windshield.

And then it's over. And Ted pulls away.

"I like you, Imogene," he says, a rather redundant statement considering what they'd just done.

But Imogene answers with, "I like you, too."

On the drive back to the Marina where her car is parked, she thinks of nothing but that kiss… and the popcorn she now owes Greta.

37

Ted

(JUNE 1963)

THE RAIN SPILLS FROM THE sky in buckets. This storm hit later in the day than most, but it's June still, and they have yet to fall into the predictable pattern of afternoon summer storms. Odds are it won't last long, but it sure is ugly now.

"I don't like the idea of you driving home in this, Imogene." They are parked at the marina, watching the rain sheet down the windshield.

Imogene looks rather apprehensive beside him, but says, "I'll be okay. This isn't my first time driving in the rain, you know."

"Hey," Ted says, as an idea sparks within him. "I still owe you dinner. Want to come back to The Siren with me? I can make us something while we wait for the rain to pass."

He is grasping at straws; he doesn't expect her to say yes. But the corner of her mouth twitches and she says, "Yes, that would be very nice."

Ted hadn't thought to bring an umbrella, and kicks himself for the oversight, but canny as he his, he snatches his jacket from the backseat of the car. Ted and Ray share the vehicle—a 1960 Ford Fairlane—as one seldom goes anywhere without the other. But earlier today, he'd begged Ray to let him use it to take Imogene out to dinner. She had her own car, of course, but what kind of date would he be if he made her drive? Imogene hadn't allowed him to drive clear to her house, though he had offered, so they agreed to meet at the marina instead. He hands his jacket to her; a dark blue fog jacket, older than the hills, thin material, but enough to keep the rain off for a quick jaunt up the dock.

Pulling it over her head, she nods at Ted, and the two of them make a run for it.

Ted rummages through the cabinet and the small refrigerator in The Siren's tiny galley. Imogene sits at the rounded booth opposite him. The room is so cramped, he could reach out and touch her if he wanted. He senses her eyes follow his movements as she rings the remaining wet from her hair with a towel; turns out, his shoddy jacket was no match for the downpour.

Ray isn't here, which surprised them *both* when they entered the quiet boat. He must have walked somewhere, Ted thinks; dollars to donuts, he's sneaking around with Athena. Unfortunately, now it looks as though Ted planned it this way, as if he knew Ray would be out and is trying to trick Imogene into going all the way with him. He wouldn't say no if she wanted to, of course, but that wasn't his plan. Not even close.

Ted smiles at her now, but panic moves into his chest. He'd spoken fast in the car, desperate to prolong his time with her. But he doesn't know how to cook, save for a few basic meals, and he and Ray haven't shopped since they moved into the boat.

C'mon, Ted! Something in here has to work. He promised her food.

God, she is pretty.

Think, Ted!

Ah-ha!

"You ever had a fried bologna?" Ted asks, a mite too abrupt and loud; he notices Imogene startle.

"Can't say that I have," she answers with a chuckle.

Ted pulls an assortment of items from the cabinet and lines them up on the counter; if you could call the tiny square space he has to work on a counter. In his haste, he crashes and bangs into everything and nearly causes an avalanche when he tries to dislodge their one frying pan from the back of the cabinet. Imogene watches him with this amused glint in her eyes, and Ted doesn't even mind if it's because he looks like a total dip stick; he would embarrass himself a million times over to see her happy.

Twenty minutes later, he's managed to turn a half-eaten pack of bologna, four slices of white bread, and a few cheese slices into a nice dinner. Well… it's a dinner. Maybe not a *nice* one.

Imogene doesn't complain, though. For the first time since they met, she seems completely relaxed in his presence. This is a victory he does not take for granted. Imogene eats and says it's delicious, putting a blush on Ted's cheeks that doesn't come often or without great effort.

"You've Really Got a Hold on Me," drifts from the radio, and conversation is steady, but outside, the rain eases. Ted hopes Imogene doesn't notice. But just in case, he cranks the music louder. This girl is the missing piece to his puzzle. There's a bit of money in his pocket now, a great friendship shared with Ray, a new business bound to take off, and now he has a girl; someone with whom to share everything with. It's too soon to say what the future holds, but in this moment, with Smokey Robinson crooning in the background, he knows he will do his best to keep her.

38

IMOGENE

(JUNE 1963)

TWO WEEKS WITH TED. TWO *wonderful* weeks. To Imogene, it may as well be a lifetime. Work is hard. Home life is harder. It seems her mind is always with him, and there isn't space for much else.

She parks her car in the lot behind The Sheldon and exits in a lovesick daze.

"Hey, stranger," a voice says.

Imogene swings around, surprised to see Greta there. She leans against the driver door of Rhonda, arms crossed over her chest. Somehow, Imogene hadn't noticed her car in the lot. *An honest mistake*, she thinks.

"Greta," Imogene breathes, and presses a palm to her heart

in relief. "Don't scare me like that."

"Sorry." Greta straightens herself and drops her arms. "But I wanted to catch you before work. We're having a bonfire tonight at the condo. Wanna come?"

Imogene glances to her feet and rolls a piece of gravel with the toe of her shoe. "Oh, I'd sure love to, Greta. But… I'm actually supposed to go out with Ted tonight." Ted reserved them a table at the swanky restaurant inside the golf club where he works. It is rather prestigious, and Imogene is looking forward to it.

Greta clearly doesn't share Imogene's enthusiasm on the matter. She sighs. "That doesn't surprise me. You've seen him almost every day for the last two weeks. I just thought you might want to do somethin' different is all."

Here comes the guilt.

"You're right. I'm so sorry, Greta. I haven't been a very good friend."

"*Are* we friends, then?" This comes out as an accusation.

"Of course, we are. Why on earth would you ask that?"

"I called your house," Greta says.

"What?" Imogene is confused. But if what Greta says is true, then Imogene has some explaining to do.

Greta nods. Her mood takes a further dive. "I called your house," she repeats. "I hadn't seen you in over a week. You missed work. You *never* miss work. I came by to invite you shopping with me and Christine, but you weren't here."

"How did you get my phone number?" Imogene asks. She'd been so careful not to let her home life and her life in Daytona collide. A wave of betrayal flows through her, but it's Greta who looks most hurt.

"Wow," she says, with a look she's never used on Imogene before—a look like disappointment. She shakes a thought from her head and answers the question. "Mr. Pickman gave it to me. Told me you were sick. That's why you weren't in. So, I asked for your phone number so I could check on you."

"Oh," Imogene says.

"Yeah," Greta plods onward. "Imagine my surprise when

your mom told me you weren't home. Says you were takin' a summer course at Stetson. Funny... first *I've* heard of that. I didn't realize they offered courses on frenchin' Ted Barret down at Stetson."

Imogene blushes with shame.

"And here's the real sad part. When your mom asked who was calling, I said, 'It's Greta.' And you know what *she* said?"

Imogene swallows but doesn't answer. Of *course*, she knows.

Greta continues. "She said, 'Greta *who?*'"

Imogene's throat tightens, and she looks to the ground, at the jagged pebble she's kicking around; she can't bring herself to meet Greta's eyes.

"Why on earth would your mom not know who I am?"

Imogene can't speak. How to explain she's lied all this time... and *why*.

"Imogene!" Greta shouts, zapping her back into the moment.

"I'm sorry!" Imogene shouts back. Tears cloud the corners of her eyes, and she tries hard to keep them from overflowing. "I never told my parents about you... or Ted. Not him, either. They... You don't know them. They wouldn't approve."

Greta pales at this and then asks, "Are you embarrassed of me, Imogene?"

A sick feeling rises in her gut. "No! Goodness, no! Greta, that's *not* it. My parents... They don't approve of anyone who isn't *exactly* like them. They expect me to be this perfect daughter who does everything she's told. And they tell me to go to work, go to school, go to church, go volunteer for the community or the less fortunate, and then go straight back home. If they found out where I've been these past two summers, they never would have let me go."

At some point during this revelation, the tears had spilled over and now fall in earnest down Imogene's cheeks. Greta looks around the parking lot with a regretful expression, as if it would mortify her to discover they were making a scene. Lucky for them both, they are alone.

"That's why I love your family so much." Imogene sniffles

and wipes her eyes. Uses a few deep breaths to calm herself. "They are *nothing* like mine. I was having so much fun with you. With your friends. My parents would have ruined it if they'd known. If I locked myself in my room all summer, reading bible verses with Susan Bostwick, they'd be only too pleased."

"Who is Susan Bostwick?" Greta asks.

"It doesn't matter. The point is… I'm sorry. I'm sorry I lied. I'm sorry I didn't tell my parents about you. I'm sorry I've been spending so much time with Ted. I'm sorry for all of it. But I am *not* embarrassed by you."

A stretch of silence spreads between them. After a moment, Greta moves toward her, and with a heavy sigh, says, "Listen… It's fine. Like you said, I don't know nothin' about your folks. If you want to keep us all a secret, that's *your* bag. But I miss you, Imogene. Come tonight. Bring Ted. Tell Mom and Pops whatever you need. But come. *Please.*"

Imogene nods. "Okay. I'll be there."

The golf club can wait.

At last, Greta is satisfied. She opens the door to Rhonda with a smile, but glances back once more before she lowers herself into the seat. A moment passes between them where Greta looks as though she has more to add, but decides against it. Instead, she nods and says, "See you tonight, then."

"Tonight," Imogene agrees.

The engine revs, Greta peels from the parking lot, and Imogene takes another minute to compose herself before her shift begins.

She told Greta she's not embarrassed by her. And she isn't. At least, she doesn't *think* she is. But keeping their friendship a secret out of fear her family might not approve, what message does *that* send? Greta wasn't wrong to reach the conclusion she had.

Same goes for Ted. Imogene is so enamored by him, yet at heart she knows her parents will never deem him worthy of her. For starters, he's twenty-five. He's also an orphan, not college-educated, and lives on a boat with another man, risking everything for a business that may or may never take off.

Imogene knows her parents will perceive these things as shortcomings and will never give their blessing. But if she *knows* these things, does she believe them *herself* on some level? How much of her parents and their beliefs have imprinted within her? How many of their thoughts and prejudices does she carry with her each day? The idea she may end up exactly like them, despite her efforts to do better—to *be* better—troubles Imogene very much.

Greta snaps her chocolate bar in half and passes the other bit to Imogene. Ted has a marshmallow waiting, browned and gooey, and he helps Imogene press it all between two crunchy graham crackers.

The night has been perfect. Imogene can't imagine that a stuffy golf club could have compared to this on any level. Around the bonfire, the energy is alive and warm; Imogene's heart soars. There has been music and laughter and food and drinks.

Now, a bottle of root beer in hand, Mrs. Green entertains the small crowd with stories of Ray and Greta when they were *just little bitty ol' things*, much to the chagrin of Ray and Greta.

Imogene sneaks a glance at Ted, at the firelight slicing across his features, and she is warm. So warm. He watches Mrs. Green with a thoughtful expression, laughing along as she recounts the day Ray went to school with a pair of Greta's little-girl-undies stuck to the back of his sweater. Ted's face is content and cool, but Imogene sees something hidden in his eyes; the same thing she herself tries to conceal whenever she is around the Greens— *longing.*

That's when it hits her. Though born and raised in different circumstances, Imogene and Ted both long for the same thing—a family like this one. To Imogene, family has always been a place of rule and order, where individuality is discouraged, and expectations are to be met without argument. To Ted, family has been a great vanishing act. The bonds he'd known weren't just broken, they were ripped without warning from his grasp. But Imogene dreams of a future with children and grandchildren, vacations every summer, ice cream, starlight, campfires, conversations over dinner; a simple and carefree life where everyone is welcome, and nobody ever leaves.

Without a word, Imogene reaches over and takes Ted's hand. He looks at her then. Golden flames twinkle in eyes the color of chocolate.

Ted and Imogene may not have been blessed with the family they'd hoped for, but *now*, just maybe, they can be that for each other.

39

TED

(JULY 1963)

ALONG MAIN STREET, AMERICAN FLAGS hang with pride from light posts, and most businesses sport one or two of their own. Ted and Ray have just returned from distribution night at The Office. Forty dollars this week. Not great, but certainly not terrible considering they haven't been on a job of their own in a couple months now.

On their way back, they stop at the deli for a late dinner. They sit out front on a wooden bench, watching city workers set up barricades for the Independence Day parade tomorrow morning.

"So, before I forget," Ray says through a bite of his salami on rye.

Ted watches Ray reach into the pocket of his trousers and withdraw a long, rectangular box. Ray clears his throat and passes the box to Ted without meeting his eyes. "I got you a little somethin'."

Ted takes the box with a jolt of surprise. "What for?" he asks.

"For getting us off the ground with The Siren. I couldn't have done it without you."

They had booked their first two fishing tours last week. The first of many, Ted hopes.

He opens the box and peers inside, a lurch of shock courses through him. "Ray. Where'd you get the money for this?"

Ray just winks. "Don't worry about it. Now you're official, boss." He slaps Ted on the shoulder and takes another bite of his sandwich, looking pleased with himself.

With one last admiring glance at the gift, Ted slips the box into his jacket pocket and taps his chest where it now rests. "Thanks, man," he says, a tightening in his throat. "Truly."

The boardwalk is busy. Not a surprise, as this is the primo place to watch the big fireworks display. Crowds are hardly Ted's favorite thing, but Imogene seems at ease, and that's enough for him. She bobs along beside him, hair tied up in a blue scarf, lips painted a brilliant shade of scarlet. Ted recently told her how much he loves her in lipstick, and she's worn it every day since; like a secret code to tell the world, 'I'm Ted Barret's girl.' But the red shorts she's wearing tonight make it hard to concentrate on anything but those incredible legs. Add in the white blouse, and she is America incarnate; Lady Liberty as played by a Radio City Rockette.

Alongside him and Imogene is Ray, Greta, this girl Marybeth, Christine, and some Buddy Holly looking dork Christine brought to try and ruffle ol' Ray's feathers—Steve or Sam or something. It smells of summer—of fried food and salt and gunpowder and rain.

A scorcher and still two hours from sunset, Ted sweats

through his shirt, though he can't place the blame on the heat alone. A good amount of perspiration comes from nerves. No one knows, but tonight, during the fireworks, he plans to tell Imogene that he loves her, and if that ain't enough to make a man sweat, he don't know what is.

It's soon, he realizes. They only met a month ago. Perhaps she'll think him a total clod, but he knows what he feels, and he needs Imogene to know that *she* is his girl. There will never be another for him… no matter *how* she responds tonight.

Ted, Ray, and Steve/Sam buy the girls lemonades to cool off. Imogene sips hers slowly, a peaceful smile on her lips that Ted drinks in like water. Her eyes flick to his, and Ted's chest tightens with a rush of devotion. Unable to wait a second more, he opens his mouth to tell Imogene exactly what she means to him.

But before he can, Imogene tenses and squeezes Ted's hand so hard his knuckles grind together. A small gasp escapes her. His full attention is on Imogene, but her eyes fasten on something in the distance, and from the fear on her face, it's not a good something.

"Imogene Louise Elkins!" a shrill voice tears through the air, slicing through the crowd, clear as a bell.

"Oh no," Imogene mutters. In less than a blink, she's dropped his hand and moved several steps away from him.

A short, heavy-boned woman stomps through the crowd, face red, nostrils flared. She may have been an alright looking woman once, Ted thinks, but with her features all twisted in anger, it's hard to tell.

By this point, Ray, Greta, and the others have noticed the situation, and everyone pauses, standing in an awkward half circle around Imogene, who is more scared than Ted has ever seen.

"What in Heaven's name are you doing here?" the woman asks, and her eyes snap to each of them as she appraises the scene. An older gentleman dressed in a smart shirt and hat files in behind the woman; there is anger in *his* face as well, but more controlled.

"I—" Imogene stammers.

"And *what* are you wearing?" the woman demands.

"Shorts, Mama," Imogene answers, voice barely a whisper.

No. This *can't* be Imogene's parents. Surely not.

"Shorts! You call those shorts? More like a swimsuit, I'd say. And *boys?*" She turns to Ted and the other two guys with such scrutiny and distaste that Ted cowers beneath her stare.

"You're supposed to be volunteering at the church, Imogene," she continues. "I go down to bring you some supper, and Pastor Jim says you haven't been by all day. Can you imagine the embarrassment? Went down to the theater, and Mr. Pickman says he heard you talkin' about coming out here today. I say, 'no sir, that can't be right.' Yet, here you are, makin' me out a liar. So, is that what you're doin' now, Imogene—lyin'? Lyin' about volunteering at *church* so you can run around with boys, dressin' like a harlot? Do you have no respect for yourself? For us? For the Lord?"

How Mrs. Elkins got all that out without hyperventilating, Ted doesn't know.

"I'm sorry, Mama," Imogene mutters, but can't quite meet her mother's stare. "These are my friends, and I—"

"—Friends?" Mrs. Elkins interrupts. "Well, we never met these friends of yours. And I don't like my daughter keepin' friends with grown men. Now you're coming home with us right this instant. Let's go."

Imogene freezes in place, eyes wide in terror. Ted is beyond scared himself, but he can't stand to see Imogene this way, so he takes a breath and moves to defend her, as any good man should do. "Mrs. Elkins, ma'am," he says, "I assure you—"

"—Oh, you *assure* me. You hear that Frank?" She turns back to her husband for effect, fire in her eyes. "He *assures* me."

Now she steps closer to Ted; another flush of embarrassment ripples over his skin. He shrinks in her presence. "First of all, young man," she says through clenched teeth, "I don't believe I was speaking to you. This is between me and my daughter, and I certainly don't need no *assurance* from grown men who prey on young girls."

For someone who keeps referring to Ted as a *grown man*, she sure has a way of making him feel small and helpless as a child.

"Mama, he's not—"

"—Say goodbye to your *friends*, Imogene, and get yourself to the car, before you make me say something I'll regret."

Imogene casts another pleading glance in Ted's direction, eyes two hazel pools of despair. She shakes her head in defeat and shrugs. Jaw slack, Ted watches her go. He so badly wants to say something. To help her. But what can he do?

Ted winces as her mother's fingers dig into the pale flesh of Imogene's upper arm. Mrs. Elkins steers Imogene through the crowd and away from their group, who can only look at each other with gaping mouths and pure disbelief.

40

IMOGENE

(JULY 1963)

IMOGENE MUFFLES THE SOUND OF her cries with her pillow; she hugs it tight against her body, her face pressed into the floral pillowcase.

The entire ride home, Daddy drove in silence. Eyes glued on the road ahead, he'd offered Imogene not even a glance in the rearview mirror. The moment they stepped through the front door, he disappeared into his office, unable to face her for even a second.

Mama, however, was a different story. She spent the car ride reprimanding Imogene until her voice grew hoarse, and she repeated points already made. At home, Mama sat Imogene at the kitchen table and forced her to read aloud from the bible.

For a full hour, she kept her there, and when Imogene set in to crying, Mama told her, *Speak clearly, now. Or I'll have you start over again.*

Afterwards, Imogene went straight to her room, and it's here where the tears fall unbridled down her cheeks.

The embarrassment she feels is earth shattering and complete. After today, Ted will never want to see her again. The certainty of this causes an indescribable ache in her stomach. He must think she's a child. A scared little girl. Never mind that she's a grown woman; that means nothing when she cowers to her parents at the slightest sign of disapproval. Why hadn't she stood up for herself? Now everything she cares for, everything she's gained, all the things that have become hers the last two summers, will vanish. *Poof!* Just like that.

Her body coils further around her pillow, and the sadness consumes her, washing over her in shuddering waves.

From somewhere beyond the perimeter of her grief, Imogene hears a few faint knocks. She settles herself and listens close. At first, she thinks it must be her imagination, but a moment later, the taps come again from across the room. No denying it this time; something is rapping against her bedroom window.

Imogene gathers herself and moves toward the sound, where she pulls her curtains back the tiniest bit and peeks out, then rips them open the rest of the way, hand clutched to her mouth. Because there on the lawn, shoulder to shoulder, are Greta and Ted, each wielding a lit sparkler. Silver glimmers spit in every direction, arching, descending, and fading before they hit the grass. The relief to see them there brings a smile to her tight, tear-stained face.

Greta waves and motions for Imogene to open the window.

Imogene passes a nervous glance at her bedroom door. If Mama heard the knocks, too, she might come to investigate. When Imogene left her, she'd still been in the kitchen, but the house is silent now. Perhaps she's gone to bed; it's near ten o'clock, after all. So, with slow, controlled movements, Imogene raises the panel of her window. There is a loud *pop!* as it dislodges, and she winces against the sound. Her heart stills in her chest. No one comes to the door, thank goodness, and she takes that as a sign to continue. The window raises the rest of the way without difficulty or sound.

Greta moves forward and shuffles around the tall shrubs Mama planted along the side of the house last spring.

Astonished, Imogene asks, "What are you guys doing here?"

Greta shrugs and says, "You missed the fireworks. So, we thought we'd bring the fireworks to you."

There are no words. Imogene shakes her head. Stunned. "But how did you know where I live?"

"Mr. Pickman," Greta says. And then, "He's a real blabbermouth, by the way. You should really have a talk with him about your privacy."

A rogue tear escapes Imogene's eye, and she laughs, wiping it away. "Thank you," she says. "This is wonderful."

Greta's attention flicks to Ted. She clears her throat and says, "Well… it wasn't *all* my idea."

Imogene allows herself to meet Ted's eyes; she'd been too frightened to face him before now. He watches her with a bashful expression.

Greta turns to go, cursing as her blouse hooks on a rogue stem from Mama's pesky bushes. She crosses to take the dying sparkler from Ted's hand and nudges him with her elbow.

There is a moment, as he crosses the yard, when the fear returns to Imogene. What will she say to him? What will *he* say? What *could* he say to ease the sting of what happened?

But the panic dulls as Ted reaches the window and takes both of Imogene's hands in his own. He's looking at their hands clasped together, and then he's looking at Imogene.

"Imogene," he starts, "I'm real sorry for what happened earlier. But mostly, I'm sorry I did nothing to stop it."

"Don't think that," Imogene says. "What could you have done? I lied to them, *and* to you. It was my fault. *I'm* the one who should be apologizing."

Ted shakes his head. "No. You shouldn't have needed to lie in the first place. I don't blame you for doing it; your mom is terrifying." He shudders as he says this. "But you're a grown-up, Imogene. They have no right treatin' you that way."

A sad smile touches Imogene's lips. "No, you're right. But unfortunately, my parents don't share that opinion. And as long as I live under their roof, they make the rules."

"Then get out from under their roof!" Ted almost shouts this, and Imogene has to press a hand to his mouth to silence him. She laughs then—a hopeless laugh—because Ted doesn't know how often she's dreamed of doing that very thing.

"And go *where?*" she asks.

Ted looks younger now; a child about to suggest something he knows is silly and is sure to be met with a resounding, *No.* But he says it anyway. "Well… live with *me.*"

Imogene laughs again—she can't help it—which causes Ted to blanch. "What? On the boat with you and Ray?"

Ted's head falls, and his voice comes out in a whisper. "We ain't gonna be on the boat forever, Imogene."

"I know that. I'm sorry. I didn't mean it like that. It's just… you know I'd love to live with you." It's funny to hear it spoken out loud, but Imogene knows it's true. "Honest I would. But we don't have a plan. There's got to be a plan, you know. You and Ray are only working part time at the golf club, and when I start at Stetson in the fall, I won't be working at all. The Siren is going to do great! I know it will. But, until it does…" She shrugs. The last thing she wants is for him to think she's making excuses, but she knows she's right. Girls don't just run off with men without a plan… or a *ring.*

A new resolve enters Ted's expression. He squeezes her hand tighter and says, "I'm gonna do right by you, Imogene. I swear it. I'll get you out of this place and give you the perfect life. Just wait and see."

"Any life with you would be a perfect one," Imogene says.

Ted leans across the windowsill and plants a kiss on her lips. "I love you, Imogene Elkins," he says, his breath warm on her cheek.

Imogene's heart stops in her chest. When it beats again, it is stronger. *Changed.* It is with this new breath of life she replies, "I love you too, Ted Barret."

———

When she wakes the following morning, two thoughts fill Imogene's mind.

First is Ted—it's *always* Ted. Will always *be* Ted. But today is different. Last night, he'd made her promises. Promises she hopes she can count on him to keep. These promises will guide her through the rest of today and every day that follows. But, more than anything, she needs these promises to pull her through what she prepares to do next.

Mama, who starts each day the same, will be in the living room tidying up; when the living room is clean, she'll move on to breakfast and the dishes.

Today, Imogene woke determined to tell Mama the truth— the *whole* truth—before she leaves for work. Scanning her room one last time, she takes a mental inventory—purse, keys, cash— to ensure she has everything needed for the day. Once she leaves, she expects she won't be back for a while; Mama will need time to cool off.

But Imogene is surprised to find her mother on the sofa, sipping a cup of coffee and looking a touch bedraggled. Daddy's coffee mug and morning paper still lie on the coffee table where he left them.

Mama hasn't tidied up at all.

At this, Imogene's confidence falters; her mother is clearly in distress. Maybe today *isn't* the best day to come clean.

Mama appraises Imogene from her place on the sofa. A weariness sags her mouth and eyes. For a moment, Imogene thinks her mother looks sorry and that perhaps she might apologize. But then she says, "Nice to see you put on something respectable today."

Imogene tenses, but she tugs at the hem of her shirt and pulls herself up, tall and proud. In that one snide remark, she makes her decision. Today is the day.

"Mama," she begins, "you were right. I shouldn't have lied

to you and Daddy."

Mama readjusts her seat on the cushion. She's always been a proud woman, but seems almost smug at Imogene's admission.

"But," Imogene continues, "I shouldn't have needed to lie. I'm eighteen. A grown-up, Mama. I can have any friends I'd like."

"Grown!" Mama snorts out a laugh. "Come to me in ten years and talk to me about bein' grown. All you kids think you're grown the minute of your eighteenth birthday. I'm only tryin' to protect you."

"I don't need protecting," Imogene mutters, eyes falling to the beige carpet beneath her work shoes.

"Like Hell, you don't! You don't know nothin' of the world, Imogene!" Mama shouts.

Imogene's blood boils. With a deep breath, she squares her chin and says, "Ted—the boy I was with—*he's* a grown-up. He's twenty-five! And he's not just my friend. We've been going steady all summer. And we're in love. And Greta? The girl who called here the other day? She's my best friend in the entire world. Last summer when I said I was spending time with Susan Bostwick—"

Mama's eyes grow wide as saucers, already predicting what Imogene will say.

"—I was with *Greta,* not Susan," Imogene continues, watching Mama's face turn red as a turnip. "I haven't been taking summer courses at Stetson, either. I've been with my friends. I love being with them, Mama. I'm *happy* with them. And I'm sorry I disappointed you and Daddy, but I'm going to keep seeing them. In fact, I'm going to meet Ted right now before work. I'm telling you this. I'm done lying. And I'm going to be fine, Mama. You raised me fine, and I'm okay. But Mama, I'm going to do what I want now."

Mama's face is blank, mouth agape. Her bottom lip quivers as though trying to form words.

Imogene takes this moment of indisposition and makes for the door, but before she leaves, she turns back to her mother. "Oh—and by the way… Greta likes girls, the same way that I like boys, and it doesn't make her a bad person."

"Imogene!" Mama finally finds her voice, but Imogene has shut the door and is walking down the drive to her car. A proud smile pulls at her cheeks.

As a graduation present, Ray had gifted Greta a brand-new Kodak Instamatic camera. She's been obsessed with the thing. This morning, the girls drive to the marina so Greta can take pictures of the boats.

While Greta clicks away, Imogene and Ted sneak off for a private walk.

Hand in hand, they stroll along the dock.

"You want a big wedding?" Ted asks her.

"A wedding?" Imogene laughs. "Ted Barret, what on earth are you talking about?"

Ted stops walking and spins Imogene around to face him. Wild twinkles stud his dark eyes.

"I'm gonna marry you, Imogene." He says this as a fact. Absolute. "I can't spend my life with no one but you. It wouldn't be right."

"I'd love to marry you one day," she says.

With an awkward bobble from heel to toe and back again, he scratches the side of his neck and says, "I don't have much to show for myself right now, but with you by my side, I can do anything. I *can*. And one day I'll have enough money to give you the biggest ring and the nicest wedding you can imagine. Doves! You want doves? You'll have doves!"

Imogene can't help but laugh at this. She shakes her head and wonders how this impossibly perfect man found his way into the belly of her dismal life and lifted her hopes to the sky like bubbles in a fizzy seltzer.

"I just want *you*," she says. "No ring. No doves. Just you."

When they rejoin the others, Greta is popping a fresh roll of film into her camera, and carefully stuffs the old roll into her pocketbook for safekeeping.

Ray is busy on board. Ted says he's trying to repair the windings on a fishing rod—whatever *that* means.

Ted skips forward and snatches the camera from Greta, who makes a desperate grab for it, eyes wide as though he intends to drop her most prized possession right in the water. But instead, he says, "You got enough of the boats. Let me get you girls in a picture."

Greta grumbles, and Imogene waves the idea away. But eventually, they both agree. Greta sits on the dock in front of The Siren and pulls Imogene down beside her, where she lands with a *THUNK* and a giggle. Ted takes a few backward steps and squats low to get more of the background in the shot.

"You three look beautiful!" he shouts.

"Three?" Greta questions.

"Yeah. You, Imogene, and The Siren... not necessarily in that order."

Imogene and Greta call Ted a slew of names and dissolve into laughter.

Between his own laughs, he shouts, "Okay. Here we go! One... two... three!"

And the shutter clicks.

41

IMOGENE

(JULY 27, 1963)

IT WAS A SATURDAY.

A day Imogene will remember for the rest of her life.

In fact, she will spend *years* replaying this day in her head, unable to think of anything else.

She will remember the heat. The voice that crackled from her stereo warning of the elevated heatstroke risk; *the hottest day of summer so far, folks. Take care out there.* Imogene will recall her annoyance that the theater would be extra busy that day, as people looked to escape the blazing sun with a nice indoor activity instead. In that moment, there was no way to know she would never work another shift at The Sheldon.

Without even trying to, she could call to mind the exact

condition of her room that day. The details that shouldn't matter, but do, because this is the day her entire life flipped upside down. And everything about this day, even the insignificant things, burns into her memory like a brand on cattle. For years, she will close her eyes and see the bare mattress on her bed (she'd just taken a load of clothes from the dryer and stuffed her sheets into the wash); the stereo on her dresser that had wrapped with the weather report and now played "One Fine Day" by The Chiffons; her yearbook from senior year set beside the stereo. She'll see her nightstand with the round, black alarm clock, the slender lamp with baby-pink lampshade she'd had since she was twelve, the bottle of hand lotion, her car keys, the receipt for the pastry she bought herself the morning prior. Her clothes, her records, her makeup and barrettes, her textbooks for college in the fall. All of it... so meaningless.

The clock shows 10:30am.

Imogene is folding her clothes and putting them away when someone bangs on the front door. The banging is loud and insistent; she could swear the walls are rattling. She drops the shirt she'd been folding—a violet pajama top—and runs to the front door.

Mama runs in from the kitchen, drying her hands on the apron at her waist. "What in Heaven's name?" she says in response to the knocking.

Imogene is the one who answers the door.

In those first moments, it is impossible to tell what's going on, but Imogene's stomach sinks, nonetheless.

Greta.

Greta is at the door, eyes bloodshot red and oozing fresh tears. *Had she driven here in this state?* On her face is an expression Imogene has never seen—on *anyone*, let alone thick-skinned Greta. The two girls stare at each other for a second, and Greta tries to speak, but the words won't form.

Imogene will never forget the grotesque way her mouth worked as she tried to get the words out, as if iron fists were squeezing her lungs, ringing her breath out like a sodden dish rag.

Imogene is aware of her mother in the background, of the rapid fire of questions that hail in their direction, but the exact words are lost to Imogene. Whatever is happening right now, it's not good. And Imogene's attention is wholly on her friend.

"Greta?" As she steps onto the front porch, she keeps her voice low and soft. If this is a personal matter, she's sure Greta won't want to discuss her problems in front of her mother. "What's going on? What's wrong?"

Greta takes several deep breaths, shaking through each one. You'd never guess how hot it was from the awful way she shook.

"There... been... an *accident*, Imogene," she begins. "A fire. It's—it's The Siren... they found it burning this morning... and..."

At this, Greta crumbles and folds in on herself. She braces herself with her hands on her knees and emits a cry of complete anguish that sends a tremor through Imogene.

"A fire?" Imogene's heart thuds against her chest. Deep, terrified thumps. "What happened? Is everyone okay? Where are the boys?"

Greta's eyes are fixed on the wooden planks of Imogene's front porch, but her head moves back and forth, dark hair swishing around with her erratic movements. When at last she raises herself to look Imogene in the eyes, it's clear this visit brings no good news.

"They... found Ray—he... he..." Her eyes glass over again, but she shrugs, looks everywhere but at Imogene. Tries to steady her breaths, to pull herself up a little straighter. Tough. So tough. Even in despair.

Imogene waits on pins and needles while Greta gathers herself enough to say, "He didn't make it."

And then she falls to the ground, shaking and crying, and Imogene falls with her as a loud *No!* escapes her lips.

"He was burned so bad—but they... it's him... it's him, Imogene."

Imogene doesn't want to ask. She doesn't think she can stomach the answer. But she must. When she speaks, only one word comes out. "Ted?"

Greta shakes her head again, and Imogene's heart stops dead. "No sign of him yet," she says.

Relief floods through Imogene. And guilt, of course. How could she feel such relief while Greta mourns her brother on her parent's front porch? But relief is what she holds to because relief means *hope*, and the alternative is more than she can bear. Maybe Ted wasn't on the boat. Perhaps he was somewhere else. Please, God. Let him have been somewhere else.

Greta shakes her head again, though. She has more to say.

"But Imogene… they found his jacket."

"How—how do you know?" Imogene asks.

"Mom and I were out at the docks when they pulled up the wreckage. I saw it. The blue one he always carries around with him. I wouldn't think anything of it, except—"

"Except *what?*"

Greta looks ill when she says, "It was all covered in blood."

42

IMOGENE

(AUGUST 1963)

THE FOLLOWING WEEKS ARE A BLUR.

Greta left, as expected. Her family packed up and returned to Virginia to bury Ray. Imogene wanted to drive up for the service, but it was such a long way, and she didn't want to travel far in case there was news of Ted. But of course, there wasn't.

Days passed with no sign of him.

Imogene held onto hope for as long as possible. Longer than most people would bother. When you love someone, that's what you do. You close your eyes to all the ugly. Silence the part of yourself searching for the wrong in a situation. But after a time, one must acknowledge the truth. And the truth is: if Ted were alive, he'd have come for her by now.

Another truth: the recovery divers who take to the water each day are no longer on a rescue mission, but a search for a body. The local news has made this painfully clear. But then, what if Imogene doesn't *want* them to discover Ted's body? To find him would give her closure, sure. But if they never do, she can pretend he's still out there somewhere.

It's silly, of course. Either way, he's gone. Imogene knows this. Her world will never be the same.

After two weeks, the police call off the search.

A week later, on August 21, a memorial service is held in Ted's honor.

The morning of the service, Imogene wakes in a daze. She dresses, curls her hair the way Ted likes, and carefully paints her lips with his favorite cherry lipstick. As she moves through these mechanical motions of routine, today is an ordinary summer day. For the briefest moment, Imogene is dressing to see *him*. But a single glance in the mirror and reality sets in. With the spell broken, her composure crumbles.

She tells herself to stop and pull it together. A box of tissues is nearby, and she snatches three in fast succession, drying the wet from her eyes. After a quick re-powdering of her nose, she adjusts her dress, checks her reflection one last time, and makes her way to the living room.

Mama refused to go with her to the service. The rejection stings but doesn't surprise her. She wishes Greta was here, though, so she wouldn't have to be alone today. But if alone is how she's meant to do this, then alone she'll be. She'll do it for Ted.

Mama sits on the sofa, thumbing through Sunday's paper. "I'm heading out," Imogene says.

Mama lifts her eyes from the page, as if this were any other morning, and says, "Imogene… Sweetheart… I know you think you loved that boy. And it's a real shame what happened to him. It is. Believe me when I say that. But… you see… sometimes the Lord works in mysterious ways. Things may not make perfect sense to us at the time, but it's His will, after all. And you can't argue with His will."

Mama's eyes brighten then, and her posture straightens. That's when she says the thing that will stick with Imogene for years to come. She says, "Perhaps now you can focus on your schooling in the fall without the… *extra distraction*, hm?"

A distraction.

That's what Ted was to her.

Mama hasn't lost a wink of sleep over this, not even from the devastation it's caused her daughter.

She may not have said it in so many words, but Imogene knows. Mama is *relieved* that he's gone.

With a clenched jaw, Imogene turns for the door.

———

Ted's service is at Saint Mary's.

Cathy Marsh, Ted's former foster mother, organized the ceremony in his honor.

Without a body to bury, the altar instead displays a long, wooden table, decorated with photos of Ted and two grand arrangements of flowers: red and white roses, pale carnations, and yellow snapdragons.

On shaky legs, Imogene approaches the table.

Three framed photos. That's it.

The first photo shows Ted around age ten, a pair of oversized sunglasses worn upside down on his face, and an oversized grin to match. In the second, he's older—thirteen or fourteen—sitting on the floor of his room with a book in his lap. This photo was taken into the sun, and shadow obscures most of his face. The third—the most recent—shows Ted around age sixteen; he stands in front of a white door, dressed in a smart shirt and tie. Imogene guesses this was before a school dance or perhaps a wedding. There's not much of a smile in this one, just a slight hitch to one side of his mouth, as if he didn't want to stand for the photo in the first place and was hoping the person behind the camera would hurry and click the shutter.

Imogene reaches out to caress the image of Ted's face, but

the glass is cold beneath her fingertips—*too* cold—and she yanks her hand away.

Imogene stares at the table a moment longer and shakes her head. How can this be everything? No photos of him from recent years? She knows he was never especially close to Cathy Marsh, and they had limited contact with each other since he went his own way. But still… three photos? A whole beautiful life, and they could manage nothing more? Imogene's stomach roils, and she clenches her throat to stop the angry tears from flooding over.

She finds a seat at the back of the room. The large open doors offer a feeble breeze and, oddly enough, the farther from the altar she is, the closer to Ted she feels.

Cathy, now a fleshy woman in her sixties, and a few others of varying ages—foster children, past and present, Imogene suspects—squeeze themselves into the first two rows. *You didn't even know him,* she thinks.

As the minutes tick by, a few other stragglers find their way into the church and scatter themselves throughout the pews, but Imogene doesn't recognize a single face. *Did* I *even know him?* she wonders.

Perhaps thirty people are in attendance.

At the end of a short and impersonal service, Imogene gets the sense she's being watched. She glances to the right. Sure enough, a man gawks at her from across the next row.

No longer concerned with decorum, Imogene abandons her usual politeness and stares back, hoping the man will look away in embarrassment. But instead, he offers her a sad smile and a curt nod.

The man is older, thirty or so, with fair skin that looks even paler against his crop of dark hair. His hair is slicked back with something greasy, and he has a scruff of facial hair that could stand a bit of professional maintenance. No matter how long she stares, Imogene is positive she has never seen this man before—yet he looks at her as though he knows her.

The man lifts a gray bowler hat from his lap and stands.

Afraid he may try to strike up a conversation, Imogene

snatches her purse from the pew beside her and leaves the church in a hurry.

For days after the service, thoughts of the memorial table trouble Imogene.

Three photos.

She aches to return to the beginning of summer, to take so many pictures of Ted he begs her to stop. Pictures of him on the boat, with the prideful smile he always wore when out on the water. Pictures of him dressed up for dinner and dressed down while he worked in the sun. Pictures of his face in the early morning light. Close-ups of his freckles, his long, lean fingers, the dark hair that grew beneath his belly button. Pictures of the way his eyes lit up whenever he looked at her. Pictures of him in the rain, dripping and laughing. Pictures of everything. Every last moment.

But Imogene imagined there would be more time for all that stuff. Shouldn't there have been? It isn't fair. So much of his life hadn't happened yet. Time isn't something you should fret over when you're young. There should have been *more* of it.

More time for Ted.

More time for *them*.

43

EMELINE

(MAY 31, 2019)

THE WATER LAPS AGAINST THE dock, but the sound is hollow to Emeline's ears, the edges dulled, as if she were listening through a conch shell. The silence that follows Greta's story lingers among them.

Greta puffs out a breath of relief; Emeline senses she hasn't spoken of that summer in many years.

"Oh my gosh, how awful," Belinda croaks.

Greta nods, slapping her palm a few times on the wooden post at the end of the dock. "That isn't even the worst part," she says, and her voice turns dark. "What I can't get past is the whole thing stank of somethin' fishy from the start, and we never figured out what.

"On the morning of the accident, my mom cornered the medical examiner as he came off the dock. He hadn't done the official report yet—we were still on the scene, and he'd only taken a quick look at Ray—but he told us the first thing he noticed was a deep laceration on Ray's throat that seemed suspicious for a fire. Told us something seemed… *off*—that was how he put it. Then, when the details of his report came out, he'd changed his whole attitude. Said the cause of death was smoke inhalation due to—what the police suspected to be—an accidental fire. My mom called the office and demanded to speak to him, to ask why he lied on the report. He tells my mom that he didn't lie. There *had* been a laceration on Ray's throat, but not as serious as he originally thought, and certainly not in a way to suggest foul play. He tells her that Ray was exposed to the elements for an undetermined amount of time—the boat had all but sunk by the time help arrived—and the laceration may have been due to exposure. He tells my mom she'd do well to accept the whole thing as a tragic accident and make her peace with it. Bull*shit*, I say! Pardon my French," she adds, with an apologetic glance in their direction.

"And what about the jacket?" Wyatt asks, punctuating his question with an exaggerated shrug. "The blood on the jacket? What about *that*?" Wyatt loves a good conspiracy theory and is quick to jump to Greta's defense.

"Exactly!" Greta says, playing into it. "I saw the thing with my own eyes! They didn't deny they'd found it—they couldn't! But they maintained that Ted might have hurt himself attempting to save the boat, or himself, or Ray. There was the possibility of sharks, of course. The blood may have been from a prior accident, even. They lived on the boat, after all, so you'd expect his jacket to be there, wouldn't you?" She stated this as a question, but the inflection in her voice says she doesn't believe a word of it herself.

She continues. "It was a pretty story, but the whole thing felt wrong. I told my mom, 'The medical examiner is lying about Ray. You realize that, don't you?' There was the obvious lie— the coroner's report. Then there was the jacket, and the fact that they found the boat over twenty-five miles farther than they ever took their fishing tours, and at *night,* which they never did! There was more than one detail not lining up, and in my experience, that means *someone's* being a phony bologna."

Greta sighs, face flushed as she relives the anger of that long-ago summer. Emeline can understand her frustration; having a million questions and no one to answer them, knowing the only people with knowledge of what happened that day are dead and gone, their secrets gone right along with them.

"Did you fight it?" Wyatt asks, and his brown eyes beam with passion for the cause.

Greta lets out a humorous snort. "Oh, Sweet-pea. Back then, there wasn't much of anything someone like me could do. And my mother, she was so tired at that point. She aged about ten years that summer. I couldn't blame her for not digging deeper. For wanting to put it all behind us. It was an open wound, gushing blood all over the place for *months.* We were both fading. And Ted… well… unfortunately for him, orphans don't exactly have a whole lot of people lined up ready to fight for them. All he had was your Gram."

"And did she?" Emeline says. "Fight for him?"

Greta falls silent. Looks away. Looks to her feet. "No," she says. "No, she didn't. It's possible that… *ahh,* I doubt it—but maybe if I would've come back, the two of us could have figured it out. *Nancy Drewed* the whole damn thing. But that was the last year we stayed at the condo. In fact, your Gram and I never saw each other in person ever again. She moved to Georgia a few years later, met your granddad, started her life. But we wrote to each other all the time, every couple weeks, until… well…" Greta shrugs, stuffing her hands in the pockets of her slacks.

Emeline has a sour taste on her tongue. Not unlike the gut feeling Greta had all those years ago, something about this doesn't sit right with her. How could someone just abandon the person they call their best friend? How could they go an entire lifetime without seeing each other? Gram had never even *spoken* of Greta, and they'd heard every story of Gram's childhood at least three times over.

Or had they? Emeline thinks. *Did they know Gram at all? Or just the version Gram* wanted *them to see?*

She shrugs the thought away and turns her attention back to Greta. "You said you wanted to see her? To meet her kids, to meet *us?* So, why didn't you? You tracked her down when you were younger, got hold of her address, showed up at her house that night on the Fourth of July. So why didn't you do the same after she moved away?"

Greta laughs at this, as if the answer is so obviously obvious it may as well be tattooed on her forehead. She nods along in agreement. "Your Gram must have suspected I'd do that very thing." She chuckles, though not in a facetious way. "She wrote to me from a PO box, all the way to the end. I never had her actual address. I tried to search for it once or twice without luck. Didn't help that she never told me Wilfred's last name. Your Gram kept the name Elkins whenever she wrote."

As Greta talks, Emeline punches out an inconspicuous text to her mother:

Did Gram have a PO box?

A few moments later, her phone vibrates against her palm. Emeline swipes the screen and reads her mother's reply:

No. Why?

Emeline slips her phone into her back pocket. "Baker," she says. "That was his last name… *Gram's* last name."

Greta nods. Her eyes focus on Emeline, and the weight of her stare presses into her. Greta looks ready to cry, but swallows the emotion back and says, "Well then… now we know."

44

BELINDA

(MAY 31, 2019)

A LOST LOVE.

This revelation comes as a surprise to Belinda, as Gram never alluded to such a thing in all the years they'd known her.

The tale of their ill-fated romance might have been rather poetic had it not ended so tragically.

Had Gram thought of Ted often? she wonders. *Had she ever caught herself watching their grandfather, imagining the life she might have had if she'd married him instead, if she'd never lost him?*

Belinda doesn't believe in soulmates, not in the sense of there being just *one*—one special person you're destined to spend the entirety of life with, forsaking all others. To meet *the one,* and then lose *the one,* somehow dooming yourself to love only those never meant to be yours, is a notion she simply can't stomach.

To Belinda, soulmates are everywhere. Sometimes as romantic partners, but not always. Friends. Business partners. A weekend fling. Anyone whose soul speaks to yours, who drums to your beat, who is an extension of yourself; two brushstrokes on the same canvas—glorious on their own, but together... a *masterpiece.*

So, was their grandfather another of Gram's soulmates? Or just someone who appeared at the right moment, a suitable substitute for the real thing? To settle out of convenience—or necessity—is perhaps Belinda's biggest fear. The reason she is forever moving. Forever changing.

They'd returned to Main Street and now stand on the sidewalk outside The Salty Siren's front door.

Belinda looks at Greta with a mixture of pity, admiration, and curiosity. "When did you come back, then? And why *here,* of all places?"

Greta smiles, and her small eyes turn to the sign above the door. "About eight years ago," she says. Wistful. "I'd just retired, but I couldn't stand the silence. The monotony, you know? Guess I've never been much good at sitting still." She shrugs and then grins. "I figure, I'm still young! I've still got somethin' to offer the world! This place came on the market, and it felt like kismet. I had an epiphany, see. I'd come here. I'd open this place. I'd name it after my brother's business—the business he never got the chance to grow—and I'd do him proud. I'd do it in his honor."

Belinda loves this. *Can siblings be soulmates, too?* she wonders. Sure! Why not? Ray was most definitely Greta's soulmate. Decades after his death, and he's still there, stretching and pulling at the part of Greta to which he will always belong.

"I bet he's looking down right now, smiling at you," Belinda says.

Greta shrugs this away. "Ah, I don't know about that one. We did real well the first six years or so. And then, not-so-well. This last one has been tough. Not sure how much longer the ol'

Siren will stay afloat."

"Oh, I'm so sorry to hear that," Belinda says.

"Ah, don't be. I've had a good run. And I'm tough as old boots. Whatever happens, I'll be all right. But I'll tell you one thing, I'll go down with this ship. Make no mistake about that."

The waitress—*Cami*—pops around the corner, dark hair pulled back in a messy ponytail. "Oh good! You're back!" she says to Greta, relief in her voice she tries to disguise. "Everything is good here, totally fine. But I *do* need you to authorize a few comps."

Greta inhales through her nose, out through her mouth. "Frank again?"

Cami gets this sheepish grin and nods. "Undercooked a few fried fish."

"How in the hell?" Greta mutters and rakes her hands across her face. "I swear that man will be the death of me."

"I'll handle it, I'll handle it," she says then, and waves Cami closer, "Come her for a sec, will ya?"

Cami obliges and stands beside Greta with her hands clasped in front of her. Greta drapes an arm around Cami's bare shoulders. "I never properly introduced you to this young lady here," Greta says. "This is Camila Suarez. I've known her family for years. Her grandmother was Christine Delgado." Belinda calls to mind the image of a teenaged Greta, Gram, and a star-eyed Christine romping along the beach.

Cami smiles and nods, and Belinda notices the extra-wide grin she extends to Wyatt. Wyatt catches this, too. He's blushing.

"Your grandmother sounds like an amazing woman," Belinda says.

Cami nods. "She was."

Greta jerks her head toward the door. "Go on in, Cami. I'll be right there. Don't let Frank kill no more of my customers, please."

Cami salutes and disappears through the open door of The Salty Siren.

"Well, I gotta get myself back to work," Greta says, stuffing her hands in the back pockets of her slacks. "You kids are welcome to hang around as long as you'd like. But, before I go, there's one more thing I need to tell you."

Emeline asks, "What's that?"

Greta opens her mouth to speak, but at that moment, a middle-aged couple exits the restaurant, giving Greta a few appreciate slaps on the shoulder as they maneuver around their group. "Delicious as always, Greta," the guy says. Greta grins. Raises her hand and gives them a polite wave. As the couple climbs into a blue Mustang parked at the curb, Greta's attention falls back to the four of them, who watch her with eager faces. "Your Gram said in her letter that I should tell Belinda to get her ring cleaned while she's in town?" She says this as a question, apparently trusting Gram's judgment as well as the four of them do so far. "She said her insurance should still be good at the jewelers. Ask for Hank, she said. Does that mean anything to you?"

Belinda gasps at this. "Yes! Yes, it does, Greta. Thank you! Uh… Gram left me a ring in her will… a ring from my grandfather. I'm sure that's what she means. Right?" Belinda looks to the others for encouragement but gets nothing. "It must be. The box says Lancome or Lancer or something like that on it."

"Lancaster's," Greta nods.

"Yes! That's it! Is that nearby?"

"Sure is, yeah. Lancaster's Jewelers. You'll find it a few miles south on Peninsula Drive. But," she glances at her dainty wristwatch with a frown, "they closed at five. If you plan to pay a visit, it won't be till mornin', I'm afraid."

Geoff's head falls at this, and Emeline releases a quiet, almost inaudible, sigh.

Greta watches them a beat longer. "I'm so glad I finally got to meet you all. I hope it's not the last time. And I'm truly sorry to hear about your Gram. She was one of a kind."

Greta clears her throat, and Belinda notices the shine of tears pooling in her eyes. "Look, if you kids are hungry, go on in and order whatever you want. It's on the house."

Greta turns and heads for the front door, but before she

passes through, she pauses, and glances back with a warning: "Just… maybe steer clear of the fried fish baskets."

45

GEOFF

(MAY 31, 2019)

SO MUCH FOR GETTING BACK on the road tonight. He should have known it wouldn't be that simple.

Agitation twists in his gut.

Greta offered to buy them dinner. Geoff would have preferred to take something to go and get as far away from people as possible, but as usual, he'd been outvoted. So here he sits at The Salty Siren, shouldered up at the bar with the others, feasting on mediocre sandwiches and some dry-ass wings. Every so often, Belinda and Wyatt make small talk with the hot waitress. Geoff hates small talk. It's so meaningless. Emeline alternates between watching the sportscast on the television above the bar and scrolling through her phone. Geoff does the same, still seething over the need to spend the night here, and on a *bus,* of all places.

Given the circumstances, he'd considered the advantages of booking a hotel for himself, but when he mentioned this to Emeline, she'd shut him down at once. *Like hell you are,* she'd said. Geoff reminded her she's his sister, not his boss, to which Emeline replied with a curt, *No.* To that, Geoff muttered that he'd do whatever he wanted. But deep inside, he knows he'll end up on that Goddamned bus.

Geoff glugs his way through his third beer, hoping to quell his irritation beneath a buzz of Bud Light, but somehow this only makes things worse. His mood darkens and thuds away behind his eyelids. Heats his neck. Cranks the long muscles of his shoulders into tightropes.

Of the four of them, Geoff is the only one with a proper reason to hurry home. Why should Wyatt rush back? Mom and Dad's garage isn't going anywhere. The same way Uncle Danny has a job waiting for him no matter what. Because why not make life *that much* easier for Wyatt, right? Belinda is more or less living as she always does, driving around without a plan or care in the world. And Emeline? He's sure she's just *itching* to get back to Tennessee and live that single mom life. Finalize that divorce. Boogers and screaming and a part-time job, a shadow of the career she *could* have had if she hadn't settled.

Geoff does a mental eye roll and wonders how he's survived this family for so long. How is it that he lives so motivated and captivated with purpose, while the rest of them are content to be ordinary? Okay, fine—he's different. But why treat him as if it's wrong to want more for yourself? Since when is that a crime? What it boils down to, he thinks, is jealousy. Whenever Geoff succeeds, it forces them to look inward, to evaluate the things they must be doing poorly. And no one enjoys coming face to face with their flaws and weaknesses. People are so quick to complain about their shitty circumstances, when the fact is, a few simple changes to their daily routine could solve a great majority of their problems. But lesser humans are afraid of change. Because change requires *accountability.* And accountability means to acknowledge your role in the problem and be willing to put in the work to fix it. And who wants that, right? It's so much easier to whine and play the victim. So instead of placing the blame where it belongs—on their sorry life choices and lack of drive—people like this turn a sour eye to those who have what it takes.

People like *Geoff*.

Without a doubt, his family questions his worthiness. They disregard his achievements. Undermine his obligations. Act as though his entire life in New York is his juvenile and elaborate way of saying, *I'm better than you, and I'm going to prove it.* And maybe that was true when he first moved away. But now, the life he has is *his*, and he couldn't care less what they think. Geoff doesn't deserve the shit they give him. He really doesn't. Because he's worked hard. He started from the ground up, and he's sacrificed more than most are willing to—staying in when others partied, missing birthdays, and holidays, trips home, investing instead of splurging on frivolous garbage, living within his means when he could have gone balls-to-the-wall crazy—and because of that, *yeah*, you better believe he deserves every damn thing he's got! None of this makes him the enemy. And yet, his family treats him as if he somehow wronged Wyatt by leaving and making something of himself—like it's *his* fault Wyatt messed up his life. Like he abandoned the lot of them, chose money—chose *Lila*—over his own flesh and blood. But Geoff has abandoned no one. In fact, he's *tried* to make his family see the error of their ways. Tried to ignite them with a flash of his own spark. Raise them to his level. But they scoff at every suggestion, push him to the outside of their world, and then wonder why he prefers to go his own way. He realizes they may never understand him. But, at the very least, shouldn't they be *proud* of him?

Oh well. Who cares? They drag him down, they always have.

Lila has never treated him this way. His success is *her* success. Their dreams one and the same. Whenever he calls from work with good news, he's met with an enthusiastic, *Way to go, baby!* And later that evening, a bottle of wine to toast to, shared over a home-cooked meal. Her eyes glisten with pride as he gushes over their lives and what waits for them in the not-so-distant future, and he can almost hear the milky tone of her voice when she says, *We're going to have it all, babe. I love you so much.*

He should have got on the plane when he had the chance.

"Where are we supposed to park this thing?" Geoff asks once they make their way back to the bus.

"I know a place," Belinda says, her sing-song voice hitting his eardrums in all the wrong ways.

Fifteen minutes later, Belinda pulls the bus into a small beachfront parking lot sandwiched between two tiny rental cottages a few miles north of the restaurant.

"I know the landlord here. He's cool," Belinda says, killing the engine.

Given the questionable company she keeps, Belinda's judgment on who's *cool* or not is unreliable at best. Throughout dinner, Geoff watched her send multiple texts to Denver-The-Soap-Pusher, grinning like a buffoon when her phone pinged with a new reply. And now the loser is *here*, loitering outside the bus in another loose Henley and striped linen pants, a ridiculous smirk on his skinny, grass-fed face.

And Birkenstocks.

My God, is he *trying* to be a walking stereotype?

Geoff keeps a watchful eye on him as he waits for Belinda to change clothes; they are going out for drinks, she says. Geoff tries to imagine what a hippy-freak like Denver might indulge in on a Friday night. An organic cider, he bets. Or a hemp-infused oat and barley beer. Who knows? Dude probably bathes in CBD oil.

Geoff sits at the small kitchen table that lowers into a single bed—the bed *Wyatt* claimed for himself earlier today. *The little bitch.*

After a while, Belinda emerges from the bathroom on a wave of coconut body spray that trails out in a fog behind her. It reminds Geoff of a scent Lila wears, and his stomach roils with missing her. "Be back later," she calls. "Make yourselves at home!"

Right, Geoff thinks.

Emeline sits cross-legged on the bed and makes a video call home to talk to the kids, though Mom won't get off the screen long enough to let them speak. Instead, she gives Emeline a play-by-play of their day while the crotch goblins shriek in the background. The cacophony that blasts from Emeline's phone speaker is ear-piercing.

Across from him at the table, Wyatt is reading, flipping the pages of his book with unnecessary vigor.

Left with nothing but his thoughts, Geoff fights the urge to reach for the phone in his pocket. He's been obsessive in checking it; a pointless effort, as he hasn't heard from Lila since the last text he received at the funeral. Knowing his phone will show him nothing new, he resists the temptation to look. May as well save himself the disappointment.

A small part of Geoff believes if he were to rush home this very instant, he'd find her waiting for him. They'd sit and talk, save their relationship, and this whole awful weekend would be behind them. But another thought grows and swells inside him, stronger than the others. And he knows the extra day it takes to complete this trip won't matter in the slightest. Lila is gone. After the year of hell they've gone through, he's lost her. And he's lost with what to do.

Geoff gets to his feet, mutters to no one in particular, "I'm going for a walk," and exits the bus.

46

EMELINE

(MAY 31, 2019)

EMELINE SPEAKS TO CONNER AND Aimee and assures them both that Mommy is fine and good and will be home soon, and she reminds her mom to please not pump them full of sugar and to get Aimee in bed no later than seven-thirty or it will throw off her whole schedule and be hell on Emeline for the next two weeks as she tries to regulate her. Only after she ends the call does she realize she and Wyatt are alone on the bus.

He's angled his body into the booth, left shoulder pressed against the wall. There's a book in his hands, but his mind is somewhere else. He fidgets. Looks out the bus window. Plants his eyes back on his book. Emeline is well-versed in her brother's moods and senses when something is bothering him; she can almost hear the gears of his brain turning round and round as he works out his thoughts.

It dawns on her then that he hasn't spoken over two words to her since earlier at the beach. Wyatt is a quiet guy, but not *that* quiet.

"Everything good, Wyatt?" she asks in her knowing big sister voice.

He glances over his shoulder at where she sits on the bed. "Fine," he clips, and turns back.

Emeline sighs. So, *this* is how he's going to play it.

"You sure? You've been quiet."

Wyatt's shoulders raise and lower. "Nothing to say, I guess."

Emeline hates being brushed off, but Wyatt may be taking things with Gram harder than she thought. A rush of sympathy wells up inside her. "Listen," she says, "I realize I've maybe been a lousy sister lately, but you know you can talk to me, right?"

At this, Wyatt snorts.

Sympathy gone, defenses up, she asks, "What's *that* for?"

"Why would I talk to you?" Wyatt swings his body around to face her now, eyes sharp with accusation. "You don't talk to *me.*"

"Sure I do," Emeline says, though as the words leave her mouth, she can't recall the last time she and Wyatt sat and talked at length about their lives.

"All that stuff at the beach today about Armie… that was all news to me, and you told *Belinda,* of all people. Belinda, who lives in a state of eternal happiness and thinks people have depression because they don't eat enough whole foods." Emeline watches him roll his eyes.

"You could have come to me with that stuff. You know I would have understood," he adds.

Emeline knows he is right. She *hadn't* told him. Why hadn't she? They always had the most in common, she and him, and he *would* have understood better than Belinda. They used to talk often. But then, that was before…

"Nobody talks to me about the serious stuff anymore," he says. "Like… no one trusts me. Not after…"

"That's not true, Wyatt."

"It is!"

"Not for me! I never for a *second* believed those drugs were yours. You *know* that. But…"

"*But.* Here we go." He rolls his eyes again.

"*BUT*—you wouldn't tell anyone who they *did* belong to. That doesn't make sense. If you would have just *told,* they wouldn't have put you away for it and you…"

"Just stop, Emeline! Stop. I can't do it. And I told everyone that back then. I made a choice, and I'm living with the consequences. I just didn't think everyone would still treat me like a reject three years later. Least of all *you.*"

He gets that wounded bird look again, and Emeline's face burns hot. "Don't you dare," she mutters. "Don't you even dare. Choosing to keep my private life to myself is not a personal attack on you, so stop acting like I'm this horrible person who shut her brother out of her life. You can't sit around in a little bubble of isolation and whine when people don't share things with you. For the last three years you've made yourself a ghost, Wyatt, so don't complain when we can't see you."

Emeline feels the prickle in the back of her throat that often precedes tears. But the last few years have left her with an impressive new skill: the ability to cry in mixed company with no one the wiser. She often does this at home as Armie sleeps in peaceful slumber beside her; if he notices, he never lets on. There was a morning last month when Conner woke earlier than usual. He greeted Emeline in the kitchen with a sleepy hug, but his eyes crinkled with worry as he pulled away and took in his mother's face. *Your eyes are all red and puffy,* he'd said. *Have you been crying?* The coffee machine had Armie's full attention, but he turned at Conner's question, seeing Emeline for the first time that morning. Her throat clenched, and she fought the urge to pull him close again, because this sweet, perfect boy saw her and he knew, he *knew* in two seconds what her own husband hadn't noticed in *years.* Instead, she'd told him, *Of course not, Sweetie. It's only allergies.* Armie's gaze lingered a moment longer before he returned to more pressing matters—adding an unhealthy amount of sugar to his steaming cup of Folgers. Whether he believed her, who's to say? But Emeline's feeble lie was enough to suffice both husband and son, as neither brought it up again.

Now, she throws herself on the bed, careful to face away from Wyatt, and lets the tears fall. Crying takes the edge off, relieves some of the crushing pressure—like cracking the lid on a bottle of soda; it may not take the bad feelings away, but it gives them room to move around, and sometimes that's enough.

It's only eight o'clock, but this has been one of the longest days Emeline can remember. The pillow beneath her cheek is damp and cold, but she closes her eyes and drifts to the sound of Wyatt's occasional page flips.

Rest does not come easy for Emeline these days. All part of being a mother, they say. But whenever she dozes, she lingers on the edge of sleep, set to spring into action if the need arises. Emeline wakes around nine-thirty to the sound of thunderous snores. On the floor beside her, Geoff has wedged himself into the small space between the table and the kitchen cabinets, a thick comforter pulled up to his chin; harsh, snorting breaths puff from his gaping mouth.

Half-conscious, Emeline scans the bus and sees that Belinda is still on her date, and that no one has bothered to collapse the table into bed form. Wyatt's book is still there; a scrap of paper sticks from the pages to mark his place, but Wyatt himself is nowhere to be seen.

The tiny AC unit Belinda has on the bus does a better job of cooling the space than Emeline expected. Gooseflesh covers her arms. She moves beneath the sheets and a crocheted quilt that holds the spicy scent of incense, and dozes again.

Around ten o'clock, the sound of distant giggles interrupts her slumber for a second time. With the back of her fingers, Emeline touches the thin curtain that hangs from the back window of the bus and moves it aside. The source of the giggling is immediately obvious. Belinda and Denver are in the parking lot, illuminated by moonlight and the glow of a distant streetlamp, bodies smashed together in a sloppy embrace. Denver's hands roam free, and she allows it, melting into his touch and his kisses. Emeline watches as Belinda bends and arches, allowing him full access to any part of her he desires. Her hands are in his hair, and he presses his lips to the hollow space between her throat and clavicle.

A hot blush touches Emeline's cheeks, mixed with the dry tightness of her earlier tears.

When Denver's hand travels up Belinda's thigh and disappears beneath her dress, Emeline lets the curtain fall, and her blush grows into a quiet rage.

This is a public parking lot, for crying out loud!

Belinda isn't some hormonal teenager. She's twenty-five; old enough to make smarter choices. At that moment, Emeline resents her cousin. She is disgusted. She is irritated. She is… jealous.

God, admitting that to herself is embarrassing and just… silly. But that's the closest word to what she feels. *Jealousy.*

Because Emeline hasn't given herself to someone in that way—so free and uninhibited—since before the kids were born. And here's Belinda, still young and vital enough for a parking lot grope session, while Emeline wasted her "hot years" getting married, starting a career, and having kids. She didn't live enough. She realizes that now. And now it's too late.

Belinda does whatever she wants whenever she wants it and never worries about strings or consequences or what people think of her. Emeline has tried to live this way, convinced herself that she could. But it's not in her. Worry comes as naturally as breathing.

But then, Emeline and Wyatt were always the darker, more introspective ones. The ones more interested in the *why* of things than the *how.* They shared that bond from a young age, both weighing every choice they made as if it alone would decide their entire fate. Now *Geoff,* he always had his plans. Even as a kid. There was never any choice other than one that delivered him his perfect vision. He's entirely one dimensional that way. No

Plan B*'s*, no *what ifs*. Just the life he wants and whatever it takes to get him there. Where doubt thrives in Emeline and Wyatt, Geoff has nothing but confidence and a strong, unyielding—almost obsessive—purpose.

But Belinda... well, she has no plans at all. College wasn't even a blip on her radar—and that was by choice, not because she isn't bright enough—nor is marriage. She could never pinpoint a career to pursue or a city to settle down in or even a single color to paint her bus (each wall is a different shade of pastel: soft lavender, pale yellow, minty green, and cotton candy pink; a visual representation of her scattered brain). Over the years, people have called her flaky and indecisive and immature and confused. But that's the thing with Belinda. She's not confused at all! Her indecision is a decision in itself, and she makes no apologies for it. She just... lives life.

Like life is simple.

Like all anyone ever needs to do is just... *live*.

Emeline can't fathom herself ever being so self-possessed. Part of her will always exist behind a wall, she expects. And Emeline knows, whatever she chooses to do, no matter how sound her decision may seem, a *what-if* will always dwell in her heart. Never settled, always wanting more.

Emeline can't have been sleeping long. The sound of someone fumbling with the lock on the bathroom door jolts her awake. It's the disoriented type of wake where she's uncertain she's even been asleep at all, though she can't remember the last few moments, and a sheen of drool clings to her chin, so she must have been.

Denver pops out of the bathroom and looks rather disoriented himself. With frantic, roving eyes, he looks to see if he's woken anyone. But Geoff is out cold, and Wyatt hasn't returned from wherever he's gone. Emeline watches him from behind her blanket; she's in the shadow, he can't see her face. After a moment, he tiptoes down the steps of the bus and back to Belinda.

After Denver leaves, Emeline slips into a deeper sleep. This time she drifts long enough to dream of summer at Gram's house.

The four of them are there, but no longer children. Each at their current ages, they run around the backyard. They shriek and wail through a game of hide and seek, as if still those little kids from the past. Gram watches and laughs from the shade of the porch, rocking back and forth in her favorite rocking chair, her cross-stitch balanced on her lap. She looks as good as she ever did. The way Emeline remembers her. Emeline is the seeker but has found no one and is frustrated. As the oldest, she was always the best at games. But Dream Emeline struggles. In desperation, she looks to Gram, who smiles and points to the small cabin Grandpa made them from wooden pallets he'd taken from work: Camp Baker, they'd called it. It was their headquarters. Their home base. Gram presses a slender finger to her lips, a playful warning in her eyes. *Don't tell them I told you.* Emeline creeps toward Camp Baker with a rush of excitement and lifts the metal latch on the door, quiet as a mouse. Then she throws it open, ready to surprise whoever hides within with a giant *Gotcha!* Instead, she finds Belinda... making out with Denver. Belinda turns at the sound, startled but not embarrassed. Giggles spill out of her. *Oops... sorry, Emeline! Mind giving us some privacy?* Emeline turns, confused. The door of Camp Baker slams in her face. Stricken, she looks back to the porch, but it's empty now. The rocking chair rocks in the breeze, but Gram is gone. The happy squeals and laughter have silenced. Now Wyatt sits alone by the lake, smoking something from a pipe, running his hands along the tall blades of grass that grow along the shore. Geoff paces in the distance, shouting into his cell phone. She's on the verge of calling out, to ask *What about the game?* but an incessant banging pulls her attention to the front yard where a man hammers a For Sale sign into the ground beside the driveway. Mom and Dad are carrying boxes from Gram's front door.

Emeline makes the slow drift into consciousness, but as she surfaces, the banging gets louder. She soon realizes the sound comes from the bus, not from her dream. Her eyes spring open, and she finds Belinda in a panic, tearing through drawers, turning over bags. Geoff and Wyatt are coming to as well, roused by the commotion.

"What's going on, Bee?" Emeline mumbles in her scratchy sleep-voice.

"My ring!" Her head shakes in bewilderment. "Gram's ring! I can't find it."

47

GEOFF

(JUNE 1, 2019)

Through groggy, sleep-caked eyes, Geoff can see it's still dark. He lights the screen on his phone. *4:27am.*

Still heavy with sleep, he dislodges his shoulders from his spot on the floor and pulls up to a sitting position. Belinda is half deranged, flipping through drawers and cabinets, switching on lights without concern for her sleeping guests.

"I can't even *see* anything with all this *stuff* in the way," she mutters, as she kicks aside the bags that litter the floor.

Emeline asks Belinda what's wrong. Belinda bumbles out something about a missing ring.

"What about a ring?" Wyatt asks, rousing from the fold-down bed beside Geoff.

Wyatt raises onto his elbows. He has this dopey, restful look on his face, up there on his pedestal, all stretched out and comfortable. Geoff wants to punch him.

"The ring, Wyatt!" Belinda snaps. "Gram's ring! It was sitting right here on the counter, and now it's gone!" She jabs a finger at the space beside the sink.

"Could it have fallen down the drain?" Geoff asks, picking a bit of sleep crust from the corner of his eye and flicking it away.

Belinda rolls her eyes. "In the ring box, Geoff? No. It didn't fall down the drain."

"I didn't realize it was in the ring box, *Belinda.* Why wasn't it on your finger?"

"I took it off before the beach. I didn't want to get it all sandy and forgot to put it back on. But I remember setting the box right here on the counter."

"Okay," Emeline says, and nearly crushes Geoff's finger beneath her foot as she stands from the bed. "It's got to be here somewhere. We just need to spread out and look for it."

Geoff snickers at the advice to *spread out*; you can't stretch your arms to either side on this stupid bus without touching someone else.

"Come on." Emeline steps over Geoff with a sigh and smacks him in the back of the head. "Be useful for once."

So, they *spread out* and search every nook and cranny, anywhere a ring in a ring box might slip. But it's nowhere to be found, and soon, they abandon the search.

"How could it have just disappeared?" Belinda collapses on the edge of Wyatt's bed. Her forehead drops into her palms. Strands of her long blonde hair dust the floor of the bus.

Geoff asks the obvious question. "Could someone have taken it?"

Belinda's head snaps up, an irritated blaze in her eyes. "Who would have taken my ring?"

It may be the stress of being here, or sheer exhaustion, or the constant belittling from his family, but Geoff has had enough. "For starters," he snips, "that fucking moron you're dating."

Belinda reddens. "*Denver?* Okay, first, I'm not *dating* him. Our connection is on a spiritual level. And second, there is no way on Earth he took Gram's ring. He knows how special she is to me. He wouldn't do that. Don't call someone a thief just because you don't like them."

Geoff snorts. Shrugs his shoulders. "Trust the loser then. See if I care. But he's shady as hell, that's all I'm saying."

"He was with me all night! Don't you think I'd notice if he swiped my ring?"

"Actually," Emeline's hand raises in interruption, and guilt sweeps over her face. "He was alone on the bus last night for a time."

"What?" Belinda says.

"He came in to use the restroom, I guess. He seemed… kind of out of it. And like… I don't know… like he was hiding something."

"We had a few drinks," Belinda says. She stands now and paces (as well as one can pace in such a tight space). "And, yes, he came in to use the restroom, but you were all in here too, and he came right back out and…"

"Stop defending the dude! It takes two seconds to steal something," Geoff says. "Where is he right now?"

"Back in his van, I imagine."

"Yeah, but where was he *going*? Home? Where does he live?"

Belinda pauses. Her eyes meet Geoff's and then flick away. "In his van," she mumbles.

Geoff exhales in a long sigh, rubbing his eyes with the heels of his hands. "Dude lives in his van?"

At this, Belinda's face swells red-hot. He's only seen her this fired up perhaps twice in his life. Most recently, when he was seven and her ten; Geoff had accidentally killed a lizard with a stick, and Belinda swore he'd done it on purpose.

"Yes, Geoff, he does! He lives in his van. Not everyone has the same idea of success as you. Sorry he doesn't live up to your standards. But at least he's happy. You've been miserable the entire trip!"

"Oh, I'm sorry. Last I checked, I came here to bury my grandmother. I wasn't aware I should be enjoying myself."

Wyatt picks this exact moment to insert his opinion. "Don't suddenly act like Gram matters to you," he says. "You hadn't been to see her in two years."

Geoff burns with anger. At the rude hour. At Belinda for her naïve stupidity. And at Wyatt, who is the very *last* person he needs to hear from right now. His hands shake as he says, "I had school, Wyatt. And a good job I couldn't up and leave. And a girlfriend. And a home. Unlike you, I had *responsibilities*. I'm sick and tired of you acting like you're better than the rest of us because you stuck around. You really think that means you loved Gram more?"

"Yeah, as a matter of fact, I do. You should have been there to help, and you know it. But you left, Geoff, because you're selfish. And you've always *been* selfish."

"And you stayed because you didn't have a choice. Because you messed up and ruined your life. We left! Yes! But we *all* loved her. You don't get to miss her more just because you moved into Dad's garage."

Wyatt's jaw clenches and unclenches, face a deep shade of scarlet. Geoff has rattled him. *Good.* But he doesn't give up. "At least I was there to help. That's more than *you* can say."

Geoff blurts out a laugh. "Oh my God! Is that what you think you're doing there? *Helping?* How can you still not see it? You're a burden, Wyatt! One more person for Mom to worry about. You aren't *helping* anybody."

"That's not true," Wyatt says, and shakes his head stubbornly. "She's grateful at least *one* of her kids is there. The rest of you can hardly bother to pick up your phones."

Geoff steps toward Wyatt, makes the most of his height to stare down at his brother and says, "And when we *do* answer… why is it that Mom always begs us to come home and visit? If you're such a big help, then why does Mom need *us* so badly?"

"Shut the hell up, Geoff! You don't know the first thing about what I've been through."

Geoff puffs out a derisive snort. "I know everything you've been through, you brought on yourself."

"Enough!" Emeline's voice slices through the bus, and

everyone falls silent. After a beat, she turns to Belinda. "Can't you text him and *ask* him if maybe he saw the ring?"

"Do *not* text him that," Geoff says, turning on his sister.

Belinda's phone is in her hand, but she makes no move to use it.

"Why not?" Emeline cuts him a shrewd glance. "What's the harm in asking?"

"If he has the ring and we tip him off with our suspicions, then we've given him a nice little head start to get rid of it, haven't we?"

At this, an exasperated snort comes from Belinda, but no one speaks.

Finally, Emeline sighs and says, "Where does he park his van? Does he have a usual place?"

Belinda's eyes dart around, frazzled, cornered. A frightened doe in the crosshairs of a hunter's rifle. "You want us to go there? To his van? That's ridiculous. I—" She shakes a thought away. "Fine. Okay. *Fine.* He—he parks at his cousin's place. An apartment complex a few streets away. But I'm telling you, bothering him with this is a waste of time."

"Well, if it is... that's great. We've ruled him out," Emeline says in a calm voice. She's trying to appeal to Belinda's sensible side, to quash the tang of hostility before it befalls the entire bus.

But no matter how hard he tries, Geoff cannot quiet his seething rage. His anger is a tinderbox, set to blow. Belinda had been the spark; Wyatt a whole damn inferno. That the bus hasn't gone up in flames is no small miracle.

Everything is such a mess right now.

At least catching this asshole with Belinda's ring will give him a place to direct his pent-up aggression.

Geoff shoves his foot into his shoe, fully awake now, buzzed with adrenaline. "And if it's *not* a waste of time... mark my words, that bastard will be sorry."

48

WYATT

(JUNE 1, 2019)

EMELINE SUGGESTS TAKING THE BUS, but Geoff says no, they should walk. The bus will be too noticeable, and if Denver sees them coming, he might panic. They need to catch him unawares. Belinda argues that ambushing someone in their van at five in the morning should be more than enough to catch that person *unawares*.

Wyatt hates to admit that Geoff is right, however... he knows from experience that the sudden appearance of certain vehicles will set your pulse to thumping faster than anything.

So, on foot they go.

Belinda is a firecracker of irritation and clearly feels they've already accused Denver of the crime. She walks in a huff and refuses to meet their eyes. This early in the morning, traffic is light. Dawn is close; Wyatt can sense it. But for now, the world is quiet, the *CLIP CLOP* of Belinda and Emeline's sandals and the occasional puff of breath the soundtrack to their wayward mission.

When he glances at Emeline, he sees the effects of their argument earlier on the bus. The tight set of her jaw, the swollen shadows that frame her eyes. *Has she been crying?* Beneath that, she seems indifferent to the entire situation, determined to settle it one way or another, with no personal stake in the matter.

Geoff, though… he's invested in this. He's out for blood.

Geoff—as Gram phrased it—always had a *mean streak.* Sometimes he did things just to elicit a reaction. To prove his power over us. *I could do this terrible thing if I wanted to… but I won't. I could… but I won't.* One summer, Geoff was swinging a giant stick around the yard. Belinda, oblivious to the rest of them, had spotted a lizard basking in the sun on the trunk of one of Gram's spruce trees and taken a shining to it. Belinda always loved animals, even the gross and scaly ones. Well, Geoff sees this and comes over and starts hitting his stick against the tree, each swing drawing closer and closer to the lizard. "Stop it, Geoff! You're scaring it! You're going to kill it!" Belinda had shouted, eyes welling with tears out of fear for the helpless little reptile. Geoff laughed and kept going, making a cruel game out of it, laughing harder the more upset Belinda became. "I'm not…" *WHACK!…* "going to…" *WHACK!…* "kill it." *WHACK!* Belinda wailed, face red, fingers raking through her hair. She jumped at Geoff and tried to force the stick from his hands, but he swung one last time. *WHACK!* To this day, Wyatt can remember the way the lizard's tail kept on twitching, even though it was already dead, and the slimy red gash where its throat lay open, smashed against the tree bark. Now, Geoff isn't evil. His behavior would be easier to explain away if he were. But it was an accident, because Wyatt can also remember the absolute horror on Geoff's face after it happened. He dropped the stick and tried to shrug it off, to play it cool. He pulled a face and said, "Why are you crying? It's just a stupid lizard!" But a wicked pink had colored Geoff's cheeks, and Wyatt saw the wet sheen of tears pool in his eyes moments before he rushed off into the trees.

Geoff's *mean streak*—or whatever makes him do the stupid crap he does—is out in full swing tonight. But his mood has been off the entire trip. Despite his claim of being distraught over Gram's death, there's more to the story he isn't telling them. The aggressiveness, the drinking, the mood swings. Not to mention this distrust he has for Denver. It's more than concerning… some may even say suspicious.

After a twenty-minute trek past blinking traffic lights and darkened storefronts, the four of them, panting and sweating, turn onto a street with two long rows of single floor duplex apartments. Tan paint job with white trim, kind of dumpy, by no means nice. From one unit, Wyatt hears faint shouts, and a television blasts at full volume from another. The parking lot itself is quiet. Every fifteen feet or so, a bright, cool-toned streetlamp. No sooner does the light from one melt into shadow, when another emerges to pick up the slack.

"There it is," Belinda sighs and points to a blue Chevy Astro van in the distance. "Go on, then. Go and make complete fools of yourselves."

Geoff, without hesitation, storms ahead of them and approaches the van. He peers first into the driver's window and then moves around to the sliding door and knocks. Three loud, thumping knocks. Belinda wraps her arms around herself. Embarrassment radiates from her, and Wyatt wonders if this whole thing is a mistake.

A few feet behind Geoff, the three of them wait in silence. But nothing happens.

Impatient now, Geoff cups his hands above his eyes, presses his face to the window. A sheet is attached to the inside of the window, for privacy most likely, but something snags the corner of the makeshift curtain, leaving a gap in which to snoop.

"Jesus Christ," Geoff mutters against the glass.

"What? Is he in there? What is it?" Emeline whispers.

Geoff steps back, victorious. "Come see for yourself."

Belinda stays put, but Emeline and Wyatt inch forward and take curious turns at the window.

When Wyatt's turn comes, he's relieved to see no sign of Denver. Instead, he sees a van that has been completely gutted. No seats, just open space. On the floor, against the far wall, is a twin mattress; bare, a white sheet crumpled in a ball on top, and a sad, flat pillow without a case. Scattered around the mattress is what can best be described as complete filth: shopping bags, food wrappers, discarded clothes. A few cardboard boxes labeled *SOAPS* in black permanent marker. And then, an assortment of random items with no business in the van of a soap salesman: a stack of five sneaker boxes; two dozen sunglasses piled on top, two large paintings propped against the back door, a basket full of orange prescription bottles, another basket of what looks like various cell phones and parts.

Wyatt leans back from the window and sighs, sharing a glance with Emeline, who appears to have drawn a similar conclusion. In the next moment, three heads turn in unison to Belinda; Geoff with a smug grin, Wyatt and Emeline with mirrored expressions of apology and guilt.

Belinda looks on with wide eyes, but purses her lips, bracing herself to excuse whatever they saw in the van.

"Told you, didn't I?" Geoff gloats. "Tell me that ain't the van of a thief! Tell me right now!"

No one answers, but Belinda's hackles are up, and Wyatt suffers through her discomfort as if it's his own. This whole thing makes his skin itch. But regardless of his sympathy for Belinda, and the unpleasantness he feels over being here, he must admit it doesn't look good for ol' Denver.

Now, could there be a perfectly plausible explanation for the items he has in his van? Sure. But Wyatt is quite interested to hear what that might be. And, perhaps more than that, is his interest in Geoff's obsession with nailing this guy. There is more than one shady character in this scenario, and Wyatt is determined to get to the bottom of it.

Belinda, without much choice in the matter, pushes forward with a dignified sigh to look through the window for herself. For five full seconds, her eyes scan the back of the van. But she quickly retreats and shakes her head. With a dismissive wave, she says, "Okay, wow, you guys don't even know what that stuff is or why he has it."

Everyone is silent, but Belinda keeps talking, working through it in her mind.

"Shoes and glasses, okay, whatever. They're obviously his."
Silence.

"And the paintings. You know… I think I remember him mentioning once that he was friends with someone who owned an art gallery and…"

Geoff gives off an exasperated grunt. "Oh my God! You can't be serious right now! Look, I get you don't want to believe your boy toy is a thief, but you can't just *trust* people, Bee. There are people out there—*bad* people—who prey on people like you. Anyone with eyes can see that guy is seedy, and a quick peek in his van proves it. You've got to be more careful with who you let in, or you're going to get seriously hurt."

"So, I should just assume everyone I meet is out to get me? *Poor, sweet, gullible Belinda.* Is that it?"

"Yes!" Geoff snaps. "In today's world? Yes! You absolutely should. It's every person for themselves out there. Everyone has an agenda. Trust me on that."

"What about *you*, Geoff?" Belinda snips. "Do *you* have an agenda? You wandered back to the bus the same time Denver and I showed up last night. Where were you that whole time? Hm? Could we be suspecting the wrong person here?"

Geoff laughs at this. A wild laugh, eyes half-crazed. "Are you kidding me right now? Yeah. *I* took the ring. *Me.* Not Denver, the guy you've known for five whole minutes who has three dozen prescription bottles in his little camper van here."

"You said I shouldn't trust *anyone.* Shouldn't that include *you?*"

"I meant you shouldn't trust know-it-all, wannabe hippies who live in a parking lot. I didn't mean your own family!"

"Where *did* you go last night?" Wyatt asks, jumping at the opportunity to hear his alibi. After all, he's taken an enormous interest in pinning this whole thing on Denver, and is presently evading Belinda's question. Of course, Denver is guilty. Wyatt would stake money on it. But screwing with Geoff is too much fun, and falsely accusing him of something as serious as thievery might just be the sweetest karma on Earth.

Geoff doesn't find this very funny. All traces of humor vanish, and Wyatt soon regrets opening his mouth.

"*Wow*—yeah, okay… I went for a walk, like I told you I was going to do. And where were *you*, brother? Because when I got back to the bus, you weren't there, either."

"What?" Belinda mutters.

"Oh yeah, he took off! You didn't know? Gone a while, too. Pawn shop maybe? Needed some extra cash for a fix? I wonder what a ruby ring would pull in?"

"Shut the hell up, Geoff," Wyatt says through gritted teeth. He should have known this would turn back on him. He'd underestimated his family's lack of faith in him.

"Enough. Both of you." Emeline raises an authoritative hand.

But Geoff is undeterred by this. He wants blood, and he'll get it… by fair means or foul. "No, seriously," he says. "Where were you? We're all pointing fingers all of a sudden, right? So, let's hear it."

"Same as you," Wyatt clips, blood pumping fast through his veins. "Walking. I don't sleep much."

"Yeah, walking… *right*," Geoff snorts.

"So, you can go for a walk, but I can't?"

"I'm not a fucking cokehead!"

"Neither am I, asshole!"

"Not what it says on your record, man!"

"*Enough!*" Belinda's voice tears through the parking lot, echoes off the low apartment walls, and empties into a silence that makes Wyatt realize how hard he's breathing.

Belinda takes a deep inhale of her own and says, "Listen… I don't know *what* to think right now, but… I *know* Denver. He wouldn't do this. He *couldn't*. Wyatt… I…" She searches for words, struggles, presses her fingertips into a steeple and says,

"If you took it—just… I won't be mad. I swear. But… tell me so I can get Gram's ring back. *Please.*"

Wyatt is sure he misunderstood. Is Belinda accusing him? Sweet Belinda? His cousin? The girl he'd do anything for—*has* done everything for? Goosebumps bubble over his arms. He shakes his head in disbelief.

"Are you serious?" he says. To her. To all of them.

With a heavy expression, Belinda watches him. Silence has fallen again. No one comes to his defense. Three years of mistrust, and it still stings. "Please tell me you don't honestly think I would do something like that, Belinda."

She shakes her head, eyes wide and watering. Her actions say she doesn't believe it, but her words say something else. "I don't *think* you would—but… if you *did*…"

There it is. Reasonable doubt. And that's enough to render Wyatt small and worthless. As if everything he's done since his arrest has been for nothing.

"I didn't take the ring!" Wyatt shouts. "What is even happening right now? Why am I suddenly in the hot seat? This doesn't even make sense!"

Geoff just shrugs. "Motive, man."

Belinda looks at her feet. She agrees with him. With Geoff. This can't be real.

Wyatt steps forward, takes Belinda's hands in his own, forces her to look him in the eyes. "Do you honestly think I'm on drugs, Bee?" he whispers. "Answer me. Do you?"

Again, with the conflicting emotions. Her head shakes no, but she says, "You said you weren't… but…"

Wyatt's hands are shaking now, and he drops Belinda's, taking several steps backward. Her arms flutter as though she wants to reach out for him, but she doesn't. No one does. For *years* he has avoided the truth, keeping what happened that night to himself. But being confronted this way, something breaks inside of him.

Belinda continues. "It's just… *Quentin.* I mean, he was your best friend, wasn't he? Him and his loser buddies—they were trouble. We all knew it, but—"

"You hung out with druggies, bud. What'd you expect?" Geoff offers this piece of wisdom with another careless shrug. It's abundantly clear that Geoff just wants to see someone hang tonight. It doesn't matter who.

Belinda looks ashamed, but confident as she continues. As though she's had these arguments inside her for years, locked away in case she ever was to need them. But she cuts them loose now and airs them out in front of everyone. They think they know him so well. They have no idea.

"I'm not trying to accuse you of anything, Wyatt. All that stuff happened a long time ago, and it's not fair to judge you for it now. But… under the circumstances… if someone gets bit, you question the dog first, right? You don't start with the goldfish. It—it wouldn't make sense."

Wyatt shakes his head, trying to make sense of her ridiculous analogy.

"Me being the dog, right?" he says. "And your buddy Denver being the goldfish? Because I'm obviously an addict. I'm cracked out of my mind and so desperate for a fix that I would pawn my own *grandmother's* ring. Is that it, Bee? Look me in the eye! Am I on drugs?"

She stiffens, pulls herself up straighter. "I don't hang out with those kinds of people, Wyatt. So, I have no idea what that would look like."

Wyatt snorts. "Oh man, isn't that the truth?"

He meant to say it quieter, or not to say it at all, but *dammit*, why won't they just leave him be?

"What's that supposed to mean?" Belinda asks.

"Nothing. It doesn't mean anything."

"It means *something*. You said it."

"No. I'm just upset. Forget it."

"You can't go making cryptic comments without explaining them," Geoff says.

"I'm not," Wyatt's voice is soft as a whisper. He tries to swallow the rage that has been simmering inside him. How much longer can he do this?

Belinda's jaw tenses. "I'm aware that Denver smokes pot, if

that's what you're insinuating. I'm not dumb. But marijuana is hardly a drug. I mean, honestly, it's 2019. Cannabis use doesn't make someone a thief. And associating with people who smoke it doesn't make me a bad person."

Wyatt snorts. He can't help it. She's missing the point. Of course she is. "I wasn't talking about marijuana. I wasn't talking about Denver. Or any of your dumb friends." Wyatt wants to shrink inside himself, disappear into a void of nothingness.

"What are you talking about, then? Are you accusing *me* of taking drugs? I know what you guys think about me. But I'm not some dumb hippy, you know. This isn't the sixties. I'm not like… going to marches and taking LSD with strangers. Whatever you think I am, I'm not."

Wyatt stays quiet. Blood thrums behind his ears. A knot twists away in his stomach.

Then Belinda does something she never does. She yells. "If you've got something to say to me, just say it, Wyatt!"

"Your dad, Belinda! Not you! I was talking about your dad! *Jesus!*"

That's it. Wyatt has snapped.

In the moments following his outburst, a fog overtakes him. *Did he say that out loud? Had he heard his voice ricochet across the parking lot? Or had he screamed it in his head?* Please *let him have screamed it in his head.*

The expression on Belinda's face is his answer. She pales, and behind her blue eyes, Wyatt sees a million thoughts zoom past. "What does my dad have to do with this?"

Wyatt sighs. If he could gather his words, stuff them back into his mouth and swallow them down, down, down, he would do that. But he can't. It's time to come clean.

After a breath he says, "Because the drugs in my car were *his.*"

There it is again. That disembodied feeling that comes from speaking aloud a long-held secret. It's a heaviness and a lightening all at once.

"What?" Belinda mutters.

"The drugs they found in your car… those were Uncle

Danny's?" Emeline asks. She looks shaken.

But whatever intrepidity led Wyatt to confess is gone. The guilt takes hold now. Consumes him. He didn't want to tell Belinda this way. He didn't want to tell her at all.

"That's not true," Belinda says, bottom lip quivering with defiance.

Wyatt drops his gaze to the pavement. "It is," he says. But there is no time to get into it now.

"Belinda?" Denver exits one of the apartment doors, unsurprising considering the racket they've been making. "What are you doing here?"

Belinda looks as though she might be sick. But everyone waits for her answer.

"I..." she swallows hard, eyes glazed. "My Gram's ring... it's—it's missing."

Denver gives a few quick blinks, taking in the group of them. "Oh... man, I'm sorry Belinda. That's terrible. Can I do anything to help?"

"Yeah. You can let us look in your van, asshole!" Geoff says, seeming to remember *why* they are standing in this grungy parking lot at five in the morning.

Denver turns a disbelieving eye on Geoff. "Excuse me?"

"You heard me. The ring is missing, and we know you took it."

"What?" Denver's attention is back on Belinda. "Belinda, you don't think I had anything to do with your ring disappearing, do you?"

It's obvious that Belinda is struggling to stay in the present moment right now. She mutters, "I... I don't know..."

Wyatt wants to hug her. He wants to take it back. This is too much for her. But all he can do now is try to protect her from whatever else is coming their way... and get back that ring.

"Yeah," Denver clears his throat. "Of course. You guys can look around. I don't mind." He steps toward Belinda, who won't meet his eyes; she tucks her chin to her chest, arms hugged tight against her body. "I'm so sorry," he says, and touches a hand to her arm. "Your Gram meant so much to you. I can't imagine what you must be going through right now with her ring unaccounted for. I really hope you find it."

Belinda says nothing, just nods.

Denver moves to unlock his van and slides the door open with one big tug. When his untidy space comes into view, a sheepish grin breaks across his face. "Sorry about the mess." He snatches up a handful of clothes from the floor, attempting to clear a path. "I wasn't exactly expecting company," he adds with an insinuative glance at Geoff.

"Oh, no need to clean up on our account." Geoff steps forward with purpose, ramming a shoulder into Denver as he pushes past him. Denver stumbles backward, clutching the disused clothes to his chest as Geoff hoists himself into the back of the van.

The atmosphere is tense. Anger pops and sizzles off Geoff. Humiliation a dark cloud over Belinda. The low hum of anxiety vibrates off Denver. Emeline fades into her usual haze of displeasure and self-absorption.

While Geoff rummages around, eyes only for the task ahead of him, Wyatt keeps a close eye on Denver.

It's odd that he doesn't go to Belinda, he thinks, or even offer her so much as a glance. Instead, Denver stands by the van door in wait, as if expecting there to be questions. When his gaze *does* leave the van, it's to scan the apartment building behind him, the sidewalk, the back of the complex.

"Man, you got a lot of stuff in here," Geoff's voice calls out from the dark center of Denver's hideaway.

A laugh escapes Denver, but catches in his throat. He looks nervous. His voice, however, is cool and light as he says, "Yeah, sure do, my man. Like I said, if I'd expected to entertain tonight, I would have tidied up a bit."

Geoff's face is in the door now. "Lots of shoes you've got in here." He lifts the lid of one box with his finger, peers inside, lets it fall shut.

"Yeah, I'm a bit of a collector," Denver says.

"Hm… you don't say." Geoff nods, pretending to mull over this information. "Funny though, because I've only ever seen you in Jesus sandals. These are some pretty expensive sneakers you have here."

Denver shifts the wad of clothes around in his arms. He looks more confident now, prepared for a long interrogation. "I collect, like I said. You wear them out, they lose their value, don't they?"

"And these sunglasses here?"

"I collect those, too."

Geoff plucks a pair off the top and waves them out the door. "You collect *ladies* sunglasses?"

Without missing a beat, Denver says, "Gender norms are completely outdated if you ask me. I like what I like, I don't put a label on it."

Wyatt stifles a grin. Denver has an answer for every question, and his quick replies are driving Geoff straight to madness. But as the veins in Geoff's neck continue to bulge, Wyatt is doing what he does best. He observes.

Dissolving into the background is Wyatt's specialty. People often say things to him like, *Geez, don't sneak up on me like that*, or, *Shit, man! I didn't even see you there.*

Earlier, Emeline called him a ghost. Perhaps she isn't wrong about that.

Yet again, Denver shuffles the clothes in his hands. *It's a big pile. Why doesn't he just set them down?* Wyatt thinks. He shuffles them again. And again. Still refusing to set them down, he moves to adjust his pants, and Wyatt doesn't miss Denver's hand, pausing at his pocket a moment too long.

"Paintings?" Geoff continues.

"Gifts for my mom. She's a big fan of contemporary art."

"Lots of cellphones for just one person."

"Oh yeah, I'm sure." Denver laughs again, his confidence soaring at this point. "I do repairs on the side. Soaps are great, but they don't always pay the bills. This is just a little something I picked up over the years. I'm a bit of a renaissance man." This is the moment Denver chooses to glance back at Belinda. He actually *winks*.

"All these pill bottles?"

"Pill addiction is a serious concern. I'm crazy-passionate about the cause. I also run a community drug-take-back program with my mom. A few times a year we collect old and expired pills, take them to the proper depositories. Make sure they don't end up in the wrong hands, you feel? That box there, I'll be dropping off tomorrow."

It's not even a good lie, but Geoff fumes.

Wyatt watches.

Even though Geoff continues to dig through his personal items, still throwing out questions like a hot-tempered prosecutor, Denver's nerves have settled. The answers he gives are concise, and well-delivered. Denver knows whatever they're looking for isn't in the van. But at the beginning, when they first arrived, he hadn't been so sure.

Wyatt knows what Denver has done. And as much as he likes to see his brother outsmarted, this isn't about him. It's about Belinda.

"Your pocket," Wyatt says in a tone that verges on boredom.

Denver jumps and looks back at Wyatt as though only just realizing he was standing there. *Ghost, see?*

"What?" Denver asks.

"Your pocket. You pulled something out of the clothes you're holding, and you put it into the pocket of your pants." Wyatt takes a few steps closer. "Mind showing us what that was?"

Denver's eyes flick to Wyatt, back over his shoulder to Geoff who's crouched in the door of his van with a threatening glare trained in his direction, and then, in a movement too quick to have seen coming, Denver drops the pile of clothes and throws a hard punch into Wyatt's left eye. Wyatt hits the ground before the throbbing pain even registers.

One of the girls screams out. Wyatt can't tell which. Geoff emits an animal-like shout and throws himself from the van, grabbing for Denver as he attempts to flee on foot.

Half-blinded by the tears streaming from his left eye, Wyatt watches a blurry Geoff close his fingers around the collar of Denver's shirt, spin him around and send a punch of his own straight into the bridge of Denver's nose. Denver falls to the ground, greasy blonde hair sticks to his face with sweat, and his eyes clench in pain. Geoff takes this moment to climb on top of Denver and sink another blow into the angled slope of his jaw.

"Where's the ring, you little bitch?" he growls through his teeth.

Wyatt pulls himself into a sitting position, clutching the tender bone beneath his eye. "His pocket," he calls to Geoff. "In his left pocket."

Emeline appears at Wyatt's side. She worries over his face as she checks for serious injury.

Witts seemingly restored, Belinda runs to join Geoff.

With Geoff's weight pressing Denver to the asphalt, Belinda reaches a frail hand into Denver's pocket and withdraws the ring box in one swift motion. Wyatt watches her face change from immediate relief for having found it, to a crushing disappointment as she stares at a bruised and bleeding Denver.

"How could you?" she mutters.

Denver says nothing. Just stares at his assailant, blue eyes red-rimmed with hatred. The anger on Geoff's face is mutual.

"What is this worth to you?" Belinda shouts, shaking the ring box an inch from Denver's face. "Because it's priceless to me!"

Again, he says nothing.

Belinda motions to Geoff. "Get off of him," she says.

Geoff obliges but takes his time to stand and relieve Denver of his crushing weight. He steps aside but lingers nearby, presumably in case his services are needed again.

Belinda offers her hand to a now shame-faced Denver, which he takes, and allows her to pull him to his feet. Eye-to-eye, Belinda stares him down with an expression that—much to Wyatt's surprise—is one of self-assurance, not needing of anyone's help.

"I trusted you," she starts, voice quiet and controlled. "I *defended* you. I thought we were friends. This ring…" She holds it up to him again. Allows him to see it. "This is all I have left of my grandmother. And to you, it's what? Money? A trade? Whatever is going on in your van, I'm not going to tell anybody.

None of us are." She glances back at the others as she says this. "And I won't tell about the ring either. You have to live with these choices you're making. Not me. But if you ever lay a hand on a member of my family again, I will destroy you myself."

Wyatt's mouth twitches into a grin.

"You make me sick, Denver. Never speak to me again." She turns her back and walks away.

"Belinda, I…"

She swings back around, venom in her eyes, a finger raised to him in warning. "*Never.* Again."

At last, Denver is quiet, Gram's ring is back in Belinda's possession, and the four of them walk away, a bit worse for the wear, but whole.

49

BELINDA

(JUNE 1, 2019)

S THEY CROSS THE INTERSECTION that leads to their campsite, the sky lightens to a gentle blue, and the misty morning dew dampens Belinda's hair and turns her skin soupy beneath her clothes. A new day.

They made the return walk in silence. Belinda used the time to ground herself with deep breathing exercises but couldn't quiet her mind the way she needed. She is hot and ashamed and unbalanced.

And alone. So alone.

How could she have been so wrong about Denver? Who *else* has deceived her over the years? And her dad—what Wyatt said can't be true, can it? How did she miss the signs? Then again, hadn't she suspected something wrong from the start? She had. But she turned a blind eye and kept driving and traveling and pretending everyone was fine without her.

The moment the bus comes into view, Belinda pushes ahead and takes refuge in the bathroom before the others even reach the door. A quick shower will help recenter her. At the very least, she can prepare herself for the inevitable conversations to come.

Ten minutes later, Belinda pulls a soft pink summer dress over her head, towels the wet from her hair, and emerges from the bathroom. Shoulders still stiff with tension, she braces for a barrage of Geoff's *I told you so's,* and everyone else's sad, disapproving looks.

Silly Belinda, always making the wrong decisions.

Too simple to see what's going on right in front of her.

Thank God she's not our sister.

Will she ever grow up?

But the scene she steps into stops her in her tracks.

Wyatt sits on the bed at the back of the bus, wincing as Emeline presses a wet cloth to his face. There is a small red gash on his cheek where Denver slugged him, nicked him with one of his rings. The skin there is ripening into a nasty purple bruise that deepens the already gaunt shadows beneath his eyes. Geoff has returned the spare bed to table form; Wyatt's sheets are folded neatly and stacked on the tabletop in front of the window. Geoff sits sideways in the booth, long legs filling most of the aisle. He concentrates on his hand, flexes his fingers as he ices his knuckles with a few iced cubes wrapped in a paper towel.

"Look at you two, fighting like a bunch of kids," Emeline chides. But her voice holds an air of humor, which makes Wyatt and Geoff exchange a mischievous look and smile.

They actually *smile.*

At *each other.*

Belinda hasn't seen them do that since… well… she can't remember when, exactly. But it's this very moment that sends her heart soaring, and a soft giggle escapes her lips.

Three sets of eyes meet hers, and Belinda freezes. *Here it comes,* she thinks.

"Hey, Bee," Wyatt says.

Belinda exhales a sigh of relief. "Hi," she says. "How's your…?" She motions to her cheek.

Wyatt's hand shoots up to his face. "Oh, it's not so bad," he says.

Belinda nods. What can she say? She's lost for words.

"Well, my hand hurts like a bitch. Thanks for asking," Geoff snorts. But when Belinda turns to him, he grins.

"Sorry," she says.

Geoff gives his fingers another experimental flex. "Don't be. It was worth it."

"You were right about him," Belinda mutters, turning from the others, and she realizes, for the first time, how tiny this bus truly is.

She'd baited Geoff, and now she waits for him to take it.

But he doesn't.

When their eyes meet again, he's watching her. With sincerity, he says, "I wish I hadn't been. I don't know what you saw in that loser. I mean, *honestly*. But… you liked him. And I'm sorry it worked out like this."

Belinda just shrugs. She *had* liked him. But it doesn't matter now.

Stepping over Geoff's legs, she sits opposite him in the booth and watches Emeline finish her administrations to Wyatt.

The energy on the bus is hard to explain. Obviously, there are things they need to discuss, and the threat of serious conversation hangs in the air like a storm cloud. It *will* unleash, but when? Yet the pangs of dread have—for now, at least— washed from Belinda's mind, and all she feels is pride. Pride for her family. They did this for *her*. Woke up and walked ten blocks at five in the morning to recover a ring that *she* lost, ending up bruised and bloody in the process. And now, with the perfect opportunity to throw it in her face, they refuse. The scene before her is both tragic and beautiful, and she can't help but bask in its glow. Because she was wrong—*so* wrong. Whatever happens in life, whatever darkness she needs to face, she won't have to do it alone.

"Wyatt?" she says.

His eyes snap to attention.

"What you said back there about my dad… can you… can you tell me what happened?"

Wyatt hesitates, looks at the others, then back to Belinda. He clears his throat. "Do you… maybe want to step outside and talk in private?"

Belinda thinks this over for a second—but *only* a second. "No," she says, tucking a strand of damp hair behind her ear. "We're all family here. We should *all* hear it. No more secrets."

50

WYATT

(JUNE 1, 2019)

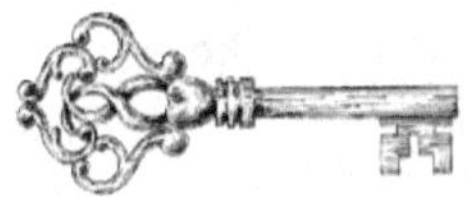

NERVES ARE AS MUCH A part of Wyatt as his hair color or shoe size. But this moment's nerves are not his alone (although to share this with the others after all these years is enough to unsettle his stomach), he's nervous for Belinda as well. How will she handle the truth, and what will she think of her dad once he tells her?

Wyatt takes a deep breath and wipes his palms across his jeans. "Well, first, you should know there aren't any hard feelings toward your dad. I don't blame him for what he did. And you shouldn't either." Wyatt feels this is important for Belinda to understand.

She nods, but it's hard to miss the tension in her shoulders, the way she wedges her fingers beneath her thighs to keep from fidgeting.

"Well, it started about a year after you really started traveling," he begins. "When you left for longer stretches at a time. Aunt Dea—uh… your mom, I mean… she'd just remarried, and your dad was kind of lonely, I guess. During that time, he tried to get closer to my dad, but… well… you know how my dad is. They never really had that close of a bond. That was totally my dad's fault, of course. He's always been bitter that your dad took over Gramp's company. Deep down, he knew it should have been him. But… his choice."

Wyatt shrugs and continues. "But, uh… one night your dad was over at the house, trying to get my dad to go shoot pool with him. But, as usual, my dad said no. *It's late, I need to get up early tomorrow, blah blah blah.* And then he says, 'Hey, why don't you go out with Wyatt? He's about to meet some buddies out that way. I'm sure he wouldn't mind you tagging along.' I was going to meet Quentin and a few of the guys out near Baytree, and Dad just up and volunteered me to take him. Not that I minded," he rushes to add. "I like your dad. He's awesome. But, it was me and a bunch of other kids my age, and it seemed a little weird to bring a parent with me, you know?"

Wyatt wipes his palms again. He sweats when he's nervous.

"Uncle—uh… your dad… he seemed a little unsure as well, but he said okay, he'd go. He promised to stay out of my way and not cramp my style. That made me laugh, and I told him nobody says that anymore. And he laughed back and said, 'yeah, that sounds about right. In that case, I'll try not to talk much either.'"

Belinda tuts out a small laugh at this, and Wyatt wishes there were more witty anecdotes to come. Unfortunately, there's not much humor in the events that followed.

"When we showed up that night, Quentin was acting stranger than usual—pretty sure he was already messed up on something. That's what I want you guys to understand," he says, addressing the others. "I knew what Quentin was—what he was into. But we'd been best friends since we were six, and I didn't want to throw that away just because he was going through some stupid phase or whatever. Quentin was a good guy. Or, at least, he *used* to be. But I never enjoyed hanging out with him when he was like that. I hated it, and I wished he would stop. Whenever I got around him, I was always on edge. And, as it turns out, I had every reason to be."

Wyatt remembers that evening well, and each that spawned as a result.

That first night, it had been Wyatt, Uncle Danny, Quentin, Ricky, Dean, and two guys Wyatt hadn't known that well. It hadn't taken long for Quentin to get all kinds of chummy with Danny. Compliments spewed out of him, and he kept Danny glued to his side. Wyatt reckoned there was an agenda to this behavior; Quentin was definitely up to something. But Danny ate up the attention. It was as if he felt young again... or *cool*. Who knows?

Sure enough, before night's end, Quentin sidled up to Danny and asked if he'd go to the package liquor next door and buy beer for everyone. Now, Uncle Danny isn't a dummy, and Wyatt saw him weighing the risk.

Wyatt turned to Danny then and said, "You don't need to do that. He's being stupid. Just ignore him."

Quentin gave a playful shove to Wyatt's shoulder. "Oh, come *on*. Don't be such a lame ass, Wyatt."

"It's illegal, you idiot. This is my uncle."

The guys booed and jeered and called Wyatt a thousand unsavory names he'd heard a million times before. That's where Uncle Danny spoke up and said, "Now, come on, guys. That's not fair. It's okay, Wy, I remember what it's like to be young. I'll just... yeah—yeah, I'll do it. It's not a big deal." Danny slipped back into dad-mode for a moment and added, "But you can't be flaunting it all over the place if I get it for you, you understand?"

"Oh, yes sir!" said Ricky, giving a stupid salute.

The other guys nodded like obedient little puppies while their eyes bulged with excitement.

Wyatt wasn't sure what possessed Uncle Danny to do it. Was it the high that came from being needed and appreciated? Or had he gotten a taste of his spent youth and wished to savor it? Or perhaps, the simplest explanation, that he didn't want to be seen as the loser uncle and embarrass Wyatt in front of his friends. Whatever his reasons, he walked into the corner store that night and bought them the beer. And that, in Wyatt's opinion, was the start of Danny's problems.

For months after that first night, Quentin continued to invite Danny out with their group. The first few times, he'd invited Danny through Wyatt, but at a certain point, the two of them had exchanged phone numbers and Wyatt's involvement was no longer necessary. There were even a few occurrences where Wyatt declined an invitation because of an early class, and they'd all gone out without him.

A strange jealousy overtook Wyatt on those nights, even though, by this point, he'd gathered that Quentin didn't care about Danny. All he wanted was someone to buy alcohol for him and his dumb friends. But as sure as Wyatt was in this knowledge, Uncle Danny was oblivious to the truth. He'd changed, slipped into the rhythm of Quentin's world: his laid-back style, his stupid Justin Timberlake haircut, his sluggish mannerisms, that clipped, aloof reaction to life. Danny believed they were buddies. That they wanted him around. That somehow, it was possible he fit in with a bunch of eighteen-year-old kids.

Then Uncle Danny's transmission blew two weeks before Christmas. He had to have the whole thing rebuilt. Of course, when Danny asked Wyatt's father to borrow one of their cars, his request was met with a big fat *no*.

"I only need it during the day, to get to and from work. I can bring it back in the evenings. It's not a far walk home. I don't mind," he'd said.

Wyatt's father sighed and shook his head with forced empathy. "Ah, Danny, I wish I could help. But with me and Frannie's work schedules, we need to keep both cars. The timing won't work out, I'm afraid."

And then—*once again*—he volunteered Wyatt for the job. "Hey," he'd said, eyes flashing as though he'd formed the most brilliant idea. "Why don't you take Wyatt's car? He's on winter break right now and doesn't really need it, do ya, bud?"

Dad nudged Wyatt and added under his breath, "It's just for a week or two," as if that in any way helped.

Wyatt had just started dating Prisha, and it annoyed him to see his car get bogarted when his parents had *two* cars of their own to lend out. But Danny needed transportation, and it seemed Wyatt was the only sympathetic person in the family.

And it wasn't so bad. In fact, he barely even missed his car until that Friday night before Christmas, when Danny returned it late. Wyatt needed to pick Prisha up for dinner; they were celebrating their three-month anniversary. Now he was going to be late.

Danny showed up with a million apologies, but Wyatt didn't have time to hear them. The second his fingers closed around the keys, he made for the car and was gone.

Ten minutes later, Wyatt's phone vibrated in the cup holder. Danny's name flashed on the screen.

"Hey."

"Hey, Wy! Glad I caught you. Listen, I left something in your car. I just... I just realized. Shit. I'm sorry. Can you... do you think you can swing back real quick?"

"What? No. I'm sorry, but no. I'm already late."

"I've got fifty bucks on me. It's—it's yours. You can take it for the extra trouble. Use it for dinner. Treat your girl to a nice evening. Least I can do. Hm?"

Wyatt gave this an honest thought. With an extra fifty bucks, he could spoil Prisha with appetizers and dessert. Or he could whip into the store for flowers and a giant box of chocolates— the fancy kind. He checked the time on the clock and shook his head. "Danny, I'm sorry, but no. We have reservations I'll be lucky to make as is. Is it that important? What is it?" He looked around the car as well as possible while driving. "I don't see anything in here. What am I looking for?"

There was a pause on the other end, and then Danny laughed. "No. No, of course it's not important. Have a good night with Prisha. Don't worry about it, pal."

"Okay, well, I'll swing by after I drop her off and you can check on… whatever it is."

"Okay, sounds good. Have fun and… you drive super careful, okay?"

"Okay, see ya." And Wyatt hung up the phone.

In hindsight, if he hadn't been so focused on Prisha, on getting to dinner, on making a good impression and not totally blowing the longest relationship he'd ever been in, he might have noticed the panic in Danny's voice. The strangeness of the entire thing. But, as it was, he continued through his evening, oblivious.

On the way home, Wyatt took the long way, holding Prisha's hand across the center console, heart soaring. But before they went too far past the main strip, flashing red and blue lights sliced through the night. A line of cars slowed to a stop in front of them; a DUI checkpoint. Wyatt, being only eighteen, had nothing alcoholic with dinner, so this delay in their evening shouldn't have caused him a moment's worry, yet his skin prickled with nerves. Wyatt kept his cool. His foot lifted off the peddle, a slow and steady coast to the checkpoint. Much to his relief, the officers stopped the car two ahead of them—a sporty red hatchback. Another officer, who held the leash of a massive German Shepherd, approached Wyatt's window. He motioned for Wyatt to pass to the right of the stopped car and continue through the checkpoint. Wyatt nodded at the man through the window and hoped he didn't look as guilty as he felt, but before he so much as turned the wheel, the giant dog lunged forward and went berserk, barking and clawing at Wyatt's door. The officer's eyes widened in surprise as he heaved on the leash.

The officer reined in the dog and stared, dumbstruck, at Wyatt through the window of the car, eyebrow arched in question. For a moment, it was as though he were deciding what to do with this sudden development. *Is this going to be worth the mound of paperwork involved?* Time slowed as the officer scratched his bushy brow with the nail of his thumb, and then he motioned for Wyatt to pull up to the side and step out.

That's when they searched his car.

Within moments, they had pulled a bag of cocaine from the compartment on the driver's side door.

A *gram* of the shit.

A second-degree felony.

At once, his thoughts shot to Quentin, but he hadn't been in Wyatt's car for months. *Or* had *he? Uncle Danny might have taken him out somewhere.*

Wyatt had been so sure he could explain everything to the cops. Seeing as how the drugs weren't his, he only needed to tell them. Which he did. Many times. In fact, he maintained the belief that he'd get himself out of this entire mess, right up to the moment he saw the handcuffs. And that's when it hit him. *Everyone* says the drugs aren't theirs, even when it's plain to see they are. The cops didn't believe him. Why should they?

They told him to turn around, and he did.

Told him to put his hands behind his back, and he did that too.

"Please. I'm telling you; I have no idea how that stuff got in my car. I've never done drugs in my life. It isn't mine."

The officer had hold of his wrists. "You've mentioned that."

The handcuffs were icy and heavy as they slipped around his wrists. Terrified, he choked back tears.

A female officer had escorted Prisha from the car and asked her to turn around as well, put her arms behind her back. Silent tears rolled down her cheeks, and when her dark eyes flicked to his, Wyatt saw the terror and confusion and disgust painted on her face.

"What—no… wait—why are you arresting her? She didn't do anything!"

The officer behind Wyatt sighed, breath visible in the chilled December air. "Look kid, you're telling me the drugs aren't yours. They may be. They may not be. They might be *hers*. I haven't the foggiest. Figuring that out is a job for the guys at the station. My job is to get you there."

"But… they aren't hers! She had nothing to do with this!" Wyatt yelled.

"They'll sort it out," the officer said, sounding altogether disinterested.

At that moment, the officer with Prisha reached for her cuffs and panic took hold of Wyatt. He didn't have a plan, but he had to do *something.* "Wait," he begged, in a voice so soft he wasn't sure he'd spoken at all.

He tried again. "Wait. No. Stop. They're mine… THEY'RE MINE, I SAID!"

The officer with Prisha paused, looked back at Wyatt, and over to the other officer.

"They're mine," Wyatt said for a third time. "The drugs are mine. Let her go. She didn't know. It was stupid to have them in my car. But she… she wasn't involved. They're… they're mine."

Prisha watched as he confessed, shaking her head in disbelief. The look she gave him—as if he were a monster—broke his heart. Wyatt mouthed the words, *I'm sorry,* as they led him away to the cruiser. The other officer took Prisha home, and Wyatt got a fun ride to the police station.

Later, after what seemed like hours, they allowed Wyatt to use the phone and, of course, he called his mom and dad, who were pissed beyond words.

Next day, when they released him, the first thing he did was call Danny. Wyatt's suspicions still pointed to Quentin. That Danny must have driven Quentin in his car without telling him. At that point, it still didn't register that the drugs might have belonged to Danny himself.

But his uncle admitted everything.

Much to his surprise, though, the bulk of the conversation involved Danny begging Wyatt to take the fall, instead of discussing the obvious elephant in the room—Danny's apparent drug problem.

"Please, Wy. God, I'm *so* sorry. I can't believe this is happening, but *please…* you can't say anything to anyone. You're eighteen. They won't send you to jail—not for a first offense. Most you'll get is a slap on the wrist. Worst-case scenario, a few fines. And I'll pay them! I swear! If they… if they bust me for this, they'll put me away. They will. I'll lose everything. Your grandfather's business. *Belinda*, I—I can't."

Belinda watches Wyatt with unblinking eyes. Tears cloud her irises, and Wyatt knows if she blinks, the tears will have no choice but to overflow. He tries his best not to look at her because he hates how much his words are hurting her.

Wyatt swallows. "Your dad—he couldn't do that to you, Bee. And neither could I. He wanted to make sure you could always come home whenever you wanted, that he'd be able to take care of you. He didn't want to abandon you like… like your mom did. The entire idea of confessing to something I didn't do was terrifying. But I didn't want to make things worse by throwing him under the bus. So, I went along with it, admitted to the whole thing in court. Only, your dad was wrong. It wasn't just a slap on the wrist I got. It was a five-thousand dollar bail that Gram had to pay because Danny didn't have that kind of money. Oh… and the six months in state prison, of course."

Belinda puts her face into her hands, rocking herself back and forth. "This was all my fault, Wyatt. I never should have left him. He needed me, and I… I left him. Just like *she* did. God! What's wrong with me? I'm so sorry."

"No," Wyatt says, and he reaches out to take her hand. "It wasn't your fault, Bee. It was mine. All of it was mine. If I wouldn't have taken him out that night, none of this would have happened. I shouldn't have let him get in with Quentin. I should have ended it when I had the chance. I blame myself. I blame myself for *so* damn much. For your dad. And for Gram, too."

"For Gram?" Emeline asks. "Why on Earth?"

Wyatt sucks in a big gulp of air. "The night before my court date… that was the night Gram first got sick. The night of her first episode, I mean."

Sad faces stare back at him, waiting for him to elaborate, which he's not sure he wants to do. But he's come this far. May as well go the distance.

"Gram came to the house around ten that night. This was back when she still drove. But she never drove *that* late, you know that—the glare bothered her. But here she was at the door, ringing the bell like a madwoman. It was me who answered."

Wyatt presses his palms together, fingers wringing nervously. Whatever he thought sharing these events might feel like… it's worse. Much worse.

"She was all messed up," he says. "Her hair was falling from her pins, and it looked like she'd done half an eye in eyeshadow, then given up. When she spoke, she called me by another name—Misty or Richey or something—I couldn't tell because she was slurring a bit, but she kept saying things like, *The nightmares are back. What do I do? It's too much.* It terrified me. I had no idea what she was talking about. Mom and Dad sorted her out, made her a warm milk, and she calmed down—came back to her senses. But then, she couldn't remember what happened, how she got there. None of it. I kept thinking, what if she'd gotten into an accident on the way, or ended up somewhere else, somewhere far away, or… God, *anything* might have happened. The next week they diagnosed her with the dementia."

"Yeah, but you can't possibly think any of that was your fault?" Emeline says.

Wyatt shrugs. "Maybe the stress of everything going on with me made her like… snap."

"No. It was just poor timing. Not your fault, man." Geoff says and his sincerity takes Wyatt by surprise.

"I'm sorry for being a dick, earlier," Wyatt says. "It's just… you guys got the luxury of leaving, you know? You got to keep her. To keep her in your mind exactly as she was. You didn't have to *see*… not like *I* did… to watch her deteriorate right in front of you."

Geoff's eyes fall to his feet, but Emeline speaks. "I always forget that part. You shouldn't have had to deal with that alone. I'm sorry."

"My dad—" Belinda interjects, "is he still… you know, is he…"

The thought fizzles out, unfinished. But Wyatt understands.

After four months served of a six-month sentence, Wyatt was back home. No girlfriend. No college. No job. And no one who wanted to hire a kid fresh from jail. As luck would have it, Wyatt knew someone who owned a business, and that someone was the very person who'd landed him in jail in the first place. Given the facts, Danny had zero qualms in giving Wyatt a job.

These days, they see little of each other outside of work, but for Wyatt, that's more than enough to form a solid hypothesis of how Danny spends his free time.

Belinda's suspicions show in her eyes before Wyatt can answer.

"I... I can't say for certain. I only ever see him at work. But, from what I see of him there, I... I'd say he is, yeah."

She nods, her fears confirmed.

"Look, he has a problem, Belinda. But his problem is not *your* problem, got it?"

Still nodding, she says, "It has to be *someone's* problem, though, because he hasn't gotten better. My mom walked away from us, and she's not coming back. So... maybe I need to instead."

For a moment, Wyatt expects her to cry. But in the same instant—like a flipped switch in her brain—the fog lifts, and she's back to her old self again.

"Well, I'm hungry," she says. "Let's go get breakfast."

51

GEOFF

(JUNE 1, 2019)

GEOFF PICKS AT THE REMNANTS on his plate. Belinda had only a few bites of avocado toast and left the rest of her breakfast untouched; Wyatt snags a strip of bacon from her plate as the waitress clears their things away and refills their coffees.

They'd ended up at a busy mom-and-pop diner, stuffed into a booth much too small for four people. It's still early—a few minutes past eight—so there's an unfortunate amount of time to kill before Lancaster's opens.

With full stomachs and an exhaustion stemmed from too little sleep and too many emotional conversations, they sip their coffees in silence, willing the caffeine to bring them closer to their normal selves.

Earlier events had proved an adequate distraction, but now Geoff is back in his head. From time to time, snatches of quiet conversation reach his ears—mindless nonsense—and he tries his best to follow along, but his thoughts are louder than anything else. Thoughts of Lila, of the mess his life has become, of what he'll return home to—or rather, what *won't* be there—roil through him like a sickness. So, he sips his coffee—limbs heavy, pulse thick, chest so tight it aches—and tries not to lose himself completely.

For the entire flight to Mom and Dad's, Geoff considered how much he intended to share with his family about Lila and their recent struggles. In the end, he'd kept their problems to himself. After all, he'd only be in Georgia for two days, and then he'd go home and straighten it out. But now, Geoff realizes things with Lila have spiraled beyond his control, and the others will find out, eventually.

Geoff clears his throat. "Well… in the spirit of sharing things…"

Everyone inclines their heads. The weight of their attention is more than Geoff can handle just now. He takes another sip of coffee and returns the mug to the table with more force than intended; a pale brown wave swells up and over the lip, splattering the speckled Formica tabletop. Like a reflex, Emeline plucks a napkin from the center of the table, lifts Geoff's cup, and soaks up the mess. "Go on," she says, and daubs the side of his mug as well.

Geoff tries to crack his neck, but can't. "Well… I'm sure you guys have concluded that something is going on with me and Lila."

Around the table, eyes flick from his—save for Emeline, who meets his stare head on.

Geoff straightens, squeezing his shoulder blades together, and a sigh mingles with a long puff of breath.

"The truth is," he starts, "I haven't spoken to Lila since the funeral. She isn't visiting her family in Dallas. Actually, I'm not sure *where* she is, but my guess is she's been moving out of our apartment."

This—the *real* reason Geoff agreed to come on the trip. He'd made it as far as the airport drop-off lane before telling the Uber driver to turn around and bring him back. Not for Gram. Not because he was dying to unravel some silly mystery. And definitely not to spend more time with his family. But because he was *terrified*—of going home to face the thing he feared most. The thing he already knew to be true.

"Why? What happened?" Emeline asks.

Belinda adds, "But you've been together since high school."

"Yes, I'm aware of that," Geoff says, with more than a hint of annoyance. "And I don't know *what* happened. It's been an awful year, sure. But not bad enough to tear us apart—to make her want to leave me."

Emeline leans forward, elbows on the table. "What's been going on with you two?"

"Well, for starters, back in November… Lila found out she was pregnant."

"Oh my gosh!" Belinda gasps.

"Congrats, man," says Wyatt.

But Geoff turns out a hand to pause their celebration. "Let me finish."

Silence falls.

"Lila found out in November. It wasn't planned. I was— *we*—were completely blindsided. When she took the test, she cried, and *not* the happy kind. I kept my cool in front of her— I'm the man, I had to be strong. But inside, I was dying. Like, I'm twenty-two. She's twenty-one. We can't be parents. And we're not even married yet! That isn't—it's not how it's supposed to go. We're supposed to get married, enjoy it for a few years—travel a bit, build a nest egg—and *then* think about kids. And we were on track for it, too. This messed up the entire plan. So, she made an appointment to get checked out. I thought it could be a mistake, right? These things happen. But the doctor said no, she was definitely pregnant—perfectly implanted, strong heartbeat, all that." Geoff waves a hand at this. None of that matters anyway.

"The next several weeks were a blur. Then, one day around Christmas, she called and said her stomach hurt and she was swinging by the doctor to have it checked out. I honestly thought nothing of it—it was a *stomachache*. I was at work, so I couldn't go with her, and I'd gotten so swept up in coding this new app, I'd forgotten to call back and check on her later. But I figured, if something were wrong, she would have called me. So, I finished my day. But when I got home that night, first thing she said is she'd lost the baby."

Emeline sucks her bottom lip between her teeth, eyes slick and glistening. But Belinda is the one who speaks. "Oh, I'm so sorry, Geoff," she says.

Geoff nods. Unsure what to say. "It's so weird. Like… she was pregnant when I left for work that morning, and then she just… *wasn't*. It doesn't make sense. What could have happened inside her body to make a baby just… die like that? But Lila was fine. No tears. *Nothing*. When I got home that night, she was on the couch watching TV—an episode of Hell's Kitchen—and she made us salmon and jasmine rice for dinner and even joked around. She did her awful Gordon Ramsey impression. *Come here, you! Look at this! It's raw!* We both laughed, and then I wondered if I should have felt bad for laughing. But she was totally herself and stayed that way for weeks.

"But things took a turn. Out of nowhere, she was like… depressed—stopped eating, stopped showering regularly, didn't want me to touch her. She'd get better for a while and then *boom*, it hit again, worse than ever. The moods came in waves. But she withdrew from me, even on the good days. That's when the panic hit. I assumed her change of heart had to do with losing the baby; there was no other explanation. But what I can't understand is why she got so upset about it. For me—I hate to say it—but there was a little breath of relief when it happened. Like *whew*, now we can move on and have a baby when we're actually ready for one, you know? I mean, she hadn't wanted a baby either, so I told her—"

"You didn't." Emeline's face is grave, as though he'd just confessed to some heinous crime.

Geoff blinks a few times in annoyance and continues. "*I told her,* 'I understand you're upset about what happened, but honestly, it's for the best. Neither of us were especially thrilled to be parents. We weren't ready. Now, we can focus on each other—like before—and have a baby one day when we're better prepared.'"

"Oh, Geoff," Emeline mutters, and her face falls to her hands.

Geoff's face stings with embarrassment, and he's not sure why. "What? What's wrong with that?" he asks.

Wyatt sighs, and Belinda averts her eyes completely.

Geoff suddenly feels much too large for this table; he wants to get up, to stretch his legs. "There is nothing wrong with what I said. It's true. She *knew* it was true. I've always been very direct with Lila, and she appreciates that about me—she says so."

But Emeline shakes her head. "You're such an idiot."

Heat sprouts from Geoff's neck, and a frantic twitch starts above his right eye. "It wasn't like that. Lila had been upset long before I mentioned anything about losing the baby. You guys can't judge the situation when you don't even know her."

"You don't understand the first thing about what she's going through," Emeline accuses.

"Oh, and you *do*?"

Two snaky veins throb beneath the thin skin of Emeline's forehead. "As a matter of fact," she says, "yeah—I do."

Geoff's brows pull together as he searches for a snarky comeback, but only finds confusion.

After a beat, Emeline sighs and says, "I had a miscarriage in 2016. After Conner, before Aimee."

"Oh my God, Emeline. I didn't realize," Belinda says, hands clutching her mug as though attempting to warm her fingers through the tepid ceramic.

Prickles of shame flare up over Geoff's skin. "I'm sorry. I didn't realize."

"It's okay. We didn't tell *anyone*," Emeline says, throwing Wyatt a conspicuous glance.

"How far along were you?" Belinda asks.

"Almost three months." Emeline's attention then falls on Geoff. "It was—like you and Lila—*not* planned."

A moment of quiet settles across the table where Geoff can hear the noises of the diner with impeccable clarity: the sluggish morning conversations; the scraping of plates, discarded food plopping into the trash; wet slurps from the booth behind them; the tinny refrain of a handheld video game; a waiter rattling off the specials.

The tunnel of sound narrows back to his sister, and she continues her story.

"I'd already been struggling with the whole motherhood thing. Conner was the neediest baby and I... I loved him so much. But I was a terrible mom. And then to find out I was pregnant again four months later... was a gut punch. I cried myself to sleep every night. I mean, my belly button sagged below my waistband, and my stomach still jiggled like a big bowl of Jello whenever I walked, and stupid me had gone and put another baby in there. I was *so* angry—with myself, with Armie, with the world—you can't imagine how angry I was. I just... I didn't want to be a mom again. Maybe someday, but not so soon. I would have given anything to just *not* be pregnant. But when I lost him—it was a boy—I felt nothing but guilt. And do you know why?"

Geoff shakes his head, speechless.

"Because I couldn't stop thinking... what if I'd somehow wished the baby away? Could he sense how much I didn't want him? It's irrational, I get that, but it didn't matter. I hated myself for a long time, believing I'd somehow brought it on myself. It was a little person—*my* little person—and I'd hated him." Emotion shatters Emeline's last few words, and wet streams of tears roll down the hollowed pits of her cheeks. In a rush, she wipes them away. Scans the room to ensure no one has noticed her moment of weakness.

After a stabilizing breath, she continues. "So—it's true that Lila may not have wanted the baby. But she didn't need you to remind her of that. Because I promise you, Geoff, she never *stops* thinking about it."

Geoff's throat clenches and retracts. Throughout the entire struggle with Lila—the fear of losing her, of starting over—he never once shed a tear. He hadn't cried over Gram, either. Truth be told, it's been many years since he had an honest cry. But right now, just for a moment, he's worried he might.

"I *am* an idiot," he says.

Belinda lays a hand on his forearm, her pulse fluttering beneath the tiny bumblebee tattoo on her wrist. "It's not too late to fix things," she says.

But Geoff shakes his head. "No. No—it is. After I said what I did, Lila shrank farther away from me. I can pretend she didn't, but… she did. Even the way she looked at me was different. Where there used to be love, there was this… deadness in her eyes. I wanted to fix it, and I didn't know how. So… I pulled a Hail Mary and bought a ring. I proposed to her last week."

No one asks for her answer, and their silence tells Geoff they know it wasn't good.

He continues. "She told me we should take a break, that she wasn't sure she wanted to spend her life with me anymore. I begged her to give me a chance, to let me make things right. She told me she'd consider it, but I could tell her heart wasn't in it. Three days later, Gram died, and when Lila said she wasn't coming with me to the funeral, I worried she wouldn't be there when I got back. And, judging from the radio silence I've received from her, I'd say I was right."

Across from Geoff, Wyatt doesn't move, but when he speaks and says, "I'm sorry, man. That sucks," it comes across as sincere. And for once, Geoff doesn't want to punch him.

"Yeah," Geoff agrees, and for a lack of anything better to say, adds, "Yeah, it majorly sucks."

52

BELINDA

(JUNE 1, 2019)

SHE'LL WORRY ABOUT IT LATER. This mess with her dad. And it *is* a mess. Yet, she can't say the news comes as much of a shock. More, the confirmation of her worst fears: keeping away from home doesn't stop bad things from happening, it simply passes the burden to someone else. She'd known her dad was handling the divorce poorly, and she'd still left. *How could she?* She'd seen the dishes piling in the sink. The late notices he tried to hide behind the record player. The strange phone calls taken at odd hours. The agitated tap of his heel against the floor when stuck somewhere for too long. She'd known his behavior was off for *years*, yet she'd walked out the door again and again, took herself as far from the suspicions and guilt as possible. And there *was* guilt. So much guilt. Because deep down, Belinda knew *why* she'd stayed away for so long: she was selfish… and afraid. Afraid of going home and getting stuck. Afraid she'd be the one to fill the space her mom had left. That her best years would be stolen, to care for someone that *should* care for themselves—care for *her*—and that her future was being written without her consideration or consent. But mostly, she was afraid of herself. Because if Belinda thought, for even a second, that her dad truly needed her there, nothing could keep her away. Not even the loss of her freedom. Her dad knew that. And so did she. So… they pretended. The worse things got, the more they acted as though everything were fine. At home, conversation never veered toward heavy subjects, and visits became shorter and shorter with longer spaces between. Her dad never complained or asked for anything more, and they always said goodbye with a hug and a smile and a *See you soon!* This last time, she'd been gone so long, she'd almost forgotten the world she left behind, the one that kept spinning without her. Wyatt's confession had been the rude awakening she'd needed.

But she'll worry about it later. This isn't the time or the place. They are here for Gram.

She checks the time on her phone, shielding the screen from the sun. "Five till," she says to the others.

They stand at the big glass doors at the front of Lancaster's Jewelers. A man bobs toward them from inside, a shiny set of keys swinging from one hand, a Styrofoam coffee cup in the other. His lips are pursed and—while unable to hear through the thick glass—Belinda thinks he might be whistling. As he moves closer, she can see the man is slight, with short, sandy blonde hair combed to one side—mid-forties, she thinks. The man startles as he notices the group of them through the glass, and with an amused expression, hurries to unlock the door.

"Wow. I can't say I've ever opened to a crowd before," he chuckles, and takes them in one by one. But when his eyes fall to Wyatt's bruised and battered face, his smile slips.

With a hint of trepidation, he steps to the side and ushers them into the store, asking, "How exactly can I help you?" as they file in past him.

"Hi there," Belinda says, taking the lead. "Our grandmother, Imogene Baker, sent us."

The man's face doesn't change; the name obviously means nothing to him. But Belinda clears her throat and continues. "Well… she recently passed, and I acquired this ring." She reaches into her bag and withdraws the maroon-colored ring box, extracts Gram's ruby ring and hands it to the man. The man has moved behind the counter now—either to better serve them, or to distance himself from Wyatt's questionable appearance—but he reaches for the ring at once and sets to examining it under a small magnifier fit between his thumb and forefinger.

"Hm," he says, turning the ring over in his hand. "This is quite a beautiful piece," he mutters, though he speaks more to himself than to them, lost in the art of inspection. Belinda studies him; the meticulous way he rotates the rock; the tiny nubs of bitten fingernails; his complete unawareness of their presence as he sees things in the stone invisible to their untrained eyes. And then the trance breaks. He sets the magnifier on the glass countertop beside him and returns the ring to Belinda.

"Yeah," he says, taking a sip of his coffee, wincing at the heat of it, and then taking another sip. "That's a fine piece, most definitely. I can tell it's an heirloom—at least sixty, maybe seventy years old. The color on the ruby is vibrant and clear—I detected only a few inclusions in the stone. And the setting is lovely as well. Looks like a fourteen-carat gold band. Of course, the inscription would lower the value a bit, but all things considered—yeah, I'd say you could get close to two-thousand dollars on the ruby alone."

"Oh, it's not for sale," Belinda quips, and she stuffs the ring back into its box. Protects it against her chest, as if the man might fly across the counter and pry it from her hands.

"No, no—of course not," the man stammers. "Sentimental value is worth far more, I know."

"Right. Yes," she agrees, letting out a slow breath of relief.

"Anyway, the reason we're here—our grandmother mentioned I should come and have the ring cleaned while I'm in town."

The salesman screws up his eyebrows. "Your grandmother, who—who passed, you said?"

"Yes." Then, realizing his confusion, she adds, "I mean, *she* didn't tell me to come here, not directly anyway. I mean, *obviously.* She told her—oh, never mind. It's a long story. She has insurance here—it should cover it."

With another skeptical glance, the man slides his coffee farther along the counter to the computer system, which looks frightfully in need of an update, and waves for them to join him. "Okay, well, let's just take a look, shall we?"

The man presses a thousand buttons and types in a million codes, the process nearly as mesmerizing as the ring inspection. More typing and scrolling around with a—oh, wow, does that computer mouse have a *wire?*

"Let's see… Baker, you said it was?"

"Yes. Imogene Baker."

They wait while he searches. But the man's brows crease for a second time when he utters, "Hm," followed by, "I'm not seeing anyone in here by that name."

"Oh! Try Elkins. Imogene Elkins. That was her maiden name," Emeline offers, looking pleased with her contribution.

"Ah, yes, I bet that's it," the man encourages, though a few moments later his expression sours once again, and he says, "Unfortunately, I'm not seeing anyone by that name, either."

"How strange." Belinda searches the faces of her cousins, but they shrug and shake their heads.

At that moment, Belinda remembers something. Something Greta told them. "Hank! She mentioned we should ask for Hank. Are you Hank?"

At this, the man's eyes widen into great blue saucers, and then, in a soft voice, he says, "I'm Stanton. Stanton Lancaster. Hank Lancaster is my father. He retired ten years ago. I run the place now."

"Oh, I see," Belinda says, and a fresh wave of fatigue washes over her. What she wouldn't give for the comfort of a bed. But no, there is something for them to learn here—a reason Gram insisted they come—and Belinda suspects that Stanton Lancaster isn't a man in the know. So, she asks, "Could we—is there a way to get ahold of your father by chance? I'm curious if he somehow knew our grandmother."

Stanton smiles, eyes darting amongst them. He checks his watch. "Let's see. It's 10:15, so… he probably just settled in front of the TV to scream at reruns on the Game Show Network," he chuckles. "I'll give him a call."

Belinda's heart leaps in her chest, and from the restless shuffles amongst her cousins, they, too, are anxious to see what information Hank Lancaster can give them, if any.

Stanton swipes at his cellphone screen a few times and presses the device to his ears, taking another long drag of coffee. A moment later, he rolls his eyes. "We've been open for fifteen minutes, Pop. How could I have already burned the place down?"

After a beat, he smiles and continues. "No, I'm here with a few young kids who believe you may be an acquaintance of their grandmother." A pause. "Imogene Baker, or… or Elkins?" He looks at them to confirm, and they nod. Another pause.

A lingering gaze in their direction.

"Really? Right now? Are you sure you're feeling up to—" Stanton is obviously interrupted. He sighs. "Okay."

Stanton ends the call and quietly returns the phone to the front pocket of his pants. After a moment, he says, "It would seem my father has been expecting your visit. He told me to send you to the house at once."

Twenty minutes later, Belinda pulls the bus into a long and winding driveway that leads to an impressive house on the Halifax River; two stories, the sharp angles of mid-century architecture, fresh white paint, and more glass than walls.

They exit the bus into a clean and manicured yard. As they approach the lavish home, Belinda notes the spotless shine on the windows. Even the doorbell is gleaming; Emeline rings it with her knuckles so as not to smudge the glossy finish.

The chime of the bell echoes from within, and somewhere inside, a dog barks and doesn't *stop* barking—a large dog from the sound of it. A few moments pass, and the door cracks open only a fraction. An old, graying man with a cane, peeks out. Though he uses this cane less for balance, and more for swatting at the dog, trying to pry him from the door. A gaping, drooling mouth, attached to a head as big as a horse, has appeared in the crack above the man's knee.

"Get back, you damned fool! Go!" the old man shouts, landing a blow on the dog's rump that sends him whimpering into the depths of the home, nails clicking across a hard floor. Belinda winces and hopes the poor beast is okay.

With the dog safely disengaged, the old man throws the door wide, taking a moment to give their group a once-over. When his soft green eyes land on Emeline, he pauses, and a weathered hand clutches at his chest. "My God, it's like seeing Imogene all over again."

Emeline turns a pretty shade of pink at the comment.

Then, the old man turns to Wyatt and, all softness gone, says, "What the hell happened to you, kid?"

Wyatt's jaw drops, but he doesn't answer.

It doesn't matter, anyway. The old man isn't waiting. "Never mind," he says. "Come in, come in. I don't know how much longer I'll be alive, and we've got a lot to cover."

Without another word, he turns and hobbles off into the sprawling home. The door swings on its hinges behind him.

For a moment, the four of them only stare at each other. Then, in silent agreement, they shrug and follow the man inside.

53

TED

(JULY 26, 1963)

The day before the accident

TED HAS BEEN SOARING FOR WEEKS.

His relationship with Imogene couldn't be better. Business continues to flow in for The Siren, and he and Ray have been skirting by at The Company, collecting generous payouts on distribution nights despite not having worked a job of their own in several months.

Today, Ted relaxes on the deck, tan legs outstretched, bare feet propped on a tackle box. As the sun heats his skin, the radio beside him plays hit after hit.

Between songs, the radio folk talk of the massive earthquake that hit Yugoslavia overnight, killing well over a thousand people, the numbers climbing with each new update. A shiver washes over Ted as he imagines the destruction to which those poor people had woken. He sends a silent prayer of thanks that he had *not* woken to death and despair, but to a gorgeous view, a thriving business, and a woman who loves him.

It's a damn near perfect day.

Ted hears footsteps on the deck below, and a moment later, Ray stalks up the ramp with a tired face and a sour expression.

"What's up with you, man? All good?" Ray ignores Ted's question and sulks past, disappearing through the open door of the salon. From inside, Ted hears the refrigerator door rattle open and the clanking of bottles.

After a moment of deliberation, Ted releases a drawn-out sigh and follows Ray.

Propped against the counter, Ray pops the cap on a bottle of beer.

Ted tries his question again. "You good?"

"Yeah—yeah, fine," Ray answers, and he takes a long swallow of beer, a look in his eyes the furthest from fine Ted has ever seen. "Just tired. Gonna go have a rest, I think."

And with that, Ray disappears into his tiny stateroom at the back of the boat and lets the door shut behind him.

Ray hadn't emerged from his room for the rest of the day, which put Ted in a rather crabby mood; he was left alone to clean the deck in preparation for an early morning tour, sweat and the foul stench of mucky water coating every inch of his body.

As he stuffs the cleaning supplies back into the storage closet and entertains thoughts of a nice, cold shower, a throaty cough resounds from somewhere behind him. Ted whirls, surprised to find Louis Steinfeld standing at the end of the dock, peering up at him through the large, round frames of his glasses.

"Louis," Ted crosses to open the hatch and drop the ramp for his fellow brother. But Louis waves him away and stuffs his hands in his pockets.

"No—no need," Louis says. Ted notices that a thick sheen of sweat has flattened the dark hair to Louis's head, highlighting the patches where he's already gone thin. "I just came to deliver a message."

"Oh? What is it?"

"Marty needs to see you and your buddy tonight at eight-thirty. He says don't be late."

Now Ted is confused. Marty has never called them in on a whim. "Why? Did he say?"

"None of my business, kid," Louis clips. "Just get yourselves there."

With that, he turns and moves up the dock with a speed to suggest he desires to distance himself from this errand as soon as possible.

Two hours later, Ted and Ray park in front of the old run-down meat market and are now climbing the twenty-odd stairs to the vacant space at the back of the building that acts as The Company's main headquarters.

For the entire ride, Ray had been a bundle of nerves, half from his worry over what Marty might soon unleash on them, and half, Ted figures, from whatever screwed up his mood earlier in the day. Whatever it was, he hadn't shared it with Ted, nor had he recovered from it. And anything involving The Company sets him on edge, regardless.

They do the secret knock and are at once let in, not by one of the usual door guys, but by Marty himself. Now Ted finds himself sharing in Ray's apprehension—Marty *never* answers the door.

An enormous grin—toothy and wide as a shark's—breaks out on Marty's face. "Right on time," he says, and hurries them inside.

At first glance, they are alone. Whatever this business is, it concerns only the three of them. A moment later, however, as Marty herds them into his separate office space in the back, Ted takes notice of a fourth man. Propped against the wood-paneled back wall, arms crossed in front of his chest, the stranger watches them enter with a cocky snarl. The man is soft-jawed, with fair skin, and dark, coifed hair—older than Ted; late thirties, he'd say. Ted doesn't recognize this man, but he certainly isn't a member of The Company.

Beside him, Ted senses Ray withdrawing, wanting nothing more, he knows, than to spring for the door.

But Marty has moved in behind them, and his giant body at once makes the space—makes *them*—feel much too small.

"Have a seat, boys. Have a seat," he says, as he moves around the table and situates himself in his usual chair.

The other man doesn't flinch. Just watches.

As Ted finds his seat, he clears his throat and says, "I, uh— got to be honest... it surprised me when you called us in tonight. Is—is everything okay?"

Another smile shoots across Marty's face. "Oh, no need for concern, boys. In fact—" He leans onto his elbows and hitches forward. "I've got a big opportunity for you."

"For us?" Ray asks.

"Oh, absolutely," Marty says, leaning back in his chair and pressing his fingertips together. "There's no one better for the job, in fact, and you'll understand why in just a few moments."

Ted's mouth falls dry, and he's unable to speak. There's a spark in the air he can't place—the itching excitement that slithers over Ted's skin, the wild gleam in Marty's eye, the nervous energy erupting from Ray, all mingled together.

To Ted's right, Ray's leg bounces in fast succession.

"You boys ever heard of Walter MacNeil?" Marty asks.

Ted can only shake his head no, but Ray answers, "I have, yeah. He's a seafood guy, right?"

A riotous laugh explodes from Marty as he repeats, "A seafood guy." He turns to the man against the wall and points a playful finger at Ray. "A seafood guy. You hear this kid?" The other guy lets out a slight chuckle, but still looks as though someone pissed in his cereal this morning.

Marty continues laughing. The corner of Ted's mouth

twitches, but Ray is silent.

After a moment, Marty composes himself and continues. "He's not *just* a seafood guy, Raymond. He's *the* seafood guy. MacNeil Seafood, Inc, owns and operates twenty-five fishing vessels and the biggest fish processing facility on the east coast. Over seventy-five percent of restaurants on the Atlantic coast of Florida get their seafood supply direct from ol' Walter."

At this, Marty turns to address the other party in the room. "Now this here is Larry Patrick. For seven years, he's been Walter MacNeil's domestic."

The men exchange glances, but no one moves a muscle.

Marty sighs. "Well, shake hands for Christ's sake!"

Larry steps forward, extending his hand first to Ray, and then Ted.

"There. That's more like it," Marty says with an amused smirk. "Now then, as I was saying, Mr. Patrick has been working for MacNeil for seven years. Ain't never had a problem with the man in all that time... until a few months ago, when MacNeil started getting stingy with Larry's paychecks. Now, if you saw the size of his estate you'd know, money ain't an issue for this fella... greed is."

Larry returns to his perch against the wall, arms crossed as if he'd never moved.

"So, Larry here is lookin' to get what he's owed, and you boys are just the ones to help him get it."

"How so?" Ted asks. This sounds like a much larger job than they're used to, with a far greater risk.

"Well, it would *seem* MacNeil has been keeping a few million pennies from ol' Uncle Sam. Last I checked, that there's a crime. Mr. Patrick says he keeps the money holed up in a safe in his study. He suspects there's close to five-hundred-thousand clams in there."

Something heavy drops into Ted's stomach. He can't even fathom that much cash.

Marty keeps talking, and Ted wills his ears to listen. He struggles to find his breath.

"Mr. Patrick is selling us this rather private information for our help in the matter. Whatever we uncover tonight—"

"Excuse me?" Ray interrupts, and Ted doesn't miss the flash of annoyance on Marty's face at being cut off mid-sentence. Ray blanches. "I'm sorry, sir, but did you say *tonight*?"

Marty's expression softens, and he says, "Absolutely, my boy. Tonight is the night."

Only now does Larry step forward to speak. "My boss is in Miami this weekend. He won't return until Sunday afternoon. If we're going to move, it has to be now."

"So, here's what I'm thinking," Marty goes on, regaining control of the meeting. "We use your boat. The MacNeil estate is right on the Halifax, so you'll park at the dock and approach the home from the rear. Larry will supply you with a key, so no breaking and entering. Now, Mr. Barret, you're one of my best safe crackers, so you'll be the one to do the extracting. Mr. Green, you will act as lookout from the back. And Mr. Patrick, you'll be on lookout from the front."

"He'll be coming with us, then?" Ray asks, throwing an icy nod at Larry.

"Of course. If anything goes sour, he knows the place better than anyone. You'll be glad to have him there. Trust me on that. Now, Mr. Barret, once you've loaded the money into the bag— and I have no doubt you will succeed in this—" he adds with a wink, "you'll have to move on to the tricky part. MacNeil is no fool. An ADT Telewave system protects his home. These things specialize in detecting intrusion. You'll have the code to deactivate the alarm on arrival, but for this to appear as a robbery and keep the suspicion off Larry, you're gonna have to set off that alarm when you leave. A simple window smash should do the trick. Once that thing sounds off, though, I reckon you'll have about ten minutes to get your carcass down that dock and out of sight."

Ted swallows. "I don't know, sir. This seems like a job for someone more experienced. We've only been on a few small jobs. Surely there's someone better equipped for this. Mickey— or Louis, maybe?"

Marty waves this away. "Nonsense. You boys have proved

your capabilities to me plenty. It's about time I give you a bit more responsibility around here. And this job is damn near perfect for you. You two have a fishing boat. A fishing boat pulling up outside a seafood man's place won't draw any eyes. Ain't no one else in The Company with a fishing boat, is there?"

Ray has gone silent. Ted shakes his head and says, "No sir, it's just—I appreciate the opportunity, but I don't think we—"

"You know," Marty interjects, and his eyes narrow as if mulling something over, "come to think of it, I guess *I* own a bit of a fishing charter myself. Well… at least twelve-hundred bucks of one, am I right?" He laughs again, but this time, Ted doesn't sense a shred of humor.

Marty watches Ted and Ray squirm in their seats. The silence stretches to an almost unbearable limit. Then, Marty sighs and says, "Listen, I tell you what… this job is a big deal to me and to Mr. Patrick here and, well, to *all* your brothers here at The Company. But you're right. Of course, yes, you're right. There's more risk involved in this than what you're used to, so let me make you a bargain, okay? Mr. Patrick has requested one hundred and fifty thousand dollars for the information he's providing and for his part in this evening's festivities. My personal cut of the haul, if Larry's estimation is correct, will be around one hundred and seventy-five thousand. Because of the *delicate* nature of the job, I'd like to offer you boys fifty percent of *my* cut, rather than making you share the scraps with the others. That will give you each around forty-five thousand big ones. How does *that* sound?"

For the tenth time tonight, Ted's breath catches in his throat. *Forty-five thousand dollars.* In a few brief hours, that money could be *his.* Sure, there's a risk—a *colossal* risk. But it sounds pretty straight-forward. He's sure he can do it.

His brain turns over again and again as he envisions what he might do with that kind of money. He thinks of Imogene, of her family, of his promise to get her out of there, to give her an extraordinary new life. He could *easily* get her out with forty-five thousand dollars to his name. He wonders if Ray reckons the same thing.

Marty's eyes flick between them. "What do you say, boys? Are you in?"

Ted passes a glance to Ray, who has a sick paleness to his skin. He can't get a read on him, but can guess what he must be thinking. *This is stupid, man. Let's just go. Before something bad happens.*

But Ted turns back to Marty and says, "We're in. Yes—we're in."

With another carnal grin, Marty locks eyes with Larry and says, "Fantastic! By morning light, we'll all be much better off! Well… perhaps not Walter MacNeil," he laughs. Then, "Mr. Patrick, can you grab the bag, please?"

Larry crosses the room and lifts a large, black duffel bag from the floor. He returns to where they sit and plops it on the table. "Now, I went ahead and took the liberty of packing walkie-talkies. We'll each have one, and these will make it easier to communicate once, uh—Ted, is it?—Right. Once Ted's in the house. And one other thing…"

From the front of the bag, Larry withdraws a black handgun—a violent looking little thing—and Ted's heart skips in his chest. Ray scoots his chair back abruptly, blue eyes shining with a sudden flash of fear.

"Whoa, sorry," Larry says, slowly placing the gun on the table, and sliding it with careful consideration over to Ted. "Should have given you a warning, I guess," he shrugs. "This is for you. I've packed it in your bag. Don't see any reason you'd need to use it. But… you know what they say—a stitch in time saves nine. You ever use one of these?"

"Of course. Yeah. I've used a gun," Ted says, though he has not, in fact, ever shot a gun. When you're nine and your father dies and you end up in foster care, there aren't many opportunities to learn the ins and outs of firearms.

"Good. It'll be right here in your bag." Larry lifts the gun again, more deliberately this time.

Ted nods, but already feels the doubt seep through him. *How did he get here?*

But before Ted can slip too far into his feelings, Marty shoots to his feet and claps his hands twice together. "Alright then!

Enough with the schematics! I don't know about *you* fellas, but I'm ready to get this show on the road!"

The car ride back to The Siren is tense. Ray is a ball of furious nerves and looks as if he may vomit at any moment.

"I told you. I told you, didn't I?" he kept saying. "We took his money. I knew he'd throw it back in our faces. He owns us, Ted. He *owns* us. This is exactly why I wanted out in the first place."

Ted's own stomach twists in knots, but the vision of that money in his hands, the look on Imogene's face when he surprises her with a ring, tells her to pack her bags and come with him, is enough optimism for him to cling to. She won't approve of how he got the money. The Company—and Ted's involvement in it—has, by good fortune, remained a mystery to her. But she'll forgive him once she sees the money. He knows she will. And he and Ray will be okay. This is easy. In and out. Instant riches.

"Ray, we've got this, man. We've got it. Think of Athena. Right? Think of the life you can give her."

Ray snorts. "You were right about Athena. What sort of life could we ever have? No one wants to see us together. It doesn't matter what I want."

"Sure, it does," Ted says.

"It doesn't." The face Ray pulls is all fire and finality, and Ted falters.

But just then, Ted notices a familiar shape stumble from the Irish joint he'd taken Imogene to on their first date. "Is that Mickey?" Ted asks.

Ray squints through the windshield. "Looks like him," he says. "Miserable drunk."

"Maybe we should give him a lift."

Ray snorts in obvious disagreement, but Ted is already slowing the car.

Ted rolls down the window and coasts beside the staggering

form of Mickey Lancaster. "Hey Mick. You need a ride, pal?"

Mickey looks as though he'd started drinking at noon and hadn't quit. Bits of dark, stringy hair fall into his eyes, his face gaunter and paler than usual, almost translucent beneath the streetlamps. Half his shirt is untucked from his pants, and he looks at Ted with a sluggish, out-of-focus stare.

"Hey! Ted! Thanks, man! Yeah, a ride would be swell. Real swell." In a few inebriated steps, he's at the car, fumbling with the handle on the back door. He doesn't *climb* into the car as much as he throws himself inside it. In an instant, the entire automobile fills with the smell of spilled ale, body odor, and sauerkraut.

"Where to?" Ted asks, checking the rearview mirror to decide the odds of Mickey spilling the contents of his stomach into the backseat of his car.

"Oh, you know what?" Mickey slurs. "Cillia's over on Beach Street would be great. Thank you."

"Another bar, Mick?" Ray asks.

A Cheshire Cat grin breaks out on Mickey's face. "Well, sure. The night is young, and so am I," he croons, and he throws his arms and legs wide, colliding with the duffel bag that shares the seat with him.

"What's with the duffel?" he asks.

Ted and Ray exchange wary glances. The MacNeil job is a tremendous opportunity, and Ted is sure that guys like Mickey, Louis, and Sinclair would eat escargot straight off Marty's big toe for a chance at a haul this big. But Mickey is Marty's right hand. Of course, he's aware of the job. And Marty hadn't explicitly told him *not* to tell.

After a moment's meditation, Ted decides it will be okay and says, "It's for the MacNeil job."

Mickey nods, eyes heavy as he processes Ted's answer. "Oh—yeah, that's right. Right. The MacNeil job. When is that again?"

"Tonight," Ray clips, the perturbance in his voice hard to miss.

"Right. Tonight," Mickey says, head nodding a few too many

times. "Yeah, that's right. I remember now. The day got away from me, I guess. Well… good luck with that."

The car falls silent for a minute as Mickey stares out the window, either lost in thought, or—more likely—rapidly losing consciousness.

"You know what?" Mickey says. "You can just let me out right here."

"Here?" Ted asks. At present, they are on a residential street, still three miles from Cillia's. "Are you sure?"

"Yeah, yeah, I'm sure. Here's great. Thanks, pal. I appreciate it. You're a keen guy."

Mickey mumbles more thank you's and compliments as he exits the vehicle, slamming the door behind him.

Ted and Ray watch Mickey Lancaster stumble off down the road and disappear into a cluster of shadows.

54

TED

(JULY 27, 1963)

The day of the accident

I**T'S JUST PAST MIDNIGHT. TED** zips his jacket and watches Ray, who sits on the small sofa in the salon, pluck nervously at his fingernails. Larry will arrive any minute to deliver the key and go over last-minute instructions. The atmosphere on The Siren is somber, punctuated with brief sparks of anxiety and tiny prickles of fear. But even as the creepy crawl of nerves tickle Ted's flesh, he envisions the money that will soon be his, the life he will build with Imogene.

Ray runs his thumb along the line of his jaw, a clouded look in his eyes as he works his finger into the little crater on his chin. "I still don't know about this, man," he mutters, almost too low to hear. He must realize—same as Ted does—that his feelings are irrelevant. They are in too deep, and the only way out is *through*. Best they can do is get through it as fast as possible.

Ted watches his friend give over to terror and is at once reminded of his own responsibility tonight.

"I'll hurry," Ted says. "I promise. We'll be out of there before you can say Jack Robinson."

Ray's eyes meet Ted's, and he nods once. It's plain he's not convinced, but he says nothing more on the matter.

Twenty minutes later, a few knocks on the salon door send Ted's pulse into a frenzy. On unsteady legs, he crosses to let Larry into the cabin.

"Hey, man," Ted says with his best attempt at friendliness.

Larry moves into the room with purpose and, skipping the pleasantries, says, "Where's the duffel?"

Ted points to the blue upholstered armchair in the corner where the empty bag awaits.

In two long strides, Larry is there, pulling a folded paper from his pocket. "This is the code to the alarm," he says, and he holds the paper to Ted's face, voice slow and loud, as though speaking to a dimwit. "Do not lose this. You lose *this*, and the entire plan goes down the shitter. Got it?"

"I got it." Ted clips.

Larry continues. "And *this*," he says, withdrawing a small, shiny object from his pocket, "is the key to the back door. Do *not* misplace this. It's my personal copy, and if it goes missing, MacNeil will be sure of my involvement. And that wouldn't turn out so well for you if that were to happen. Understood?"

Threats now. *Great.*

"I won't lose the key. I know what I'm doing."

Larry nods, unsure, but offers a slight crook of his lip that, for him, might pass as a smile. "Right. Well, Marty said you were the best choice for this. I suppose we'll see, won't we?"

As Larry stuffs both items into the side pocket of the bag, a small beam of pride shoots through Ted at the notion of Marty placing him above the others. Of course, he'd always hoped to be the best at something *not* involving thievery and safe-cracking, but he'll take what he can get.

"Where's your pal?" Larry asks, dark eyebrows knit with suspicion.

"He went up to the cockpit to prime the engine."

Larry nods. Then, "Ya'll got any beer on this thing? My damn nerves are shot to hell."

"Sure thing." Ted pops around the corner into the galley and withdraws two beers from the refrigerator. At that moment, the boat roars to life beneath his feet; the churning of the water sends Ted's guts into a similar condition.

He returns to the salon and hands Larry a beer. "Thanks," Larry says, and drains the bottle in four large gulps.

It pleases Ted to see nerves sinking their teeth into Larry as well. He can't imagine they aren't *all* a bit apprehensive with a job of this magnitude looming over their heads.

Larry wipes his mouth on the back of his hand and passes the empty bottle to Ted.

"Now, when you leave here, you're going to head north on the river. You'll cross under the Main Street bridge. The MacNeil mansion is about thirteen nautical miles on the right. Keep your eyes peeled for a long dock; it looks newer than others in the area, but just in case, I've tied a post with a length of yellow cloth. Take that off before you leave. Do *not* forget it."

Ted nods, hoping he can remember everything in the rush of escape.

Larry continues. "I'll be out front in my car the entire time. If anyone approaches from the front, I'll send immediate word. We've got walkies. But emergencies only, yeah? If it's not life or death, keep it silent. And we sure as Hell won't be using real names, got it? I'm Alpha, you're Bravo, your pal's Charlie."

Ted nods, mouth dry despite the beer.

"I don't foresee any problems, but we need to be quick. Walkie us when you open the safe. Keep it brief. I'll give you ten minutes to load up and get the hell out of Dodge before I split to pick up Marty. We'll meet you back here at the docks. Be quick. Do *not* make us worry about where you two are."

Ted nods again. As confident a nod as he can muster.

At the door, Larry pauses, takes a good hard look at Ted,

then shakes his head and says, "I hope to God you're as good as Marty says."

––––––––––

"There!" Ray points ahead as Ted slows The Siren, pulling her alongside the dock marked with a yellow strip of fabric. He swallows the lump in his throat and wills himself to stand from his place in the captain's chair and trade places with Ray.

"Well… here we go," Ted says.

A look of cold fear passes over Ray when he says, "You be careful in there, man. I'm serious. I don't like this."

"Ah, don't worry." Ted waves him off with a cool shrug. "It's gonna be a piece of cake. Just keep this thing running and don't you dare leave without me."

Ray gives off a slight chuckle at this. "I've got your back," he says.

Ted places a hand on Ray's shoulder, and they share a loaded nod. Ray's says: *Please, don't do anything stupid in there.* And Ted's says: *I'm not going to let you down. I promise this will all be worth it.*

With one hand, Ted dislodges the walkie on the back of his pants. "Alpha. You in position?"

A few moments of silence, and a crackle of static. "I'm here. All quiet from the front. You're good to go."

Ted swallows, returns the walkie to his waistband, and tosses the empty duffel over his shoulder. In a few moments, this bag will overflow with money and Ted will be a hero. It's this thought he defers to as he moves away from the boat and up the long, strange dock toward the mansion. *This* thought that carries him through the low iron gate that leads into the backyard of MacNeil's sprawling estate, past the sparkling pool, around to the backdoor, and allows him to—almost mechanically—unlock the door, deactivate the alarm, and step into the house as though he belongs there.

Ted doesn't waste precious moments on looking around, but from where he's entered, he can see that the mansion forks off in several directions. This central part of the home is cavernous, with tall, dark walls. To his right, he sees the staircase, and heads there at once, taking the polished wooden stairs two at a time. The whole of his focus is on reaching the study, locating the safe, and getting to work.

At the upstairs landing, Ted slips into the first door on his left and finds the study—right where Larry said it would be. Inside are sharp angles and clean, shiny spaces, walls of deep espresso and several expensive looking rugs. To the left is a wall of built-in bookshelves that boasts a neat display of books—of the boring and encyclopedic nature, Ted guesses, based on the dull-colored bindings. MacNeil's desk is to the right. Dark wood, an expansive writing space littered with papers and folders. The far wall is floor-to-ceiling windows with thick ivory curtains that drag the ground; someone has pulled these shut in MacNeil's absence, though Ted imagines the seafood mogul as a conniving and secretive man who keeps them closed on a permanent basis. MacNeil's desk faces a giant art piece: a portrait of a woman in a low-cut gown, powdering her decolletage, pale lips pulled into a coy smile.

This is what he came for.

Quick as a fox, Ted moves to the painting and drops the duffel to the floor. He drags a finger along the right edge of the frame and locates the latch with ease. As the painting swings out from the wall, Ted's eyes fall to the safe concealed behind it. A small sigh of relief escapes him when he sees the safe is a Schwab Corp; this is a popular brand he's had plenty of experience with.

Ted withdraws his stethoscope from the bag with careful hands. Sinclair Parks had purchased the stethoscope for Ted at an estate sale soon before Ted's first job with The Company. He then taught him how to use it, how to press it to the safe and listen for the delicate clicks and pops that will betray its owner's unique combination code. It is this very thing Ted listens for now.

There is no air in the study; sweat has formed on Ted's brow and a drop makes its way down the bridge of his nose. He wipes it away with the back of his hand and continues, willing his ears to listen closer, harder. But it's difficult to hear anything over the sound of his own heart pounding in his chest. He's not sure how much time has passed, but it's taking longer than expected, and his hands shake.

At long last, the final number clicks into place and Ted hears the reassuring sigh of the locking mechanism as it releases, and the door of the safe pops open. A breath catches in his throat as he peers inside. Stacks and stacks of money climb the walls of the safe, and Ted guesses that five-hundred thousand is a conservative estimate of what MacNeil has hidden away in here.

Head in a daze, he reaches for the walkie. "I'm in," he says, and his voice sounds so big shooting out of the silence that he startles himself. Then, barely able to control his excitement, he adds, "And it's *a lot*."

"Woo!" Ray's voice shoots from the walkie and sends an adrenaline-fueled laugh rumbling through Ted's chest. "That a boy! Now hurry up in there."

With a wild grin, Ted yanks the mouth of the duffel bag open and tosses handfuls of money inside as quick as he can manage. There's so much of it, it's as though the safe is endless. Ted only has ten minutes before Larry leaves for Marty. He needs to hurry.

Static ripples from the walkie, and Ray's voice fills the room once more. He says, "Hey, there's someone at the end of the dock."

Ted is so focused on the task that he first regards the interruption with annoyance; they aren't supposed to be using the walkies this much and Ted needs to hurry. But the panic in Ray's voice when he radios back and says, "They're walking toward the boat," reminds Ted of the severity of this mission.

Ted snatches the walkie from the back of his pants. "What? Can you see who?"

"No, I can't see who. It's too dark. What do I do?"

"Do you have a weapon?"

"Not on me."

Dammit. Why doesn't he have a weapon? Why had no one thought to supply him with one? Why hadn't Ted thought to?

Ted's pulse quickens as he tries to think. "Okay—listen.

Climb down and grab the knife. In the salon. In the drawer—the top drawer. Go. Hurry!"

"Okay. I'm on it." Ray mutters, his voice crackling a bit from interference.

Blind to whatever is happening on the dock, Ted picks up the pace; blood thrums in his ears so loudly he nearly misses when Ray calls back a minute later. "Never mind," he says. "It's only Lar—I mean *Alpha. Son of a bitch.* That was terrifying," he breathes, relieved.

Ted's own breaths level for a moment, but then he radios back. "Wait—Why the hell is he at the dock? He's supposed to be watching the front."

"Beats me. Let me find out."

In the silence that follows, it hits him. He is exposed. Larry, for reasons unknown, has abandoned his post six minutes early, and the front of the house is now unattended. Sweat soaks through Ted's jacket as he continues to work. The earlier euphoria has evaporated, and now all he wants is to be rid of this place.

Ears still sensitive from their work with the stethoscope, Ted registers the sound of a door opening and closing somewhere downstairs. He pauses. Listens. With trembling hands, he grabs for the walkie.

"Charlie? Is Alpha still with you?"

Silence.

"Alpha? Be my eyes, man. I think I just heard a door downstairs. What's going on?"

Again, no reply. *Fuck the codenames.*

"Dammit, Larry! Where are you?" he hisses. A message that, same as the others, goes unanswered.

Moments pass where all Ted hears is the thud of his own heartbeat, then a few blasts of static on the walkie send a thrill of hope through his chest. "Hello? Can you repeat that? What's happening down there?" he stammers.

Footsteps, now. Ted is sure he hears footsteps coming up the stairs.

The walkie stays silent. Then, another crack of static and a

voice. *Ray?* A broken word slips through the speaker. "Er......
un." And a shiver climbs up his spine.

That's it. Ted can't sit around and wait for help. And he can't
get out without running into whoever is on the stairs. It's now
or never. His fingers find the side compartment of the duffel
where Larry stashed the gun. Ignorant on how to use it, he's sure
he can manage if he needs to. But his hands meet nothing but
emptiness. In a panic, Ted scans the floor, moves the bag to the
side and searches underneath, thrusts the money against the
edges, and runs his hand along the bottom of the main
compartment. But the gun is not there.

Ted's brain can't assemble the information fast enough, and
suddenly, he feels lightheaded and out of control.

"Looking for this, Ted?"

Ted whips around to the door of the study, where Larry now
stands, cradling the missing gun in his hands.

Relief comes first; a soaring rush of it. Ted's breath pushes
out in a shuddering burst as he says, "Thank God. Where did
you find that?"

But before Larry can answer, Ted's relief gives way to a
darker sensation. It's not the gun that troubles him, or that Larry
isn't rushing to return it, but rather, the way Larry *looks* as he
stands there holding the vile instrument in his hands. Because
now, Ted can see the fresh blood that splatters the front of
Larry's yellow pinstriped bowler shirt. And the expression he
trains on Ted turns the sweat to ice on his skin. "What happened
out there?" Ted asks, barely recognizing the sound of his own
voice. "Whose blood is that?"

Larry moves into the room with slow, purposeful steps. "I
needed to tie up a loose end," he says. "It's handled now.
Nothing to concern yourself with."

Ted's eyes search Larry's for signs of the truth, of what
happened at the dock while Ted was holed up in the study. "Did
someone get hurt? Where's Ray?"

At this, Larry laughs. Actually *laughs*. Ted doesn't find any of
this amusing. He is terrified. He feels as helpless as a child, and
he wants to go home.

Larry's laughter fizzles out, and then his eyes widen into a look of mock surprise. "Oh, man! You mean you haven't heard? Oh boy, you're not going to believe it. Okay, I'll tell you, but I warn you… it's a doozy.

"Ray Green… you know Ray—that weak little pantywaist who only ever pulled lookout jobs? Well… he actually had the guts to stage a *robbery* at the MacNeil mansion. Used the chartering boat him and his friend owned. Couple of cocky little bastards, they were. Must have known MacNeil was out of town. Figured this was their big chance. Stealing a man's hard-earned fortune? Pathetic," he snorts.

Ted listens as Larry paces the doorway, tossing the gun around in his hand, face alight as he spins this weird tale. Confused and stunned, Ted finds himself glued to the spot.

Larry keeps talking.

"Little did they know, Mr. MacNeil had *me* stayin' here while he was away for business. I mean, did they *honestly* think he'd leave this place unattended? Good thing I was here, too. I came back from grabbing a pack of smokes from the corner store and caught Ray's buddy red handed. *Ted*, it was—Ted Barret. He was stuffing money into a bag right out of the old man's safe. There was a third guy, too, but I didn't get a good look at him. Now, let me tell you, I've never been so scared in all my life! Both these guys were armed. I wasn't. Lucky for me, I remembered the gun Mr. MacNeil keeps under his desk."

Larry holds up the gun in demonstration. Eyes it the way you might admire a pretty girl.

"Got to it just in time," he says. "Ted, the crazy bastard, was coming at me with a knife. But I pulled the trigger before he could damage me *too* bad. The other guy, though? Took the bag and ran. I fired at him as he took off for the stairs…"

Swift as anything, Larry turns and fires a shot straight into the stairwell. Ted jumps, petrified, the blast ringing fresh in his ears.

"… but I missed," Larry continues with a shrug. "He made off with most of the cash."

None of this makes sense. Ted is bewildered. More than

bewildered—he doesn't feel real. None of this is real. The pieces won't fall together fast enough. But he's scared beyond words. He knows that much. And he knows Larry is a filthy backstabber.

Ted musters what courage he can and says, "I have no idea what you're talking about, but this isn't a game. Who do you think you're dealing with? When Marty finds out you—"

But Larry interrupts his threat with more wild laughter. "When *Marty* finds out? Who do you think's idea this was, huh?" The hysterical laughter continues. "Well... *my* idea, but Marty's for including you two imbeciles."

Out of everything, it's *these* words that cause Ted to blanch. He is angry and scared, yes, but now he's pained with deep betrayal and embarrassment. This sudden shift in emotion clears his head enough to repeat the question he should have focused on the moment Larry stepped through the door. "Where's Ray?"

With a grimace, Larry shakes his head. "You know... it always surprises me with these guys, the trust they place in each other. Can't understand that crimes are best committed alone. When multiple people are involved, someone always gets greedy." Larry clicks his tongue. "Third guy must have decided he wanted all the money for himself and killed his pal when they got back to the dock. Sad. Can't trust a soul these days, can you?"

Ted has had enough. He reaches for his walkie. "Ray?" he speaks into it, eyes still glued on Larry. But Larry just stares back, that unsettling grin pasted on his face as though he were a mannequin.

Terror rises in Ted's throat, but he tries again. "Dammit, Ray! Answer me!"

This time, Larry's laugh is subdued. He shakes his head in amusement. "Oh, man. You're not getting it, are you? You know, I pictured myself enjoying this more, but frankly, at this point, it's become sad." He breathes out a sigh. "Okay, let me make this easy for you."

At this, Larry raises the gun and aims the barrel right at Ted's chest. Ted's eyes widen. Icy fear consumes him. When Larry speaks again, his voice is void of humor. "This was a *setup*,

Teddy. Do you know what a setup is? I'm going to kill you, Ted. I'm going to kill you, and then I'm going to take this money here—thanks for fetching that for me, by the way. Beautiful job. And I *do* mean that—I'm going to take this money, and I'm going to split it fifty-fifty with Marty. That was the deal. And I'm sad to say that you and your little pal are just necessary casualties of the job."

Larry's thumb finds the hammer and cocks the gun, eyes showing not a shred of remorse. "Sorry, Teddy. It's nothing personal. I hope you understand that. It's just business."

Ted's eyes clench, a ball of dread drops into his stomach, and thoughts of Imogene fill his mind. If he is to die here tonight, he wants her face to be the last he sees before he goes.

The shot rings out then, a shattering blast of violent sound.

Ted waits for the pain, for the lead to splinter his bones, turn them to shrapnel in his chest. But it doesn't come.

Instead, he opens his eyes to see Larry fall to the ground, that smug grin at long last wiped from his face. And just behind the fallen form of Larry Patrick is Mickey Lancaster, gun barrel still smoking.

55

TED

(JULY 27, 1963)

MICK'S GUN HOVERS THERE, AIMED in Ted's direction, but his eyes are on Larry, who attempts to sputter words through a mouthful of blood. Mick's lips draw tight as he watches the man die at his feet; his final breath comes out in a strangled gurgle.

Ted can't breathe. Too many thoughts hit him at once. *Why is Mick here? Is he in on this, too? Will Ted be the next with a bullet in him? Where is Ray? If he survives the night, what is he to do now that someone has been killed? Will he go to jail? And if he does, what happens to Imogene?*

But Mickey interrupts his thoughts when he lowers the gun and—*finally* looking at Ted—says, "Are you okay?"

How could he answer that question? Of *course,* he isn't okay. None of this is okay. But Ted says, "Fine. Yeah. I'm fine. What is this?"

With a sigh, Mickey stuffs the gun into the back of his trousers and crosses farther into the room, stepping over Larry's splayed legs as if they were nothing more than a puddle on the street. He's close enough now that Ted can smell the alcohol sweating out of him.

"I knew something was up when you mentioned the MacNeil job earlier," Mickey explains. "I hadn't heard of any jobs at the MacNeil place, and trust me, I hear of *all* the jobs. I thought, it could be that Marty is trying to cut me out. But once you dropped me off, I paid a few visits to the other big cheeses— Louis, Sinclair, Gene—and it was pretty obvious they weren't in the loop, either. That's when I pieced it together." Mickey studies Ted for a moment, then puffs out a sigh and mutters, "Which I can see you still haven't done yourself."

The room falls into silence as Mickey drops his head and rubs the bridge of his nose with thumb and forefinger. His voice is soft when he says, "I was afraid something like this would happen. But I didn't realize how far he would go. This was a setup, Ted. Marty and Larry, they… this was all them. None of us knew. Believe me."

"I'm sorry. I'm trying to understand. I—why did you come here, Mick?"

Mickey shrugs. "I don't know. But I'm glad I did. I knew something hinky was going on, so I came here and waited. When Larry showed up, I got a real bad feeling. The guy is scum. A liar, a gambler, a cheat. But he works here, so I wouldn't have thought ill of it, except I knew you guys were here, too… or would be. Trouble is, I didn't know you'd taken the boat, so I was watching the wrong side of the house the entire time." Torment crosses Mickey's face.

"I saw Larry walk to the back of the property, and five minutes later, he comes back and walks through the front. I gave it a minute before I moved around back to see what he was up to. That's when I saw your boat parked down at the dock. I ran down hoping to find you guys, hoping you were okay, but when I went inside, I…”

Mickey trails off, throat muscles bobbing beneath the tight flesh of his neck. But when his dark eyes meet Ted’s, there is the ghost of an unspeakable horror, and that haunted look is enough to paralyze him.

“Ray,” is all Mickey utters. He communicates the rest with a sorrowful shake of his head.

Realization dawns slowly for Ted; a tiny flame of what he’d feared the moment he saw the blood on Larry’s shirt. But now the reality of it grows and grows. Consumes him in an inferno of unbelievable grief. “No,” he breathes.

He’s not aware that he’s falling until his knees crash to the ground. Ted presses his palms to his eyes, hard enough to see stars swim before him, and then asks, “How?”

Mickey sits beside Ted, the heels of his black Oxfords digging into the wooden floor. “Does it matter?” he asks.

“It matters. I need to know what happened to him.”

Mickey blinks—decides—and then, in a distant voice, says, “Larry slit his throat. He bled out before I got to him.”

At this, Ted’s entire body goes rigid, and tears cloud his vision. They spill over, drenching his face in unrelenting torrents. Ted hates crying. And more than that, he hates to be *watched* while crying. But tonight, he doesn’t care. He can’t. Fortunately, if Mickey thinks less of him for it, he doesn’t say. In fact, he looks near tears himself.

“How could Marty do this? Why would he want us dead? I don’t—I just can’t make sense of this. This can’t be real.”

Mickey shakes his head, reaches out a hand as though he might comfort him, and then decides against it, pulling his hand back to his own knee. “Marty wanted money, Ted. That’s all Marty wanted—all he’s *ever* wanted. His whole ‘brothers’ thing is such horseshit. Seriously—he’s the boss, and that’s it. He’s never seen any of us as brothers.”

Ted won’t allow himself to believe it. The idea of betrayal is too much. “That can’t be true,” he says. “Maybe Larry lied. Maybe he went off plan to keep the money for himself. Marty might not have even known he—"

Mick interrupts him with a snort. "What do you think happened to the last two guys? The one's whose place you and Ray took?"

The mention of Ray's name sends another tremor of anguish through Ted. As for Mick's question, he can't answer. He has no idea what happened to the other guys. He'd never asked.

Mickey takes a deep breath and says, "Marty heard through the grapevine that these guys were going rogue. Planning something on their own. That information didn't sit too well with Marty, so he sent me and Steinfeld to sabotage the job. We were supposed to scare them off—make them leave town. One got the message and split, but the other put up a fight. Louis got carried away and shot the guy. Now Louis wouldn't be able to tell you much about the man he shot, but I can. His name was Henry Alpin. He was thirty-three. He wore glasses because of astigmatism. He worked in retail. He had a wife named Margarite and two baby girls at home—twins. They were planning a family trip to Key West in the summer. And now there he was, dead in the back of my car."

Lost for words, Ted just stares.

"I didn't sign up for this, you know—murder. I'm aware I don't have the best reputation in town. And I've gotten myself into more jams than I can count, The Company included. But murder? That's not me. It wasn't then, and it's not now.

"I figured, when we got back to headquarters, Marty would lose it on Louis for breaking protocol and putting us all in danger. But he actually *praised* him. Told him he respected him for doing what needed to be done, for *'preserving The Company's good name.'* I saw Marty's true colors that day. I learned then that he was never to be trusted, and never *ever* to be double-crossed... unless you had a death wish.

"Now, I'm not always the quickest guy. I realize that. I didn't see it until it was too late. But I *did* see it—the twinkle. Marty was furious at Henry and his buddy for planning a side job, for duping their brothers out of a payout—for duping *him*. But there was this twinkle in his eye whenever he spoke of it, like he recognized the value in such a scheme. So, I kept a watchful eye on him, waiting for the day he'd pull something like that on his own. Little good it did, of course. Because I still wasn't quick enough. And I'm sorry."

"You saved my life," Ted says, and yet, as the words leave his mouth, he thinks of the life he *didn't* save.

"Well, the night isn't over yet," Mick says. "We've got a long way to go."

"We've got to call the police." Anger washes over Ted like a tsunami. He's practically shaking with it. "Marty needs to pay for this."

Mickey laughs, a cackle of despair. "Have you not listened to a word I've said? We can't call the police."

"There's nothing else to do, Mick! Two men are dead because of Marty Camargo! One of them my best friend. I won't sit back and let him get away with this. I can't."

"You can and you will! You call the police and tell them the truth, you implicate not only us, but everyone at The Company. At the end of the day, Ray is still dead. And I'm sorry for that. God—you have no idea how sorry I am. But you and I going to jail won't change anything. The fact is, *we're* here, Ted. Not Marty. They would need to tie him to this somehow and I promise you, Marty knows what he's doing. He is a master at playing *man behind the curtain*, and before anyone can prove his involvement, he will have already sent someone to punish us. Only, we'll be in jail, won't we? So, who do you think will pay the price for our loud mouths, hm? Our loved ones. Our family, Ted. That's who!"

For the thousandth time tonight, Ted thinks of Imogene. Of her lovely hair that falls around her face in almond waves... soaked in blood. He shudders at the idea of someone finding her, hurting her, causing her even a moment's harm... because of something *he'd* done.

Mickey stands, hovering over a slumped and broken Ted, and says, "I got things I've got to live with, Ted. And now, so do you."

"What do we do?" Ted mutters.

"We're getting you out tonight. We deal with the house and the bodies, and then… we make you disappear."

At this, Ted rockets to his feet, heart beating in painful thuds. "Whoa, whoa, what do you mean *disappear?*"

Mickey meets his eyes straight-on, and says, "Ted Barret is dead. He died on that boat with Ray."

Ted moves mechanically. He can't stop to think about what he's doing, or he'll be sick, or cry again, or take off and run away, straight into Imogene's arms, the only place he truly wants to be anyhow.

He and Mick moved Larry's body downstairs and stuffed it into the trunk of Larry's car. Now, on hands and knees, they scrub the blood from the floor of MacNeil's study with bleach found in the downstairs closet. Mick cracked a window to air out the smell of disinfectant, but the chemical tang of it still coats Ted's tongue and nostrils.

His arms ache from the scrubbing. He pauses and stretches out his fingers.

"There's got to be another way, Mick," he says, as desperation seizes his heart.

Mickey blows out a puff of air, shakes a mess of dark hair from his eyes. "If you can think of one, please let me know. If Marty finds out you're alive, I promise you won't be for long."

"I can't leave Imogene. Not without an explanation. What if I just go to her and tell her I'm okay and that I need to leave for a while, but not forever? Then she'll—"

"Come on, pal. You know better than that."

"I love her," Ted says, and feels the hurt of it tighten his chest.

Mickey nods. "Then don't do that to her. Don't put that knowledge in her head. If she knows the truth about tonight, she's a liability. And that's a dangerous thing to be. If you want to keep her safe… if you want any chance of a future with her… you can't have gotten out of this alive. There can be no doubt.

None. Do you understand me?"

Ted swallows hard and his vision blurs with fresh tears. But he understands. He does. "So, what's the story, then? Larry is dead. Obviously, Marty's plan didn't work. So, what's the story?"

Mickey sits back on his heels in consideration. Then he says, "Marty put a lot of faith in Larry. He figured this would go without a hitch—blindsiding a couple young guys with only a few small jobs under their belts with the promise of riches—it should have been easy. But what if Marty underestimated you?"

Ted blinks, confused.

Mick continues. "Where things fell apart, nobody knows. But Larry ended up dead, and you missing… with all the cash."

"I don't want the money, Mick. I want to go back to before. I want this to disappear."

"Me too, pal. But it's too late. There are bullet holes in the Goddamn wall, a missing domestic, and a man waiting for his payout who is probably already suspicious that it's taking so long. So, let's pick up the pace and get out of here, yeah?"

Ted nods and returns to scrubbing.

<hr>

Ten minutes later, Ted climbs into Mick's car and Mick into Larry's. Ted is told to follow Mick south along the river to where his brother lives.

"Hank will help us," Mick assures him.

Ted nods. Too tired and scared for another argument.

As it turns out, Mick's brother lives in an impressive home on the Halifax, six miles from Walter MacNeil's place. Before Ted can even exit the car, a tall figure emerges in the towering doorway and crosses the lawn to greet Mick, who arrived moments prior.

"Hank," Mickey nods.

In a bored voice, Hank says, "It's two in the morning."

Hank Lancaster is young—younger than Ted, even— perhaps twenty-two or twenty-three. He has a soft, pale face and rich brown hair; wavy and well-maintained. Despite the unthinkable hour, Hank is dressed; black slacks and a white fitted t-shirt. Based on appearances, Ted figures Hank as a guy who's been pampered most of his life, but his expression is no-nonsense when he looks them over—at their sweat-soaked clothing smeared with blood—and says, "What is it this time, brother?"

"There's something in the trunk here I need to make disappear. The car as well, while you're at it."

In response to that, Hank asks only one question: "How gone are we talkin'? Recovered in a few days gone, or—"

"*Gone*, gone," Mick replies.

Hank nods.

"And my friend here needs identification." Mick jerks his head in Ted's direction. "And for you to forget you ever saw him."

Hank trains a wandering eye on Ted. Mulls something over in his mind. After a moment, he nods. "Come with me," he says, and he turns on his heels and makes for the house.

Ted follows.

Inside, the spotlessness of the home takes Ted by surprise. The style, he supposes, you might call *minimalist*. White, clean walls; shiny tile floors; simple furniture; no paintings or photos on the strikingly barren walls. To Ted, the house feels cold and empty and, despite the mugginess of the evening and the nerves that have kept him sweating for hours, he shivers.

Hank leads him into a cramped back room that was likely meant to be a storage closet or food pantry. Hank pulls a string that dangles from the ceiling and the room lights, revealing cardboard boxes stacked along the back wall and a long wooden table against the left, littered with papers and stacks of mail. Ted lingers in the doorway while Hank crosses to the boxes, removes the top box from the stack, and rifles through the second. Every so often, he glances back at Ted, shakes his head, and continues his search. For what—Ted hasn't the foggiest.

After several minutes more, Hank straightens and crosses to the table, slapping a flimsy paper folder in front of Ted.

"There you go," he says. "If I had more time, I could have

got you a better match, but as it is," he rolls his eyes, "this is the closest I've got."

Ted opens the folder, and he is staring at a face not unlike his own. Longer hair, paler skin, and none of his signature freckles, but the face shape matches and the eyes as well.

Behind him, Hank studies the image over Ted's shoulder. "Not an *exact* likeness, but close enough that no one will ask questions. Identification card, Social Security card, and birth certificate are all in there. Anything else you need is up to you. And I assume it goes without saying… you didn't get any of this from me."

Ted nods, once again at a loss for words. He worries he might be sick and tries his best to swallow the urge.

Hank must be not altogether convinced of Ted's understanding of the matter, because he adds, "Look, my brother obviously trusts you, or he wouldn't have brought you here. And I trust my brother. But I don't know you from Adam, so let me make myself clear. If I do you this favor and it costs me or my brother even a *moment* of trouble, I promise you will live to regret it."

Ted nods again, mouth dry as he stares at the assorted items in his hand, at the stranger's face looking back at him.

"Well then…" Hank pats Ted on the shoulder. "Enjoy your new life."

56

EMELINE

(JUNE 1, 2019)

THE FOUR OF THEM SIT wedged together on Hank Lancaster's outdated white leather sofa.

Across from them, Hank lounges in a newer, gray rocker-recliner that seems out of place from the rest of the sleek décor. A recliner of *function*, not style, Emeline decides. To Hank's left is a small end table and, to his right, a bulky oxygen machine with clear tubes sticking out. Though—despite several rather concerning coughing fits—he hasn't touched the machine since they've been here.

If you ignored the old man's raspy voice and the constant pauses for water, Hank was an excellent storyteller, and the four of them had been captivated while he spoke and hung on his every word.

At present, Hank rocks back and forth, spinning Gram's ruby ring around and around in his gnarled, weathered fingers.

It has been several minutes since anyone has spoken.

"So," Belinda says, "Ted Barret *didn't* die in the accident, then?"

"To anyone who mattered… yes—yes, he did," Hank says. "But to the few of us in the loop… Ted was very much alive."

"Damn," Geoff mutters under his breath.

Emeline chimes in then. "Did Gram know? Surely, if she had known, she would have searched for him."

Hank nods, the ring still twirling round and round. "Oh, your grandma knew, to be sure. *Eventually*, that is."

"Did she ever find him, you think?"

Emeline watches the old man, watches his lips curl into an amused grin.

After a moment, he says, "I would expect she did."

"What makes you say so?"

Hank smiles at each of them, one by one; the smile of a man who enjoys the secrets he keeps and is unlikely to give them away all at once. "Well," he says, "if she *hadn't* found him, you four wouldn't be sitting here today, would you?"

The silence that follows tells Emeline that the others are just as confused as she is.

With a grunt of effort, Hank pulls himself to the edge of his chair and says, "The name I gave to Ted Barret that night… it was Wilfred… Wilfred Baker."

57

TED

(JULY 27, 1963)

WHEN TED IS AGAIN ABLE to move, he returns to the yard. Mick emerges from the detached garage; two large cans of gasoline swing at his side. Hank watches from the shadows, hands stuffed in his pockets. He assures his brother that both the car and its *contents* will be handled by daybreak. Mick nods. "Thank you, Hank. I owe you one."

"Don't you always?" Hank says with an amused snort.

"Yeah, well—" Mick scuffs the ground with his shoe.

Hank presents a set of keys and slips them into the front pocket of Mickey's shirt; keys to a small motorboat docked out back, he explains. "A *loan*," he adds with a stare of warning.

Mick thanks his brother once more and tells him he'll return the boat first thing in the morning.

Morning.

The entire idea of sunrise and what it will bring is a concept Ted can't fathom. In the morning, Mick plans to return alone. And if he does, that means Ted has actually followed through with this ridiculous plan. To become another person, assume a new identity, start a brand-new life. How can he? He's not Wilfred Baker of Georgia. He's Ted Barret. And Florida always has and always will be his home. His entire past is here. His future. *Imogene.* Just the thought of her twists his stomach into knots. When will he see her again? How can he leave knowing that tomorrow she and the rest of the city will believe him dead? How can he do that to her—put her through the pain of losing him so completely?

Next Ted knows, he and Mick are in Hank's motorboat (funny, he can't recall boarding), and are puttering along the Halifax River. Their speed is slow, and Ted wishes they could hurry, but they mustn't draw attention to themselves.

Ted is so out of it, so bone-weary, he can't tell where on the river they are, but when The Siren becomes visible in the distance, Ted's heart thumps a hollow beat. The vessel sits at the end of MacNeil's dock, still and silent as a ghost. But it's the grisly scene he imagines *inside* that curdles Ted's guts like soured milk.

They were *just* here, Ted thinks—he and Ray. They should be celebrating right now. How, in mere hours, did things go so terribly wrong?

Mick clears his throat. "I'll uh… I'll take the charter. So, you don't have to… you know—so you don't have to see—"

Ted nods. He understands. No need to say another word.

Beneath everything, Ted is grateful for Mick and the protection he's offered him tonight; protection from more than *one* thing.

The boat slows as it approaches the dock. Mick grabs the gas cans, hoists them onto the dock ahead of him, and then makes to climb out himself. But a thought must cross his mind, because he turns back. "Give me your jacket," he says.

"My jack—What? Why?"

In a calm voice, Mick explains. "Your jacket is covered in blood. If they find it, it will help our story."

Ted's eyes fall to his favorite blue bomber jacket. Sure enough, Larry's blood soaks the front in grisly red streaks. So, it's odd this image should conjure the memory of his first date with Imogene—of the rainstorm—and running through the marina. The elated squeals pouring out of her as she clutched his jacket above her head.

What has he done?

With a sigh, Ted unzips the jacket and hands it to Mickey. He takes it with a somber nod and turns for The Siren.

"Wait!" Ted shouts.

Mick pauses again.

"The pocket." Ted's hand lunges forward in desperation. "There's something in the pocket I need to keep. *Please.*"

With a look of uncertainty, Mick returns the jacket to Ted, who fishes his hand in the inner pocket. A moment later, he withdraws the gift Ray gave him the night before the Fourth of July: a blue and gold fountain pen. Ridiculously expensive—a token of thanks and a sign of their imminent success—Ray had used his first big payouts with The Company to buy it for him. Ted clutches the pen in his hand and passes the jacket back to Mick without meeting his eyes.

A moment of silence passes, and when Mick speaks, his voice is leaden with sympathy. "We'll get you through this, pal. I promise."

Ted nods, eyes filling with tears for the hundredth time tonight. He is past the point of caring.

In a blink, Mick's face returns to business, and he issues instructions. "Follow me. Stay far enough back to ward off suspicion and keep the motor as quiet as you can. When I stop, *you* stop. I'll do what needs to be done, and then I'll swim out to you. We'll figure out the rest then. Got it?"

Ted nods again, unable to do anything else.

———

How much time has passed? It feels like hours.

Ted has followed Mickey out into the Atlantic, farther than he and Ray have ever taken their fishing tours. With no signs of slowing, Ted has no choice but to settle into his thoughts. And tonight, that is a dangerous place to be.

Ted is vaguely aware of the duffel bag full of money at his feet—more aware *still* of Ray's body growing cold in the boat in front of him. There is the un-real knowledge that he'll never see his best friend again. And that his family will never learn the truth of what happened here tonight. Ted is leaving everyone he loves and cares for with painful, unanswerable questions, and he alone has set these terrible events in motion. And rather than take responsibility for what he's done, for the devastation he's caused, he is running and leaving everyone else to gather the pieces.

He fights the urge to turn back. To go home. Face the music. But Mick's voice keeps slipping into his thoughts, reminding him he's doing this for Imogene. To keep her safe. There are no other options.

Finally, The Siren stalls in front of him. As instructed, Ted stills the motor on Hank's boat, plunging himself into an unnerving silence. As Ted waits, time behaves by its own rules; moments stretch toward the infinite horizon, swallowed by the dark. For the longest time, Ted's only companion is the thunderclap of waves. The roar of his savage thoughts. Then, he sees Mick dart onto the main deck of The Siren and jump over the side; he hits the water with a nasty splash. Ted hoists himself forward, heart pounding, and scans the dark water for Mickey. He puffs out a breath of relief when a dark head breaks the surface and begins to swim.

Mick is panting when he reaches the motorboat, and Ted helps pull him up and over the side. Mickey rights himself, catches his breath, clothes soaked and stuck to him like a second skin. It is only now that Ted sees the first lick of flames spread over The Siren.

Mick lifts his shirt and pulls a wad of tarp from inside the waistband of his pants. It's been folded several times and wrapped thoroughly with tape. Mick hands the parcel to Ted, who takes it with a look of confusion. "What's this?" he asks.

"I went through Ray's pockets before…" he trails off. "I, uh… I found a letter. Thought maybe you should have it."

Ted looks at the parcel as if it's a bomb set to detonate. "What does it say?"

"I didn't read it. Not my place."

Ted nods, his eyes on the bundle of tarp. He's more than curious to discover what Ray might have been carrying around with him, but he can't force his fingers to open the package. He's not ready. Not yet. Besides, the fire has caught, and Ted can do nothing but stare at the dismal scene before him.

They sit for a while like that. Ted watches in terror as the blaze continues to grow, a wild wall of twisted flames raised against the night sky.

The enormity of what they've done, of what he must *still* do, finally snaps into place. "That's all that's left of my old life, isn't it?" Ted asks.

Mick watches him from across the boat, black hair dripping with sea water, face creased with the memories of the night. "At least you get to say goodbye to it," he says. "Take a few minutes more. But then we've got to go."

Ted steers first. He needs to do something. Keep himself busy. Across from him, Mick counts the money in the duffel bug. He works in silence, but now and then he breathes a sigh of amazement and shakes his head.

The humidity aids in Ted's overwhelming discomfort. Even in motion, with wind whipping his hair, the night clings to his skin. He isn't sure of the time. Must be three, four in the morning at this point. But Ted can't think of sleep after what he's done. For now, the water is quiet. But in another hour or so, the first fishermen will venture out to start their day. Wherever Mick is taking him, they best hurry and get there.

At last, Mick returns the final stack of cash to the duffel bag and zips it shut, slow and steady. He leans forward, arms on his knees, hands clasped in front of him, and waits for Ted to meet his eyes. "Five hundred and sixty-five thousand," he says.

Mick's eyes glimmer at the number, but this news does zilch for Ted. Last night, the prospect of forty-five thousand dollars had thrilled him. Now over half a million sits at his feet and he couldn't care less. He nods, saying nothing.

"Let me take over for a while," Mick says.

They switch places, and the boat tilts dangerously beneath them. Ted plops onto the aluminum seat at the bow of the pint-sized watercraft.

Another silence settles between them. Ted can't allow himself to think just now. He can't. "Why—I mean, how did you end up working for Marty, anyway?" Ted asks.

Mick sighs. "I, uh—suppose you might say I hit a bit of a rough patch. I drink a bit, see. I get a little carried away. A few years ago, my family cut me out of the business because of my... *habits*. But it took a bit before folks around town got the message I was no longer toting Lancaster money in my pockets. One night after—uh... *several* drinks, I suppose I bought a few rounds for some folks at the bar... like... seventy-two rounds, to be exact. Only, I didn't exactly have the money to foot a bill that size. At the end of the night, I'd racked up over two-hundred bucks on my personal tab. Jerry, the owner, he knew me. Knew I was good for it. Only, I wasn't. Not anymore. So, I walked out. Two nights later, I'm sloshed out of my mind, and just dumb enough to go back. Two guys grab me and drag me back to the kitchen, and there's Jerry, demanding his money. When I told him I didn't have it, that I'd work off the tab, he said he didn't want a drunk stinking up his kitchen—he wanted his due. The boys that grabbed me must have thought that sinking their boots into my rib cage a few good times might jar some change loose." He snorts at this recollection.

"Anyway, in the middle of my beating, in walks this man. He's massive. All business. I'd never seen him before. But Jerry knew him, and so did the guys acquainting their heels with my kidneys. Just like that, the beating stopped. After a brief inquiry as to what I was being punished for, the man offers to pay my debt and even pay upfront for another round of beer for the both of us. Then he helped me up, dusted me off, introduced himself as Marty Camargo, and took me out to the bar where we sat and drank and talked. Marty said to me, 'You know, I got a way to keep cash in your pocket and boys like that off your back.' The rest, as they say, is history…"

Mick trails off, eyes on the water ahead.

"He bought me for two-hundred bucks and a beer," Mick says. "And I let him."

Ted swallows, lost for words.

"See, with new recruits, there's two types of guys Marty sniffs out: guys with big dreams, and guys who already squandered their dreams away. Both can be bought. When a man's dreams are on the table, I reckon there's not much he *wouldn't* do to protect them… even sell his soul straight to the Devil."

And what was Ted's dream worth? The life of his best friend? Losing Imogene? His own identity? No. It wasn't worth any of that.

"Where are we heading?" Ted asks.

"I'm familiar with a small pier in Jacksonville. It's as good a place as any. We aren't far. Maybe twenty minutes."

Ted nods. Mick is right. It doesn't matter where he goes. Wherever he lands, he'll be a stranger.

And then Ted remembers the bundle of tarp in his pocket. He pulls it out and turns it over in his hands, debating whether to open it now or wait until he gets wherever he's going. Decided, he cracks open the tape and pulls back the wrapping. Mick watches him, pretending not to, but doesn't say a word.

Inside is an envelope, folded over twice. On the front, in black ink, is the word: *Raymond.* Ted opens the envelope and pulls out a piece of paper. It is a note from Athena, dated yesterday.

Raymond —

I'm sorry. I don't know what else to say. I wish things were different. You know I do. I love you with all my heart. In a different world, we'd marry, buy a little house somewhere far away, and raise our child together. But we both know my parents will never allow it. I'm scared, Raymond. I don't want to lose you or the life we created together... even if we didn't mean to. But my parents are right. They will never accept it in this world. A baby with a white father and a black mother? What kind of life would it have? Still...

Dad says he's taking me somewhere up north in a day or two where they can "help" me. But I know what that means. It means when I come home, I won't be pregnant no more. I'm so scared. I don't want this. I want the baby. I want you. I want you both. I pray you'll still love me when I get back. I pray you will forgive me. I hope I can forgive myself. I love you. Always and forever. ~Athena.

Ted must have stopped breathing while he read the letter because his lungs burn when he sucks in a gulp of air, and he feels faint.

Beneath Athena's note, Ray had scribbled a response, but hadn't finished.

Don't do this, Athena. Please. Don't let them decide this for you. For us. I love you and I love the baby, whoever he or she ends up becoming. And I will give you both an amazing life. The most perfect life ever. Please trust me. This is our responsibility and our choice... not theirs. I get a say in this, too. Please don't let them do this. I promise I'll

His words stop there.

Athena is pregnant with Ray's child.

It doesn't seem real, yet it explains Ray's funk yesterday. He was sad and afraid and angry and likely felt there was no one in which he could confide. So, he tried to put his thoughts into words, to get one last message to Athena before she went and made a huge mistake. But now, she'll never get that message. She'll never know how he felt, how much he wanted the baby, how much he loved her.

More tears sting Ted's eyes, and he doesn't try to stop them.

After a moment, he composes himself and says, "Ray's girl is pregnant."

"Oh, damn," Mick mutters.

"Her folks want her to abort. Her dad is taking her today or tomorrow. But Ray wanted to keep it. He wanted…" Ted can't bring himself to finish. He lets his fingers trace Ray's handwriting, hating himself more than he ever imagined possible. "Can you look into it, do you think?"

Mick nods, his bloodshot eyes slick with suppressed tears. "I will. Yeah. I'll see what I can do."

"Thank you," Ted mutters.

A few minutes later, Mick pulls the boat alongside a strange pier. Everything here is quiet and dark; one lone light post flickers over the dock. Mick climbs out and ties the boat to an empty hitch. He then extends a hand to Ted.

As Mick pulls Ted to his feet, everything hits him at once. This is no longer a hypothetical situation. What's happening to him now is very real. And in a few minutes, he will be alone. No one to talk to. No one to share his secret with. He won't even be Ted anymore. He checks his pockets for his pen, Ray's note; all that remains of his old life. He's tucked the folder with his new identity into the back of his pants, covered with his t-shirt. Inside, his heart judders, his bones are heavy and tired. This is a nightmare from which he will never wake. Panic rushes through him.

"Mick—I'm… I'm not ready. I can't—I can't do this."

Mick places his hands on Ted's shoulders and looks him in the eyes, and in a slow and direct voice, says, "You can. You can do this. One step at a time, yeah? I'll go back… just until the dust settles. I need to get a handle on how Marty reacts when the news breaks. Make sure he doesn't suspect anything. If he does, I'll do my best to deter him. One week. I will be back here in *one week*. Noon. Here at this dock. Can you make sure you're here?"

Ted nods.

"Good. Just get somewhere safe and lay low." Mick jumps into the motorboat and tosses the duffel up to Ted.

"Whoa. No! I don't want this. Keep it. I'm serious—I want nothing to do with that."

Mick raises an eyebrow. "And how are you going to live without money? Think realistically, pal. Take it. I'll get my cut in a week when we meet again."

Mick starts the motor, and the sound reignites Ted's nerves. A fisherman and his son are heading down the pier now, getting an early start to their day. The boy carries a tackle box. He can't be more than six. Ted tries hard to straighten the features on his face, to not fall apart again.

"Keep an eye on Imogene, Mick. Can you—can you please do that for me?"

Mick nods. Sincerity floods his expression. "I will," he says. "You have my word. No one will lay a hand on her."

58

BELINDA
(JUNE 1, 2019)

S HANK FINISHES ANOTHER CHUNK of his story, the four of them are once again moved to silence. Bits of their history, things they've always known to be true, are far more complex than they ever suspected.

Geoff is the first to speak.

"So, you're telling us that Ted Barret, who supposedly died in 1963, is in fact our *grandfather*, Wilfred Baker? And Gram just never told us any of this?"

"That's the long and short of it," Hank says, his attention still fixed on the ring in his hand. He turns it over and over, inspecting it in much the same way Stanton had earlier, his own eyes no doubt keener than the magnifier his son had used. "I never thought I'd lay eyes on *this* thing again," he muttered.

"So, the ring *is* from your shop, then?" Wyatt asks.

Hank nods. "Certainly is." Before he can elaborate, he breaks into a fit of coughs and spits something nasty into a wadded-up handkerchief. After a moment of looking rather winded and worn, he tosses the handkerchief to the table beside him. Belinda wonders how many times he's used that napkin and stifles a gag.

"Sorry," she starts. "But what I'm not understanding is how our grandfather bought this ring from your store here in Daytona when he left town that night and never returned."

Hank chuckles. "Well, first of all, I never said he didn't return, did I? And second, your grandfather didn't buy this ring."

"Sure, he did." Belinda reaches to take the ring from the old man. Maybe she was wrong, and his eyes *weren't* as good as they used to be. Clearly, he'd missed the inscription. "Right here," she says, turning the ring so he can see the engraving inside.

Not wanting to embarrass the man after the kindness he'd shown them, she keeps her voice light and sweet. "*I + W*, see? Imogene and Wilfred. So, that means he had to have bought this *after* the accident. After he changed his name."

Hank trains his eyes on the inscription and chuckles again. "Ah, yes, I get how you would think that," he says, and shakes his head in amusement. "Sometimes it's easier to see things the way we want to, isn't it? Problem is, you've been looking at this all wrong."

The old man sucks his teeth, takes the ring between his thick fingers once again, flips it upside down, and hands it back to Belinda. "Not *I + W*, I'm afraid. *M + I*. Mickey and Imogene. My brother bought this ring for your grandmother back in 1964."

59

WILFRED

(AUGUST 3, 1963)

ILFRED TURNS INTO THE PARKING lot of Fresco's Seaside Bistro in Jacksonville. Beyond the restaurant is the pier where Mickey dropped him off last week.

The truck he drives is a beat-up 1957 Chevy, bright orange. The automobile was driven hard and sold cheap and is registered to one Wilfred Baker. The whole thing is still unbelievable to him.

After Mick left, Wilfred sat on a bench at the pier for a long while, unsure what to do or where to go. Finally, an hour past sunrise, an old man gave him directions to the bus station, and he'd taken a Greyhound seventy miles north into a coastal town in Georgia called Brunswick. There he found a cheap family-run motel and got himself a room. For the past week, he'd mostly slept, walked, and drank.

But now he is eager to see Mick. To find out what people are saying about the robbery and the fire, but mostly, to hear of Imogene. He prays Mick will bring news of her.

Mick arrives ten minutes late. The sight of him puttering up to the pier in Hank's old boat takes the sting from the nerves that have lurched within Wilfred since he left the mansion. But adrenaline and the need for information is what fuels him. He is halfway down the pier before Mick can even climb out and secure the tiny vessel to the dock. In place of a greeting, Wilfred says, "How's Imogene?"

Mick smiles. "She's fine. As well as she *can* be, all things considered."

A flood of relief at once yields to a sudden rush of loss and regret. "So, she thinks I'm…"

Mick nods. "Yeah. Yeah, everyone does, pal. But that's good news. That's what we want, right?"

Wilfred nods, though he isn't sure he wants that at all. He was not thinking clearly that night.

"And Ray?"

Mick purses his lips. "Let's walk," he says.

They find themselves in the front seat of Wilfred's truck. An Elvis tune croons from the radio. People pass by the truck on their way to the restaurant for lunch, and others carry little take-home bags on their way out. A seagull happily chomps on a fry outside Wilfred's window.

Over the next twenty minutes, Mick tells Wilfred everything that has happened in his absence. He listens. Hears the words. But it feels as if Mick speaks of someone else. Not him. Not *his* life.

"They found The Siren before I even made it back. I'd just returned the boat to Hank, made sure he'd… taken care of everything on his end, and was heading home to clean up when I saw the flashing lights. They were towing the boat to shore. I wasn't sure they'd even *found* Ray until later when the news broke about a recovered body.

"Now Marty… he was a tough one. When I got to headquarters around noon, he'd heard of the accident. Pretty sure the whole town had by that point. I played dumb. Asked him what you two would have been doing out there. Asked him if he'd sent either of you on a job. But he denied it. Said he didn't know. He was angry, though. I could tell. They found your jacket, but Marty didn't seem convinced you were dead. Here's where it gets funny: when Larry didn't turn up, Marty sent me out to look for him. Fed me this line about Larry owing him money. Easiest job he ever sent me on," Mick laughs. "When I reported back, I told him Larry was gone and hadn't been to work in days. In fact, someone robbed MacNeil's place while the old man was away for business, and Larry was the likeliest to have done it. Just like that, Marty changed his opinion. Now he was telling the guys that you and Ray probably got mixed up with some bad men and gotten yourselves killed. So, that's where we are now. I can't be sure, but Marty is likely under the assumption that Larry double-crossed him, killed you both, took the money and ran. He's been in a right foul mood, I'll tell ya."

"And the accident? What are they saying happened?"

Mick shakes his head. "No one knows for sure. The big mystery is what you guys would have been doing out that far. But that's good! They've been sending searches out every day, although most folks know the odds of finding you alive is slim."

Wilfred swallows, shuddering.

"There's something else," Mick says, an air of apprehension in his voice.

Wilfred just stares. How much worse could things get?

"Well… Ray. He was… *burnt*, of course." Mick speaks hesitantly, aware of every word choice. "But… the medical examiner was circling around the cut in his throat. Luckily, he's a friend of the family. Known him since grade school. So I went down that afternoon to speak to him. He said his opinion was that the accident looked suspicious, and he hoped his findings would help the police get to the bottom of it. I… may have paid him off to change that opinion."

"You *what?*"

"I had to. If I hadn't, there… there would have been an investigation, Ted!"

"It's Wilfred now, in case you forgot." He doesn't hide the bitterness in his voice.

"Wilfred. Right," Mick stammers. "Sorry."

"So, you're telling me there's someone out there who believes Ray was *murdered?* And who now knows *we* were involved?"

Mick shakes his head. Adamant. "That *I* was involved. Not we. He, like everyone else, thinks you're at the bottom of the Atlantic Ocean right now."

Wilfred squeezes his eyes shut. Drops his head.

"I'm sorry," Mick says. "That was insensitive. But, no, he changed his report. No one will be the wiser. I promise."

"How on earth did you afford that?" Wilfred asks, for it's common knowledge that Mick's family cut him out of their finances when he started drinking himself silly and soiling the Lancaster name.

Mick flushes. "Like Hank said… I always owe him one."

Wilfred nods. *Hank.* He should have guessed.

Then, remembering, he says, "Athena! Did you find out anything? About her? About the baby?"

Mick turns solemn. "I looked into it, yeah. She's… she's gone, pal. Her mom says she's gone to a girl's camp and will be back in two weeks. Wherever she is, I doubt she even knows about the accident yet. But as for the baby, it looks like we're too late."

Wilfred nods again. After a week in the dark, he'd hoped that news from home—answers to the many unknowns—might rid this horrible weight in his chest. But he feels heavier than ever.

"Is that it then?"

"For now," Mick says.

Wilfred pulls the duffel from beneath his seat and passes it to Mick. "Your cut," he says, staring out the window at the ravenous seagull.

To his right, he hears Mick unzip the bag, and then, "Whoa! No. This is way more than half, Wil."

"It's all of it," Wilfred agrees. "Minus what I took for the truck and enough for another month's rent at the motel. The rest… I told you—I want no part of it. I never want to see that money again. It's yours."

Disbelief flashes in Mick's eyes. He taps the duffel a couple times. "I… I don't know what to say."

Silence fills the cab, and it stays that way for a moment, until Mick says, "I'll keep watching over Imogene for you. I will. I'll call and check in with you next week. Okay?"

Wilfred only nods.

With a soft, tired voice, Mick says, "I'm sorry, Wil. I am. I'm sorry this is happening to you. I mean that. You don't deserve it. I wish to God I would have gotten to the dock before Larry that night. I hesitated. And because of that, Ray is dead and you're here. This is all my fault, and I'll never forgive myself."

Wilfred watches Mick's eyes fill with tears. The guilt he must feel doesn't surprise Wilfred in the least.

But he's wrong about everything.

"No," Wilfred says, eyes drifting out the window once more. "Ray is dead because I got him mixed up in something neither of us should have been involved in. He wanted out a long time ago, and I convinced him to stay. He's dead because of *me*."

60

IMOGENE

(SEPTEMBER 1963)

A MONTH HAS PASSED SINCE Ted's memorial.

A month.

Though time has moved much slower than that for Imogene.

Since the accident, she has received two letters from Greta. Neither said anything of importance. She used to be so good at making small talk, her words painting a vivid picture of her life in Virginia. But now Greta is as lost as Imogene, doing her best to stay afloat in the wake of tragedy.

School started two weeks ago, and Imogene is trying. Honest, she is. But sitting there in class as her nasal-voiced professor drones on and on—about anatomy, recognizing the signs of infection, the practices for safe medication administration—is too much for her.

For Imogene's entire life, she's known she wants to help people. Was sure this was her way to earn a place in the world. But then she'd met Ted. And lost him just as fast.

The official story is that Ted and Ray were both killed in a horrible accident, in which their boat caught fire off the coast of Ormond Beach. What happened that night remains a mystery, and odds are they will never get the answers they seek. Imogene and the Greens must live the rest of their lives worrying over the events that led to the death of those two beautiful souls, with so much life and love left to give.

Why were they out there?

Did they try to save each other?

What were they thinking in their last moments?

Did they know they were dying?

Was it quick?

Did they suffer?

Imogene can't bear to imagine Ted in any level of pain. Yet she does. She thinks of it constantly. Whenever she closes her eyes, she sees his body sink in the ocean, lungs full of water and smoke, sharks and barracudas tearing him limb from limb. And with that, her heart breaks anew.

Imogene couldn't save Ted from his cruel fate. She can't save the Greens from the nightmare they are surely living. And she can't save herself from the sadness and grim fantasies that consume her every waking moment.

She can't save anyone.

61

WILFRED

(JUNE 1964)

TED BARRET IS A DISTANT MEMORY.

Only two people, Mickey and Hank Lancaster, know that Ted is alive and well. Everyone else either believes him dead or calls him Wilfred.

As it turns out, Wilfred and Ted are nothing alike. Wilfred plans. He calculates. He doesn't make mistakes. Ted dreamed. Wilfred has nightmares. Horrible nightmares. The kind that wakes him with such tremors he sits in a cold sweat for hours, stunned, unable to move. It is a rare day when Wilfred clocks more than a few hours of sleep. Ted loved to relax, to breathe in the day, let it drift over him however it pleased. Wilfred works hard and keeps pushing and fills his days with movement to avoid the thoughts; all the thinking he wishes he could stop.

After that first meeting with Mick, Wilfred found a job at a fish processing plant and saved his money; money he'd earned the honest way. Money that *hadn't* cost someone their life.

Mick's phone calls came like clockwork every other Saturday at ten PM. These calls became the marks on the calendar that drove Wilfred forward. Mick talked of Daytona, the people he used to know. There was a memorial, he said. Cathy Marsh, his foster mother, had put it together. This moved Wilfred, as he hadn't spoken to his foster mother in years and always thought she never especially cared for him. According to Mick, Imogene had attended alone; he'd sat across the aisle from her.

Three months ago, Sinclair Parks died of a heart attack. Wilfred told Mick he was sorry to hear this, though if not for Sinclair, he and Ray would never have found The Company, and Ray would still be alive, so he guesses he isn't that sorry at all.

Apparently, Wilfred lacks empathy as well.

But the stories of Imogene are what keep him waiting by the phone, tapping his foot as he listens for the first note of the ring.

She'd started school last fall. She works evenings at Edmund's Drug near the university. Mick says her hair is shorter now; she cut it and wears it loose. And she still lives at home with her parents in Deland. This last bit tears at Wilfred's heart, because here is the evidence of his broken promise to her. He was supposed to take her away from there. But he'd failed her.

Tonight is Saturday.

When Mick calls, Wilfred gives him a new address. Next week, he's moving two hours west to Valdosta and getting on in construction. Rumor had it there was a surge of growth out there and plenty of work to go around. More work with better pay.

A stroke of good luck had led Ted to a studio apartment above a barbershop. Affordable rent. Water and electric included. Another breeze of good fortune blew him to a unionized construction company. The crew was to begin work on a residential neighborhood and was desperate for day laborers.

"I'll get a phone and send word as soon as I can," he tells

Mick.

Mick wishes him luck and hangs up the phone.

62

IMOGENE

(SEPTEMBER 1964)

IMOGENE, ENCUMBERED WITH BOOKS AND fatigue, trudges across the bright green lawn of the university. She sees her car in the distance, waiting in the busy lot. There is nothing she wants more than to get inside. To stop smiling. Stop pretending. To drive for a while in silence.

Davey Lumsden falls into step beside her. "Hey Imogene," he says with a sniffle. Davey is always sniffling. Allergies, he says. "Heading home already?"

Imogene offers a polite smile and nods. "My early day."

Davey's expression crumbles. "Oh, that's too bad. I was going to ask if you wanted to grab a burger with me after you finished. I forgot you don't have Rogan's class today. Maybe I could accompany you to dinner or something instead?"

Imogene blinks in surprise. She had guessed that Davey was interested in her; he'd been less than subtle with his attentions. But this is the first time he's asked for a date outright. Imogene would not call Davey handsome. But he isn't plain either. He has straight, red hair that always looks freshly shampooed, cut like George from The Beatles. Rail thin and tall, he towers over Imogene, but he dresses smart and has a lovely smile.

But he's not her type.

Or perhaps he is.

Who knows anymore?

"Oh, I'm sorry, Davey. I'm actually not feeling very well today. I think I might head home. Maybe another time." Imogene takes her leave and walks with hurried steps to the parking lot.

"Oh, okay, sure," he says, and she tries to ignore the disappointment in his voice when he adds, "Feel better, Imogene."

———

But Imogene doesn't go home.

Instead, she drives to Daytona, just as she's done every Wednesday afternoon for the past month. Classes end early on Wednesdays, and her parents go out with their church group after service. The evening is hers.

The White Horse Saloon faces A1A and the beach, and it is here where Imogene huddles over a pink drink and lets her thoughts go fuzzy.

The first time she came here was after an unsettling dream, in which Ted appeared to her. Of course, she often dreams of Ted, but this one had been so *real.* He'd held her, and there was the stroke of fingertips on skin, the unmistakable heat of his body through their clothing. When he spoke, breath warmed her face. When he kissed her, her lips seemed to burn from it. While she lay alone, snug in her bed, her mind delivered a version of Ted so close to the real thing that when she woke, she swore she could still feel the places his hands had touched. The memory of him ignited her from the inside out. She was alive. Effervescent. Just as she'd been before. The day wore on and—though she'd tried to hold the feeling, to trap it in her chest—by mid-morning, the glow of the dream had faded. She'd lost him.

So, she came here.

To Daytona. To the beach.

She is not sure why, exactly.

She supposes it was to walk around, to be back in this place, to be near him again. Back to their past. To those feelings from last summer before everything crashed to a halt.

But being here only reminded her how much time had passed, and how little they had of each other.

For the past year, time has played such cruel tricks on Imogene. The nights creep along at a pace so despairingly slow she fears she'll never make it through. In the quiet of her room, she suffers through the heavy thrum of each heartbeat as it echoes off the empty spaces Ted used to fill; each breath harder to take than the last. And yet, during the day, huge chunks of time disappear as she loses herself in thoughts. Hours gone to the dark recesses of her mind. And she wonders how she can carry on this way, feeling so much so deep for so long.

But that dream had corrected the timeline. Brought Imogene back to herself. Right back to last summer. So vividly did he appear to her. Every tiny detail of him restored in perfect clarity. But as she stood there at the beach on that first day, she'd tried to summon his face again, and could only manage a hazy, watercolor version of the real thing.

And that was scariest of all.

Because she *knew*... she was forgetting him.

Without another thought, she'd run across the street, right through the doors of The White Horse Saloon, and ordered a drink.

Imogene had never drunk in a bar before—or *anywhere*—but she didn't know what else to do. At first, she felt nothing. So, she ordered another. But when she stood to use the lady's room, the floor tipped ever so slightly beneath her feet and blurred the edges of everything around her—softened them. It was pleasant, she thought. It was like… dreaming.

So Imogene returned to the bar and ordered another.

Now, four weeks later, Imogene finds a sense of calm here. She is closer to Ted in this place. Closer to herself.

Outside, the sky goes dark. How long has she been here? How many drinks has she had? She is usually home long before now. Time got away from her.

Jacob, the bartender, who she met a couple weeks ago, wipes the counter and clears a glass. "Ready for another, Imogene?" he asks.

She gestures to her half-full glass and politely declines.

Over the chatter of the bar, a fuzzy chime rings out, and moments later, Imogene senses someone to her right. She risks a glance, and sure enough, there is a man. He leans on his elbows to hang over the counter. To speak to Jacob, who crouches to restock the glasses on the shelf beneath the bar. They share a laugh over a joke that Imogene must have missed.

She lifts her drink to take a sip, but when she returns the glass to the counter, it hits with a force much harder than intended. For the first time, Imogene worries she may have overindulged. Her brain and her hands move at different speeds.

For fear of sounding ridiculous, she decides not to ask Jacob how many drinks she's had. Jacob has been nothing but nice each time she's come in, and she'd hate for him to think he's over-served her. Or that she is a terrible drunk. Or a baby who can't hold her liquor. But she worries over the hour and the obvious issue of how she is to safely get home in this condition.

Water. That's what people drink when they've had too much, right?

"May I have a water, please?" she mutters to Jacob, who has just passed a beer to the man beside her.

Jacob smiles and nods. The man clears his throat and says, "Pardon, Miss. Is that chair taken?"

Confused, Imogene turns to the seat beside her. Her bag is there. That's right, she'd sat it there earlier when she arrived. But the bar is busier now, and no other seats remain. How did she miss that?

"No, I apologize," she says, and hurries to move her bag. The man watches as she clumsily hangs the strap on the back of her barstool.

A moment later, Jacob brings the water, and Imogene notes the concern in his smile when he places it in front of her. She smiles and takes the glass as smoothly as she can. After the alcohol, the water leaves a strange taste on her tongue, and she can take only the smallest sips.

"Rough day at school?"

Imogene startles and her head whips to the man beside her. For the first time, she allows her gaze to linger on him. The man has hair so dark it verges on black, worn long and tucked behind his ears. The fairest skin. Eyes of the deepest brown—trained on her.

Imogene could swear she's seen him before, but can't quite place it. "Pardon? But how do you...?" she stammers.

The man only nods to her bag. At the textbooks poking from the top.

"Oh. My books." Imogene's cheeks burn hot as she continues to sip her water, wondering how long before she sobers enough to leave. "Yeah. I—kind of. Yes. A rough day," she says. "You're rather observant."

The man shrugs. "It's a gift."

With one sip, he drains half the bottle, and then runs a hand over his mouth, over his scruff of facial hair. Angling his body to hers, he says, "I can do better. Are you ready?"

Imogene gives him the go-ahead with a nod and a hesitant shrug.

"You're new to drinking. I'd say..." He takes a quick assessment of her. "Less than a month."

Imogene blinks. "How...?"

But the man just laughs and points to her glass, the half-empty one that Jacob has yet to clear away. "That's a vodka and cranberry, if I'm not mistaken. Or, as most prefer to think of it, a *sissy drink*. Light and fruity. Perfect for new drinkers. And you're young. Those are college textbooks, so I'd guess eighteen or nineteen at most. So, unless you've been drinking illegally, you haven't made a career of it, like me. Am I close?"

"Close," Imogene says, and the man finishes his beer.

When Jacob brings him another, Imogene downs her water and asks for more. "Sure thing," he says, and scurries off for a fresh glass.

When Jacob returns with the water, he smiles at Imogene and turns a wary eye to the man beside her. "Thank you," Imogene says, and Jacob moves along to help another customer. The place is really filling up now.

"The bartender thinks you're pretty," the man says after a few moments. "And he doesn't care much for me talking to you. He's looked over here no less than five times."

Imogene looks at the man, raises an eyebrow, and then glances over to Jacob, who, sure enough, is staring in their direction. He turns hastily away, and a violent blush creeps up his neck. Imogene turns back to the man with an amused laugh. "How on Earth? I hadn't noticed."

He shrugs. "Well, I don't deserve credit for that one. He's doing a terrible job at hiding it."

Imogene laughs.

"But really, it's all in the details. That lady there, for instance," he says, pointing to a woman four seats over. "She's been stood up. Notice the way she keeps glancing at the door, and then checking her watch. There are two empty glasses sitting in front of her and the bartender took a third away right as I came in. So, she's been here a while, yet talking to no one. Not waiting for her girlfriends; she's far too dolled up for that. She wants to leave. You can tell. But she's not quite ready to call it. Poor thing.

"And that guy over there." He points to an older gentleman at the table behind us. "He lost his left testicle in the war. Got blown clean off. *Boom*!" He makes an explosion gesture with his hands.

Imogene's eyes widen, but as she opens her mouth to speak, the man laughs.

"Alright, I'm completely joking about that last bit. I have no idea." Another laugh spills out of him, and this time, Imogene joins.

He has a wonderful laugh, this man. As his grin widens, Imogene notices that his top teeth have a crooked slant to them. But it adds a bit of character, she thinks. An air of youth and charm. What's more, she notices that throughout this exchange, they have subconsciously angled toward one another, and their knees nearly touch beneath the counter. But her thoughts are so thick with drink, she doesn't move away.

"Mickey Lancaster," he says then, extending his hand.

"Imogene Elkins," she says, and she gives his hand a shake.

"Pleased to meet you, Imogene. That's a lovely name."

"Thank you," she mutters. She sucks her bottom lip between her teeth, testing it, but her lips are still tingly and numb. Shouldn't the water be helping?

After a third glass of water, her head is pounding and her stomach churns. "If you'll excuse me," she mutters, hearing herself slur on the *s's*. "I need to use the lady's room."

Everything is in a haze. It's as though she's watching herself from somewhere else, from somewhere outside her body. As her feet touch the floor and she takes a step, she stumbles and nearly falls. But Mickey's arms find her and pull her upright. "Are you okay?" he asks.

"I don't know," she says. "I stopped drinking a while ago. I…"

Jacob rushes over then, holding Imogene on her other side. "You okay, Imogene? I didn't think you drank that much. You can't drive home like this."

Imogene nods, only half hearing him. "No, I know." But all she can focus on is how tired she is. How desperately she wants to close her eyes.

Jacob leans close to her ear, and she cringes at the moist breath that's now on her cheek. "Look, I can dip out of here early," he says. "It's not a problem. You can come home with me until you're well enough to drive."

"No," Imogene shakes her head. A sluggish attempt, but still. "No. I'm fine. I just need to rest a bit. I'll be fine."

But it hurts to talk. Everything hurts.

"Nonsense. I'll take care of you. Don't worry." Imogene senses the exchange of power as Jacob attempts to pull her from Mickey's grasp. "I got it from here, Mick. Thanks."

But Mickey doesn't let go. In fact, his grip tightens.

There's an edge to Mickey's voice when he says, "How many did you serve her?"

"Just a few. Three. Four *tops*. Honest. Look, I'll just bring her back to my place, let her sleep it off. I live close. It's not a problem. Things like this happen all the time around here."

"I bet they do," Mickey says. He releases her arm and goes for her water glass instead, puts it to his nose and then takes a small sip. Imogene watches his face go pale with recognition and then bright red with anger. "You son of a bitch," he growls, turning on Jacob. "There's vodka in this!"

Jacob blanches. "I don't know what you're talking about."

Mickey slams the water glass onto the counter and then helps Imogene back onto her barstool, where she watches the scene through dizzy eyes.

Mickey turns back to Jacob, fuming, their faces now inches apart. "She's a nice girl, you candyass!"

Jacob's hands raise in surrender. "Whoa. Calm down. What's your bag, man?"

"Dirtbags like you," Mickey says through clenched teeth. "Although, with a face like yours, it's no wonder you can only score girls after you've gotten them blitzed out of their minds."

With a red face and clenched fists, Jacob glances around to see if anyone has heard.

"Come on, Imogene," Mickey says, one hand on her arm, one around her waist. "Let's get you home."

***

Next Imogene is aware, she's in the passenger seat of her own car. Her head rests against the window, which is cracked to let a warm breeze hit her face. It smells of rain.

Beside her, in the driver's seat, is Mickey, eyes trained on the road ahead. It's thoroughly dark now, and she can only see his face when they pass beneath the streetlamps.

Imogene fades in and out of consciousness, but it surprises her to find that she's not afraid to be alone in her car with this man. Because somehow, through her stupor, she remembers where she'd seen Mickey.

"You were at Ted's memorial," she says, turning her head to look at him, and fighting the wave of nausea that accompanies the movement.

When he glances over at her, a range of emotions flick across his face, and settle at last on sadness. "I was," he says.

"Were you friends?"

"We were. Yeah—I… I didn't know him well, but yeah… we were friends."

Imogene nods. Then, in barely a whisper, she says, "I loved him."

Mickey looks at her again with something that resembles guilt. "I'm sorry."

For lack of response, Imogene returns her eyes to window. The glass is wet, and she watches the raindrops slide down. One drop hits another on its way to the bottom and forms one giant drop, plummeting. Down and out of sight. Past the raindrops, she recognizes these streets. Mickey is taking her home. She can't recall giving him her address, but she must have.

When she comes to again, Mickey has pulled her car into her driveway. It's late. Imogene doesn't know *how* late, but thank the stars, her parent's car is still missing. They haven't returned from their outing with their church group. A breath of relief escapes her.

Mickey turns off the ignition and comes round to her side of the car. After he helps her to her feet and ensures she can stand unassisted, he opens the back door to retrieve her bag and drapes it over her shoulder. Thank goodness he'd thought to grab it, because Imogene had forgotten it entirely until just this moment.

His eyes flick to her front door. "Are you going to be okay?" he asks.

With a sleepy nod, she says, "I will. Thank you." But then she gasps. "Oh my goodness! How are you going to get home?"

Mickey shrugs. "I like to walk," he says with a soft smile.

At that moment, a rush of appreciation overcomes Imogene. For him. This stranger. Although they aren't exactly *strangers*, are they? Both had known the same man; Ted connects them to each other.

The streetlamp in front of Imogene's house lights the driveway, but Mickey stands five feet away on the lawn, face partially obscured in shadow. His fair skin is almost luminous, eyes flooded with unspoken thoughts.

He is deep, she thinks. He is lovely.

And Imogene notices her feet moving before she comprehends *why*.

She closes the distance between them. The rain has settled in the thick grass, and the damp wets her ankles, soaks through her canvas shoes.

"Imogene," Mickey says, voice almost a warning as she draws nearer.

She stops before him. In a timid motion, her hands lift and find themselves on either side of his chest. Then, she allows her eyes to raise. To meet his. He looks afraid—*terrified*, in fact. But something else is there as well. Interest?

When his hands move up to take hers, a flutter blooms within her. But no sooner do they connect when Mickey pulls her hands free of his chest and moves a half step back.

He swallows once, throat bobbing. "Go get some rest, Imogene. I'll check on you in a day or two."

Without another word, he leaves her there on the lawn, confused and dizzy.

63

WILFRED

(FEBRUARY 1965)

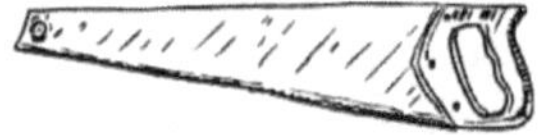

WILFRED WORKS. SLEEPS. KEEPS TO himself. And waits for news from home.

Of course, as he nears on two years after the incident that brought him here, he supposes it's foolish to refer to Daytona as *home*. But it *is*—it *is* home. Wilfred can lay roots wherever he goes, but none so deep as the ones lain in the Sunshine State. The ones tied to the gorgeous girl with the cinnamon hair, who is the closest thing to family he's ever known.

Construction has its ups and downs. It's sweaty, tough work, but Wilfred gets to be outside, so there's that. He's still with the framing crew he started with eight months ago but was promoted recently to Carpenter's Helper. The carpenter he works under—Leon—is forty-two years old and even quieter than Wilfred. For that alone, they get along splendidly.

The other guys, however, have yet to figure Wilfred out. One guy in particular—whose name, as fate would have it, is *Ted*—always gives Wilfred a hard time. On lunch break, while trying to enjoy his turkey sandwich and potato chips, Carpenter Ted peppers Wilfred with questions. *Why are you always so quiet, huh? Cat got your tongue? What—you don't like us or something? Think you're better than us? You got a girl, Baker? How come we never see you with a girl? Do you even like girls then, or should we be worried?* Each probing query is at once met with laughter and jeers of encouragement from his pals.

Last month, Carpenter Ted offered to set Wilfred up with his cousin Jane—a nice girl who just split from a real sorry guy, he'd said. Yelled at her. Called her awful names. Even hit her a time or two. Carpenter Ted said he figured she could stand to saddle up with the quiet type for once. And he'd assured Wilfred (with two vulgar hand gestures) that her melons were *ripe for the squeezing*, a statement that, in Wilfred's opinion, one should never make in regard to their cousin. Feeling cornered, Wilfred agreed to take Jane dancing that Friday night, but he regretted the choice at once. For one thing, he hates to dance. For another, as much as he longs for the touch of a woman, the thought of sharing that with anyone but Imogene makes him feel like a scoundrel—a cheat.

The night he was to meet Jane, he wrestled with his decision for hours—pacing the room, weighing the pros and cons—and in the end, he'd sat on the edge of his bed, still dressed in his dancing clothes, and watched Gomer Pyle, U.S.M.C. on television until he fell asleep.

The next Monday at work, Carpenter Ted stared daggers into Wilfred as he ate his turkey on rye and hadn't spoken to him since.

At least lunch has been quiet.

But sadly, so has the phone line.

Last they spoke, Mick mentioned that things had been hectic, and he may not call again this month. That was three months ago, and still—nothing.

Wilfred worries. But work keeps him so busy, there's not much time to dwell. A scorching summer had given way to a hotter-than-normal fall, and now, *finally*, winter weather is upon them. Yesterday boasted a high of forty-two degrees. A few guys had grumbled, but not Wilfred. He embraced it. The heat left him yearning for home, for the ocean. But the cool weather is a welcomed distraction. A reminder that he is *here*. That, painful as it may be, *this* is his life now. And he's doing fine.

But today, Wilfred comes home to a letter.

He peels off his jacket, kicks his boots to the corner of the room, and has the envelope open before his ass hits the chair.

Because the letter is from Mick.

Wil — it reads.

I'm sorry I haven't called. Things have been busy. You understand. I'm contemplating a move from Daytona. Starting somewhere new. I reckon it's time. What do you think?

I bring you news that I regret to share. I know you won't take it well, but as your friend, I need to tell you.

Imogene has been seeing someone.

She seems real happy. I'm sorry, pal. I am. But it looks as if she's moved on, and... well... maybe you should consider doing the same.

I'll write again when I can.

I hope you're well.

ML

For the longest time, Wilfred stares at the letter, chest heaving with the weight of his breaths. Then, he crumbles the paper in his hands. Throws it to the floor. Watches as it bounces beneath the foot of his bed. His face falls into his hands. Hurt swallows him whole.

No. More than hurt.

Heartbreak—again. Old wounds split open fresh.

He doesn't know what to think—what he'd *been* thinking. He'd imagined there might come a day he could return to Daytona and explain everything to Imogene. And in this vision, she doesn't hate him for what he's done. In fact, she's waiting for him, just as he waits for her.

But, in her eyes, he had died nearly two years ago. Of *course,* she isn't waiting. To be honest, he's shocked she waited *this* long to find someone new. He's been kidding himself. He knows this. Even so, it stings.

The idea of her in another's arms… it hurts too much to imagine.

No one can ever love her or care for her the way he had… the way he *does.*

But she deserves happiness. Happiness he can no longer give her.

64

WILFRED

(JULY 2, 1965)

MONTHS PASS WITHOUT ANOTHER WORD from Mick. No calls. No letters. Nothing.

Wilfred hasn't felt this alone since his parents died.

But what did he expect? For Mick to stay in Daytona forever? That he would go on watching Imogene and feeding Wilfred information on her for the rest of their lives?

No. That would be insane.

But he'd expected a slower transition—*gradual*—not this sudden and complete cutoff of communication.

Mick is the last remaining tie to Wilfred's old life, and without him, he does not connect to the world. No sense of belonging. To anyone or anything. And if he doesn't belong *anywhere*, then he may as well go wherever he pleases. Right?

So today, with nothing left to lose, and two full summers of separation from the night that claimed his former life, Wilfred fights his nerves and better judgment and drives to Daytona.

His intentions are not to disrupt Imogene's life. He only wants to see her.

By the time the highway drops him in Daytona, it is afternoon, and his hands grip so tight to the wheel they ache. Fear creeps in. Is this a mistake? Will someone recognize him? Doubtful. It's been years, and he is so changed… in more ways than one.

For a while, Wilfred drives the streets, gaining nerve, before he continues west to Imogene's hometown of Deland. Soon— *too* soon—he is in front of Edmunds Drug, the small pharmacy Imogene had been working at, last he spoke to Mick. How long has it been now? Six months? More?

As he whips into a parking spot, Wilfred notes the sweat beneath his armpits, and curses himself for not bringing a change of clothes. What does he do now? Does he go inside?

No. Too much of a risk, he thinks. But what if she's in there?

Well, what if she *is*? A busy pharmacy is hardly the place to accidentally reintroduce himself to her. No. He should wait.

So, that's what he does. He waits. And waits and waits.

Two hours pass, and no sign of Imogene.

A rumble in Wilfred's stomach reminds him he hasn't eaten since lunch yesterday. So, he starts his truck and leaves for food. He'll come back later.

———

At 4:30, Wilfred returns to the pharmacy and parks a few spaces along from where he'd been earlier. He sips a watered-down cola through a straw and resumes his waiting.

Forty-five minutes later, his heart stops cold.

The door to the pharmacy opens, and there she is—*Imogene*— the woman he hasn't seen in two years. The woman he feared he'd never see again. Yes—a woman now. Aged. Radiant. His entire body burns hot at the sight of her.

When Wilfred made this trip for Imogene, he never imagined speaking to her. He only hoped for the chance to see her. Just once. To see with his own eyes that she was truly okay. That he can leave her behind without worry for her happiness. But now that he's here—and she is *so* close—can he, in good conscience, let her walk away without talking to her?

Wilfred eases the car door open. Steels himself to step out. To call to her. That's when her hand raises in greeting, a wave meant for someone in another car a few spots to Wilfred's left. A smile spreads across her face, then. But not an ordinary smile; that's why Wilfred pauses and settles back against the seat. This smile is so like the ones she used to give to *him*. The kind of smile he hasn't seen in a very long time.

Wilfred, crouched low in the seat, turns the direction in which she'd waved. And there, emerging from a sleek black car, he sees him. Wilfred can scarcely breathe, because there, right in front of his eyes, stalking toward Imogene as if he belongs there, as if he belongs to *her*, is someone else Wilfred hasn't seen in a very long time—Mickey Lancaster.

Through the dusty windshield of his truck, Wilfred watches in horror as Mick pulls Imogene into his arms, plants a kiss on her lips, long and deep, and then leads her back to his car, the two of them hand in hand.

But it's the flush on Imogene's face, the utter contentment in her expression, that causes Wilfred to pull his door shut and wipe madly at the angry tears that sting his eyes.

His thoughts come fast and erratic. Anger. Sadness. Embarrassment. Betrayal. He feels it all at once in quantities he can hardly contain. How *could* she?

No, he reminds himself. This isn't Imogene's fault. It's his. Every terrible event of the last two years is *his* fault. *Mick.*

He trusted Mick to watch her, to make sure she was *safe*. And instead, he'd stolen her away.

Wilfred wants to follow them. To confront Mick. But he fights the urge. In his current mental state, whatever he says or does to Mick will only make Imogene hate him more. So, he takes a deep breath, puts his truck in reverse, and drives instead to Hank Lancaster's home.

The house looks the same, or at least Wilfred assumes it does. Last he was here, he was hardly in the state of mind to marvel over the Lancaster's good fortune.

Anger and adrenaline are the fuel Wilfred uses to march to the front door and ring the bell. He doesn't even care about the muddy footprints he's tracked up the gleaming front path.

A few moments later, the door swings open, and Hank is there, as youthful and put together as the last time Wilfred saw him—the night he became Wilfred Baker. Hank's face doesn't change as he looks him over.

"Well, I'll be damned," he says, with a sigh and a shake of his head. "Come on in, I guess."

Wilfred follows Hank inside and pulls the door shut behind them.

Hank leads Wilfred down the main hall and into the large sitting room in the back of the house. Off to the right is the closet-sized room with all the boxes where Hank had taken him two years ago. The door to the room is shut. But Hank doesn't go there. Instead, he crosses to the left. To the liquor cabinet in the corner where he removes two rocks glasses and a bottle of whiskey. He adds a few splashes to each glass, tosses his own back with one gulp, and hands the second to Wilfred.

Hank adds another finger of whiskey to his own glass and says, "I wondered when you might show back up here. Figured you'd have made an appearance back when he first split."

Wilfred rolls the glass in his hands, sniffs the liquor inside, but isn't much in the mood for drinking. "When who split?"

"Marty, obviously," Hank says.

"Wait—what?" A frenzy of questions assaults his mind. "Marty left town? Like… he's gone? When did this happen?"

Hank's eyes widen as he lowers the glass from his lips. "I figured my brother told you. He's been keeping you in the loop, right?"

"Apparently not so much." Wilfred's jaw tenses.

"Shit. Okay. Well… yeah. Marty skipped town about six months ago. Disintegrated The Company without telling a soul. Mickey and the guys show up one night for distribution, and the place is locked up tight. Empty. No one has heard from Marty or seen him since. Could be he ran. Could be someone finally killed the bastard. No one knows, and frankly, no one cares."

Wilfred lowers himself to the arm of the sofa. "Six months," he snorts. After some quick mathematics in his head, he adds, "And how long has Mick been dating my girl?"

Hank lets out an uncomfortable chuckle and shakes his head. "Man. My brother really stepped in it, didn't he? Imogene was *your* girl?"

"She was."

"Look, I don't know what my brother is doing. He tells me what he wants me to know. Leaves me to sort out the rest. I didn't realize Imogene was your girl. But… I'm guessing *he* did, right?"

Wilfred just nods, every muscle tensing as one.

Hank nods in return. "Mick's been seeing Imogene for… I don't know—around eight months, I'd say. He's crazy about her. And Mick, he's… changed since he met her. Quit the drinking. Been taking shifts at the shop. Our folks have been trusting him again. I don't know what your history with her is, but I know she's sure made a difference in my brother's life. And he's serious about her. Talking marriage and all that. And listen man—not to rub salt in the wound, but from what I can tell, she feels the same."

"*That's because she thinks I'm dead!*" The words come out in a growl.

Hank, unruffled, sets his empty glass on the ledge of the cabinet. "That's the thing," he says, voice even. "As far as anyone here is concerned, you *are* dead. That was the whole idea, yeah? I put my neck on the line to give you a new name, a fresh start, and for what? So you can stroll back in here two years later and rave that everyone has moved on?"

Wilfred's cheeks are burning. No one can understand what he's gone through. What this has been like for him.

"But I get it," Hank continues. "Clearly you haven't gotten the closure you need, and it sounds like my brother has done a pretty shit job of helping you through it." A thought strikes Hank then, and he sighs. "I'm supposed to meet Mick at The Perch at seven for supper. Why don't you go instead? Have a chat. It might help."

Wilfred nods, no idea what to say, but determined to not let Mick get away with this. "Yeah. Yeah—I think I'll do that," he says. And now, much more inclined to the idea of drinking, he chugs the whiskey in one gulp and hands the empty glass back to Hank. "Thanks for the hospitality," he says, and moves for the door.

"Hey Wilfred," Hank calls after him.

Wilfred turns.

"I'm not telling you what to do about Imogene, but… she's happy now. She mourned you for a long time, but now… I'm just saying… maybe pickin' at old wounds ain't the best idea."

Wilfred feels a tightening in his chest. He turns and leaves without another word.

He waits at The Perch, leg bouncing in anxious bursts beneath the table. He's been stewing since he left Hank's, imagining what he might say. Mick had been a genuine friend the night of the accident. Or so Wilfred thought. But to look back now, Wilfred sees only deceit. Mick had him at his weakest, most terrified, most vulnerable moment, and used fear to convince Wilfred that the only way out was to fake his death and assume a new identity. He'd sailed Wilfred away from everyone and everything he'd ever known, which, as an orphan, wasn't much. But still—it was *his*. Then, Mick steals the woman he loves and lies about it. He doesn't bother to tell Wilfred that Marty had vanished. That it was safe to return.

No matter how you slice it, Mick had abandoned him.

Condemned him to life in Georgia—a life he never wanted—a shadow of the man he used to be.

Wilfred grinds his teeth as he waits.

He'd asked for a table on the patio with a view of the front door, and worn a ball cap and sunglasses, on the off chance someone might remember Ted Barrett. Though it appears Mick has done an excellent job of erasing him. No one has so much as blinked in his direction.

"Aren't they?" The waitress sets a glass of ice water on the table.

"Pardon?" Lost in thought, Wilfred hadn't seen her approach *or* heard her question.

She flashes a patient smile. "I *said*, summer evenings are the best for dining outdoors, aren't they?"

"Ah, yes. They are." Wilfred pulls his lips into what he hopes is a polite grin but does not make to continue the chit chat. She takes the hint and leaves him to his thoughts.

Twenty minutes later, Mick's car turns into the parking lot. Wilfred's anger had ebbed as he sat there. But now, watching Mick saunter to the door, swinging his car keys around his finger, not a care in the world, Wilfred's contempt returns full force. Mick doesn't see him sitting there, but then, he isn't exactly looking for him, either. He expects Hank.

The chatty waitress leads Mick out the side door a few moments later and across the patio to where Wilfred sits in wait. The confusion on Mick's face lasts for a fraction of a second; as realization quickly dawns, his eyes go wide.

"Hey, Mick! Glad you made it, buddy." Wilfred plasters on a toothy smile and gestures for him to sit.

The waitress, mirroring Wilfred's enthusiasm, asks, "Can I grab you fellas a drink to get this evening started?"

Mick lowers himself into the chair across from Wilfred, a wary edge in his gaze.

"Oh, sure thing!" Wilfred says, and he shoots a grin at the waitress that sends a rosy blush across her cheeks. "I'll have a Jack Daniels and cola, and my friend here… he likes to have what *I'm* having, isn't that right, Mick?"

Mick notes the challenge in Wilfred's eyes. But he swallows and gives the waitress a soft shake of his head. "Actually, I'll just have a water please." And then, in a quiet voice, adds, "I don't drink anymore."

"Oh, that's right!" Wilfred says. The venom has slipped into his tone, into the firm set of his jaw, the strain of his shoulders. "I forgot! You're a changed man now."

The waitress, scenting the tension in the air, slips away to fetch their drinks.

For a while, the two men watch each other in painful silence. Wilfred can see that Hank was right—Mick *has* changed. His skin looks better. Healthier. The greasy flop of hair he used to sport is clean and trimmed, and his face is freshly shaved. He wears nice slacks and a sleek, cream-colored button-down. To Wilfred, he looks every bit the rich brat he was always meant to be.

When Wilfred removes his sunglasses, he looks away, unable to bear the weight of Mick's evaluation just yet. Because he knows he is worse for wear. He's suffered. Mentally. Physically. The last two years have not been kind to Wilfred. But Mick needs to see what he's done to him. What he's become. Wilfred turns and meets his stare, waiting for Mick to speak first.

"You talked to my brother," he says. It isn't a question.

"I did."

"What did he say?"

Wilfred shrugs. Indifferent. "Why don't you tell me what you *think* he said." He returns the sunglasses to his face.

Mick sighs and drops his head. "Come on, pal. Let's get on with it, huh? Do you know about Marty or don't you?"

"I do now."

"I'm sorry!" Mick says, and to Wilfred's surprise, he *looks* sorry. "I wanted to tell you. But I knew you'd come back if I did."

Wilfred leans in, chin resting on his fist. "And why wouldn't you want me to come back, Mick? What might you possibly be hiding from me that you wouldn't want me to discover if I came back to town?"

Mick blinks. "You know about Imogene." Also not a question. Mick is many things, but he is not a dummy.

The waitress returns with the drinks, a trifle on edge as she asks if they are hungry. But both men play perfect gentlemen, and say *No, thank you. We're fine with the drinks for now.* With a sweet nod of her head, she leaves them alone once more.

Wilfred takes a long sip of his whiskey and cola before speaking. To rattle Mick, sure, but more to get his emotions under control. The last thing he wants is to cry in front of Mick. Not again.

But it's Mick who speaks first.

"Wil, I don't even know what to say. I'm sorry. I did what you asked me to do. I watched her. I made sure she was safe. I never meant for anything to happen between us. You have to understand that. She made the first move. Not me."

"You're lying," Wilfred says, feeling sick at the very insinuation.

"I'm not. It's true. And… I tried to keep things friendly between us, but… it—it just happened."

"And what exactly *happened*, Mick? How far has this thing gone?"

A blush creeps across Mick's face, and his eyes go wide. Silence hangs in the air between them.

Wilfred fights back tears as he demands, "Have you had sex with her?"

The silence lingers, but Mick's head falls to his lap. When he looks up again, the answer is in his eyes. "I love her," he says.

And he does. Wilfred can see that. Feels it in the gut-punch that follows.

"I'm sorry. For everything. Every lousy thing I've done to you. But… I *do* love her. I thought—if I told you she was seeing someone and she was happy, maybe… you might leave her be. And then, you'd never have to know it was me. I did not intend this to hurt you. I thought enough time had passed. I figured you'd made a life for yourself in Valdosta. I—"

"A life for myself?" Wilfred interrupts. "What kind of life can I have? I had to start all over. I lost my home, my business, my best friend, my girlfriend. I lost everything. Do you have any idea how long it takes to *get* those things when you're on your own? When you haven't got a family to help you?"

Mick is quiet. Ashamed.

"No, I don't suppose you do," Wilfred continues, and he doesn't hide the judgment in his voice. "Well, I *did* it. I *had* it. And I lost it. Everything. In one night. Because of *you*."

Mick shakes his head, mouth agape. Lost for words.

"I don't sleep," Wilfred says, voice only a whisper. "I... Imogene—the thought of her—is the only thing that's been getting me through and you... you *ruined* her."

A wounded look transforms Mick's face. "She isn't some fling, you know. She... I want to marry her. I found us a house. A nice place north of here. I'll give her a good life, Wil. I'll take care of her. I swear to you, I'll make her happy."

What can Wilfred say? Does Mick want his blessing? He can't give him that.

"You act as though I'm really dead, Mick. Can you honestly marry Imogene knowing I'm still out there? That I was her first choice?"

Mick doesn't answer. Instead, he stares at his water glass and asks, "Are you going to tell her?"

"Do you think I should?"

Mick ponders this, and then, crestfallen, says, "I would if I were in your position. But I'm begging you not to."

65

WILFRED

(JULY 3, 1965)

THAT NIGHT, WILFRED SLEEPS IN his truck.

He hadn't brought enough cash for a motel and has nowhere to go other than back to Georgia. But he isn't ready for that yet.

For most of the night—curled in a ball on the stiff and uncomfortable bench seat, sweat dripping between his shoulder blades—he wrestles with thoughts of what his next move should be.

The responsible decision is to leave. Go back to Valdosta. Let Mick marry Imogene and move her far away. Let him give her the life she deserves. Isn't that what he himself had promised to do for her?

But he'd failed.

And now Mick can do for her all the things that Wilfred cannot. Make no mistake, Ted Barret could have given Imogene the world if he had enough time. But Wilfred Baker has nothing to offer her.

Yet every time Wilfred moves to start the truck, to drive away, he thinks, *Can I live with myself if I never tell her the truth?* Can he live knowing she will always carry the burden of what she believes happened to him? If he tells her, even if she *hates* him for it, at least she'll know. Then she can truly move on. And so can he.

As morning dawns, he wakes determined to talk to her. After that, if she wants him to go… he will go. He won't beg. He'll admit defeat.

Wilfred drives first to the pharmacy. He returns the ball cap to his head and slips inside, where he asks the girl at the counter for Imogene, trying his best not to meet her eyes. The girl says, "I'm sorry. Imogene is off today. She has class."

Back in the truck, Wilfred tosses his cap to the seat beside him as he switches into reverse and drives the two miles south to Stetson University. He finds a shaded spot on the street that faces the broad, grassy yard in front of the main building. From here, he can see the corner of the parking lot. Of course, Imogene could come from any direction. Could be on the other side of campus, for that matter. But he feels good about this spot, and there's a pleasant breeze beneath the giant oaks that line the street. So, he waits.

Hours pass and Wilfred becomes discouraged and restless. There is no way to know if she is still inside, or if she slipped out another way and is already halfway home. Or worse… with *him*. As the minutes tick by, his hope dwindles. The radio plays low in the background, but Wilfred isn't listening. He is exhausted and starving and questioning his entire purpose here, but can't tear his eyes from the fresh batch of students that have made their way from the main hall out onto the lawn. Wilfred watches as they scatter in different directions across the lush, manicured grounds.

So many of them, he thinks. There are so many people, and his eyes are so dry and heavy that he struggles to concentrate.

But then, as if by magic, a lovely girl in a pale pink dress, cinnamon hair falling just below her ears, breaks free of the crowd and heads straight for him. *Imogene.*

As she moves, her eyes cast to the ground, someone calls to her. She looks up, smiles and waves, and continues toward the street where Wilfred is parked.

He watches in amazement. Stunned by her beauty in the same way he'd been when he first saw her that day on The Siren. Back then, she'd talked about going to college, becoming a nurse. He'd been so impressed with her drive. Of the dreams she had that were so much bigger than herself. And here she is. Doing everything she said she would do. Something akin to pride flares within him as he watches her walk; the midday sun beats on her shoulders, her face, her hair. But then comes an intolerable ache that spreads throughout his chest, because he hadn't been a part of this. Of her *becoming.*

Wilfred nearly loses his nerve then. Because she'd done it—everything—without him. She didn't need him. Not in the least. But he needs *her.*

His windows are down.

Imogene nears his truck.

He only needs to call to her.

But Wilfred freezes, and Imogene passes by, continuing down the sidewalk.

He watches the back of her now as she walks away. Soon to be gone forever.

No longer conscious of what he is doing, Wilfred opens the car door and steps out. Leans on the open door for support. It's now or never, he thinks.

"Imogene," he calls, his voice so meek. So terrified. Will she even hear him?

But Imogene stops.

She turns around.

66

IMOGENE

(JULY 3, 1965)

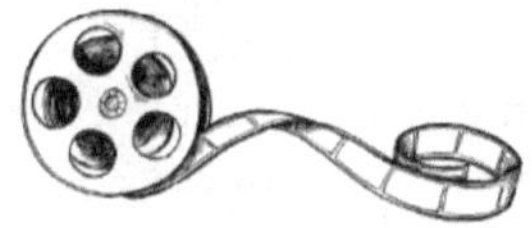

AT FIRST, IMOGENE ISN'T SURE who's called her name. A man leans against an old orange truck who stares in her direction but says nothing. There's a familiarity in his face, though. In his features. In his eyes…

Imogene's heart leaps, catches in her throat.

She's seen his face in strangers before. But this…

Older and worn, yes. Tired, she thinks. His hair, once cropped so short, now falls over his ears in unruly brown waves. He's thinner. *Too* thin. And his tan skin is now a deeper bronze. A few days of dark stubble dusts his jaw line. But despite the differences, he is, unmistakably, *her* Ted.

In a daze, she moves toward him. Slow steps inch her closer.

All the while she thinks, *This can't be happening. I'm seeing things. Ted died two years ago.*

But he's standing right in front of her. Living. Breathing. So… that means for the past two years, Ted has been *alive*. Alive somewhere. And now, here he is—returned—after all this time.

"Imogene, I…" he starts.

Imogene lifts her right hand and slaps him hard across the cheek; the force of impact stings her palm, dulled only by the terrible anger that rages inside. Ted moves a hand to where she'd struck and closes his eyes, as if to feel her punishment—accept it—again and again. When, at last, he opens his eyes, the look he gives is filled with such despair Imogene can hardly stand it.

Her own eyes fill with tears then. And in a motion that nearly knocks him off his feet, she flings herself into Ted's arms and buries her face in his chest. He smells exactly the same. Over time, she'd forgotten this smell, but it hits her now. Like catching a familiar scent on the wind and falling face first into a memory.

His arms tighten and pull her flush against his body. The weight of his chin rests atop her head. For the longest time, they stand there beneath the canopy of trees, breathing each other in.

But even as she holds him, there's a gnawing voice that says: *This isn't real.*

And yet, she can't let go. Because she is so afraid that if she *does,* he will vanish. That somehow, he was never there to start. And she can't lose him again. She can't…

In an instant, the spell breaks, and the rush of longing for Ted gives way to a crushing guilt.

Mickey.

As his name slams into her mind, a wall goes up, a divider between this new life and her old one. A reminder of current obligations. Of reality. Ted may indeed be here, but Imogene is right… this *isn't* real.

At once, she pulls away, and wipes furiously at her tear-stained cheeks, checking to see if anyone has witnessed their roadside embrace. No one has, thank goodness.

Retreating a few steps, Imogene stares at him in

bewilderment.

Ted clears his throat. "You look lovelier than ever, Imogene."

"Don't," she warns. "You don't get to say that to me. You... you can't just come back after all this time and—"

"I know. I know, and I'm sorry, Imogene. I'm so sorry for everything. What you went through, I—"

"*Where... were... you?*" The words are a growl through her teeth.

Ted pauses.

"I've been in Georgia," he says, and shame crackles every syllable.

"What? So, you just *left?* Why? Why didn't you come back to me, Ted? Why did you leave with no explanation or—"

He motions for her to lower her voice. "It's... complicated. And it's not Ted anymore. It's Wilfred. That's... that's my name now."

Imogene tries to put the pieces together. To make sense of the living nightmare she'd endured two summers ago. Why had he disappeared? And why come back? Why now? When she's happy at last. When she's finally moved on. Her heart belongs to Mickey now, who loves her dearly. And he is a wonderful guy who held her up when no one else could. Imogene believes in a future with Mickey. So how—*how*—had she forgotten Mickey the moment Ted held her in his arms? How could she do that to him? He deserves better than that. And the betrayal eats away at her. Even if the disloyalty extended only to her thoughts, and only for a moment, she is ashamed.

"I can explain everything to you," Ted says. "Please. Will you let me?"

She wastes less than a second answering him. With a nod, Imogene climbs into Ted's truck and shuts the door. To satisfy her own curiosity, she will hear him out. She will put an end to the what-ifs, and then she'll go.

She will let him go.

An hour passes in that truck, and fresh tears fall from Imogene's eyes. From Ted's as well—or *Wilfred.*

He'd told her everything. The Company. The botched robbery. The dead domestic. *Ray.* The other guy that showed up and saved Ted's life that night. Helped him change his name and get to safety. When Imogene presses for more information on this mysterious savior, Ted only says that he didn't know the guy well but owes him his life.

Imogene isn't convinced. Whoever this other man is, he is responsible for taking Ted away from her. And for paying off the medical examiner who ruled Ray's death an accident, knowing full well murder was to blame. Sure, this move had saved Ted, but it had stolen the truth from the Greens. This man, whoever he is, doesn't seem much like a hero to Imogene.

"So, what, you're back now? You're just coming back, with a brand-new name, like nothing ever happened?" Imogene asks the question but fears the answer. Afraid he'll say yes and put a wrench in her plans with Mickey. Even *more* afraid he'll say no and disappear again.

Ted shakes his head. "No. No, I can't do that. I wish to God I could, but… what happened that night… no one can find out. If it were ever brought to light, everyone involved would be done for. Not to mention, if Marty still *is* alive somewhere, he could turn up whenever he wants. And I can't be here if that happens." He shakes his head again, as if trying to convince himself of his reasoning. "No. I need to go back. I've got a life in Valdosta now. A decent job in construction. And… I've even got an apartment of my own. It's… I've started something there."

So, it seems Imogene isn't the only one whose life has moved forward these past years. She nods, silent, as these newly recovered pieces of her heart splinter in her chest.

In one swift motion, Ted angles toward Imogene, an urgent glint in his eyes. "Tomorrow is the Fourth of July. Meet me. *Please.* Come and meet me! We'll watch the fireworks together, like we should have two summers ago."

Imogene stills. Mickey's parents live in one of the swanky condos on the beach, way up on the eleventh floor, and they plan to watch the fireworks together from their balcony. Imogene has been looking forward to it all summer. But now...

"Please," Ted says again, brown eyes dark and desperate.

Oh, how she'd loved this man.

But that was a long time ago.

She should tell him about Mickey. It might be easier if he knows there is someone else. Maybe there is someone in Georgia—a girl he's been considering? If he knows she's moved on, he'll be free to do the same. But does she *want* him to do the same? Of course she does. She must. To say nothing of the kindness it shows to Mickey, to tell Ted that she's spoken for. When you're promised to someone, it's the courteous thing to do.

But Imogene decides against it.

"I'll think about it," she says. "You have to understand... a lot has changed in two years, Ted—*Wilfred*," she corrects, still struggling with the thought of him being someone else now. But isn't *she* someone else now, too? "I'll... I'll think about it."

Ted nods, shrinking a bit. "Okay. That's fair." Then, in a flash, he reaches for Imogene's hand; the sudden touch stirs something within her. "I'll be at the boardwalk tomorrow night. Eight-thirty. You'll find me in the parking lot. If you decide not to come... well... I'll understand. I will. I know I messed up, Imogene. But I've missed you so much it hurts. And I'm sure glad I got to see you again. No matter what you decide, I'll remember this moment always."

A sad smile tugs at her cheeks. And she means it when she says, "It was good to see you, too... Wilfred. I'm glad you're well."

And at that, she removes her hand from his and slips from the truck.

The drive home is silent, save for the sniffles that accompany her tears. Through clouded eyes, Imogene stares at her hand on the steering wheel—the hand Ted had held not five minutes earlier—and the ruby ring she wears there.

Mickey put this ring on her finger three months ago. A promise ring, he'd called it. Imogene had soared that day, basking in the warmth of his love. Mickey Lancaster has been nothing but good to her. And she's never had a single doubt in her mind. Not a single one. But doubts, she certainly has now.

Because Ted is alive.

He's here in the flesh and wants to see her again.

What is she to do?

She sucks in a sharp breath as she pulls into the driveway and sees Mickey step out of his car. The black Oldsmobile is parked on the street, tires half in the yard. As she crosses to him, bag slung over one shoulder, his eyebrows raise in surprise. "You're usually home by now," he says.

Imogene adjusts her bag and glances at her shoes, at the scuff of grease from Ted's truck near the toes. "Yes… I stayed late at school today—to study with Brenda and Rhianne. We have a… big exam coming up, so…" Her thought fizzles.

Mickey nods, eyes falling to the crumpled white bag in his hand. "Well, I brought you a donut from Myrtle's," he says.

Imogene takes the bag and smiles, lightening in his presence. Whenever they are together, she is buoyant. Just a happy, bubbly girl, floating above the world. "Cruller?" she asks with a wink.

Mickey smiles. Those crooked teeth still send her to the moon. "Of course," he says.

Raising on the tips of her toes, she plants a kiss on Mickey's cheek.

"You must be hungry. Shall we do dinner?" he asks.

Imogene toys with the bag in her hand and blanches. Dinner—*tonight?* Tonight, she needs time to mull things over. Tonight, what she needs is to be alone. "Actually, Mickey, I'm feeling a bit tired. I might just stay in tonight, if that's okay."

"Oh." He deflates at this, but says, "Yeah, that's no problem, Imogene. Get some rest. I'll see you for the parade tomorrow, right?"

Imogene nods. "Yes! Oh, yes, I'm looking forward to it." And just like that, the guilt returns. Imogene pulls him close, kisses his lips hard, and runs off to the front door before the tears take over once more.

67

IMOGENE

(JULY 4, 1965)

THE PARADE WAS A BLUR. The sizzling magic that usually surrounds the Fourth of July was a million miles away.

After the festivities, Mickey and Imogene stop at a fancy bistro for brunch. Mickey sits across from her in the bright, airy room, cutting into an omelet with the side of his fork. He takes a long chug of orange juice to wash down an enormous bite of egg.

Imogene's own meal goes untouched. A shred of cheese has fallen from Mickey's plate onto the white linen tablecloth, and she can't stop staring at it.

The clank of silverware on porcelain brings her attention back to the room with a start.

Mickey wipes his mouth with the corner of his napkin and regards her with a worried expression. "Is everything alright, Imogene? You've been distant today."

A blush pricks her cheeks. "I'm fine. Yeah. Everything is swell." She tries desperately hard to match her voice to the certainty of her words.

Mickey nods, but an air of disbelief hangs between them.

He knows. Something is up, and he *knows*. Imogene must try harder.

She must, because—after a restless night of reflection—she has decided to meet Ted tonight. At 8:30, Imogene will be there at the boardwalk... to tell him goodbye. After that, she'll rush to meet Mickey, and will be on that balcony before the first fireworks sound at 9:30.

So, why go at all? Why bother? If Mickey is indeed her man, why run off to see another?

Imogene had wrestled with these very questions most of the night. And she decided... if this is the last she'll ever see of Ted, she at least wants a proper goodbye. The first time had been brutal and swift—a severing with a crude blade. And yesterday, she'd fled so abruptly. It didn't feel finished. *They* didn't feel finished.

"Did you hear me?" Mickey asks.

Imogene hadn't.

"Sorry, no, I didn't. What did you say?"

A deep breath, in and out of his nose. "I asked if six-thirty was okay to pick you up tonight? Mom requested I bring you out early, so you can gab a bit before the guests show."

Imogene's pulse quickens and her skin grows hot. *Here we go,* she thinks.

"Actually... I was thinking I might drive *myself* out to the condo, if that's alright."

Mickey's eyes narrow. "Well, sure, but... I can pick you up. That's not a problem."

"Oh, I know." Imogene's words come out in a rush now. "Of course it isn't. Only—I... Rhianne invited me to this school thing. A kind of—party, I suppose. It starts late. Eight-thirty.

But I thought I might go and make an appearance. And then it's straight to you for the fireworks."

Mickey stalls, considering, and Imogene thinks she's done it—spun the perfect excuse. Mickey has met none of her classmates but has often said she should try harder to get closer to them. To be more *social.*

But instead, Mickey says, "Where's the party? I can drive you—can go with you, if you'd like. And then after, we can ride to my folk's place together."

Imogene hasn't planned beyond the fictitious party. She'll have to think fast. "No. Um… I mean, no thank you. That sounds lovely, Mickey, but Rhianne didn't specify if we could bring someone. I'd hate to be rude and bring a guest uninvited. What if they didn't buy enough food or drinks? Oh, I couldn't stomach it. I should… I should go alone."

They stare at each other, each unblinking, until finally Imogene must look away. Because Mickey has seen something in her—something close to the truth. She can sense it.

Mickey leans back, and his hands fall to his lap. "You're lying to me, Imogene. Why?"

"I'm… I'm not."

"You are. I know you."

Imogene searches frantically for a suitable explanation. But a plan evades her. Perhaps she should tell Mickey the truth.

But then, in a voice low and solemn, he asks, "Is this about Wilfred?"

The name startles her. It's been ages since they mentioned him. "Wilfred? No, I—" But a sudden notion stops her short. "Wait—how do you know it's Wilfred?"

The color drains from Mickey's face and refills with an ugly shade of pink. "Ted. I meant to say Ted, of course."

"But you said *Wilfred.* How do you know Ted changed his name? No one should have known except…" The pieces click together before Imogene can finish the sentence, and sickness overtakes her. "It was you," she breathes. "You were the one who helped him that night. *You* torched The Siren and bribed the medical examiner. That was *you.*"

In all the time she's known him, this is the first time Mickey looks terrified. "He didn't tell you about me." It isn't a question.

Imogene wants to cry. To flee from the table and never look back. But she restrains her emotions and says, "He told me *everything*. Everything *except* your name. He wouldn't give it to me, no matter how much I asked."

At this, a smirk finds the corner of Mickey's mouth and he nods, as if tasting the truth on his tongue. "Well... ain't that a bitch," he mutters.

"You lied to me... the *entire time*, Mickey. You knew he was alive, and you *lied*!

"I didn't *lie*. I just... didn't tell you. I *couldn't*. It wouldn't have been safe. For him *or* for you!"

"Oh, well, in that case, thank goodness you had my best interest in mind!" Imogene stands and throws her napkin at the table.

"Imogene, please—sit down and let me explain."

Imogene pauses. Bends to meet Mickey eye-to-eye. "I trusted you. *Ted* trusted you. You betrayed us *both*."

And with that, she storms past the inquisitive eyes of the other diners, and right out the door.

68

WILFRED

(JULY 4, 1965)

ILFRED LIES ON THE HOOD of his Chevy, back pressed against the dusty windshield, legs stretched long across the hood.

The parking lot is full, but at this hour, most have wandered to the beach or onto the boardwalk, so Wilfred is more or less alone. A few rows over, a group of teenagers kick an aluminum can across the asphalt. Wilfred can hear them laughing and egging each other on. A sad smile crosses his face as he remembers himself at that age. If only he could go back and do things differently.

But regret is a jagged pill that Wilfred swallows every day.

An hour ago, when Wilfred first pulled into the lot, he was

terrified to leave the truck. To be seen. But the more he mulled it over, the more resigned he became with the truth: Society had *never* taken much notice of him, and if even a shred of Ted Barret remained in Daytona, it was well and gone now.

So, *to hell with it*, he thought, and moved to the hood.

Now the warmth of the evening wraps him like a blanket, and the sweet, salt air swells in his lungs. And he's not afraid. Not at all.

He checks his watch. 8:29.

Will Imogene show tonight? Who's to say? His hopes are high that she will, but he tries his best to bury those hopes in case she truly *has* moved on the way Hank warned. If the night passes without her, the rejection will hurt. But no matter what happens, he will accept her choice and allow her happiness.

8:33

Wilfred hadn't told Imogene about Mickey. He'd wanted to—*God*, he'd wanted to. Truth is, he wants Mickey to hurt. To hurt how *he* is hurting. But if she knew the truth, then his win—if she were to choose him, that is—would not be fair and square. Wilfred wants Imogene to choose him because somehow, after all this time, despite everything he's put her through, she still loves him, *not* because she suddenly fancies Mick as a liar.

8:35

But if she *does* end up with Mick Lancaster, would that be so horrible? For Wilfred, yes, it would. A devastating loss. But for Imogene? Mick has the money to give her a life of excess. And he loves her—anyone with eyes can see that. Imogene could do worse than Mickey. A *lot* worse. And they've been seeing each other for eight months. Wilfred often forgets that he and Imogene had spent only a single summer together. He can't speak for Imogene, but that summer gave his life meaning. And over the years, his love for her has never once waned. He loved her *then*, and always will. What happens tonight—or doesn't—won't change a damn thing about that.

8:39

Beside him, a throat clears, and Wilfred startles, flinging himself upright. Imogene stands next to his truck with a look of unease.

She looks gorgeous in a cream-colored dress, a red barrette in her hair. A white sweater drapes over one arm, and she clutches a small purse with the same hand.

"Imogene," Wilfred breathes.

"Hello." She gives him a polite nod.

Wilfred pulls free of his trance and extends a hand to help Imogene onto the hood beside him. She tucks her dress beneath her and scoots back against the windshield.

For a while, they lay in silence. Simply gazing at the same sky, breathing the same air, and sharing the same space is enough for Wilfred. He can think of nothing better. But there isn't much time, and he needs to speak to her.

With a deep breath, he says, "I'm really glad you came."

Perhaps this was the wrong choice of words because Imogene's face at once fills with conflict. She swallows, refusing to meet his eyes, but a moment later she smiles and says, "Of course."

Nerves raise a sheen of sweat to Wilfred's brow. In so many ways, tonight feels like starting over. Everything has changed. Tentatively, he raises his left hand and reaches for Imogene's right. But as his fingers brush her knuckles, she moves her hand away. A slow movement. But deliberate.

"I'm sorry," he blurts.

"No, *I'm* sorry," she says. "I just…"

Wilfred shrugs off the embarrassment. "No need to apologize. I understand. Things are different now."

"They are!" Her voice spikes with feeling. "Yes! They *are* different."

Another silence settles over them, and Wilfred's chest tightens. For the first time, he realizes that forgiveness may not be what brought Imogene here tonight.

She exhales loudly, and he braces himself for the letdown sure to follow. But in the next instant, she reaches over to take his hand.

When Wilfred turns to Imogene, she is looking—*really* looking—at him. And in that moment, the full weight of her stare upon him, he feels… *everything*. Every good thing he's lived without for the past two years.

And before he can stop himself, he leans forward and presses his lips to hers. She stiffens, and Wilfred fears he has overstepped. But, one by one, Imogene's muscles relax, and she eases into his touch. Before long, she's taken control of the kiss, the weight of her body pushes Wilfred flat against the windshield, and the rest of the world plunges into pleasant nothingness.

Wilfred's breath comes fast and ragged, his fingers dig into every inch of her he can reach. Imogene pulls away, lips red and swollen, and studies his face. In silent agreement, they slide apart, taking a much-needed moment to regain their self-control.

Ever the planner, Wilfred had prepared a speech for how he'd hoped to ask, on the off-chance Imogene found it in her heart to show tonight. But now, words escape him.

"Come back with me," is what erupts from his lips at last.

"What?" Imogene shakes her head as if he were crazy.

"You heard me," he breathes. "Come back with me, Imogene."

"To Georgia? Te—*Wilfred*," she huffs, frustrated with the blunder. "I can't do that."

"Yes, you can!"

"I can't! You're insane!"

Wilfred shakes his head. "What's insane is spending two years without you. I never would have chosen that. Not ever. And now that I have you back, I don't want to spend another minute without you. I love you, Imogene. I still love you. I never stopped."

Tears spill over the pale rouge brushed across Imogene's cheeks, breaths heavy between sobs. Wilfred pulls her close, holds tight until the tremors stop, and she settles at last. When she pulls back, face damp and puffy, she says, "I never stopped loving you, either. It was stupid, of course. You were gone. But after I lost you, I could never love anything, or *anyone*, fully and completely. Because a piece of my heart always belonged to you."

Wilfred smiles and, in a tone so reminiscent of the man he used to be, he jokes and says, "Only a piece?"

But Imogene doesn't find this funny in the least. "I had such terrible guilt over that," she scolds. "You can't even imagine. I felt broken. Like I'd never be whole again."

Wilfred shrinks against the admonishment in her voice. In her stare.

When he risks another glance at her, she's watching him, but her thoughts are a million miles away. Her hazel eyes flare and, more to herself than to him, she says, "How... I mean, how could I even do that? Just up and leave. I—there's no way. How can I tell my parents I'm running off to Georgia with a dead man? I can't. No, I can't do that."

"No. You can't," Wilfred agrees, and Imogene arches an eyebrow in question. "Your parents can't know. If I recall, they weren't exactly my biggest fans. And if they knew what I've done..."

Imogene nods, knowing as well as he that the outcome would not be great.

She wrings her hands together and thinks. "I... I'll figure it out. But I need time—at least a week. I need to... I need to handle a few things first."

Wilfred is stunned. Can't move, can't breathe. Surely his ears deceive him. "You—you'll come with me then?"

She gives off an uncomfortable laugh. "This is absolute *madness*, you know. I... I will. Yes."

A smile pulls at Wilfred's lips, a smile so big his jaw actually *aches* from it. "Two weeks," he says. "There's a bus station in Gainesville, on twenty-third street. I'll meet you there. Two weeks from today."

Imogene shows she understands with several quick nods, her eyes glistening with fresh tears. But she smiles and kisses him again. A wild kiss that leaves him spinning.

9:30

Distant cheers sound as the first fireworks rocket into the night.

69

IMOGENE

(JULY 19, 1965)

IN THE END, SHE'D AGREED.

Of course she had.

It was Ted, after all. Or—Wilfred. She hopes she can adjust to his new name in time. Though, in her heart, he will *always* be Ted.

The past two weeks have been both emotional and exhilarating.

First, she'd handled the predicament with Mickey. Though, Imogene needn't have spoken a word; he knew what was coming.

"I *am* sorry, Imogene," he'd said. "I never meant to hurt you… *or* Ted. Despite what you both may think of me now, I carry a terrible guilt over what I've done to him, and I hate myself for it. I suppose it's only fitting that you hate me now as well."

Imogene swallowed, looking away. "I don't hate you," she'd muttered. "I could never *hate* you, Mickey. But… now that I know the truth, I simply can't see you the same way."

"I wish it would have been *me* who told you. If I could go back, I'd do things differently. I would. You know that, don't you?"

Imogene smiled, eyes misting over, and said, "Yes, I do."

She then slipped the ruby ring from her finger and offered it to Mickey. "I'm sorry," she said, unable to meet his eyes. Already, it felt as though she'd issued a thousand apologies, and this was just the beginning.

But Mickey waved her away, pushed her hand with his own. "No. Keep it. It's yours. It will never be anyone else's."

And then he walked away, and the hollowness crept in, a little light in Imogene's heart dimming as she watched him go.

Next were her parents. The truth—that she was running away with a man—of course, was unacceptable. Perhaps if it were Mickey, they may have understood—even allowed it. He comes from a good family with money, and they like him fine, even despite the age difference. But, as it was, this situation called for much creativity. Imogene sat with her parents after dinner and told them she was transferring to Valdosta State to finish her nurses' training; a professor had recommended the switch as Valdosta offers more diverse programs for those seriously pursuing a career in healthcare, as well as a higher percentage of female students.

The lie came easily. What she could never tell her parents was that she had no plans to return to school, that she no longer wanted to be a nurse, that maybe she never did. Because *that* news would not be well received. Both the continuation of her education and her devotion to God and her faith are the most important things to her mother and father. To lose either would be a personal attack on their parental efforts. True, her parents have disappointed Imogene more times than she cares to count, but they did those things from a place of love, and she has no wish to punish them for their mistakes.

She just wants out.

Daddy beamed with pride at Imogene's announcement and wished to personally shake the hand of the professor who saw so much potential in his baby girl. Imogene secretly hoped he'd never try to make good on that wish. Mama remained unsure. But both had agreed: if it opened more doors for her future, how could they deny her?

As she sorted through her room, consolidating her life into a single olive-green suitcase, Imogene struggled to keep her hands from shaking.

"But what about your things, Imogene?" Mama had said. She lurked in the doorway to her room, plucking anxiously at invisible lint on her skirt. "Surely you need more than that?"

"It's a small dormitory, Mama. And I'm taking the bus. There isn't much room for luggage." Imogene had sold her car the previous week for spending cash, said the campus and the dorms were near enough to town that she needn't waste the gas. "Besides, it's not as if I won't be back."

Imogene had promised to write and call her parents every day, and to come home whenever she could manage. But even as she made those promises, a deep-down part of her understood that contact with her family would be minimal from this point forward.

"Yes, yes, you're right," Mama said, and she turned and puttered away before emotions got the better of her. Imogene knew her mother must cry from time to time—everyone did— but she'd never seen it herself.

The following morning, as Imogene climbed into the backseat of a bright yellow taxicab, she choked back tears of her own. This was such a big, scary adventure to embark on at twenty-years of age. And although waves of adrenaline swam in her veins and electrified her brain with thoughts of the future, an equal quantity of dread slithered through and attached to the spaces between.

Mama and Daddy stood on the front porch and waved as the

taxi pulled away. Imogene watched them through the back window, getting smaller and smaller, until a left turn vanished them altogether.

Now, Imogene's leg bounces nervously as the bus slows into the station on twenty-third. Her eyes scan the window as they approach and search for his face on the sidewalk, but she can't see him. After two hours on the bus, her back aches something terrible. And the heat, mingled with the faint smell of must, exhaust fumes, and body odor, has left her with a sick headache. She pulls her suitcase into her lap and hugs her arms around the hard leather casing.

The bus stops, emitting a loud *hiss*, and the metallic rattle of doors sliding open signals their arrival.

Imogene takes a few steadying breaths while the bus empties of passengers. Finally, she stands and clambers toward the stairs. But her suitcase, heavy and cumbersome, wedges itself in the bus door. A few frustrated grunts escape her as she tries to dislodge it, growing more embarrassed with each fruitless heave. Sweat trickles down the back of her dress.

The bus driver—a portly man in his seventies, whose few remaining hairs are combed neatly to the side—stands from his seat. "Oh, let me help you there, Miss," he offers.

"Thank you," Imogene mutters with a grateful smile.

But as the driver reaches for the handle of her suitcase, a voice from behind says, "That's quite alright, sir. I've got it from here."

Imogene turns, and Wilfred is there in the doorway, a giant grin plastered on his face.

This is it, she thinks. *This is the day everything begins.*

70

WILFRED

(JUNE 21, 1966)

TODAY IS THE FIRST DAY of summer. A warm, humid Monday afternoon, with a sun fierce enough to steal your breath if you stand beneath it too long. Already, sweat pools beneath Wilfred's suit, and he'd only been outside long enough to load their overnight bags into the back of the truck.

Wilfred puffs out a steadying breath and sits on the torn cushion of their living room couch, nervously ringing his hands as he waits for Imogene to finish.

A tall, folding divider separates the living and sleeping spaces in their small apartment, and Wilfred hears Imogene rustling around behind the makeshift wall, a few sighs and frustrated grunts escaping now and then.

"Are you sure I can't help you?" he calls.

"Absolutely not!" she yells in return.

Ten minutes later, Imogene emerges; a sheepish smile tugs up her cheeks. The exertion of dressing has left her face with a slight red flush. But *my God*—she is the most beautiful woman Wilfred has ever seen. Her dress is white, but not one of those long, fluffy monstrosities other women don on their wedding day. Imogene's gown falls to mid-calf, accentuating her slim waist. There are these dainty little straps that draw Wilfred's eyes to the delicate, hollow spaces around her collarbones; how badly he wishes to kiss her there. White satin gloves extend to her elbows.

At once, Wilfred stands, though words escape him; he simply hovers there—wide-eyed, jaw hung slack like a waiting pup— and takes in her beauty.

Imogene gives off a nervous laugh and averts her eyes to the carpet. "Don't stare at me like that," she giggles and glances up from under her lashes.

Wilfred smiles then, too. "I'm sorry. I… just can't believe this is real."

She takes the few steps necessary to cross the room and reaches for his hands. He runs his thumbs along the soft, cool silk of her gloves. "Me neither," she says, voice a warm, breathy whisper.

"You look stunning, Imogene."

"Well, you're rather dashing yourself." She touches a gloved index finger to his nose.

Wilfred clears his throat. "I loaded our bags while you dolled yourself up, and Mr. Seevers from downstairs knows we won't return until mid-morning. He promised to keep an eye on the place for us."

"Well, I guess that about covers it, then."

"It does." An electrified silence settles over them. "So… are you ready to become Mrs. Baker then?"

Imogene smiles, a teasing tone to her voice when she says, "I'm already Mrs. Baker. This is merely a formality."

With that, she takes his hand and leads him to the door.

Their wedding didn't include doves, or fancy catering, or any of the two-hundred guests he had promised her. They weren't even in a proper church. But Imogene assured him those things didn't matter. All she ever wanted was to marry him. And marry him, she had.

Wilfred worried, though. Of course he did. It was a man's duty to worry. Because, no matter what Imogene said, she deserved better than someone who allowed her to marry in a lousy courthouse. Yet, as they stood together in front of the Justice of the Peace, Imogene's smile never once faltered. And Wilfred, unable to help himself, wore a similar grin. It *was* perfect. Just the two of them.

But for all his imaginings of this day, he never expected it to end as briskly as it had. In ten minutes' time, they had exchanged their vows and kissed their first kiss as husband and wife.

The Honeymoon was an overnight stay at a value hotel two miles from their apartment. The little pub in the lobby where they ate their dinner—fried fish and a cheeseburger—had surprised them with a small, round wedding cake in their honor: vanilla cake with white icing, and *Congratulations* scrawled across the top in a slanted, magenta-colored lettering. They fed each other their first bites, and the hotel staff took their photo.

Tonight, in the quiet of their room, Wilfred watches Imogene sleep. Those soft cinnamon curls, slightly mussed from earlier activities, her cheek resting hard against his bare chest; Imogene wished to fall asleep to the sound of Wilfred's beating heart. *The sweetest sound in the world,* she'd said—a sound she once thought lost to her forever. And though the happiness of marital bliss courses through him, Wilfred lay awake, staring at the ceiling. Because he despairs. And as much as he longs to unload these worries, he can tell none of this to Imogene. Because she doesn't understand. Imogene's satisfaction with him is obvious; Wilfred can feel it in the way she holds him, in the soft, contented snores that ease from her lips. And she would say as much and wave away his concerns with a kiss. But happy or not, Wilfred can never forget the life of luxury she walked away from to be with him, and the few scraps he's been able to offer her in return. She may have forgotten this, but he cannot.

So, Wilfred vows, right then and there, to be a man worthy of Imogene's devotion and to do right by her always. He may not deserve her *now*... but over time... maybe...

With that thought, he tightens his arms around her and allows sleep to take him.

71

GEOFF

(JUNE 1, 2019)

S **HANK SPEAKS, GEOFF IS** mostly quiet; the girls fill any gaps in conversation with their incessant questions, which frees him to listen… and think.

Pieces of the past snap together for Geoff in ways he never imagined. His thoughts flash to a particular day during his sixth summer. Emeline was thirteen, already becoming too cool to play with them. She now preferred to spend her days in the air conditioning, where she could text her friends or play Snake on the cellphone Mom and Dad bought her for her birthday or help Gram in the kitchen. But on this day, the three of them convinced her to play outside. The game was Geoff's idea; he and Belinda were treasure hunters, come to steal the famous gold of Camp Baker. Wyatt and Emeline were a competing group of treasure hunters, trying to get there first, to claim the glory and riches for themselves.

Geoff wanted to play, to *really* play. They were supposed to drag the game out until lunch. Make it *last*. But Emeline, selfish as she was—*still* is, he thinks—wanted to get it over with and get back inside. So, she and Wyatt cheated. While he and Belinda pretended to search for clues in the thick mess of pine-trees beside the house, Emeline and Wyatt snuck into the camp and stole the "treasure"—a bag of plastic gold coins from a pirate set Gram bought on sale after the previous Halloween.

Wyatt, being the obnoxious brother he is, ran toward the tree line and waved the bag over his head, taunting Geoff and Belinda. *We got the treasure! We got the treasure! We win! You lose! Ha ha-ha ha ha-ha.* Geoff saw red. They weren't playing right. They didn't follow the rules.

"That's not fair!" Geoff had yelled. "You cheated! Put it back! The game isn't over yet!"

Emeline came up behind Wyatt, arms crossed in front of her, and the *smugness* on her face when she said, "Don't be a sore loser, Geoff," made him shake with anger.

Earlier, when he and Belinda first disappeared in the trees, Geoff had picked up a short, sharp stick and spun it in his hand like a switchblade. "Gotta have a weapon," he'd told Belinda, "in case anyone tries to stop us." He'd then gone and found her one similar.

At that point, fueled with outrage over his ruined game, Geoff pulled that stick from his pocket and charged Wyatt. "I *said*, the game isn't over yet!" he roared, and wrapped his arm around his twin, pulling Wyatt's back flat against his own chest. Imitating what he'd seen in a movie once, he pressed the sharp point of the stick against Wyatt's soft throat. At once, Wyatt shrieked. He always *was* a little baby—never liked to play rough.

"Stop it, Geoff! You're scaring him!" Emeline shouted.

Wyatt kicked and screamed the entire time, but Geoff held tight, enjoying both the power and the game—*yes*, he would get his game one way or another. "Hand over the treasure, and he lives!" Geoff yelled, and he narrowed his eyes at Emeline in challenge.

But at that moment, Gramps appeared out of thin air and barreled down the slight slope of the backyard, heading right for them. His face was red. A scowl thinned his lips. Now, if you knew Gramps, you'd know he was the quiet sort—quiet, *not* weak—and kept mostly to himself. Whenever they played, Gramps watched from a distance and let Gram take the lead in the fun. Not once had Geoff seen him angry. But he was *sure* angry that day.

In the same swift motion, he seized Geoff's wrist and yanked the stick from his hand. Geoff dropped Wyatt in the confusion, who skittered away into Gram's arms, who had just come from the porch to investigate the shouting. "What's going on here?" she asked, voice full of worry. "Is everyone okay?"

Throughout this entire exchange, Gramps kept hold of him, his strong fingers wrapped clean around Geoff's wrist. Fear seized his tiny body. All these years later, and Geoff still remembers the altercation. The terrible ache in his wrist where Gramps latched on. The stinging embarrassment of everyone watching him get into trouble. The wild, piercing look in Gramp's eyes when he said, "You don't do that to your brother! *Not ever*! Do you hear me?"

Geoff nodded, swallowing tears.

And then Gramps straightened and looked around, as though snapped from a trance. When he saw Gram there—stroking slow circles on Wyatt's back as he whimpered into her shirt—his expression softened. And then he dropped Geoff's wrist and marched toward the garden, never once looking back. But he took Geoff's weapon with him.

For a while, Geoff could only stand there. He had never heard Gramps raise his voice and couldn't imagine what he'd done so wrong. They were just playing. He wasn't actually going to *hurt* Wyatt.

"Well… how about some ice cream?" Gram's voice broke the awful tension. Geoff nodded, his blood still pumping fast. Emeline sulked back to the house, and Wyatt screamed *Yay!* —

at once forgetting the entire ordeal.

But Geoff didn't get any ice cream. Instead, he told Gram he was tired and went to bed for a nap. In his room, he cried—quietly, so no one would hear. And that evening, he picked at his macaroni, hardly able to stand sharing the dinner table with Gramps, who seemed just as rattled. No one spoke of what happened, and Geoff was grateful.

That night, he'd lain in bed awake. He dozed off and on but was restless and sweaty. How long would he feel the sting of Gramp's words? An icky mess of knots settled in Geoff's stomach. But then, a slice of light cut across the wooden floor of the bedroom as the door creaked open, and Gram's silhouette filled the space. With soft steps, she crept to Geoff's bed, put a finger to her lips, and motioned for him to follow her.

He couldn't be sure of the time, but everyone else was asleep. The house was quiet and dark, save for Geoff and Gram and the warm overhead light in the kitchen. It was exciting, he thought, being up with her like this. She wore her long blue nightdress—the style she loved so much that she rarely changed into her real clothes until at least midday—and her long, grayish-red hair was pulled back in a low ponytail. Gram slid the kitchen chair out for him, and Geoff climbed up, watching as she pulled things from the cupboards—sprinkles, a bowl, a spoon, chocolate sauce, a container of chopped nuts, baby marshmallows, and his most favorite, a bag of Red Hots—and lined them up on the table in front of him. She then opened the freezer and removed one of those big, clear tubs of ice cream; equal parts chocolate, vanilla, and strawberry.

"What's it gonna be?" She popped the lid and hovered the scoop over the flavors.

Geoff's eyes widened. "What? *Now?*"

Surprise crossed her face. "Well now, you aren't opposed to a little midnight ice cream, are you?"

Geoff shook his head hard and picked up the spoon, using it to point at the chocolate and strawberry.

"Excellent choice," she said, and she scooped two heaping spoonfuls of ice cream into his bowl.

She slid the toppings closer to Geoff, and he decorated in concentrated silence. Gram turned for the refrigerator; the light from the open door brightened the room for a moment, and she returned a second later with a tub of Cool Whip.

As he put the finishing touches on his sundae, she lowered herself into the chair beside him. Elbow on the table, chin resting in the curve of her palm, she'd watched him eat, lips tugged into a considerate grin.

After a few delicious bites, she said to him, "I felt bad that you missed the ice cream earlier, so I thought I'd sneak you out here for a little treat." Then, after a beat, she added, "That was kind of scary this morning, wasn't it?"

His eyes gaped in surprise. Not because he didn't know what she was talking about. Because *somehow*, she'd known Gramps had scared him. Even after he'd been so careful to not let anyone see.

"It's okay," she said, sensing Geoff's discomfort. "Nothing to be ashamed of, you know. It scared me a little, too." And she said that last bit in an undertone, as if it were a secret.

"Really?" he'd asked.

"Sure," she said, and scooted her chair closer to Geoff's. "Gramps doesn't usually shout, so it's always a little surprising when he does. But... what you've got to understand about Gramps is..." she trailed off, thinking how best to phrase it.

Geoff listened as he shoveled another giant mound of ice cream into his mouth, some of it missing and dripping down his chin.

After a brief pause, she continued. "Sometimes he has bad days, see. He remembers things that happened to him a long, long time ago, and it scares him a little."

"Like, when I fell off my bike and scraped my knee and it bled real bad? I still think about *that*."

Gram smiled. "Yes. Something like that. Well... today was one of those bad days. But it had absolutely nothing to do with you. Gramps loves you very much, and he felt terrible about yelling at you. He wanted me to tell you that."

Geoff smiled a little and nodded.

"How's that sundae, my special boy?" she asked. And just like that, the day was forgotten. Geoff felt better. And the last of the icky knots faded away.

He returned to bed, mouth freshly wiped with a warm washcloth, tummy full of ice cream, and fell straight to sleep.

Geoff's attention snaps back to Hank's living room. The old man has eased himself to the edge of his recliner but struggles to get to his feet. Belinda gasps and hurries over to help, but Hank waves her off with a frustrated grunt, and eventually stands of his own accord.

Geoff slips back into his thoughts. Sixteen years later, that day at Gram's house finally makes sense to him. Gramps hadn't liked that Geoff was holding a knife—even a pretend one—to Wyatt's throat, because his *own* best friend had died that exact way. With this realization, the shame burns fresh, as though Gramps is here in this room, yelling at him all over again. If only he'd known, he never would have done that. He feels sick.

Geoff wishes Gram were here with a bowl of ice cream to make it go away. Because what he failed to appreciate on that night so many years ago, was how easily she'd taken a terrible moment and replaced it with something special—with something good he would always remember. Gram had a way of making every bad thing feel right again.

God, he misses her.

Hank had shuffled into the next room and reappears a few minutes later with a wrinkled envelope held between two fingers.

"Here," he says, and vaguely waves the envelope around in front of them, offering it to no one in particular. Emeline reaches for it.

Geoff—at the opposite end of the sofa—must move to the edge of the cushion and crane his neck to see. He can just make out the date on the stamp—2017. The envelope is addressed to Hank Lancaster, and the return address is a PO Box registered to Imogene Elkins.

Almost as an afterthought, Hank says, "This came from your grandma about a year ago. I'm supposed to give it to ya, I guess."

As Hank turns back for his chair, Emeline casts a questioning look at each of them. But what can be said? Only one way to know what's inside. Geoff gestures at the envelope with annoyance. *Come on, already!* Emeline's nose twitches in that way it does when she wants to say something nasty, but she keeps her mouth shut and opens the flap. She withdraws a folded piece of paper—a letter, most likely—and another smaller, more weathered-looking envelope.

She unfolds the first paper and quickly scans the contents. "It's from Gram," she says.

Geoff rolls his eyes. *Duh.*

Hank settles himself into his recliner with a sigh and a belch. Then, with a grunt of effort, leans to the table by his chair, slides out the drawer, and removes a glass pipe and a bag of what can only be marijuana. Geoff watches as he packs the pipe full and clicks the lighter, taking a deep drag of the stuff.

The four of them watch in bemusement.

Noticing their stares, Hank says, "What? It's medicinal." Then, "You want some?"

Belinda clears her throat, and Wyatt says, "No thanks. We're good."

Hank just shrugs and takes another hit.

"Um…" Emeline rattles the paper to pull their attention back to the matter at hand. She reads the letter out loud. "*Hank — It's been a long time. I hope this letter finds you well. As you may have heard, Wilfred passed away eight years ago. My health hasn't been great, and I fear my time here is short. In the coming months, or years, my grandchildren may come to visit you. If they do, please greet them warmly and give them the letter I've enclosed. Your brother sent this letter to me in 1967, shortly after Wilfred and I married. It's very important that they receive it.*

"*As this may be the last time we speak, I have to say that I always liked you. I never blamed you for the part you played that evening. And you were a wonderful brother to Mickey. He was lucky to have you in his life.*

Regardless of how things ended between us, I was devastated to hear of his passing. I loved him deeply, once upon a time, and I carry him in my heart always.

"The letter he sent wasn't much help to me, but perhaps my grandchildren might be interested in it. Love to you always, Imogene Elkins Baker"

Without a word, Emeline folds the letter and returns it to the envelope. She now opens the smaller one—the one from Mickey Lancaster. This one she handles with more care, as it is clearly in a fragile state. She clears her throat and reads again, *"Imogene — Congratulations on your marriage. Though I'm sure you won't believe it, I'm truly happy for you, and I hope you and Wilfred have a wonderful life together. You deserve all the happiness in the world.*

"I may no longer be yours (and though I shall go on missing you forever, I take full blame for losing you), but your wellbeing still matters to me, and I want to make sure you're always taken care of, with or without me. Should you and Wilfred ever require it, or should you ever have the need or desire to go, I want you to have the means.

"Because this is a sensitive matter, I can't risk the details being intercepted. So, if you care to accept my offer, think back to the three men on 12. It was so strange how they smiled at us on our first date. We thought then, surely they must smile because they could see the hole island from where they stood. Perhaps that was true. But they smile now for a different reason: because their heads are full of secrets. I love you, Imogene. Now and forever, M.L."

"What the hell does any of that even mean?" Geoff asks.

Emeline sits the letter on the glass-top coffee table in front of them and clasps her hands.

Hank still puffs away on his pipe. The entire room reeks of pot. It's giving Geoff a headache.

"Damned if I know," Hank rasps, as he holds in a lungful of smoke, tips his head back, and blows a slow cloud toward the ceiling

Wyatt moves to the edge of his seat. Hunched over the letter, he scans the words with quick eyes, his mind working hard.

"I'm sorry about your brother," Belinda says to Hank, smiling in that sweet, all-knowing way of hers. Geoff always hated that look. So patronizing.

But when Hank looks at her, whatever he sees softens him a bit. "Thank you," he says. "He was a good man. He loved your grandma a lot—make no mistake about that! Never married, as a matter of fact."

"Never?" Emeline asks.

Hank shakes his head. "Not from lack of trying, mind. I set him up with girls left and right, but none ever grabbed his heart the way Imogene did."

"Wait a second," Wyatt says, lifting Mickey's letter from the table. "Check this out. Look at the way he spelled *hole*."

"So?" Geoff asks.

"It's supposed to be whole—with a *W*—as in, the *whole* island."

"Maybe the dude couldn't spell," Geoff said.

But Wyatt shakes his head and pokes the letter with his index finger. "No. No, it's a clue. See... *three men on 12*. Like *Hole Twelve*. Like golf!"

At this, Hank leans forward and lays his pipe on the ceramic ashtray beside him. "Honolulu Falls," he says. "Yeah. There's this cheesy tourist trap down south on A1A. Been there for years. Some of the Company guys used to moonlight there. I know Mickey took Imogene from time to time."

With this revelation, Wyatt tosses the letter to the table and leans back, arms crossed over his chest. An I-told-you-so grin plays at his lips. Belinda and Emeline exchange a glance, and then extend that glance to Wyatt, Hank, and finally to Geoff. Their eyes are wide with the excitement of cracking another clue and getting one more piece of the puzzle.

But no one speaks.

It's Hank who finally breaks the silence. "Well... it's been great having you all, but it sounds to me like you know where you're headin' next, and it's time for my afternoon nap. You'll forgive me if I don't show you out."

72

WYATT

(JUNE 1, 2019)

BACK ON THE BUS, THEY cruise along A1A, cursing the weekend traffic and the gridlock of stoplights that has them moving at a snail's pace.

Wyatt is antsy. Adrenaline courses through him at the prospect of finding whatever Mickey Lancaster left for their grandmother—and perhaps also a smidge of pride that *he* was the one to decipher the clue. But everyone seems to be riding the same high. This trip is finally moving. Taking on purpose. And dare he say, it's actually kind of *fun*.

"You're smiling." Emeline's voice startles Wyatt from his thoughts, and he looks up to see who she's spoken to, shocked to find it was him.

Emeline stares at Wyatt with a glint in her eyes and a smile of her own. The muscles in his cheeks relax one by one; he hadn't realized he'd been grinning so wide. A blush washes over him now. "Oh, yeah," he says. "I guess I am."

"It looks good on you," she says.

Wyatt's cheeks tighten again as another smile glides into place.

"Right there! Up on the left!" Geoff is standing; his left arm rests on the back of the driver's seat as he hinges forward to see through the windshield.

"I see it. You don't need to yell in my ear," Belinda snips.

"Sorry, my bad." And Wyatt is amazed to see even Geoff is thoroughly excited.

They turn into the parking lot of Honolulu Falls, four hearts thudding in synchronized anticipation.

Unable to cruise past the cashier without tickets, they end up paying for a round of miniature golf. The course is busy. Not unusual for a Saturday, though.

Cold-blooded tourists may shrug off the oppressive heat of an open-air, 18-hole golf course at high noon, but Wyatt is melting. The manmade waterfalls scattered throughout the course tease him with their invigorating spray, and he wishes he'd bought a bottle of water from the cooler up front. Wyatt fans himself with his flimsy scorecard while they wait on the outskirts of the seventh hole; a family ahead of them is taking their sweet time, and another group closes in behind. Soon, it's going to be as stop and go as the traffic to get here.

"Go on ahead of us," Geoff says, nodding to a guy in the group who just arrived. "We're still waiting for one of our players."

The group—two guys in their teens with their giggling dates—move ahead. Geoff says, "Looks like the next group is pretty far back. If we hang here a minute, we should be good." Not that they can predict what they'll find here today—if anything—but when they get to Hole 12, it's best they are alone.

Twenty excruciating minutes later, the groups ahead of them move on, and the cousins ascend the sloping path to Hole 12.

As they approach, Emeline asks, "What exactly are we looking for, you think?"

"I'm not sure," Wyatt admits. "Something that involves three men?"

The hole in question is island-themed, same as the rest of the course, so no surprise there. This one centers around a sea-serpent attack. A giant octopus-like monster with a dozen intersecting tentacles obstructs the hole. They've climbed higher than Wyatt realized; at the top of the green, you can see most of the course below and the main road in the distance, the cars zooming past. "Let's spread out," he says.

Everyone splits up to explore the nooks and crannies for themselves.

After a moment, Geoff shouts, "Hey guys. Check this out. Might be nothing, but…"

"Three men!" Belinda squeals.

And there they are. Three tiki posts sit at the top of the hill, faces carved and painted in exaggerated grimaces. Wyatt's eyes fall to the large wooden box at the base of the posts. Nothing if not masters of theming, Honolulu Falls has disguised the box as a prop; a crate washed ashore, spilled over as part of the shipwreck scene from Hole 11. But it's sealed with a padlock, clearly used by the staff as storage.

"Do you think?" Belinda asks. And they ponder this is silence.

"Wyatt!" Emeline's voice is soft, but urgent. "Your key! The one in Gramp's wallet. It's the only gift we haven't used yet. It has to be!"

A tightness seizes Wyatt's chest as he realizes what she's implying. Of *course*, the key! He reaches into his back pocket, withdraws the wallet, opens it, and pulls the key from the worn leather flaps. The four of them share a look, and then another down the path toward Hole 11 to ensure they're still alone.

They are.

"Do it." Geoff encourages him with a nudge.

Wyatt nods and bends to the padlock, where he carefully slides the key in the chamber. But it doesn't turn. Won't even budge. His heart sinks in response. "It doesn't open it," he says, feeling rather defeated. The others sigh.

He stands then, slaps the key against his palm as he thinks out loud. "The three men. This *must* be what he meant. There isn't three of anything else up here."

An idea hits him then, and he approaches the tiki posts with a sense of knowing. He stands in front of the first tiki man, a short post with an evil grin and a Hawaiian flower painted on his head. Wyatt knocks his knuckles against the top of the post and listens. The second post is the tallest, with a broad nose and buck teeth. Wyatt knocks again. With a deep breath, he moves to the third—the shortest post of the bunch, with striking blue eyes—and knocks for a third time. The sound it makes is noticeably different from that of his brothers.

"It's hollow," Wyatt whispers, still hunched over the third man.

The others flock to his side. "Are you sure?" Emeline asks, and thumps her knuckles against the post as well.

Wyatt nods. "I'm sure. The letter, it said their *heads* were full of secrets. I got to thinking… what if Mickey meant that literally?"

Upon closer inspection, Wyatt sees that *yes*, a faint ridge runs the circumference of the post—like that of a paint can lid, but far less conspicuous.

Geoff pulls a small multi-tool from the pocket of his shorts and flicks the knife out in one swift motion. "Move," he says, and pushes past Wyatt.

But Emeline grabs his wrist. "We can't just tear into this thing," she hisses. "That's vandalism. I'm sure they've got cameras here, you moron."

They silently decide she's right, and if someone *were* watching them from a security office somewhere, how strange the group of them must seem, gathered around in a circle, knocking on their tiki posts like part of some weird, heathenistic ritual.

"Well… we better be quick then," Geoff says, and with one last glance at the path, he presses the tip of the knife to the thin ridge bordering the tiki's head. In a few slick flicks of the wrist, he loosens the cap; it was sealed with several layers of paint that now flake away beneath the polished blade.

Geoff pulls the cap free, reaches his hand into the shallow pit inside, and withdraws a folded scrap of paper and a silver key. "Holy shit," he muses.

In the distance, loud jeers and laughter on the path to Hole 12. They are about to have company.

With frantic movements, they replace the cap and rush to the exit, blazing past several stunned groups near the final hole and the gift shop. After throwing their clubs into the drop return, they practically sprint to the bus and, once inside, are all breathing hard and twitching with anticipation.

Geoff plops onto one side of the kitchen booth, Wyatt on the other, and both peer through the windows for security guards or any signs of trouble. Emeline collapses onto the bed and pushes her hair—now a frizzy mess from the humidity and the errant spray of waterfalls—away from her eyes. Belinda perches against the counter and absently picks at her thumbnail.

Geoff unfolds the paper in his hand, but his expression crumbles as he reads. "It's just an address."

"Well, that's good! That's something!" Belinda says.

Emeline pulls her phone from her pocket. "What's the address?"

Geoff reads it aloud, and Emeline plugs the numbers into Google. After a moment, she turns the phone and displays the screen to the rest of them with a look of utter delight. "It's a storage facility," she says. "Eight miles from here."

Geoff turns the key over in his hand, inspecting it. "It says 203. Unit number, maybe?"

An electrified silence settles over the bus. Then Wyatt says, "Well, what are we waiting for?"

73

IMOGENE

(NOVEMBER 1967)

MAMA DIED.

It was sudden—a heart attack—Daddy told her over the phone when he'd called with the news. News that sent an icy chill over Imogene, freezing her to the hand-me-down sofa where she sat curled next to Wilfred in her warm, fuzzy sucks, a mug of hot cocoa in her hand. When Daddy told her what happened, she'd sat the mug on the small table beside her, where it grew cold, untouched, until Wilfred cleared it away the following morning. Imogene's relationship with her mother was not without complications, but a girl only has one mama. And now Imogene's is gone. And Daddy is alone. Nothing will ever be the same again. Everywhere, things are changing. Imogene used to crave change, but now that it's happening in such momentous and final ways, it terrifies her.

Since moving to Valdosta two years ago, Imogene has seen her mother only once. She'd come home to visit last December on "winter break" and thrilled her parents with stories of school. Without batting an eye, she'd invented friends, social events, and a local church she attended every Sunday. She bragged over the glowing praise received from her professors and put on a blush when she spoke of a boy named Wilfred who had been courting her these last few months. Imogene believed if she introduced Wilfred to her parents gradually, a day may come when they might meet without recognizing him. He was so changed, after all; Imogene herself sometimes struggled to know him.

But no matter now. That day will never come.

Mama and Daddy were so proud of her that visit. Proud of the life she'd constructed from lies. She'd smiled and hugged them and accepted their praise. But Imogene drowned in the guilt of it on the bus ride home. What she wouldn't give to tell them the truth. But then, she'd settle to tell *anyone*. There is nothing lonelier, she thinks, than a selfish secret; a secret that could change people's lives if brought to the light but destroy hers in the process.

To lie to her parents had been one thing—she'd lied to them for years—but lying to Greta is taking its toll. Imogene wants nothing more than to see her best friend. To tell her everything she's learned of Ray and The Company and Mickey Lancaster and let her and her family have the peace they so deserve. But to do that is to implicate Wilfred. And Mickey as well, for that matter. And she can't do that... to either of them. She just can't. So, this limits communication with Greta to bi-weekly letters in which Imogene spins the same fantastic tales she does to her own family. Sometimes Imogene finds a pay phone in town and calls to hear Greta's voice. And when she returns to her small apartment, she falls into Wilfred's arms and tries to pretend that it's enough. That she isn't lonely. That the burden isn't really all that heavy.

Perhaps that's why Imogene is so pleased to see Mickey

approach her outside the church after her mother's funeral. He knows the truth as well. He, too, carries the burden. And in that, they are forever connected. Mickey looks good, she thinks. Taking care of himself. He's grown his hair out again, but it's clean and combed back in a neat fashion. Fresh face, tailored suit, trimmed fingernails—he clearly hasn't returned to the drink.

"Mickey," she says, wiping self-consciously at her eyes. "It's good to see you. It's... been a long time."

"Too long," he says, and pulls Imogene into his arms. Mickey's body radiates warmth, and his hug is the kind that means something; the kind that denotes a history. The kind of hug where someone pulls you so tight that, for an instant, you blend into that person, and you can't help but return their embrace with insistence. When he pulls away, Imogene at once grieves the loss of his comfort. But it's not her place to ask for more.

"I'm so sorry about your mother," he says. "I can't even begin to... I'm just real sorry."

Imogene nods, incapable of more without crying.

She watches Mickey's eyes dart around and scan the crowd of mourners that drift from the church and onto the gravel drive, hugging each other and whimpering as they split off for their cars. "Is...?"

"No," Imogene answers swiftly. "He didn't come. He wanted to," she adds, "but he thought it too risky."

"Ah, right. I suppose congratulations are in order as well." Mickey throws a discreet glance at her bare left hand. She'd removed her ring before she came. Left it in Valdosta, in Wilfred's care. But she's aware what he refers to.

Imogene motions for him to lower his voice. "My daddy doesn't know yet."

Mickey nods. "I apologize. But congratulations all the same."

"Thank you," she mutters, but searches for something to add, something to erase the guilt of admitting her happiness to Mickey. To erase that awful look of sorrow that flicks across his face. Why, though? He *wants* her to be happy. He'd always said that, hadn't he? And now she is. "How—how did you find out?"

"Oh, I spoke to Wilfred briefly last year, not long after you… you know…"

Imogene nods. Wilfred hadn't mentioned speaking to Mickey. But then, why would he? As far as she knows, he's oblivious to her romantic past with the eldest Lancaster, and she intends to keep it that way. Already haunted by the events of that night, Imogene refuses to make it worse for Wilfred by admitting to a relationship with the person who sent him away. No. That secret is best left with her; another burden, but one she can—and *will*—bear on her own.

Daddy walks up then, shuffling the gravel with his nice shoes; a fine layer of white dust clings to the toes. One giant hand finds Imogene's shoulder. "I'm gonna head on up to the house—give Aunt Fran a ride. You know she can't stand for long these days. I'll see you up there, yeah?"

Imogene nods. "Yes, Daddy. I'll be right behind you."

"Good to see you again, Mickey. Thanks for coming," her father mutters, only half looking at them. He walks on, shoulders slumped, drained from the emotion of the last few days. Imogene watches him grip Aunt Fran's fragile arm, his other hand on the small of her back, helping her navigate the patch of grass that feeds into the parking lot of the church. Aunt Fran won't be here much longer, either. She will be next. More changes are coming. Fresh tears cloud her eyes, but she wipes them away with the back of her fingers and returns her attention to Mickey.

"Imogene, I… I sure have missed you." At this, he blushes and looks away. "I wish you were here for a different reason, but as it is…" His hand slips into the pocket of his jacket and he removes an envelope. Imogene sees her name written on the front in a careful hand. "This is for you," he says. "No need to open it now. It's just… something I need you to have."

Imogene takes the envelope. Looks at it a moment before stashing it in her purse.

"One more thing," he says. "I'm moving. Leaving Daytona."

This announcement takes Imogene by surprise. Daytona and

the Lancasters are synonymous; they belong together. Imogene's mouth opens and closes as she searches for words. "Really? Why is that?"

"Yeah. I—I bought a house."

"Mickey, that's great. Truly."

"It is. Yeah. I'm excited for the change." He smiles then, but Imogene gets the impression he's not that excited at all.

For a moment, their eyes linger on one another, unspoken words and unexpressed feelings strung in the air between them. Mickey clears his throat and pulls a second paper from his pocket, handing it to Imogene. Her hand closes around it hesitantly.

"It's my address," Mickey says with a shrug. "The new one, to the new house. If you ever want to write, I'd be happy to hear from you."

Imogene offers a smile but says, "I don't know if that would be proper considering…"

"No. Yeah, of course not." He nods, looks to his feet, stuffs his hands in his pockets as a chilly fall breeze blows past the building. "But still—you know… keep it. Just—just in case.

A frown tugs on the corners of her mouth, but she adds the paper with Mickey's address to her purse.

Just in case.

Daddy has long since slumped off to bed, leaving Imogene to attend to the lingering house guests and the tidying. When the last doleful goodbye has been made, Imogene clears the serving trays and scrapes the remnants of finger sandwiches, ham salad, pigs in a blanket, and pimento cheese dip into the trash. She scrubs the pans and glasses and makes mental notes of who brought which dish so she can return their glassware. Though she moves quickly and tries not to dwell in her thoughts, Imogene can't shake the strangeness of standing here at the sink, washing Mama's dishes, drying them with Mama's hand towels, and putting them away in Mama's cupboards. Imogene thinks of her father here, alone, and the lump in her throat grows. Inside, she is desperate to return to Valdosta, to Wilfred, but cannot stomach the idea of leaving Daddy here with no one to watch over him; without Mama to take care of things, will he be okay?

With the sink empty and the counters wiped clean, her eyes trail to the clock. The soft *tick tick tick* of its mechanics echo in the silent house. She pulls on her shoes, zips her coat, grabs her purse from her bed, and makes for the door.

Imogene knew at once what Mickey referenced in his letter, though she'd smiled at his clever riddle, reminiscing on the days they'd belonged to each other. Earlier—the house fit to burst with family and friends come to mourn Mama—Imogene snuck into her old room to read the letter in private. At the time, she wasn't sure she'd dare to follow his clue. Whatever he intended her to find, she had no right to take it.

When her mind had changed on the matter, she can't say for sure, but now her frigid hands are on the steering wheel, and she's driving to Honolulu Falls. It is chilly this evening, the first good cold snap of fall. Imogene waits for the heat in her father's Buick to warm the car. But even as her fingers thaw and the air turns thick and stifling, she shivers.

When she pulls into the parking lot of the golf course, the clock shows seven, but the sky is the inky black of midnight—yet another reason Imogene prefers the summer: those extra hours of sweet sunshine. These dark seasons throw her internal clock out of sorts.

She wraps her coat around herself and steps from the car, approaching the entrance where the ticket booth and concessions are housed. With the sweetest smile she can muster, she says to the lady at the ticket counter, "Hi there. I was here earlier with my friends, and I fear I may have dropped my handkerchief. My folks are sure sore about it; it was a gift from my grandmother who passed last year. Do you mind if I have a quick look?"

The woman wrinkles her brows for a moment, presumably weighing the likelihood that Imogene is putting her on and fishing for a free game. Finally, she says, "Well, nobody turned nothin' like that in today, but… I suppose so, yeah. Have a quick look around if you like."

"Thank you," Imogene smiles again and turns for the start of the course.

"We close in thirty minutes!" the woman calls after her.

"I'll be quick. I promise. Thank you again!" And with that, Imogene scurries off.

Much to her delight, she is alone. Of course, this does not come as a surprise; it's a weekday evening and much too frigid for true Floridians. Imogene moves through the course with ease.

At Hole 12, she finds the tiki men and smiles.

What takes the longest is locating the ridge hidden at the post's top and prizing it open with cold-stiff fingers.

Even longer is the time she spends to decide whether to follow Mickey's next set of instructions, or to return the key to the tiki man's head and go home.

And yet, longer still, to decide what to do once she arrives at the storage building and recovers from the shock of what waits for her there.

74

EMELINE

(JUNE 1, 2019)

THE WOMAN WHO STAFFS THE desk at Value-Lock Self Storage hardly looks up from her computer as they pass, but they smile at her, anyway.

They have a key to the unit—they are, for all intents and purposes, *invited*—but Emeline can't help but feel as if they are about to commit a crime, that armed officers wait in the shadows to arrest them for trespassing.

With only one floor and an abundance of signs pointing this way and that, they locate unit 203 with ease—a compact unit at the end of an aisle, with a blue garage-style door. Geoff, who still has the key, stoops to work the lock.

"Wait." The words leave Emeline's mouth before she's even

sure why.

Geoff stops and glances back at her over his shoulder. "What?" he snips.

But Emeline can only shrug. "I don't know. I just… we don't know what's in there."

"That's correct," Geoff says with a sigh. "And we'd like to, yeah? So, what's the problem?"

"I… I don't know. I just—forget it. Just go. Hurry." She motions him to go ahead and to pick up the pace.

With another exasperated sigh, he shoves the key into the lock. It's no surprise when the padlock pops open; Geoff pockets both padlock and key and opens the door with a swish. The metal scrapes and echoes through the cavernous building, and Emeline's heart races.

Inside is dark; the fluorescent light from the aisle only reaches a foot or two past the door. Geoff steps into the unit and waves his hand erratically through the air. "Ah ha!" he exclaims, and a second later the space is alight; a string dangles from the ceiling that connects to a small overhead bulb.

Emeline blinks a few times, eyes adjusting to the sudden brightness. But after a moment she can see the room is empty, save for a faded black duffel bag set ominously against the back wall. She swallows once, offers a noncommittal shrug, and they all move inside.

Once over the threshold, Wyatt turns and pulls the door shut behind them.

"What are you doing?" Emeline hisses.

"Privacy," he answers with a shrug.

In two long strides, Geoff is at the duffel bag. Without waiting for direction, he kneels to unzip the zipper. Emeline's pulse throbs in her ears.

As Geoff peels back the opening of the bag, a collective gasp fills the cell-like space. There is no missing the ocean of green inside—stacks upon stacks of cash are nestled next to each other, forgotten for decades.

Geoff tests the depth of the bag, shuffling the stacks around with his hand.

"Holy shit!" Wyatt shouts in a whisper-voice.

"You guys." Geoff's voice is low and secretive. "There's got to be over two hundred thousand dollars in here."

Emeline isn't sure why they are suddenly speaking in murmurs, but she finds herself with an equally hushed voice when she says, "How in the hell is this still here? All these years later? Gram never came for it?"

"She came for it."

This small voice comes from Belinda, who has been silent as a mouse the entire time. The three of them startle at the sound. Belinda stands by the door, a letter in one hand, an open envelope in the other.

"What is that?" Wyatt asks.

"It was here on the floor. Right here." She points a slim finger to the ground by her foot. "Like someone slid it under the door. It's for us. It's from Gram."

Sure enough, the front of the envelope is labeled: *For my Darling Lovebugs.*

75

IMOGENE

(NOVEMBER 1967)

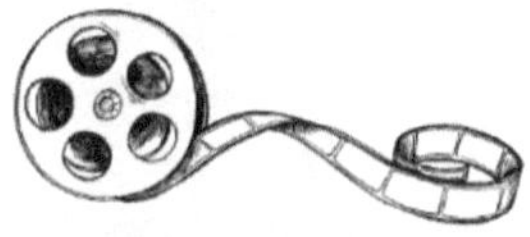

IMOGENE COULDN'T BRING HERSELF TO take it all. She shouldn't have taken the hundred thousand she did. This is the money that ruined Wilfred's life, the money that had gotten Ray killed, the money that might have destroyed a lot more. But as she stood there in that storage building, shivering in her coat, thoughts of the future filled her mind. She and Wilfred are saving for a house—a proper house with land and more than a single room—but they are years from affording more than their apartment above the barbershop. This doesn't bother Imogene much. A small space simply means she's that much closer to Wilfred, and this will never draw complaint from her lips. But things have changed—*are* changing. Every day.

As she drives back to Daddy's house, money secure in the car's trunk, she swallows her guilt and focuses on what she might say to her husband. Suppose she tells Wilfred that Mama left her some money in the will? Surely that will suffice. Prevent him from digging further or asking too many questions. The thought of lying to him is enough to cripple her. But he'd never agree to spend the money if he knew where it'd come from. Wilfred must never find out; he'd never forgive Imogene for taking it and for tricking him.

But this money can set them up right. It can even buy Daddy bus tickets or gas to come and visit.

Imogene sighs, hands gripped tight on the steering wheel. If things were different, she would have left it there. She would not have touched a single penny, gone home, and never thought of it again.

But it's not just the two of them to consider now.

Imogene hasn't told him yet; she doesn't know for sure herself. Yet she *knows*.

She is pregnant.

76

BELINDA

(JUNE 1, 2019)

AVING ALREADY READ THE LETTER silently twice through, Belinda passes it off to Emeline, who is best at reading aloud.

"*My Darling Lovebugs,*" she begins, the paper wrinkling where she grips too tightly.

"*If you've made it this far, you've already learned more of my past than I ever wished to share. But you'll be better for having learned the truth. I hope you see I was only ever human. Same as you, I tried my best, and often came up short. But it was love that first brought me to the place you now stand. Love that prompted me to take a hundred thousand dollars from the bag when my conscience begged me to run. Love that made me leave behind the rest when my brain cried,* Take it, you fool! *Love that spurred me to*" *write Greta all these many years later and asked her to slide this letter under the door of Unit 203 at the Value-Lock Self Storage without explanation, in hopes that one day the four of you might read it. And it is love—whether or not you choose to believe it—that brings you here today.*

"This money is all the remains of that fateful night in 1963. Your grandfather wanted nothing to do with it, and I can't fault him for that. Mickey dipped into it for a time, but once he'd regained access to his family's fortune, he hardly needed the cash. As for me, I took enough for Gramps and I to buy the lake house and start our lives on the right foot, but not without terrible guilt for having done so."

Belinda braces for the next line. The line her eyes returned to and hovered over when she'd first found the letter. The line that changes everything. The whole entire game.

"Now, this money is yours."

Emeline's eyes go wide, and she pauses as though she's lost her place. Belinda's own heartbeat thumps away fast as rabbit feet in her chest. Emeline continues.

"The storage unit is now in my name and paid until the end of 2020. If you don't take the bag by then, someone else will. So, please... take it.

"The journey doesn't end here, though. We've come so far... but there's more you must know. Find the answers at 55890 Willow Glen Drive, Lake City, Florida. I'll see you soon, Gram."

77

IMOGENE

(MARCH 1974)

THE CHANGES KEEP COMING. DAY after day. But Imogene handles them better than she expected. She once again embraces the changes. Even enjoys them.

Five years ago, Imogene and Wilfred bought a lovely home of their own. Three enormous bedrooms, two full baths, five sprawling acres of land, and—Imogene's favorite part—a shimmering lake right in their own backyard. She can't imagine raising a family in a more picturesque place.

The first July in their new home, Imogene gave birth to the most perfect baby boy. They named him William, after Wilfred's late father. Daddy had suggested Gene as a middle name—his grandfather's name. But Imogene had shaken her head and said,

"That's a real nice name, Daddy, but… I was thinking we'd call him Raymond."

Imogene hadn't spoken this aloud to anyone yet. She and Wilfred exchanged a look across the hospital room, little William tucked in the crook of her arm, suckling happily on a bottle, and Wilfred's eyes brimmed with tears. Daddy just nodded—not connecting the name to the accident all those years ago—and tried it out on his tongue. "William Raymond. Yeah. That's a nice strong name. Real nice, Imogene. That sounds real nice."

Four years later, in the fall, a baby girl arrived. Dea Rose.

Now the house is exactly as Imogene imagined. Two glorious children running amuck all hours of the day, swimming their Saturday's away in the lake out back, dragging through the door at sunset, dirt and mud dried in their crevices and under their fingernails, exhausted smiles glued to their faces. It is bliss. Pure, serendipitous bliss.

Yet beneath the joys of day-to-day life, beneath their many blessings, a darkness lingers, an obsidian blot on their perfect existence. Wilfred's nightmares continue to torment him. His involvement with the children has dwindled to almost nothing. And Imogene's guilt finds her at the end of each day. A circadian reminder that Raymond Green is dead because of *her*. The moment Wilfred told her the truth of that long ago day, a small voice whispered its judgment in her ear. But as the years passed, the voice grew louder, now a bellowing roar of damnation. And the voice is right, because Imogene knows Wilfred never would have pushed Ray into the MacNeil job if not for his determination to keep his promise to her. If Imogene hadn't complained so much about her home life, if she hadn't agreed to let Wilfred rescue her—practically *begged* him to—they'd never have stepped foot in the mansion that night, Ray would still be alive, and Ted would still be Ted.

78

BELINDA

(JUNE 1, 2019)

LAKE CITY IS TWO-AND-A-HALF hours north-west. Belinda, unfamiliar with the town, relies on Google Maps to get her there.

"Shut up or I'll have to start over!" Geoff shouts; Emeline and Wyatt are bickering about being hungry. Belinda's stomach rumbles as well. Now that they've stopped moving for a moment, she realizes they haven't eaten since breakfast and, rattled by their morning fisticuffs with Denver and the revelation of her father's drug problem, Belinda had taken only a few bites.

"There's some chips in the cabinet," she yells back at them.

"Seriously, shut the hell up!" Geoff snips again. The duffel bag is open at his feet, and he stacks piles of cash on the tabletop in front of him as he counts; he'd already started over once.

Behind her, Belinda hears the cabinet open and the rustle of plastic bags. A few moments later, Wyatt springs up beside her and offers her an open bag of Sun Chips. "Thank you," she says with an appreciative sigh, holding the bag between her thighs while she drives.

"Well, I was right," Geoff says from the back of the bus. "Two-hundred-forty thousand dollars total. So that makes sixty thousand for each of us. Hot damn!"

Belinda startles at this. "Wait… so, you think we should split it amongst ourselves?"

"Well, duh. What the hell else would we do with it?"

Belinda mulls this over, eyes flicking madly over the road ahead, as if the solution could be out in the trees somewhere. But an answer eludes her. All she knows is that it feels selfish to keep that much for themselves. "I don't know," she says. "But shouldn't we like… do something good with it? Something to make Gram proud?"

Geoff snorts. "Yeah, okay, you go save the world with *your* cut. Gram told us to take it."

"She said to take it. She didn't say *keep it*," Emeline comes to Belinda's defense.

"Unbelievable," Geoff mutters. "I can't believe you two are suggesting we just throw this much money away."

Emeline grunts in frustration. "I didn't say that."

Now Wyatt chimes in. "Maybe we should at least *talk* about what to do with it. Reach an agreement."

"Whatever," Geoff snorts. "But you already know *my* vote."

79

EMELINE

(JUNE 1, 2019)

OR EMELINE, THE TRIP HAS taken an introspective turn. Not that she hadn't been examining her life and dissecting the chain of events that lead to her current circumstances *long* before she got the call about Gram. But this is different. Because wherever they end up now is likely their last stop. This weekend has been the perfect distraction from the mess that awaits her at home, and now, it's slipping away. Reality looms on the horizon. Soon, she will be back in Tennessee. Alone with the kids. In the throes of divorce. And for the first time, the idea of being so far from her brothers, from her parents, from Belinda, is a tough pill to swallow.

"Do you guys remember Camp Baker?" Emeline surprises

herself with the question. A million years have passed since they last played there together, but this trip is exhuming memories long buried.

Geoff laughs, and Belinda giggles from the driver's seat, her attention focused forward, hands at ten and two.

"Of course," Wyatt says with a chuckle of his own. "Good ol' Camp Baker."

Camp Baker was the rickety old shack Gramps built them out of spare wood, old pallets he'd taken apart and stored in his garage. He'd spent months working on it, so it'd be ready for when they came that summer. On that first day, seeing it set up in the backyard was just… the *coolest* thing. Emeline had been ten that summer, Belinda six, both just the right age to consider it the neatest surprise ever. The twins, at three, were not yet old enough to appreciate it. But they would.

Gramps, who was never that involved in their games, was so excited to watch them play in their new clubhouse. On a left-over slab of wood, he'd helped Emeline write the words *Camp Baker* in white paint. Then they'd taken turns dipping their hands in Gram's various craft paints, stamping the front of the sign with colorful handprints. When the sign dried, Gramps nailed it above the clubhouse door. The four of them were so proud, and looking back now, Gramps was proud as well.

"We had a lot of good times at that house," Emeline says, a wisp of nostalgia in her voice.

"We did," Belinda agrees. "Best summers of my life."

Everyone nods in silence, likely ferreting through their mental reserves for sweet memories of their own.

After a moment, Geoff asks, "What ever happened to Camp Baker?"

With a jolt of surprise, Emeline asks, "You really don't remember?"

Geoff shakes his head no.

"Hurricane Fay in 2008. Blew it apart. A bunch of pieces ended up floating in the lake. And whatever was left…" she shrugs. "At that point, it'd been years since we used it, anyway. I think Gramps had been storing some garden equipment in there."

When Emeline rouses her memories of that summer, she recalls it well. Freshly graduated from high school, she came and went, sleeping over at her friend's houses most nights, or at home, in her own room. But she loved Gram's cooking and always returned in the evening for dinner. Belinda was fourteen and much too old for make-believe and games. And even the twins, who at eleven were still technically children, had outgrown it, their attentions turned more to video games and action figures.

"I can rebuild it for you guys," Gramps offered when they'd discovered the damage the morning after the storm. "It wouldn't take much to do it. It could be good as new."

Geoff and Wyatt had looked at each other, and then at the scattered pieces of wood, and said, "Nah, that's okay, Gramps. We don't really need it anymore."

Gramps nodded and said *Okay*, and by the end of the week, the yard was cleared and whatever remained of Camp Baker hauled away.

Now, Emeline wishes they had just let him rebuild the damn thing. She wishes she'd been at the house more that summer, and the summers that followed. That she hadn't insisted on growing up so fast. Because less than two years later, Gramps was gone.

80

IMOGENE

(SEPTEMBER 2009)

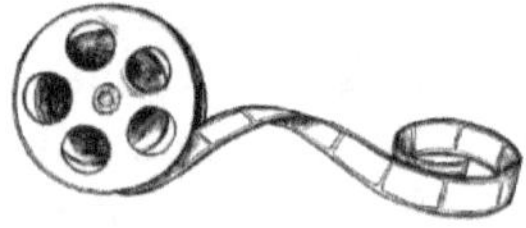

WITH THE KIDS BACK IN school, the house is quiet once again—too quiet. Imogene makes quick work of stacking a few sandwiches on a platter. She then grabs the pitcher of sun-brewed tea from the refrigerator and makes her way to the garden where Wilfred has been busying himself most of the morning. She wishes he would take it easy. High noon on a cloudless Georgia day is not the time to be outdoors mucking about in the yard.

When she finds him, he is hunched over a bean plant, grumbling. The sound of Imogene setting the lunch plate on the small metal table beneath the awning draws his attention.

"Hungry?" she calls.

"Mm-hmm," he mutters. "These beans… they look funny to you? They aren't growin' right this year. I swear, it's been too damn hot. Can't expect anything to grow in this heat."

And as he crosses to join Imogene at the table, he continues to rant over seed germination and soil temperatures and global warming and quiets only when he grabs a turkey and cheese sandwich from the tray with dirt-stained fingers and lowers into the chair with a grunt.

Imogene watches him eat, mind clearly still focused on the garden and the damn beans.

"Do you have your sunscreen on?" Imogene asks after a moment.

Surprise crosses his face. Surprise that turns at once to annoyance. With a scoff he says, "Little good that will do now, huh?"

"Wilfred, dear. You know I didn't mean—"

"I'm wearing it," he says, voice clipped and gruff. But then he looks at her and smiles. That sweet little half-smirk that still sends Imogene to pieces. Age may have grayed her husband's hair, turned his skin tan and leathery; loose bits hang from the waning muscles in his arms, sag beneath his sleepy eyes. But beneath the changes, he is still her Wilfred. And when he smirks like that, the years fold back, and Imogene is seeing him for the first time, her hand in his as he pulls her aboard The Siren.

In the middle of chewing, Wilfred says, "If you want beans again next year, I say plant them sooner. No later than April. I waited too long this year, and it got too damn hot."

"Plant them yourself," Imogene says, a defiant set to her lips.

He looks at her then, the light in his eyes fading. "Imogene… we've been over this. Let's not pretend that's a possibility."

"You don't know that it's not."

"You heard the doctor. You were sitting right there beside me."

Imogene rests her sandwich daintily on the plate in front of her. She *had* been there beside him when they'd received the news. And whenever her eyes drift shut, the doctor's words return anew. *Stage four melanoma… No cure.*

"Come on," Wilfred says, knees cracking as he stands. "Let me show you how to spread the fertilizer."

81

GEOFF

(JUNE 1, 2019)

FROM WHAT GEOFF CAN TELL, Willow Glen Drive is largely underwhelming. It started well enough—tranquil even— as a winding asphalt road surrounded by oaks and pines.

But then the asphalt ran out, and now they bump along a dirt road instead. Geoff moves to the front of the bus where the jarring is less severe.

The day has shifted to evening. Six-thirty now. Geoff is starving and tired and irritated with how the others are treating him. Like he's a selfish asshole for wanting to keep the money that *Gram herself* told them to take. But soon enough, this trip will be over, so he forces his focus onto his grandmother's letter and the road ahead.

The nasal voice of Belinda's GPS fills the bus. *"In one-thousand feet, your destination will be on the right."*

Belinda flips her blinker to signal their turn, which is unnecessary; they are alone on the secluded street and have been ever since they turned off the main road three miles back. The GPS announces, *You have arrived at your destination,* just as the bus decelerates and veers into the drive on their right.

Belinda slows the bus to a full stop. A towering metal gate blocks their entry. To their left is one of those speaker boxes with a dial pad to punch in a code or something.

"Did Gram's letter mention a gate?" Emeline asks.

"No." Belinda shakes her head and lowers the window to inspect the box. "There's a call button. Should I do it?"

"Well, I didn't drive two-and-a-half hours to just sit here," Geoff says.

With a roll of her eyes, she reaches a pale arm out the window and presses the button labeled *Call.*

A harsh ringing issues from the speaker and they fall into silence, waiting.

Another ring.

Another.

Finally, a woman's voice. Older and blunt. "Yeah? Who is this?"

Belinda blanches, but she manages to say, "Um… hi. I'm— uh, Belinda Hutson. Uh…"

"I don't know no Belinda. What business you got here?"

"Uh—we…" she trails off, eyes frantically searching for support in the faces of her cousins.

None of them had rehearsed what to say, considering they hadn't known what to expect. But Geoff can see Belinda is freezing up, so he leans over her and shouts out the window. "Hi. I'm Geoff Baker. Our grandmother sent us here… uh— sort of. She didn't tell us why, but we drove a long way, and we'd like to find out. So, if you'd kindly let us in, we—"

"Baker, you said?" the voice interrupts.

"Yes. Geoff Baker."

Silence follows, and Geoff wonders if the woman has

disconnected the call. They exchange looks and shrugs, unsure what to do.

"Hello?" Geoff calls out after another moment's silence.

A few breaths later, the voice returns. "I'm gonna buzz you in. I'm sending my daughter up to meet ya'll, so sit tight for a spell. She's right up the road."

Without another word, a buzzer sounds, then a loud, metallic *click*, and the gates ease open. Belinda shifts the bus into gear and inches forward.

Ahead of them, the drive stretches for five hundred feet or so before splitting into a wide circle laid before a picturesque southern estate.

Belinda pulls the bus around to the front of the loop.

The four of them hop out and wait for… well, they aren't sure *who* they are waiting for exactly, but Geoff is grateful to stretch his legs. He stuffs his hands in his pockets and looks around. The house is two stories. *Nice.* A white paneled exterior. Seven red brick steps lead up to the entryway. There, four rounded columns stretch up to the overhang, the peak of which exhibits classic, colonial molding. Large screened-in porches jut from both sides of the house, wide-blade fans spinning idly. And on the second floor, a balcony protrudes from the front of the house, which adds extra shade to the white double doors below.

In every direction, massive oak trees permeate the yard—a yard flawlessly manicured with grass, brilliant and green. And not the grass that just *grows* here, mind you, but the kind you must select, sod, and tend to with a certain level of skill—a skill Geoff doesn't possess himself, but *hey*, that's what gardeners are for.

The sun dips lower now and slices through the leaves, turning everything golden and pristine. The evening rays of light glint off the many windows on the front of the home, and Emeline breathes out a *Wow* beside him.

Geoff can't help but be impressed as well. If things in his life had stayed on track, if Lila had never gotten pregnant, never lost the baby, Geoff would have been able to offer her a place like this. Eventually. Two years, *tops*. But everything went to shit, didn't it?

The sound of a motor rumbling up the drive cuts through Geoff's momentary slip of self-loathing. A small silver sedan comes to a stop behind the bus, and a dark-skinned woman in her fifties steps out a moment later.

"Hi there," she says, gravel crunching beneath her tennis shoes as she approaches their group. Her hair is short and graying and she wears these hot pink cat-eye glasses and athletic wear—black leggings and a tight pink tank top. With an admiring glance, Geoff thinks this is a woman who takes care of herself; the places that normally go soft on women of a certain age are still tight and strong on her.

"Hi," Geoff says, and he steps forward, extending a hand.

"Kizzie Hubbard, nice to finally meet you," she takes his hand and offers a firm shake.

"Geoff Baker. This is my sister, Emeline. My brother, Wyatt. My cousin, Belinda."

She nods, taking them in as one. "Weren't sure you guys would ever get here. I was startin' to worry."

"No offense," Geoff says, "but you seem to know us, and yet, we don't know who *you* are. Based on our trip so far, I'm sure our grandmother sent us to your house for a reason, but rather than guess what that reason might be, maybe you'd care to enlighten us?"

"Oh, this ain't *my* house," Kizzie says, surprised. And with a jerk of her thumb adds, "I live up the road."

"Whose house is it then?" Wyatt asks, appearing at Geoff's shoulder.

"Your Gram didn't tell you?" Kizzie looks expectantly at each of them and shrugs. Then, with a smile, she says, "It's yours, of course."

82

WILFRED

(FEBRUARY 1, 2010)

HERE'S THE THING ABOUT MELANOMA: It's one of the quickest spreading forms of skin cancer. If Wilfred had caught the spot sooner, the outcome may have been different. But he hadn't, so no point dwelling on *might-have-beens*. Years of construction—of long days with the sun beating on bare shoulders—has taken its toll. Plain and simple.

Everything happened fast. The doctors warned him it would, but it was surprising, nonetheless. Wilfred is scared, of course. But not for himself—for Imogene, who tends to him as though he is simply fighting off a bad cold. She brings him soup and presses cool washcloths to his forehead and lips and mutters soft affirmations in his ear, as though he'll be right as rain in a few days' time. She takes those *in sickness and in health* vows very seriously, this one.

She knows, of course. The doctors had done their jobs to prepare her for what was to come, of what was happening inside Wilfred's failing body. But Imogene refuses to drop the pretense that they are stronger, the two of them, then whatever life throws their way—including a terminal illness. And because a wife needs to believe she can fix everything, Wilfred lets her try.

So, yes, Wilfred is afraid. Afraid of how Imogene will handle things once he's gone. And that day is fast approaching.

Wilfred is bed ridden now, heavily medicated to fight the unbearable pain. Nurses come multiple times a day to monitor the slow decline of his body and try to keep him comfortable.

Earlier, the kids came by for a visit—William and Fran, Geoff and Wyatt. It was a nice visit. William and Fran seemed happy; their usual tension set aside. The twins even gave him a hug, which they hadn't done in years. One on each side of the bed, Wilfred kissed the tops of their heads. After they'd gone, a change came over Wilfred. An energy. Imogene's eyes had brightened at this, as though, for an instant, she thought, *Perhaps he's fighting this thing off.*

But he isn't fighting. Not anymore. The change is because Wilfred knows. *How*, he cannot say for sure. But he does. The end is near. His mind has come to terms with this and has gifted this last burst of strength to share the whole awful truth with Imogene—everything he's kept hidden during their long, happy marriage.

Wilfred calls her to the bed, and she perches on the edge. Holds his thin hand in both of her own. *Her touch*—that is what he will miss the most.

"Imogene, there are some things I need to tell you. These are important things. Things I've kept from you. I'm not proud of that, and I'm sorry. But I need to tell you now, and I need you to listen. None of this *tell me next week* nonsense. This is serious. Understand?"

She nods.

Wilfred takes a deep, rattling breath. "First, I know about

Mick Lancaster. That you were in love with him when you believed me dead."

Her face reddens with surprise and embarrassment.

"But there's something about Mick you don't realize," he continues. "See, we've talked off and on for years. There's been phone calls, usually late at night, after you've gone to bed. Couple years ago, in came another call... not from Mick. From a lawyer. Mick had passed away, he said. A brain aneurism. Felt like an anvil to the chest, that news. Not that we were *friends,* mind you."

Wilfred laughs then. A small, throaty chuckle. "Hell, maybe we were," he says with a smile.

Imogene smiles, too. *Her smile.* Yes. He will miss that, as well.

"Anyway, this lawyer man told me that Mick—of all the hairbrained things he did over the years—left his house and property to *me.* Of all people! I told the man, *Thanks, but no thanks.* Told him, *I've got a house I'm plenty pleased with and not looking to leave.* The lawyer laughed a little at that and said, *Mr. Lancaster told me you'd be stubborn about taking the place.* So, Mick had given him a message to pass on to me. Apparently, he wanted me to know he bought the house with his family's money, not the money from the accident. And also, that he bought the house before I came back to Daytona. Mick bought the house for *you,* Imogene."

Imogene swallows hard, but only stares at Wilfred, unblinking. After a moment, in a choked whisper, she says, "I had no idea."

Wilfred goes on. "The lawyer said I could sell the place if I'd like. It was an extravagant home for the time, and would still be worth a pretty penny, especially being cared for as meticulously as it had been. And I'd thought, *Hell yes, I'm gonna sell it!* But, as soon as I realized the home was meant for you, selling wasn't an option."

And now, Wilfred lowers his voice and tells her the belief he's carried in his heart since 1965. "He would have been a better choice than me, Imogene. He could have given you a better life."

With this admission, furious tears spill down Imogene's cheeks, and she shakes her head. "No," she says, jaw clenched tight. "I made the right choice. Wilfred Baker, you gave me the most amazing life. I regret nothing. Not a single moment."

Wilfred moves his hand to her face and brushes a damp piece of hair—grayer now than her earlier auburn-gray, but lovely as ever—behind her ear. "But he would have taken better care of you. He *was* taking care of you, even *after* he died, damn him. And you had no idea."

Another secret propels itself into Wilfred's thoughts, and he says, "Do you remember last spring when I visited Dale in Tallahassee? From my old crew?"

Imogene nods, silent.

"Well, that's not where I'd gone at all. I went to Mick's house. To have a look around. Figure out what I wanted to do. This place... Imogene, it was *spotless*. He had this place shining from floor to ceiling. Seemed to me as if... it's probably silly—but... it felt like since he wasn't able to have the real thing, he loved the *house* the way he wished he could love *you*. He never married, you know."

Imogene shakes her head. "No, I didn't," she says. Still so quiet.

"I couldn't sell it. Couldn't even think about it. The house was yours. It always had been. But I figured I'd have to drag you out of the lake house kicking and screaming." Wilfred laughs again, coughing suddenly, chest aching something horrible. Imogene, the sweet woman, holds a glass with a straw to his mouth. After a few sips, he feels well enough to continue. "But I figure you'll do right by it. Even if you don't want the place for yourself, you'll know what to do with it. And no point arguing with me. I've already set the house in your name. You'll get it after... well..." He clears his throat, and she squeezes his hand tighter. "You know I'd stay with you forever if I could, right? I would. I'd never leave your side."

Imogene nods. She knows, of course. There is no way she doesn't.

"There's something else," Wilfred says, as the secret he's

been most guilty of keeping floats to the surface. "While I was up there at Mick's, this lady comes up. Young, pretty gal. Late forties, give or take. Introduced herself as Kizzie. Said she and her mom were real good friends with Mr. Lancaster. Said they lived right up the street. Said that after he'd passed away, they started keeping the place up as a favor.

"Well, this Kizzie took me up the road to meet her mother, and Imogene, when I walked in and saw her there, I swear my heart stopped. I think I gave her quite a scare, too."

83

WILFRED

(FEBRUARY 3, 2010)

WILFRED CAN'T HELP BUT THINK he doesn't deserve to die this way. And he doesn't mean the cancer; that's all fine and well. He means here, swathed in these warm sheets on a bed soft as a cloud. Here, in the home he was lucky enough to raise a family in, his devoted wife by his side.

Imogene.

He can't speak to her but knows she's there.

He can hear her whispering *I love you* again and again.

Can feel her hand in his, the weight of her on the mattress beside him.

He shouldn't have the luxury of a death as fine as this. After all he's done. And all he hasn't. He can only hope that when he sees Ray again, he'll find it in his heart to forgive him. And he *does* look forward to seeing Ray again.

Wilfred is not in pain. It's as though he floats between two worlds. And as badly as he wants to stay in this one, the longer he's here, the more pain Imogene must suffer. Goodbyes are meant to be short and sweet. Anything more is just cruel.

When the doctor gave Wilfred the news, they estimated his time left—best-case scenario—at a year. But six months, the doc said, was more realistic.

Wilfred got five.

84

WYATT

(JUNE 1, 2019)

"**I'M SORRY, THAT'S GOT TO** be a mistake," Wyatt says.

But Kizzie just chuckles. "I'm serious as a heart attack. And I'm glad you're here because, frankly, I am *sick* of coming up here every damn day—checkin' the mail, letting in the gardener, the cleaning service, running solicitors off—you'd think I work here."

"You don't?" Geoff asks.

Kizzie cuts him a look. "Hell to the no. I'm an RN." She glares at Geoff a beat longer before continuing. "My mother worked here for a time, back in the sixties. When Mr. Lancaster owned the house."

"Lancaster—Mickey Lancaster?" Wyatt asks.

"That's the one," she beams. "You knew him?"

Wyatt feels as though he's swimming under water, everything hazy and dreamlike. "Not personally," he says.

"But we've learned a lot about him this weekend," Belinda adds.

"Is that so? Well, me and my mama were real fond of him, that's for sure."

"Who is your mother? If you don't mind me asking?" Emeline says.

"Name's Athena Roberts."

A chill prickles the back of Wyatt's neck. He tries to do the mental math and listen at the same time.

"Did your mom used to live in Daytona, by chance?" Emeline asks.

Kizzie nods. "She did. Yeah. In her younger years. But she's lived in Lake City since before I was born."

"How old are you?" Geoff asks. Wyatt is curious as well but is aware the faux pas of enquiring a woman's age. Geoff apparently has no qualms with pissing someone off—he'd already accused Kizzie of being the housemaid, may as well continue to stick his foot in it. Fortunately, she doesn't seem to mind the question, and answers with a proud jut to her chin.

"Turned fifty-five this year. Still got it, don't I?" Kizzie cuts a pose and laughs.

Geoff chuckles but steamrolls ahead. "Yeah. Yeah, you do. And your father? Do you—"

But Kizzie lifts a hand to silence him, eyes sharp and assessing. Quiet falls among the group. "Sounds like you guys learned about *all kinds* of things this weekend."

The only sound is the occasional rustle of wind through the trees, and the gravel that crunches beneath Wyatt's shoe as he shifts his weight from one foot to the other. This far out, the lack of ambient noise is unsettling. But no one will speak without knowing how much of the story Kizzie is *actually* privy to.

Eventually, she speaks, and they get their answer. "Raymond Green. Yeah. And yes, I'm aware of what happened to him. Spent my whole life *not* knowin'—not the truth of it, anyway.

But then I met your grandfather, and he told us how it was."

She reaches into her pocket and withdraws a key. "Come on," she says. "Let's get inside. It's hotter than the devil's armpit out here."

At the front door, Kizzie stuffs the key in the lock like someone whose done it a thousand times. When the door cracks open, a blast of cold AC reaches out and grabs hold of them. "There now," she says. "Go on in. I'll pour us some tea, and we'll have a little chat."

The house has five bedrooms, three baths, a library, and an office. Everyone seems equally mesmerized, though Wyatt, who has spent the last three years living in a garage apartment with one dusty window and water pressure akin to a slow drip, may as well be having tea in the Taj Mahal.

The five of them sit in the kitchen around a large dining table. A pitcher of sweet tea rests in the middle next to a vase of fresh yellow and red flowers. Tall, floor-to-ceiling windows drench the room in soft evening light.

"I still can't believe your gramma didn't tell you about this house," Kizzie says. "She just sent ya'll on a wild goose chase and hoped you'd find your way here." A bemused laugh flies out of her, and she takes a big swig of tea, ice rattling as she lowers her glass to the table. "Then again, I only met Imogene a couple times, but… yeah, that seems like *exactly* the sort of crazy-ass thing she'd do. She was a fun old lady, that one."

The four of them exchange smiles, remembering.

"Maybe you can fill in a few gaps for us, Mrs. Hubbard?" Emeline asks.

"Kizzie is fine, dear. And I can certainly try. What would you like to know first?"

Wyatt has a question locked and loaded. "You said you met our grandfather, and he told you the truth about what happened to your father? I'm curious what exactly he told you."

"Ah," she says, "well, I met your grandfather shortly after

Mr. Lancaster passed away. This was *his* house, you see, and he left it to your grandfather in his will. He'd left instructions, too, asking us to keep an eye on the place until your grandfather either came for it, or sold it away. Took months, but he finally paid a visit. I was glad for it, too. Mama was getting on in years and didn't have the back for cleanin' like she used to, so it'd been *me* who was lookin' over things.

"When your grandpa came, I took him up the street to our house to meet Mama. And—I tell ya, when those two saw each other, it was like they both was staring at a ghost. Mama thought he'd died a million years ago, in the same accident that took my daddy. And yet there he was in our kitchen, spry as a spring chicken.

"Your grandpa told us the truth that day—about the accident, the fire, Mickey helping him escape and change his name, the whole awful lot of it. Mama wasn't too pleased with Mr. Lancaster for a while for keeping something like that from us. But she got over it quick enough… he'd done so much for us, after all."

"Like what?" Emeline asks.

"Well, for starters, he bought Mama her house."

Jaws drop around the table as they listen in disbelief.

"Yeah, Mr. Lancaster came up here in the sixties, lookin' for a house for him and his girl. My mama was working at a real estate office then, doing clerical work, and making pennies. She told me Mr. Lancaster came in one day and introduced himself. Said he was from the Daytona area. Mama said, *Small world. So am I.* And they hit it off. She didn't know him from before, but she knew his name, boy! Everyone in Daytona knew the Lancasters. Back then, me and her were living with my aunt. I was just a little thing, so I don't remember that time much, but Mama told me Mr. Lancaster didn't care for us living there. Not one bit. Now, it wasn't a *bad* place—I've seen photos—but the neighborhood was rough, and Mama and I didn't even have a room of our own. We slept in the living room, on the sofa or on the floor. So, Mr. Lancaster made a deal with Mama. Told her he'd buy her a house down the way—pay all expenses, too—if she'd keep the house up for him while he was away. It wouldn't be more than a year, he said. The house was going to be a surprise for his girl, for after they got married.

"When he finally moved in two years later, he came alone. Never did see another woman here for as long as he lived."

Kizzie's fingers wrap around her glass, and she slides it absentmindedly over the drops of condensation that float on the wood. "He looked after us always. Whenever something came up Mama couldn't handle on her own, Mr. Lancaster handled it for her. Every holiday, Mama would invite him to our place. She told him to come up and eat with the family—he was family himself, after all. But he always declined. Said he didn't want to be in the way. So, Mama and me, we'd make him this big dinner and bring it up to the house—eat with him out on the porch there, or here at the table if the weather was cold. When I had my daughter, she started coming up with us, too. Called him *Mr. Lamp-kisser* for the longest time." She laughs at the memory. "Now I got grandkids, if you can believe such a thing! And I wish they could have known him. I really do. Whether he took care of us from the kindness of his heart, or from the guilt over what happened to my daddy… Mr. Lancaster was a real fine man.

"Anyway," Kizzie sighs and refills her glass and Belinda's to her right. "After your grandpa passed, your gramma got the place. She came up not too long after. Made a few trips, actually. Her and Mama would talk some. Guess they knew each other from back when. Didn't take long to figure out your gramma was the gal Mr. Lancaster meant to bring up here all those years ago. It was nice she finally made it." A sad smile touches her lips.

"Your gramma brought these various odds and ends each time she came. Set them up in that room over there." Kizzie gestures to a closed door beside the staircase. "Then she'd leave, and each month a check would arrive to hire a cleaning crew and keep the lawn maintenance going. Last thing we received from her was a VHS tape. Now, I laughed because I hadn't seen one of those damn things in years. A note said to put it in the room by the stairs, so I did. And the same note said she was leaving the house to her grandkids. The check she sent that day was for a hefty chunk of money, like she meant it to last awhile. Then, a few days ago, a man calls to tell us Imogene had passed. And I was real sorry to hear that."

Wyatt's throat tightens. A hard little lump he can't swallow. "She left a tape?" he asks.

"She did," Kizzie nods. "Problem is, that room is locked up tight. I *had* the key, but your gramma made me mail it back to her. I assumed she had a reason and didn't think to make a copy. We could try to get a locksmith out here tomorrow, I suppose, but…"

Wyatt stands and moves toward the closed door.

"Wyatt?" Emeline stands, chair legs scraping across the wooden floors.

"I think I have the key," he mutters. And for the second time today, he reaches into his pocket and withdraws the key from Gramps' faded leather wallet.

The others close in behind him as he touches the metal tip to the lock. It slips in as though it belongs there and turns with ease. The door cracks open.

"Oh my God." Emeline's hand flies to her mouth as she scans the room.

"Oh, Gram," Belinda mutters.

Wyatt takes in everything. Every thoughtfully placed item. Framed photographs cover the walls of the room—photographs of all the summers spent at Gram's. There is the one of Emeline and Belinda sitting on a pink quilt in the living room; stuffed animals surround them, and Belinda presses a plastic teacup to the lips of a stuffed hippo. There's the one of Gramps on his riding mower, three-year-old Wyatt on his lap, pretending to steer. There is nine-year-old Geoff in mid-air, jumping from the dock into the lake, a teenaged Emeline climbing to her feet and scurrying away before the splash can drench her. And there is the shot of Belinda at age seven, Gram's cherry lipstick smeared under her eyes like war paint. And Emeline, in pigtails, standing in front of her new purple bike. There is Gramps in his garden, spraying a water hose toward the camera while Belinda, Geoff, and Wyatt run away screaming. And one of Gram in the kitchen, the four of them squashed in around her. Each of them is smiling; big, dopey, hopeful, sunburned, summer smiles.

Various toys they'd outgrown and left behind are now displayed around the room; a time capsule of their youth. The little red wagon Gramps made from wood, the tiny stool Belinda stood on to help Gram with dishes, a shelf of G.I. Joes, a basket of stuffed animals, the curtains from our bedroom hung in the window.

Behind him, Wyatt hears a sharp intake of breath followed by a muffled whimper. He turns to see Geoff with tears streaming down his face. Wyatt has never seen his brother cry. Not once. He wants to turn away, but can't, and Geoff notices Wyatt staring at him. But instead of hiding his face or trying to explain away the tears, he wipes his eyes and says, "Look."

Their eyes follow Geoff's, and there, hung above the door, is a rectangular sign. *Camp Baker* is scrawled across the front in sloppy white paint, surrounded by four tiny sets of colorful handprints.

"Oh my God," Belinda whimpers; her chin tightens and wrinkles as her own emotion threatens to seep out.

"I thought we lost this in the storm," Emeline says.

"Gramps must have found it and kept it," Wyatt mutters as tears slip silently down his cheek.

And then Geoff says, "I love you guys. I mean it. I really do. If I've been an asshole these past few years, I'm sorry. I just… this…" He gestures vaguely around the room. "How did we stray so far from this?"

"We grew up, I guess," Belinda says.

For a long moment, they seem to forget why they'd come into the room in the first place. But against the far wall is a table. A small tv with a built-in VCR is there. A VHS lies beside it. Written on the front on the tape is: *For my darling Lovebugs—*

You made it.

Emeline takes a deep breath and pops the VHS into the machine.

And a moment later, there she is. *Gram.*

They've learned so much about her since they'd last seen her face.

Gram smiles. A heavy smile. A *proud* smile. "My darling, Lovebugs," she begins. "If you are watching this video, you made it to Lake City. It's beautiful there, isn't it? I love the Spanish moss hanging from the trees and all those giant windows. Oh, it's lovely! I wish I could be there with you. Make you something to eat in that enormous kitchen." Her laugh fills the room. When she speaks again, the tone is somber. "When I got my diagnosis, I knew I must tell you kids everything. If I didn't, well, soon there'd be no one left who could. That's the thing with secrets: they get heavy. And the older you get, the harder they are to carry. For years I kept these secrets, endured their weight, sure that one day everything was bound to come out. I'd have no choice but to answer for all the lies I told. But then I got sick, and those secrets... my mind plans to erase them. *Poof!* Gone! As if life plans to give me a free pass. And I don't deserve that. Greta and Athena and their families don't deserve that. So, I called upon *you.*

"And please don't think the unfairness of the situation is lost on me. A dead woman, forcing these terrible secrets upon her grandchildren because she was too much of a coward to speak these things herself. But that's the gospel truth of it—your ol' Gram is a coward. Fear... and *guilt*... are what drove me to lie to so many people for so long. And I regret it. I do.

"But regrets are part of life, aren't they? There's room for error in every decision we make. We could let the regret eat us up. Sure. But in the end, we're all just doing the best we can, and we need to make peace with that... *I* need to make peace with that. And *you* must make peace with the fact that your Gram was far from perfect and didn't deserve the pedestal you so often put her on, though she appreciated your admiration greatly. But please… do me a favor… if *your* regrets should ever require atonement… maybe don't wait until you're dead to sort it out." Gram laughs again, but the gravitas of her words is unmistakable.

"You kids… are *everything* to me. But I suspect you know that. You are the most beautiful pieces of me and your grandfather. Each of you, so very different. Oh, you four butt heads something terrible when you were younger," Gram laughs. "But you loved each other with a fierceness far greater. You may not remember those moments of love, or those fiery little kids of yore. But I do. So, love each other. Be there for each other. Never keep secrets from each other. Because you are *family*. The one constant in life. And no matter how tough things get, no matter how alone you feel, you never ever are."

Gram's eyes close and her face lifts to the ceiling, arms outstretched. "Look around you right now. Do you feel it? I'm sending you so much love right now. I hope you can feel it."

And Wyatt *can* feel it. It is everywhere. All around them, warm as a hug, a thousand lights turning on in his heart at once. Gooseflesh erupts on his arms.

"Now, I'm sure you've figured it out by now, but I've left this house to you. I've set up something called a Lady Bird Deed, naming you kids my remaining beneficiaries, set to take over the estate after I'm gone. It's all set and done. The house is yours. You'll know what to do with it.

"I love you all. My Lovebugs. Think of me always. But *especially*, think of me in the summer. I won't be far away. And wherever I am… wherever *you* are… I am so very proud of you."

At this, her voice breaks. Gram blows a soft kiss to the camera, smiles a big, dopey, summer smile, even as tears shine in her eyes. And she is gone.

85

EMELINE

(MAY 23, 2020)

One year later

"**YEAH, WE'RE NEARLY THERE NOW**," Emeline says, one hand on her phone, the other switching on her blinker. "Is everyone there for the signing, then?…

Okay, great. Well, if there're any issues with anything, just call me. I'll have my phone on me… Okay, I will… Love you, too. See you in a couple days… Bye."

Emeline disconnects the call and returns the phone to the cup holder beside her.

"Was that Daddy?" Aimee chirps from the backseat.

"Yeah, sweetie. He's about to meet with the nice people about selling our house."

"When is he coming home?" Conner asks.

Emeline glances in the review mirror at each of her children. Conner's legs have gotten so long since last year. She smiles at the sight of them jutting from his shorts like two scrawny, rooster legs. "He'll be back in a day or two, bud. He's driving back with the last of our boxes."

"Okay!" Conner grins and returns his attention out the window. He'd insisted we ride with the windows down, and a peaceful smile now tugs on his lips as the wind blows his sandy hair in manic wisps.

Last June, when they returned to Valdosta after their first visit to Lake City, they'd gone to find Gram's secret PO Box— the one she'd used to communicate with Greta and Hank and who knows who else. The box was empty, save for one letter— from Greta. It read:

Imogene —
where the hell have you been? You haven't written. This isn't like you. Your last letter worried me. whatever crazy ideas you're having, you best knock it off! Not crazy. I'm sorry. I didn't mean that. I know you aren't crazy. But... please... I don't know what else to say except... don't you dare die on me, you old bird! It ain't your time til I say it is. I love you, Snow white. You know that, don't you? Please write back. Please.

Always,
Greta Green

The note was dated January 20, 2019—four months before Gram passed away.

Not long after the events of last summer, Emeline and Armie decided to give their marriage another shot. Couple's therapy has improved their communication with each other. And her own diagnosis of postpartum depression has allowed Emeline to better understand what's going on in her brain. Besides therapy, she's also joined a support group for moms who suffer from long-term postpartum depression. This journey is a work in progress, but things seem to be looking up. It thrills the kids to have their dad back home, and Emeline is happy as well. This reinstatement of her marriage came with one demand, however: she wanted to move back home. Tennessee was not home and could never be. Her family was here, and she needed to be close to them. Armie happily agreed.

With Emeline's share of Gram's money as a down payment, she and Armie purchased the lake house from Emeline's mom and dad and have lived there for the last seven months. Being in that house feels like Gram and hugs and every amazing summer she's ever had, and Armie and her father had just gone and bought the wood to build the kids a clubhouse in the backyard.

In the back of Gram's closet, Emeline found a stack of letters from Mickey Lancaster, dated between 1968 and 2007. The contents of the letters are not romantic, but it's obvious how much Mickey and Gram meant to each other, to have stayed in touch for all those years. She can't say whether or not Gramps was aware of the letters, but they smelled of oak and fit perfectly in the secret compartment of Gram's wooden hope chest, which is exactly where Emeline still keeps them.

Now, after months on the market, they finally have a buyer on their Brownsville house, and Armie has gone to handle the closing, since the house is in his name.

"Here we are," Emeline says, turning into the drive. The kids squeal. Aimee beats her tiny feet on the back of Emeline's seat.

A smile washes over her when she sees the tree. Belinda has wrapped the enormous tree out front with twinkling fairy lights, just like at Gram's house. When Emeline moved into the lake house, she'd left the fairy lights right where they were. She still turns them on every night, and when she does, she whispers a little goodnight to Gram.

Emeline slows the Buick and reaches out her window to press the call button. After a few tinny rings, she hears, "I'm sorry. We're not looking to buy any Girl Scout cookies right now."

"Uncle Wyatt!" Conner yells.

Emeline laughs. "Let us in, you jerk."

Wyatt laughs, too. A moment later, a *click*, and the gate opens.

Wyatt and Belinda did an amazing job hosting. Wyatt smoked BBQ ribs and a pork butt roast for pulled pork sliders. Belinda made a cucumber salad, and dairy-free mac and cheese, which was… edible. Luckily, Athena and Kizzie had come through and brought some *full-dairy* mashed potatoes and bacon green beans.

Full and happy, the guests have settled into their own little spaces of the yard, visiting and relaxing.

Emeline pushes herself on the swinging wooden bench hung beneath one of the many oaks and enjoys the late spring breeze. Aimee sits at her feet and attempts to braid pine needles with her chubby three-year-old fingers.

In front of her, the scene plays out like a movie—the part at the end when the trouble has passed, and they pause on each of the characters for a moment to see how their lives turned out, who got the happily-ever-afters.

Along the side of the house, Geoff and Conner kick a soccer ball. Emeline's dad, Uncle Danny, and Jaimes—Kizzie's grandson, who is around Conner's age—joins them.

"That's not fair! You cheated!" Geoff shouts at Conner, who has just scored a goal against his team. Geoff had let him, of course, but Conner doesn't know that.

"Don't be a sore loser, Uncle Geoff!" Conner teases and sticks out his tongue.

"A sore loser? That's it! New rule: tickles for cheaters!" He scoops Conner into his arms and tickles his ribs to an eruption of screeching giggles.

Geoff had returned to Albany, where he and Lila officially ended things. They talked first, of course, and Geoff apologized profusely for his disregard to her feelings after the miscarriage. They left on a positive note, but Lila still felt that she needed to take time away, and Geoff agreed it was for the best. Geoff kept the apartment but uses his portion of Gram's money to make frequent visits home. This time, he's here for an entire week, staying at the house with Wyatt and Belinda. He'd also sent

Mom and Dad on a two-week cruise to the Bahamas. When they came back, they were refreshed and happier than Emeline had seen them in years. For once, Mom could just relax without needing to take care of another living soul. She'd needed it for such a long time. They'd been selfish not to notice. Thankfully, Geoff did.

The door from the screen porch slams shut and Belinda crosses the yard with a tray of popsicles. She sits the tray on one end of the long row of picnic tables set up on the lawn, and calls over to the boys, "Ice pop break!"

Conner and Jaimes reach the tray first, chanting, *Ice pops! Ice pops! Ice pops!*

Belinda pulls an orange popsicle from the tray and passes it to Uncle Danny. He takes it with a smile and kisses the top of her sunny blonde head. With Belinda's portion of the money, she'd sent her father to a local rehab facility where he completed the required sixty days, and then transferred to a sober living home for another six months. He's back home in Valdosta now and doing well—sober for ten months and counting.

As for Belinda, she parks her bus out front, but doesn't take it out nearly as often. Her permanent address is here at the Lake City house with Wyatt. A few months ago, she got a job at a funky art gallery in the downtown district, and they even let her sell her jewelry from the front desk.

Belinda brings a cherry popsicle over to Aimee, who takes it with glee and shoves it into her mouth.

At one end of the picnic tables is Emeline's mom, Athena, Kizzie, and Kizzie's daughter, Malinda—who is stunningly tall and beautiful and works as a catalog model—and Greta, who bounces Malinda's tiny son, Wendall, up and down on the table in front of her.

Now, this part of the story is interesting.

Apparently, Athena inquired about Greta back when Gramps first visited, and Gramps told her that Greta had died years before. Athena, having no reason to doubt him, never looked her up. So, when we told Athena that not only was Greta alive and well, but living back in Daytona, just a few hours away, tears fell from her eyes.

At first, Emeline couldn't understand why Gramps had lied. He'd spilled the beans on everything else. But it makes a strange kind of sense now. Athena knew the truth. If she went looking for Greta, the truth would find Greta as well. And since they'd kept everything from her for so long, it was best not to wreck it. If Gramps had it to do over again, what might he do? *Regrets—* just as Gram said. He'd done the best he could at the time, and they needed to be okay with that.

The day after leaving the Lake City house, they each agreed that a trip back to Daytona was in order. They sat with Greta and came clean about everything. Gram had obviously wanted them to, or she'd never have dragged her old friend into her game. Greta remained eerily quiet while they'd told her; absorbed their words but didn't react to them. All these years of knowing there was more to her brother's death, and now she had her answers. All these years of not realizing that Imogene's mysterious Wilfred was the Ted Barret she'd known so long ago. Even so, no tears. Not even a twitch of her lip. The tears came at last when they mentioned Athena. Greta was unaware that Athena had been pregnant with Ray's baby, or that she was even still alive. "I'm... an aunt?" she asked, as tears spilled over her cheeks.

"A great-*great*-aunt, actually," Wyatt had answered.

She'd dropped her face into her hands and sobbed.

They'd asked her if she was angry. After all, she had every right to be. But Greta only said, "Oh kids, at my age, it doesn't do to hold grudges."

Greta has been to Lake City now at least a dozen times, grateful for her newfound family. She always comments on Kizzie's chin dimple. "Oh, Ray, there you are," she'll say as she kisses Kizzie's cheek.

On several of Greta's trips, today included, she'd brought Camila along with her. She and Wyatt sit together at the opposite end of the picnic tables, not an inch of space between them. They huddle over Camila's phone, each of them wearing an earbud, watching a video or something. Wyatt has this big, dorky grin on his face. He is handsome, her brother. And it seems that Camila agrees.

Wyatt took over the construction business while Uncle Danny was in rehab, and then moved to the Lake City house after he returned. He is working now to get his real estate license—far from the technology route they'd expected him to take since high school, but perfect for the new man he's become.

Unwilling to part *entirely* with his tech-savvy roots, however, Wyatt and Geoff are officially working on an app together. It was Wyatt's idea, and Geoff jumped at the opportunity to help. They'll call the app *2econd Chance,* and it will help connect wrongfully accused teens and first-time offenders with local employers. Part of the reason for Geoff's extended visit is to have a *thorough brainstorm-sesh* with his brother.

Wyatt gave his entire cut of Gram's money to Greta, so she can keep The Salty Siren afloat for as long as she wants. At first, she refused to take it, but eventually agreed. The bar is well and good and even got a new fryer, so no more undercooked fish.

A shriek from Aimee draws Emeline's attention back to her daughter.

"Get it off! Get it off!" she yells, flapping her sticky popsicle hands like a maniac as a black dot flutters into the air and lands on the bench beside Emeline.

"Oh, it's just a lovebug!" Emeline says, and she lets the tiny creature crawl onto her finger. "It's harmless."

Aimee hops up and hovers over the black and red bug now lapping her mother's fingertip. It flies off, and Aimee giggles.

Emeline watches the bug circle Aimee's head a few times before drifting off toward the rest of the picnic. This is the first lovebug of the season she's seen, and she knows why it appeared today, of all days.

"I know, Gram," she whispers. "I'm proud of us, too."

TANYA RUMFORD is a native Floridian and former photographer. She resides in the Tampa Bay area with her husband, son, father, two pups, and two rescue kitties. For more information, check out www.tanyarumford.com.

@thetanyarumford

/tanyarumfordauthor